Lottie's Legacy

a whydunit spanning four generations
by

Sherry Schubert

Published by Sunway Press
P.O. Box 5825
Twin Falls, Idaho 83303-5825
www.sunwaypress.com

ISBN 978-1-7329026-0-2   (pbk)
ISBN 978-1-7329026-1-9 (ebook)

Dedicated
to

Nana

and mothers who harbor deep secrets

This novel is based on the discovery
of a packet of 100-year-old love letters
and photographs.

Books by Sherry Schubert
Puffin Island
Celtic Compass, Part I
Celtic Compass, Part II
Celtic Circle~for Better, for Worse
Celtic Circle~Forever
Lottie's Legacy

Lottie's Legacy

Some mysteries begin with a murder.

Others, with a secret.

Some crimes are intentional.

Others are accidental,

Or the result of omission from lack of knowledge or naiveté.

Some mysteries are solved.

Some criminals are brought to justice.

Or all... or none... of the above.

Following is such a story.

1968

Mysteries often originate with a dead body.

> White female, age 69. Height: 5 ft, 5 inches. Weight: 135 pounds. Eyes: vivid blue. Hair: gray with an auburn tint.

Or an open grave.

> A 3ft x 8ft x 6ft deep hole in the ground emitting a pungent humus odor from recently turned dark sandy loam.

An unfamiliar, isolated location.

> A foreign land—the Deep South—not in a town or even on the edge of one, but along a dirt road between two insignificant dots on a map.

Or an eerie graveyard.

> An old cemetery of about ten acres with some graves predating Civil War times. A dilapidated wrought-iron fence surrounding the burial grounds assumes the slumped, forward bend of its aged inhabitants and the rusted demeanor of its more than 100 years of service holding back intrusive wiregrass. Air heavy with heat and humidity oppresses ghosts hidden among wisps of Spanish moss hanging from live oak trees, their knotted trunks bulging over the fence as if to escape.

An unanswered question.

> Why?

Or the crunch of footsteps on a gravel path and an elongated, burly shadow creeping up from behind through misty morning light.

A terrified scream. "Aagghh……"

> Mine!

"Apologies, ma'am. I didn't mean to frighten you."

The shadow has a voice—a deep, calm, friendly one.

"I just strolled over to meet the new neighbor. I come every year on September 19, my birthday, to show gratitude for those who gave me life. I know most of the families in these parts, but I never did make the acquaintance of these folks near you."

The shadow has a logical reason for stealing up behind me. I turn to face a man of tall stature and authoritative bearing. He carries his broad shoulders confidently, has thick, wavy brown hair, wide cheekbones and smile, and kind, familiar eyes.

"Over there is my grandmother Lottie." He points two spaces to his right. "The empty plot here next to her with the wooden name stake is for her son, my father." He waves his finger past me in the opposite direction. "Your family? Please introduce me to your family."

I turn back and peer deep into the forbidding black hole with a casket at its bottom. "This is my mother, and the two others are her parents."

"How fortunate. One tends to wonder whether his neighbors will be friend or foe. I'm comforted to imagine my papa nestled between two loving mothers."

I calm my trembles and inhale deeply. There is nothing sinister about the man. I owe him a reply. "Does your father live near here too?"

He shakes his head. "Sadly, no. My father didn't make it back from the Great War. He died fifty years ago, a few months before I was born. He never set eyes on me. My grandmother sincerely believed he would come home one day in some form when science catches up with our curiosities, so she picked out this particular spot for the two of them. I have no idea why. Her 'mind was set' she said, and made me promise to adhere to her wish. Just one of the deep secrets she carried to her grave."

My story is much the same. After returning from my grandmother's funeral a few years back, Mom insisted that she be buried with her parents... here... in Alabama... a place I had never heard her mention. But that is too much information to share with a stranger, so I offer, "Today is my mother's birthday too. Her sixty-ninth."

His eyes spark as if he has unearthed a golden nugget. "You don't say! I woke up this morning with a visceral feeling that my fiftieth birthday would be very special in an unusual way. Now, lying at my feet is a person with whom I share the most important event of my life. That's not a coincidence. That is a cosmic connection!"

I shiver. He is beginning to sound creepy. I want to leave, but I am not finished here yet.

He grasps my hand and shakes it heartily. "Thank you. Thank you for coming from...?"

"California."

"California! Thank you for coming all this way to make my half-century birthday so special!" He drops my hand abruptly. "Pardon, ma'am. I didn't mean to startle you with my familiarity. I'm so overcome with my good fortune, it didn't occur to me that you might not feel the same. My apologies."

"Accepted. I wish you a happy day." I wait for him to leave, but he does not.

"Thank you. It will be, even more so, now that fate has intervened to bring us all together. Say, how long are you staying? Can you come to my party tonight?"

I smile at his renewed enthusiasm and shake my head. "Thanks for the invitation, but I have a plane to catch this afternoon."

"Oh, dear. My wife and kids will never believe me when I tell them that by chance I arrived at the cemetery just in time to meet a lovely woman saying her farewells to her mother who shares my birthday. They'll accuse me of conjuring up a story to make my day seem more exciting. They generally leave me alone to do my 'gratituding' as they call it, but they expect me to be the life of the party in the evening. Tonight's will be one big bash with all the family and lots of friends. Sorry you can't join us, but I'll share our amazing story just the same."

"Sounds like a good time. Will your mother be there too?"

He turns serious. "Sadly again, no. I've never been told the circumstances of her death shortly after I was born. Whenever I asked my grandmother about her, she gave me the same stock answer. She did not know my mother well—had only spent limited time with her on two or three occasions—but remembered her as pretty, sweet, gentle and loving. Then my grandmother would grow teary-eyed and make reference to that 'horrid Spanish Flu epidemic.' So my grandmother Lottie took me in and raised me up and here I am—one grateful, happy man."

"She sounds like a dedicated, loving woman herself."

"That she was. I know nothing about her family or where she grew up, but she was a hard worker every day of her life, first with my father on a farm near here and then with me in the city. Her fingers were always busy—office machines, quilting, gardening. She worked past retirement age and stayed with us long enough to meet her two great grandchildren, then died at her desk. But enough about me and mine. Tell me about your mother."

I hesitate. I do not know where to begin. How do you encapsulate all that a mother means to you in one sentence? I do not even try. I feel my eyes welling up with tears and fumble in my purse for a tissue. I am too late. I am a soppy mess and embarrassed beyond words. I really need a hug, but my mother is no longer there to stretch out her arms and comfort me. A handkerchief appears out of nowhere and finds its way into my hand.

"I'm sorry," the man says as he turns away. "I shouldn't have asked. Your mother's death is too raw yet. I remember that feeling."

I attempt to compose myself and fluster with the crudely abused cotton square in my fist. I cannot possibly return it in such a condition.

He seems to sense my bewilderment and turns back to face me with a soft, empathetic smile. "No bother," he says. "Keep it. You'll need it more than once today." His eyes widen to convey a sudden inspiration. "Tell you what. I know just the thing. Peach ice cream! My grandmother's secret remedy to chase the glums away. The best ice cream shop in the whole state is just up the road in Troy. Please be my guest for an unforgettable treat."

I hesitate again. I am an emotional mess but not so far gone that I would jump into a car with a strange man in a strange place and drive off to who knows where. But he has been so kind that I do not want to appear ungrateful. "I appreciate the invitation, but I can't leave. Those men over there are due to drive me back to Montgomery to catch my plane. They are anxious to get going, but I won't leave until Mom's grave is filled in. They say some fellows will come along later and finish the job. That is not acceptable. I need to see it completed for myself." I dab my eyes with his handkerchief. "The thought of rain... birds... mice... animals... strangers peering in...." I wipe my nose. "So we're at a standoff."

"I understand absolutely." He strides with purpose toward the black vehicle and calls out over his shoulder, "I'll see what I can do."

I overhear bits and pieces of his conversation with the men from the mortuary.

"Do you fellows know who I am?"

"Yes, sir," the taller one replies. The other nods.

"Then trust me when I tell you that there is no law that says mourners must leave a cemetery before a grave is filled in. This fine lady came all the way across this country to bury her mama the way her family is used to, and it is up to you and your business to provide that service. Do you understand me?"

The two fellows nod.

"Then let's put our heads together and see what we can do to solve this problem."

The three men pace around the hearse while discussing my plight. My new acquaintance claps his hand to his forehead, points down the road, and shakes his head at the fellows' intention to walk together in that direction. The shorter stays behind to endure a lengthy lecture until the tall fellow returns with two young men and four shovels. He and his cohort remove their black suit coats and toss them into the vehicle. I am soon surrounded by five strange men, standing over an open grave in a very strange place. I am motioned aside.

"We'll want to stand over here, well away from men flinging shovels full of dirt."

I stammer an apology for causing so much trouble.

"No problem. Those fellows deserved a good talking to. Turns out that *lunch* is at the root of this ruse."

I voice my surprise. "Lunch!"

"That's right. Lunch. Their desire for you to 'hurry along' has nothing to do with custom here. Seems they were anxious to return to Montgomery in time for a full lunch hour. I reminded them... politely... that if they don't have a job, they'll be free to eat lunch all day long. Then I persuaded them to pitch in and help the hired labor. Once their work meets your approval, I offered to treat them to the best down-home cooking they'll ever find south of our capital city while you finish your goodbyes the way you planned."

I feel my face redden. I reach for my purse for the second time this morning and pick through it for my wallet. I am stopped abruptly with a glare.

4

"No. Your vulnerability is your contribution. These fellows need to learn that compassion is their primary responsibility if they plan a future in the grieving business. Mine is demonstrating how to return kindness for kindness—one of my grandmother's rules to live by."

The only sounds for several minutes are the shooshings of dirt onto shovels and then sliding off. At last, the fellows ask for approval. I look toward the man standing beside me, and he gestures that it is for me to give. I do and thank them for a job well done. The tall fellow pays the two laborers who then head back down the road. He and his cohort brush themselves off, return to their vehicle, and wait for their escort.

"You take the time you need," he says. "I'll be back in a flash."

Alone. I want to be alone, but a quiver of anxiety creeps up my spine. All vehicles drive away together. What if no one returns for me? Where do I go? How do I find my way back? Was I foolish to believe I could cross the continent by train with nothing but a purse, overnight bag, and casket to close this chapter of my mother's life alone?

I kneel at the head of Mom's grave and recount all the things I should have said and never found the time to—the thank yous, I'm sorrys, I love yous, you're the bests, I'll never forgets, do you remember whens and wasn't it fun when we.... In the end I reflect. In all our years together, and in all our conversations of wonderment and curiosity—like where do clouds come from—I never once asked "Where did *you* come from?"

I hear a car drive up and footsteps on the gravel path. They do not frighten me this time. They are familiar. The man returns with two cups of ice cream, three scoops each, and a broad, self-satisfied grin. "Try this."

I lick the melting treat from its spoon. "Thank you."

"Feel better?"

"Yumhumm. This *is* very good. Hits the spot."

"Nothing like fresh peach, and this is the best I've found. After all the hoopla, the fellows did a pretty good job. Nice and smooth. Are you satisfied?"

I nod. "Pretty much. Mom's memorial at home was so bright and colorful with lots of friends. I didn't realize how barren and lonely this small cemetery would seem."

"Aha. Hold my ice cream." He gulps a big spoonful, hands me his cup, and walks the few paces to his grandmother's grave. He rests on one knee and fumbles with the bouquet he left there earlier. "These will split three ways, easy." He replaces some on her grave, some on his father's reserved plot, and brings a nice handful to me to place on Mom's. "That's better, don't you think?"

I try to thank him again, but, again, I get the glare.

"Another one of my grandmother's first lessons was that 'sharing feels good,' and I do feel good. This encounter with you has been a

5

delightful beginning to my big day. I'm the one who should be saying 'thanks' here. Why don't we take a stroll around these intimate grounds? You'll find we're a pretty friendly bunch once you get to know us."

While he introduces me to the inhabitants and shares an abridged biography of most, I realize I have misjudged this haunting place. My mystery scenario does not hold up. The dead body is in good, pleasant company. The open grave is properly closed and decorated. There is a certain charm in this isolated location, away from the hurly-burly of everyday, in a neighborhood of folks and their loved ones who come to honor them. And consoling ice cream is "just up the road." The bends in the fence surrounding the eerie graveyard now look like smiles. Colorful garden flowers abound. The mist has disappeared, and sunlight shimmers through the hanging moss to create shadow puzzles on the ground. Our footsteps along the gravel path sound in tandem and companionable. I do not hear my own scream, but the songs of birds and… music? Yes, faint refrains of gospel music. A church is not visible, but there is a small crowd of people in the distance. "Is that a picnic?"

He shakes his head. "Probably a colored burial at their cemetery across the road and down some. They have their own place. Segregation's tentacles reach even to the dead. Maybe by the time my son and his girl have lived their lives on earth, they'll be allowed to be buried next to each other in the same cemetery. Something to hope for."

"Why wouldn't that be possible now?"

He sighs deeply and gazes in the direction of the music. "My son wants to marry a colored girl. She calls herself an Afro-American. She jumped onto his back during the March to Montgomery in '65, and he's marched to her drumbeat ever since. I'm not opposed on racial terms, but on legal ones. Interracial marriage has been against the law until recently. I try to tell them that the Civil Rights Act may be the law of the land, but not in Alabamans' minds yet. Best hold off for a while. In our family, we don't break the law. We use it, but legal go-arounds are still too risky for them, and any children will have their own set of challenges. They got all excited by the recent 'Loving' court decision. The husband was white; the wife, part black and part Cherokee, and…."

"I'm part Cherokee—on my mother's side," I chime in. "At least that's what she told me once."

"A lot of folks claim that when they are 'mixed' and want to 'pass.' Be careful who you share that with around here. Many mixed-race folks go ahead and check the 'white' box, but by previous law and still in the minds of many, *any amount* of black is 'black.'"

"What does 'pass' mean?" I ask.

Several moments crawl by as he contemplates how to frame his response. "A person of one race may be born with physical attributes that enable him to be accepted as a member of a different race. Blood vs. appearance, so to speak. If he chooses to 'pass,' he may gain rights and privileges but will live a life of denial and deception. *Appearance* has no *legal* standing."

We find our way back to the friendly grouping of three decorated graves. "Thank you so much for guiding me through this morning's frustrations. I apologize for not being more congenial. Mom's choice to be buried here was such a shock to me because Dad's grave is in New Mexico where I grew up. But fulfilling her wish makes my sorrow easier to bear." Out comes the handkerchief again. "I appreciate your kindness in making that happen… and for this…" I wave the hanky and use it to wipe my eyes, again. "…and for the wonderful peach ice cream."

His smile is repeated at the crinkly corners of his blue eyes. "Absolutely my pleasure. You are wise to be cautious in an unfamiliar place like Alabama. With all the riots and marches that have popped up recently, I would expect as much from my wife, and she has lived here for most of her life."

A black vehicle appears at the side of the road.

"Here come the fellows to drive you back to Montgomery. I'd offer to take you myself, but I have a feeling you're still a little uncomfortable to be riding around with a stranger in a strange place, so we'll stick with your plan. I'll follow along for a while to make sure they find their way to the airport."

I gaze at my mother's resting-place for the last time and hear a soft whisper in my ear. "Don't you fret one minute about leaving your mother alone. We'll watch over her for you and make sure she is remembered on special days. Maybe next time you come…."

"Oh, I doubt I'll be back," I sniffle. "We can't afford for me to be flying off every year, so I'll wish you a happy birthday now and for all those in your future. I don't know if I'll ever have the chance again."

He leads me out to my ride. "You will. And you'll come here. And we'll meet again and get to know one another a little better. Maybe share some more peach ice cream." He smiles and waves as we drive off.

I glance at the rearview mirror, and he does follow. I dab my eyes again and recollect the events and the emotions of the day. My initial fears seem so insignificant now. Only the unanswered question of 'why here' remains. I resign myself to never solving that mystery until a sudden notion strikes me. A second mystery arises. Who was that man? I never asked his name. I glance at the rearview again, but he has disappeared.

Lottie's Story

PASSING

Carlotta Lombardi skipped her way along the red dirt path through town on her way home from work as she did every day at dusk. Oblivious of the gnats that danced around her ankles and bare toes, she wore an "I have a secret" smile and her eyes gleamed in anticipation of telling it. Careful not to attract attention, she kept her eyes down but scanning to the right and left. They caught sight of a small group of young men in dirty overalls that smelled of machine oil and molasses. The hooligans whooped and shouted, clapping one another's backs and pointing to a body hanging by rope from the sturdy lower limb of an old oak tree. A sign tacked to it read, "Keep to yur own side." She froze as the limp form swung from side to side, the handkerchief in its back pocket fluttering behind—the one she gave him on his twenty-second birthday. Reflexively her hand gripped her throat to strangle the anguished cry that she dared not allow to escape, "Noooo! Not Jim Boy! Not my husband!"

Her skip became a trudge as thoughts lightninged through her head. No tears. Do not run. Ignore. Become invisible. Who found them out? How much did they know? What would they do to *her*? She bypassed the two-rut road leading to her family's farm and headed for their rendezvous spot in the hollow, the place where they exchanged marriage vows and joined together once a month during the light of a full moon.

For eight moons they had followed the same routine: leave work late; go to bed early; sneak out after dark; make their separate ways west along the road to Bainbridge. When the moon played with light and shadow, they met up to follow a hazardous sloping path over tree roots that reached out to trip them, beyond curled diamond back rattlers settled for the night, and past orange fox eyes that blinked at their intrusion. They nested in leaves and dried grass behind a stone outcropping and laid their plans… their plans to move north where a white woman and mulatto man might have a chance. This night she intended to tell him there would be three on that trek. Tears finally burst from her eyes and sobs joined owl hoots through the trees. She clutched her belly. Now there would be only two. Daddy could not come.

*

Lottie let her anguish play out, then tried to replace it with memory… happy memory… until a deer's rustle in the weeds or the sad lament of a whippoorwill jerked her back to despair and reality. She and Jim Boy were in their late teens when they met. They had been aware of one another for many years as everyone who lived in a small Georgia town near Cairo in the 1890s would be, but they never spoke until the day she walked into the general store with a notepad in her hand. She was a farmer's daughter; he, the shopkeeper's helper. She had conned her father into a year in Savannah with a cousin to learn office skills including typewriting; he had virtually no schooling but did have a strong back, mild manner and quick mind.

She arrived at the general store in response to hearsay that the man who owned the town's new shop and syrup factory was looking for help with his accounts and payroll. Lottie produced her credentials and added that she could also type his letters, orders and bills so there would be no errors in understanding. The owner left for a back room and returned with one of those newfangled type machines that a traveling salesman talked him into buying but never taught him how to use. She demonstrated. He clapped Jim Boy on the shoulder and smiled. "I think we have a team." The boy smiled back... at both of them.

In the course of their daily work they rarely spoke beyond "Good Morning" or "Good night" and the occasional "Bud Parsons needs help with his bill" or "Miz Stoffel wants to place a special order." That is, until the day that same Miz Stoffel's special order could not be found and Lottie was asked to help.

She returned with a package boldly labeled and apologized. "Here you go, Ma'am. It was hiding behind the salt." After their customer left, she turned to her coworker. "You can't read, can you?"

His shoulders drooped; he lowered his eyes and shook his head.

"Well then, we need to fix that." And they did.

In down times with little traffic and after Jim Boy's cleaning and stocking chores were finished, the two reviewed letter sounds. Then they attacked the disaster that was the stock room and rearranged products alphabetically so Jim Boy could find anything easily. Soon, the little store and office were running so efficiently that the owner spent more and more time at his factory which he much preferred. After all, he only established the store as a convenience for the workers on a daily schedule who now did not have time to drive their wagons to a larger town nearby.

Their minutes-long sessions turned letters to words, words to thoughts, and thoughts into hopes until the unthinkable happened. The letter "e" type bar on Lottie's machine broke clean off. Jim Boy tried to fix it, but every time she hit the "e" key, its bar flew across the room. That doomed her free time because she had to replace every missing "e" on a typed page with pen and ink. Not only that, but the new letter had to be a precise replication in style and size as the typed would have been.

Jim Boy offered to help. Lottie said he had to read and understand well first so that he could determine whether an empty space was an "e" or an "ee" or just a space between words. After weeks of study, he was ready for a test. She typed a paragraph from a magazine story and let him fill in the missing letters. The result, "Good job!"

On a particularly frustrating morning with a stack of orders to process, Lottie voiced her anger at her "blasted machine!"

The owner overheard and asked what the problem was. The boy replied, "She lost her 'e'." Noting his boss's eyebrow-dance of confusion, he offered a short explanation.

"You order yurse'f a new one and throw that hunk a metal out as soon as it comes. You hear?"

She did hear. She did order the newest model. But she did not throw the old one out. She hid it behind some catalogues on a top shelf in her office in case of....

*

Lottie's eyes welled up again and she moaned. "In case of what? All our hopes are gone." She reached out for Jim Boy's comfort and grasped only a handful of dried weeds. A rustle in the grass caused her to sit up and press her palms to her eyes to staunch the flow of tears.

In their few years together at the general store they had never spent more than an hour a day in conversation, and those only in snatches of a few minutes at a time. They had never strolled together from one end of town to the other, sat on a front porch and talked, shared an ice cream or a kiss. They did share a longing for time... time to become more than acquaintances. Time to become friends. And they did share the understanding that appearing together in public was impossible. That's when they decided to find a place that would be theirs only.

Jim Boy did the searching. As a young boy with no friends on either side of the color line, he had had ample time to explore the fields and woodlands in the area. Corn and tobacco were popular new crops, and a pocket of sugar cane farms produced raw product for the new syrup factory. The woodlands were his favorite, though, alive with critters and birds. Once he spotted a secluded place in the hollow, he checked carefully for brown thrasher nests in the grass before choosing it. In future, the spurting bird song would signal the time for the couple to leave and make their way back up the steep path with just enough moonlight left to find their way.

The first two full moons when they visited, they talked the nights away comfortably and found they had more in common than they expected. They both liked dewberry tarts and peach ice cream, moss-draped trees and patches of violets after a summer rain, and learning new things. They railed at the inequities of a social system where the rules had changed but the realities had not. Why should two people who cared for each other not be able to express that affection rather than hide it? By the third full moon they resolved to marry, move to the north, and begin a new life together.

On the fourth full moon, they met in the hollow to conduct their own ceremony of silent longings, whispered vows, and spoken promises. They sanctified their marriage by standing together with her small Bible pressed between their chests, holding one another so tightly that with each beat of their hearts they could feel their souls mingle with the Holy word and with one another. It might have been minutes. It might have been hours when, finally sapped of strength, they came apart pronouncing themselves surely sealed as husband and wife in the eyes of God and this congregation of His creatures.

Lottie opened her Bible to its page of records where she had copied the salient births, marriages and deaths from her grandfather's time to the present—all in different script. They paused before inking their fates with their autographs. If this were to be their legal record, any hint of prejudicial lineage could bring harm or even death to one or both of them and their children to come. Their eyes spoke in agreement and they knelt to fix their signatures. In that moment Carlotta Lombardi became Lottie Lombard and Jim Boy—no surname, but he had lived and worked around the Richards place for as long as he could remember—became James Dickson, married the Fifth day of October, 1898. They created their own family.

They did not consummate their marriage on the night of their vows. They had promised so much to one another that before they knew it, the brown thrasher's song reminded them of the sun's early rise. They must wait for the next full moon when again they would have light enough to travel the steep path from the hollow.

That same song brought Lottie back to reality. With no one to push from behind or pull from the front, it was up to her alone to navigate the difficult path toward the road to town. She turned up the hem of her skirt to wipe her face and eyes, pulled brambles from her hair, and put one foot in front of the other. This morning she must be on time to work with her feelings in check. Two lives depended on her initial reactions to the horrific news about her coworker. Play out the plan, she decided; then give in to her grieving.

Three days later, Lottie and her family assembled with other town folk, factory workers and farmers on the north side of the road, across from the black cemetery where a smaller group had gathered to lay to rest that boy who worked in the general store. The county sheriff stopped by to pay his respects to Lottie's boss, shaking his head with "Nobody seen a thing. We'll likely never find out who done it."

She scanned the small crowd for possible suspects and noticed the four or five she had seen near the hanging tree. They were not whooping or shouting, but they did wear smug looks, especially when they caught her staring at them. One whispered just loud enough for her to hear, "Serves him right."

Antagonism had always existed in their tired little town, but everyone respected "the boss," a short, graying, no nonsense kind of a guy who moved with the times. He gave his sharecroppers, black and white, a fair deal and floated them when harvests were bad. He diversified the crops he supported; built the syrup factory when industry began to take hold and boys from large families needed employment; expanded his store's hours to accommodate those workers who needed refreshment after long days on a sweltering job; and gave a bold young woman a prime position in a man's world.

Today that positive, try-to-do-the-right-thing man stood with shaking shoulders and tears in his eyes. What the whole town knew but never spoke about in public was that twenty-two years ago the boss sent his youngest girl to college in Atlanta and she returned for the summer with a baby on the way. When his beautiful blond, blue-eyed, peaches-and-cream daughter bore him a caramel-skinned grandchild, his world fell apart. But he put it back together again—too many folks depended on him. His daughter returned to Atlanta and had not been seen in town since. The baby was placed with a local farm family until he was old enough to help around the home grounds and later, the store. In quiet moments the boss allowed flashes of pride to cross his face at what a fine man that boy *could* be, but now he would never know. He watched from across the road as his grandson was buried that day.

*

For the next few weeks, Lottie arrived at the store with her gangly, overgrown sixteen-year-old brother in tow. He was lured by the promise of earning pocket money for tidying the storage room and setting out special orders before school. If he returned to clean up the place after school and his own chores were done at home, he could earn a little more. In truth, his company was worth any price; she did not feel safe walking alone on the road.

The boss, Mr. Richards, showed up midmornings in a stupor, looked around to confirm that the place was running smoothly, and shuffled out until later in the afternoon. He soon turned over the job of locking up as well as opening to Lottie. He had more pressing thoughts on his mind. Once he realized how well she and her brother managed the place, he barely stuck his head in. He preferred factory hum to block out the thoughts of regret churning inside his head.

After six weeks without Jim Boy, Lottie was ready to make her move. School was out, so her brother had all day to work at the store if he wanted. He did. The money was more than he could earn at any other job in their small town. He was already quick with numbers and could read well. And he worked every day on his handwriting. He even started to practice pecking on that typewriting thing in the office. Lottie decided that he was ready for her to make her move.

On the chosen day, she dressed in three layers of clothing with her best dress on top, the one she wore when they wed—blue with tiny yellow flowers. She put on shoes with white stockings—unusual for a workday in southwestern Georgia's oppressive summer humidity. She filled her carpetbag with undergarments, cloth for diapers, small blankets, and a shawl. And her Bible containing the family's history. Her story? She had arranged with her boss for a couple of weeks off work to travel to Savannah and help her cousin following the birth of a second child. No questions. Big family. Oodles of cousins and kids of all ages. Have a good time and carry love to the relatives.

At the store, she waited for her brother to busy himself in the supply room before reaching for a small packing crate she had squirreled away under her worktable. She spread a thrice-washed potato sack on the bottom, then moved her chair to the shelves, removed the old catalogues, and lifted the broken typewriter from its hiding place "in case of..." and filled in the blank. "In case we/I need to flee and need to put food on a table once we stop." She quickly stuffed more clean sacking on top, tacked down the lid and wrapped light rope over and around the box. She placed her carpetbag on top, her hands on her hips, and sighed.

Her boss poked his somber face through the doorway. " 'Bout ready to take off? Got someone to take you to the station?"

Lottie turned quickly and nodded.

He wiped his forehead with a handkerchief, then removed an envelope from the pocket of his overalls and offered it to her. "I never told you how much I 'preciated yur help these last three years, especially these last weeks. I cudna survived without you and yur brother."

"He'll do a good job for you." She smiled and hesitated to accept his offering.

"Go ahead, please. I wrote a note telling how smart you are, good with figures and can type up a storm, and as honest as can be with nary a penny or a peppermint stick missing. Maybe this will help you with whatever comes next."

As she reached for the envelope, Lottie noticed a flicker of understanding deep in his eyes. "Thank you. I... I don't know what to say."

"Nothin' fer *you* to say. *I* cuda loved that boy more. I'm just thankful he knew some happiness in his short life. Good luck to ya." With that, he wiped his eyes with his handkerchief, turned and walked out.

Stunned that she had not fooled her boss at all, she opened the envelope and fingered its contents: the letter and six months' wages. He was such a kindly man. Now his words, "honest as can be," stung. She placed her hat with the blue ribbon on her head, pinned it in place, and picked up her carpetbag and the crate with the typing machine that was not hers.

Once her brother had unloaded the store's order and loaded some cypress barrels of sugarcane syrup for transport, he hailed his sister over to say goodbye. The supply wagon that she had arranged to take to Cairo to catch the train east to Savannah was ready to roll. He helped her up by the driver, handed her the bag and then stowed the crate in the bed. "What the heck you got in this thing? It's heavier than you are," he joked.

"A jug of syrup, of course, some peaches, and a few jars of Mom's pickles and peanut butter," she smiled with a wink and handed him the keys to the store. "You take good care of her and Dad."

"And you stay out of trouble, Sis. See you in a cupla weeks." He waved as the wagon pulled away.

She waved back until he was out of sight, then sighed with relief. At least she had the family fooled for the time being. No telling when, if ever, she would see them or that hot, dusty town again.

The driver dropped some of his load and his one passenger at the train station. "As you know, I go back to yur place from this direction every Tuesday and Friday around noon, so when you want a ride home just stand here and wave yur hankie at me and I'll find room for you with the rest of the bundles of cotton." He chortled at himself, displaying an arc of tobacco-stained teeth. At her smile in return, he added. "You have a good time in Savannah with yur cousin. Maybe you two can slip away long enough to dip yur toes into that big Atlantic Ocean." He rapped his reins against the two horses' backs and with a "giddyup" was on his way.

Lottie wondered if she had packed her hankie... or if she would need it. She walked up to the station window and bought a ticket, then sat on her crate in the hot sun and waited. Why did she wear so many clothes? Before long she would be a dishrag ready for the wringer, she thought. The train to Savannah pulled in not much later. No one got off. No one got on. The train departed heading east. Lottie sat sweltering in the sun... waiting.

Another hour in the heat found Lottie dripping with sweat and reaching for the hankie she hoped was at the top of her carpetbag. A second train pulled in. No one got off. One passenger got on. The train departed, bound for Alabama and parts west and north. The ticket agent locked up his window, mounted his mule and headed home. He was paid to wait for only two trains a day.

*

The wooden seats in her passenger car were far from comfortable, but Lottie made no complaint. She was on her way. She lowered the window to allow a draft to cool her off—hot air, to be sure, but refreshing. And the faster the train moved, the stronger the breeze became. She gripped her elbows and hugged herself tight, hoping that no one had recognized her... seen her. Her mind rolled along the tracks in time with the wheels: *Please let... no one... see me.... Please let... no one... see me.... Please let no one see me.... Please let no one see me.... Pleaseletnooneseeme.... Pleaseletnooneseeme.... SeemeSeemeSeemeSeemeSeeme....*

That was it! The catalyst to the heinous act that wrested Jim Boy from her! She had been seen. With him. In public. She remembered the specific event so clearly now. Late afternoon. What the two of them called the "rowdy crowd" entered the store at the end of a hot workday looking for food and fun. Jim Boy was stocking shelves. She was near him taking inventory. The rowdies called to him when they were ready to pay up. He put his hand on her back to guide her out of his way as he walked to the cash register. He touched a white woman. What seemed so natural at the time, condemned him.

The mournful wail of the train's whistle nudged her anger aside to make room for the guilt and shame welling up inside her. Why had they not gone public? Stood their ground against the hooligans and the community? Shouted out, "You folks live your lives and let us live ours. There's room for everyone here. Where's the crime in loving one another? We're all the same inside." Why did she not push the rowdies away? Scream for help when she spotted Jim Boy hanging there? Maybe there was breath, life left in him and he could have been saved. Why did she not insist that they walk together whenever they wanted? Wherever they went? Why was the world so cruel to people who looked different but felt the same? *What could I have done? What could I have done?*

The train's rumble belched no answers, so the shame continued. She should have gone to her boss. Hugged him. Grieved with him. Stood beside him at the funeral and held his hand. Had the courage to cross the road and lay flowers on Jim Boy's grave in front of the whole town. Lottie was so ashamed that she did not have the guts to do the right thing when it counted, to stand up for those trapped in a world whose laws may have changed but whose practices and prejudices had not. Equality might be a step too far at present, but everyone deserved a fair shake. She vowed to do whatever it took to achieve fairness for her child.

Despite the high temperature and humidity, Lottie shivered. She trembled so violently that she finally reached into her bag for the shawl and wrapped it tightly around her shoulders and chest. She feared her body was reacting to nerves and hoped that her anxiety would not affect her baby. In an attempt to relax, she rested her head against the window and stared blankly at rich farmland whisking by. Fields of peanuts and sweet potatoes, corn and cotton, and grazing cattle were only a verdant blur.

Deep metallic clanks roused her. The train was crossing the Chattahoochee River. A wave of relief washed over her with the last clank. She was in Alabama. Safety. A new beginning. But the relief did not last long. A deep anguish swelled within her and rose through her chest, threatening to erupt. She pulled her shawl across her mouth and nose to conceal her agony. She fought to keep her tears beneath her eyelids, but they fought back and streamed down her cheeks, drenching the shawl and the bodices of her dresses.

Drowning in her grief, Lottie was oblivious of the cotton and peanut fields and mixed pine forests along the route and the small girl staring and pointing at her from across the aisle until the conductor passed through the car announcing their stop at Troy. Lottie took stock. She was a mess and needed to clean up before the train reached Montgomery. She wiped her face with the shawl, then stuffed it into her bag and placed that on top of the crate, gripping both in preparation for disembarking to find water.

She was last in line to stumble down the steps of the car with her load and head for the pump around back of the station. She was the only one with baggage, but she had learned on an earlier train trip not to leave anything behind even for a minute or it would not be there to greet her when she returned. She "lost" a hat and favorite book that way. Better to lose a seat than valuables.

When her turn to refresh finally came, she let the cool water run over her hands, splashed it onto her face and allowed a dribble to snake down beneath the collars of her three dresses. She cupped her hands again, filled them and gulped, then swallowed again and again to cool herself inside and out. She shut off the pump, smoothed her hair away from her face, picked up her crate and bag... and heard the train's whistle as it pulled away from the station.

She ran but was no match for a steam engine. Frustrated and angry, she dropped her load to the ground and gave the crate a kick as if *it* bore responsibility for picking *her* up and carrying her back to the train on time. It did not apologize, so she collected her things and tramped slowly to the small station and a conversation with its master. He informed her that the next train to Montgomery was the following day, same time. Sorry. But the conductor did look for her before giving the go ahead. A little girl told him that the lady who was crying picked up all her baggage and left the train, so he gave the signal. Sorry.

Sorry could not help her decide what to do for the next twenty-four hours, so she looked for a spot in the shade and dragged herself and her paraphernalia there to wait it out until either a very good idea or a miracle rose from the heat waves. She chastised herself for being so thoughtless. Despair was no excuse for abandoning good sense. How in the world did she expect to travel all the way to Indiana, find a job and housing for two, and make a life for them both if she could not even catch a train? She allowed her head to droop to her chest and her eyes to close as she pondered a future that had no form.

A tap, tap and clearing throat brought Lottie back to the sweltering present. An older man leaned down to her, gray hair, light tan that stopped at his collar, slight stoop, and with his hat in his hands. "Pardon me, Miss, but do you need he'p? My wife Ida Mae over there..." He waved his hat in the direction of a horse cart and the figure standing next to it—a skinny beanpole of a woman more than a head taller than her husband, same age, same hair hidden under a bonnet, same stoop. "...says that when she got on the train at Dothan, she seen you all upset and wonders if you might be needin' some he'p." His wife climbed into the cart, folded her hands in her lap and lowered her eyes. "You waitin' for a ride that didn't show? Can we give yuh a lift somewheres?"

Lottie gazed up into his kindly eyes and swallowed her pride. "Actually, I'm waiting for the next train to Indiana."

His eyes laughed for him. "Well, now, that'll be a long un. Not 'til tomorry. I don't recommend spendin' the night alone out here. There's usually a room free above the bar, but I don't recommend that neither. Yur welcome to come home with us. We got us a nice porch and a good dog who'll keep the foxes from nibbling yur toes." He stretched out an arthritic hand to help her up.

"How can I resist?" she replied.

"The name's George," he stated. "George Rider."

"Lottie," she said and took his hand. "Lottie Dickson. Nice to meet you, George."

He picked up the crate and led her toward the cart hollering, "Scoot y'self over, Ida Mae. We got us company for supper."

Her assumption that "home was just down the road apiece" turned to apprehension when it was not. They left all traces of civilization behind and looked forward to crossing three bridges before arrival. George babbled all the way. Ida Mae smiled sweetly and nodded as her husband described the area. Good ground, mostly sharecropped. The man he worked for was a circuit solicitor gone most of the time on his rounds. George did not work a farm anymore but functioned as caretaker for his boss's land. Nice man. His wife had passed on three years before, so Ida Mae fixed meals for him and took them up to the big house whenever he was home for a few days. She kept his place clean and tidy too. "Maybe he'll ride in later this evenin' and you'll have a chance to meet him."

Just a short way outside of Banks as she was told, the congenial trio turned down a tree-lined lane toward a modest two-story white house with large front porch, sizable lawn and profuse flower beds. George tended the lawn and Ida Mae, the flowers, Lottie learned. They passed a small barn and equipment shed and stopped in front of a cabin.

"Here we are, ladies. Stay put 'til I can he'p yuh off." He came around the cart and lifted Lottie down. "Light as a feather." And then his wife. "Light as half a feather, Ida Mae," he smiled lovingly. Then he hefted the crate. "This here is heavier than three times both of yuh together. What yuh got in here? Bricks?"

Lottie hesitated. She could not very well use the line she did on her brother—syrup, peanut butter and pickles—for good manners required her to share any food in thanks for their hospitality. "No. A typewriter." At their confused looks she continued. "A machine that copies handwriting to look like words in a book. I hope it will help me find a job when I finally get to Indiana."

George shook his head and clucked his doubtful approval while setting the crate carefully on the porch beside a rocking chair. Ida Mae invited their guest inside to settle while she started supper—buttermilk biscuits with sausage gravy, fried okra, and tomatoes with maybe a spoonful of leftover peach cobbler if her husband had any left over after she was gone for the night.

Lottie wanted nothing more than to strip off her dresses and sit under running water from a pump, but with no food to contribute to the meal, she felt obliged to offer her help in the kitchen. She was a practiced biscuit maker she told her hostess. She unpinned her hat and laid it aside, donned an apron and was soon up to her wrists in flour.

Some time later George leaned his head in the door. "Put another cup o' cream in the gravy, Ida Mae. The boss just rode in. I'll see to his horse and let him know we brung a stray home with us so he don't reach for his rifle when she goes sleep walkin' in the night." His loud chortle followed him to the barn.

Even more time later George leaned his head in the door again. "Put another plate on the table, Ida Mae. The boss is comin' to supper here. Says he wants to meet a vagrant who lugs a machine around with her." He chortled again and was gone.

Lottie froze. The thought of coming face to face with a man studied in the law when she was a runaway gave her the shivers again. She found a moment to wash her face, comb back her hair, pinch her cheeks and tidy her many layers of clothing. They gave her a plumpish look which might be to her advantage with a man and his rifle on the premises.

She need not have worried. The man in question, Mr. Benjamin Tyrell, was middle-aged and on the medium-height and stocky side with a mustache, full head of brown hair long at the collar and graying above the ears, a gentle face and sorrows hidden deeply in his brown eyes. He knocked before letting himself in and hung his white hat on the stile of a kitchen chair out of habit.

Somewhere between sopping up the last of the gravy and waiting for Ida Mae to spoon out two helpings of dessert divided into four with chopped fresh apple and cream to stretch them a little further, the conversation took the turn Lottie expected from Mr. Tyrell's first appearance at the door. "Tell me, Miz Dickson. What inspires a pretty, single young woman such as yourself to venture alone into unknown parts far away from home?"

"I'm a widow, so necessity."

"Really. How so?"

"My husband and I planned together to move to Indiana with the hope of finding better jobs. We had almost enough money saved when he was killed in an accident."

"I'm sorry to hear that." His eyes signaled that he was, truly. "And you're from?"

"Different towns in Georgia. I took some classes in Savannah so I could work at a local general store doing accounts and correspondence."

"And your family. You didn't want to stay near them to help you...?"

Lottie shook her head. "Mine may not be a popular opinion of the times, but at some point every young woman, married or not, should be prepared to take care of herself and any children. Then, at least she'll have choices. That time came to me sooner than expected."

He could tell that she was being less than candid with details of her past, and she could tell that he could tell. Finally she said, "You, as well as I, know how difficult it can be to share important moments in your story when every word you utter carries with it a piece of those special memories that will no longer belong only to you. I've wept enough for one day." She noticed his eyes begin to moisten. "For the moment, I'm embarrassed that my 'I'll be stronger on my own' position didn't factor in how to read a train timetable carefully or how to listen for a conductor's call." Smiles and chuckles traveled around the table. "So, tell us, Mr. Tyrell, one interesting encounter of your recent circuit."

He scooped up the last of his peach cobbler, wiped his mouth with a napkin and tilted his chair back. "I'm not free to discuss specifics," he said staring right into her, "but I will tell you about one nice old guy who is driving me crazy." He launched into a lengthy tale about a man, now a widower, who contacted him by letter waiting for him at the County Courthouse about every three weeks. He told "Benjamin" to stop by on his rounds on week one; expecting a result by his round on week two; and after thinking about it for a week, required a redo and thus another letter on week three.

"His issue, if you can tell us?"

"A rewrite, addition to or deletion from his Will. The darned thing is this thick now," he stated, demonstrating with a space between his forefinger and thumb. "It takes a whole weekend just to hand write a new document for him to change again and again and again. My wi... I used to have help, but now I muddle through on my own."

"Did you ever consider making your circuits longer so you would see him every two weeks instead of one?" Lottie asked.

He nodded. "I did, but he's lonely. Doesn't get much company that far out. And to beat all, he has practically nothing to pass on to anyone!" Smiles and chuckles traveled around the table again. He tilted his chair forward and took a deep breath. "I guess I continue to play his game because he reminds me to be grateful for what I have."

A calm silence settled over the group as all four pondered what they were grateful for that day, and good food shared with good company was noted by each.

The lawyer signaled an end to the evening by standing up and reaching for his hat. "Mighty fine meal, Ida Mae, as usual. Many thanks. I enjoyed the company," he said with a glance toward Lottie.

"Hang on, Mr. Tyrell. I have an idea brewin'. Why not take a look at that typo machine of Lottie's? It might be a way of easin' yur workload." George did not wait for a reply. He was out the door and back in an instant with the crate and set it in a clear space on the table. He untied the rope and pried off the lid. When Lottie removed the sacking, the other three stared at the unusual contraption that was supposed to transform ink to printed word.

Mr. Tyrell shook his head. "I don't see me learning how to use such a thing where the letters are all mixed around."

"It's easy, once you learn the keyboard," Lottie said. Do you have time for a demonstration?"

Three heads nodded in the affirmative.

"I only have a few sheets of paper, and the ribbon might be a little dry, but I'll do my best," she said while winding the spools back and forth with her fingers. She inserted a piece of paper and began, *In th b ginning God cr at d th h av ns and th   arth.*

The man shook his head again. "I recognize what that's supposed to say, but it sure doesn't make sense from where I'm standing."

"It will, if I can find my pen and ink." She scrounged in the corners of the crate, whipped the paper out of the typewriter, replaced all the missing "e"s with perfect size and type, and handed it to him for inspection.

He studied it carefully for several moments. "This is incredible, but is it really faster than writing by hand if you have to replace all the 'e's?"

"Most people don't have to. Machines come with a full set of letters. I broke that type bar some time ago and had to find a way to get by." Now that she felt more at ease in the company of this very nice professional man, a gleam found its way into her eye. "Are you up for a challenge?"

George and Ida Mae exchanged a "what's up?" look. The attorney shrugged a "why not" and nodded.

"Good. Handwriting man against broken machine. First paragraph of the Bible from memory." She ripped her paper in half and waited for George to find a pencil for his boss to use. "Our host will give us a start signal."

George beamed, waited a few seconds, and shouted "Go!"

Lottie was almost twice as fast, but Mr. Tyrell was a gracious loser. "Impressive performance," he said while stuffing both papers into his shirt pocket. "Many thanks again. I'll say my goodbyes now. I have a lot to think about tonight." He smiled, donned his hat and left.

George and his wife stood speechless at what they witnessed in their little kitchen. He finally came around to address the situation at hand.

"Let's get you settled for the night. Ida Mae, find Lottie a quilt and pillow. You come on out to the porch and he'p me move these rockers together. After the day you've had, you'll probably fall asleep before we're done." He gave Sparky the dog a scratch behind the ears and orders for the night. "You lie down right there at the top of the steps and don't let no one or no thing near this little lady of ours. Got it?"

The dog yipped his understanding and curled up right where he was told.

When all was quiet inside the cabin and the gas lamp turned off, Lottie slipped out of two of her dresses, found her way to and from the outhouse and the pump, and draped the thin quilt lightly over her body. Alabama nights seemed to be no cooler nor less humid than Georgia ones, but that did not keep her from falling asleep the minute her head touched the pillow. For a bad start, this day proved to be a very good one.

*

Lottie awoke to Sparky's deep growl. She opened her eyes just a slit to the dark of a moonless night. Her ear, however, picked up bootsteps approaching the cabin. With no adequate way to defend herself, she reached for a shoe, then heard another sound, a "Shhh, Spark. Only me." Tail thumping followed, so the stranger must be familiar she realized, but the voice did not sound like George's. Next came, "Go wake up that body you're guarding." A warm, fuzzy muzzle nudged her arm and a slobbery tongue licked her hand. She sat up to find Mr. Tyrell standing at the foot of the porch steps.

He tipped his hat. "Morning. You up for a challenge?"

She pulled the quilt to her chin and tried to appear offended, but a snicker sneaked out. "As you can see, I am not up yet, but I am willing to listen."

He stepped onto the porch and pulled the rocker from beneath her feet to sit face-to-face. "Now, I know you're set on getting to Indiana as fast as you can. George will take you into Troy today and make sure you don't miss your train, if that's what you really want. But if you will consider staying here a day or two to mull over other options, I might have a proposition for you."

Her eyebrows shot up.

He flushed and cleared his throat. "I mean, an offer. I might be able to offer you some choices to think about." He placed a sheaf of papers on her lap and tapped them. "This here is the Will I talked about last night. Could you type it up for me? Fresh paper is on the bottom."

Lottie examined the pile of handwritten pages with parts lined through and notes in the margins. "Definitely a challenge, but I'll give it a try. How soon do you need this?"

"I'll take whatever you've got by the time I get back."

"May I ask how many days you'll be gone and where?" She imagined being stuck in the rockers for a week with only a dog for company.

He smiled and laughed as he left the porch and started back to his house with a jaunty step. "Late afternoon. Tell Ida Mae to have her frying pan ready. For the first time in more than three years, I'm going fishing on a Saturday!"

"How far along did you get with those papers I gave you?" Mr. Tyrell asked during a meal of catfish, fried potatoes, collard greens, and fresh carrots.

George pointed his fork across the table. "Lottie here had that work done by midday. Then she he'ped Ida Mae finish the laundry that's been piling up. Got most of it ironed too. And just wait 'til you taste her rhubarb sauce." He smacked his lips and smiled at her. "We're mighty glad she decided to stay another day."

"Me too. I'm looking forward to that sauce. But first, I'll have second helpings while Lottie tells us how she got along with my chicken scratches. Any problems?"

"I finally got the hang of your scrawls, but..." Her face flushed. "...I'm embarrassed to admit that I didn't know all the words."

He rested his chin in his hand. "Hmmm. Never thought of that. So, what did you do?"

"I counted the letters and left space enough to fill in the correct ones when you have time to tell me what they are."

"Right after that sauce. With your pound cake, Ida Mae?" She nodded shyly. He looked at those gathered around the table "Excellent! I love sitting down to a fine meal with you folks. It's always so friendly here."

Ida Mae cleared a space on the table. George readied the lamp in case the session drew on till dark. Lottie spread out a clean dishtowel to guard against any leftover grease, then placed two piles of papers on it—the originals and her typewritten copies. Mr. Tyrell hefted the typing machine next to those. He and Lottie sat side-by-side at their workstations. George and Ida Mae took places across the table and stared at the strange goings on in their little kitchen for the second evening in a row.

The attorney was quite impressed with how professional the Will appeared: straight margins, crisp printing, accurate spelling and punctuation. As he proofread her work, he noticed that Lottie had taken the liberty of correcting his grammar a time or two. All the missing "e"s were perfectly inked in place. When it came to the words she did not know, he could see immediately why. They were legal terms—no way to guess, if his writing was not clear—and very few of them, at that. When they came to such a gaping space, she fed the paper into the machine, lined it up and filled in the letters he read. After, he explained to her what the word meant.

When they had finished and put the Will and papers aside, he asked, "How were you able to do so much deciphering on your own?"

She shrugged. "It's like a puzzle or a game of words with missing letters. Best guess of how the sounds must be connected. Once you get used to missing 'e's, you can try something else like 'sh's or 'th's and see what makes sense with how a word is being used." Her voice dropped to a bare whisper and her hands fell into her lap. "I once taught someone to read that way."

Her reaction did not escape the attorney's notice. He paused before he asked, "Wasn't this whole process a bit cumbersome... a bit awkward for you? Take a lot of time?"

"I didn't mind. I like learning new things. But it would have gone faster if you had just read to me from your notes. I could have taken it down in shorthand and typed from that."

"Shorthand? Haven't heard of it."

"A method of writing using symbols instead of words. You've probably seen it and just didn't realize it. In a courtroom. The man who sits to the side and takes notes of what people say. He uses shorthand so he can keep up with them. Then he'll type it up later from those notes. Shall we give it a try?"

Lottie grabbed a pencil and the back of a used piece of paper. Mr. Tyrell began dictating a paragraph filled with legalese that he used frequently and only paused when he noticed one of her eyes close and the eyebrow above the other arch. He soon learned the cue: please spell. And she only used it for proper surnames and the word "abrogate." She showed him the notes. He could not make head nor tail of them. Then she read the paragraph back to him and at the nod of his head, she typed it up. Perfect!

He rested his chin in his hand again. "Hmmm. You've been taught well. The possibilities...." He stacked his papers and replaced the machine in its crate. "George. Ida Mae. Lovely evening once again. Thank you. I'd like to have a private talk with Miz Dickson. All right with you if we use the porch?" He did not wait for an answer but grabbed her by the elbow and ushered her outside. He pulled the rockers face-to-face and gestured for her to sit.

"I don't mean any of what I'm going to say as criticism or insult. Judging character is my job as an attorney. In my experience, for a single young woman like you to be coming from nowhere in particular and going to where she's not quite sure can mean one of two things. She's running away from something or running to something. If she's running to, she's in a hurry and wouldn't hitch a ride with strangers going a direction not planned. She'd head on to the place where folks were waiting for her. She wouldn't stop for an overnight or an extra day like you did without trying to get in touch by telegram or letter with whoever is waiting. Same is pretty much true for running away. Can't risk stopping. So where does that leave you? Where do you fit in?

"I don't need to know the particulars, but I do need to know if you are running from the law."

She shook her head. "No Sir."

"You sure? If I'm supposed to uphold the law, I can't afford to be disregarding it or abusing it. I cannot risk my good reputation, so I'll ask again. Are you running from the law or anyone else who's likely to show up in the middle of the night with a shotgun pointed at my head?"

No one would come after her. No one would realize she was gone until she did not come back after a few weeks. No one would suspect she would not return except her boss, and he would not tell anyone why. "No sir," she repeated.

"I'll take you at your word, then. I'm also guessing you don't really know where you're going. You have a general plan but no people or job waiting for you. True?"

"Yes sir."

"To your credit, you have a very professional manner, are well-spoken, very skilled and have lost your southern drawl, but you are southern farm stock, born and raised. Yes?"

She lowered her eyes. "Yes. What was your first clue?"

"No offense. Probably the layers of dresses you were wearing when you got here. Only reason for that is you don't want to carry extra baggage or don't have extra bags. Any young woman as well trained as you would have more and/or expect someone to carry it for her. Put that together with your knowing your way around a kitchen and how to iron my linen shirts and most of all your not being phased by sleeping on a porch in rocking chairs—that's the sign of hearty stock. But also of a smart young woman who is trying to break away. So maybe we can work out a situation that would benefit both of us."

This man was a keen observer, Lottie realized. Better tread carefully.

"Since I lost my wife, I haven't stopped to take even one breath of fresh air. Work. Work. Work. Keep busy. Stay on the road so I don't have to go home to that empty house. But I'm getting tired of running. I want to stay around here more. Build up my practice in the small towns around Troy and in Troy itself. I'm tired of riding all day and writing all night.

"And I think you came along at just the right time—maybe for both of us. But I need to ask you one more question. Can you keep a secret?"

"Yes," she replied confidently. Her entire life was one big secret now. She dared not break confidence with herself or anyone else.

"Good. Most of my work is contracts, property agreements and such. But some documents are very sensitive. Personal. And cannot be compromised, spoken about or shared with anyone.

"So here's my offer. You stay here with us for the next few months on a trial. At the end of a week, I'll bring you the work I've collected and you'll have the following week to complete it. I'll check it over, then bring you more and so on. If you're interested, we'll talk about compensation. I know you're anxious to get on to wherever you think you're going, but maybe a stop here will give you time to think things through. You don't have to answer just yet. Sleep on it. We'll talk more tomorrow after Sunday dinner. I assume you'll stay through dinner."

The offer was not the problem for Lottie. The next few months were, as her baby kept growing inside her. But "next few months" was an indefinite period of time. She could work hard, save her store wages and add to them, then leave a month before her baby was due. She would have enough money to take care of herself until after the birth, and once she found a job she would be in a much better position to keep it. "I must stay through dinner. I'm making the dessert."

*

Lottie begged off of accompanying the three to church in Troy. She needed the time to bathe, wash her hair, and rinse out some clothes. Could she please use the large wash tub out by the pump? Ida Mae nodded. Lottie would spend some time with the Good Book once she felt cleansed enough to touch it. If Ida Mae would tell her the menu, she would start the Sunday Dinner to be ready on their return from Troy. Agreed? The older couple nodded and headed their cart up the lane.

Freedom. Half a day of freedom. Lottie could not believe her luck. She wasted no time in heating buckets of water on the cast-iron stove and hauling them back to the pump—filling, heating, and emptying again and again—until both the depth and the temperature of the water were tolerable. She stripped and stepped into the tub that was just large enough for her to sit cross-legged. Dribbles of water over her head, down her face and shoulders, onto her back and chest pooled on her swelling tummy. She covered herself in sweet-smelling suds and massaged her stomach searching for signs of life inside. She would begin showing soon. Time to think about loosely binding her middle with a long, wide strip of diaper cloth. Then the dam broke. Her body bathed in as many tears as cups of soapy water. "No!" she cried. "I don't want to be sad. Today I want to be happy. Today I have a chance to make life a little bit better for us. To give *you* a fair start in this world."

She pulled her dirty clothes into the tub with her, leaving her middle dress aside to wear. She scrubbed and scrubbed to remove travel dust, soot, sweat and grease stains from them. From hair to toes to cuffs and collars she scoured and then rinsed in fresh, cool water from the pump. She drip-dried while wringing out the clothing and dropping it in one bucket while she bailed wash water from the tub with the other until the vessel was light enough to upend and rinse. Satisfied that she had left the area tidier than she found it, she stepped into her middle dress, filled the empty bucket with water to rinse her feet again once she reached the cabin, and trod carefully across the damp paving stones leading back.

Next chore: Dinner. Ida Mae left the fixings for fried chicken, potato salad, peas, skillet cornbread, dill pickles and Lottie's chocolate pudding with cherries. Stoke the stove. Start the chicken and potatoes. Hang the laundry. Turn the chicken and cool the potatoes. Shell the peas. Mix the cornbread. Start the pudding. Test a clean dress to see if it is dry enough to iron. Not yet. Cut up the potatoes and herbs. Make the dressing. Add the chocolate to the pudding and cool it. Test a dress again. Just about. Remove chicken to a platter, cover and set on a warm spot on the stove. Clean the fry pan for the cornbread. Find a space on the stove to heat the iron. Grab a dress, ready or not. Fill an empty bucket to soak the one she's wearing. Iron the dress. Dress the salad. Open the jars of pickles and cherries. Uggh! Ooof! Where was her brother when she needed him? Uggh! Success! Thicken the cherry sauce. Set the table. Change clothes. Brush her hair. Plop dirty dress and towel into bucket. Take a deep breath. Listen for the mule cart. Here it comes. Put the peas on the stove to boil and the batter in the skillet to fry. No time for the Good Book. Save it for bed. Dinner's ready! Whew. So much for her half day of freedom.

The gathering around the table was more congenial than usual, more relaxed. While they waited for the peas and bread to come to the table piping hot enough to do a hunk of butter justice, George and Mr. Tyrell bantered about the folks at church that morning and the issues they brought with them. Both rolled up their sleeves, crossed their arms on their chests, and leaned back to add to their comfort.

"The preacher must have delivered quite a message this morning for you two to be wearing such smiles," Lottie said.

The attorney turned to her with a grin and a glint in his eye. "Perfect. 'Seek, and ye shall find.' Open your eyes. You might find just what you've been looking for. The message to me? It's time for the dark days to be over. Let some sunshine in and move forward. And I plan to do just that as soon as we get those platters of food on the table and some business settled between the two of us."

George and Ida Mae exchanged startled stares. Lottie jumped up to fill the table. No further specifics were given until time for dessert. Mr. Tyrell pushed back his chair and stood. "Mighty fine meal as usual. Many thanks. Lottie and I are going to step outside for a minute. Don't dive into that pudding until we get back." This time he escorted her off the porch and a ways further down the lane.

"I hope you've thought about my offer. I'd love for us to work together as a team. There's plenty enough for both of us to learn. Will you accept?"

Lottie stared into his kindly eyes. "I have thought about your offer. I'd like very much to stay and help you for a few months. But I cannot commit longer than that. I need to be further north before winter sets in. And I don't want to inconvenience George and Ida Mae too much longer. If that is agreeable, then I'm happy to sign on."

He broke into a huge smile that had been hiding beneath his mustache. "I can't tell you how pleased I am. You'll have room and board, of course. On our farms we grow, raise or receive in payment almost everything we need. You'll take meals with George and Ida Mae." He turned her to point further down the lane. "See that small cabin behind the trees? Only a one-roomer. Not much to look at but tight and sturdy. Hasn't been anyone in there for years. We'll clean it up and rustle a table and chairs and a bed. I'm sure I have an extra gas lamp somewhere and we'll find a small stove—big enough for a kettle and some heat—before the rains come. I can't pay you much until my business grows some, but how does a penny a page sound?"

Lottie's eyes grew saucer-wide at his generous offer.

"Okay, how about two pennies a page? I can't go any higher just yet."

"More than satisfactory," she said. "And, thank you."

They hurried back to the cabin to share the good news. "Bring on the chocolate pudding, Ida Mae. George, no nap for you this afternoon after dinner. Lottie will be staying with us for a while longer, so we have a cabin to whip into shape!"

At the end of the next week, Mr. Tyrell brought a few documents to use as examples, a pile of notes, and a legal dictionary. "How about a dictation session after supper tonight?"

"And fishing for you on Saturday?"

"That's the plan."

At the end of two more weeks, Mr. Tyrell brought a pile of notes and a box of ribbons. "I checked around the Pike County Courthouse until I found a typewriter and asked where to buy ribbons. The man ordered me some from Montgomery. No excuses now! Dictation after supper?"

Lottie handed him a pile of completed documents from the previous week. "Proofreading and corrections first?"

He nodded, but when he returned he had only one correction, dictated his notes and left to ready his fishing gear for Saturday.

At the end of another month, Mr. Tyrell returned midday Friday leading another horse. "Not for you. For me. I'm going to try riding a little farther and a little faster. If George can meet me Wednesdays midday at the Brundidge junction with a fresh shirt, fresh horse and the work you've finished, I can trade him for the work and notes I have so far.

28

And when I return Friday with only a little more work, I can have the full weekend off."

"Why not come back for Wednesday nights to make the switch?"

"Too many extra miles and hours for me and my horses. Besides, if I can feed you work and hit the courthouse with finished documents twice a week, the turnaround will be faster and we can take in more. Good idea?"

Lottie smiled and nodded, thinking of all those pennies piling up.

At the end of the next month and a few adjustments to his circuit, Mr. Tyrell agreed that the midweek handoff was working. He had added a few new clients.

"More work. More pennies!"

At the end of the next month, Mr. Tyrell had added a few more clients. "Word is getting around. Business is picking up. By the way, I brought you a present."

Lottie couldn't contain her delight. "A new typewriter! With an 'e'! Now I can get my work done in half the time."

"Use the extra to get some rest. You're looking a little tired and peaked lately."

Lottie pulled her shawl more tightly around her shoulders to drape down her front.

At the end of her eighth month, Mr. Tyrell dragged in so late on Friday night that he did not have the energy or enthusiasm to work. "Save it for Saturday," he said with downcast eyes.

"Is there anything I can do on my own? Then you could hit the streams early tomorrow morning as usual, and we could make short work of the rest in the evening."

He shook his head in frustration. "There's that cotton pickin' Will again."

"No problem. I practically know it by heart after three revisions. It'll be ready for you when you return. Go ahead and enjoy. Just bring back enough fish for our dinner."

His eyes smiled for him.

After two days of rest, relaxed times along a stream bank, and Ida Mae's hearty meals, the attorney was in a jovial mood and so appreciative of Lottie's conscientious work that provided the opportunity for him to recoup. She did not have the heart to tell him she would leave on the coming Saturday's train north. She excused herself from the table early and returned to her snug little cabin to contemplate the journey ahead without Jim Boy.

*

Lottie awoke to a light rap on the door. She had no idea how long she had slept, but no daylight shone through her window. Must be the wind, she decided, and rolled over.

The rap sounded again, followed by Ida Mae's soft voice. "Lottie, you awake? We needs to talk."

Those were the first two complete sentences Lottie had heard the woman speak since they met at the train station. She grabbed her shawl and scurried to the door. "Is something wrong? George?"

"No. He's asleep. Told him I's goin' to the privy. C'n I come in?"

Lottie nodded and pointed toward the table. She lit the lamp and sat across from the woman, staring at the map of wrinkles that surrounded her tired eyes. "How can I help you?"

"Not me. This is 'bout how I c'n he'p you." Ida Mae reached across the table to pat Lottie's hand. "I wan'cha to tell me when yur time comes sos I c'n he'p you."

"I... I don't understand."

"A young'n' like you shouldn' be birthin' alone. I'll he'p."

Lottie's heart screeched to a stop at the sudden realization that she had been found out. "How do you know?"

"Dearie, a woman can tell."

"Mr. Tyrell. Does he...?"

Ida Mae shook her head, causing her gray curls to dance around her face. "No. Men don't recanize the signs like a woman do. But you needs tell him before that baby comes. It's only right he should know."

"I was going to leave the end of this week so I wouldn't have to tell him. Spare him his disappointment in me. I'll be long gone before...."

"In my 'sperience, babies gots minds o' their own."

Lottie was shocked. George never spoke of their children, and Ida Mae hardly spoke at all. "Do you have children? Where are they?" As soon as she saw the sadness in the woman's eyes, she wished she had not asked.

"Three. Two boys and a girl. My oldest, he were killed in the War. He'd be bare fifty now. My other boy died of the tetanus. And my beautiful little girl died giving birth. Both her and the baby. So I knows you shouldn' be on yur own when yur time's come." She gave Lottie's hand another pat. "That's why I brung Sparky with me. He's to stay with you nights, and if you needs me, you tell him to go find George. He'll come to us right away."

By her own calculation, her baby was not due for about a month, but Lottie could not bring herself to hurt the woman who had taken her in by refusing her thoughtful offer. "That's very kind of you, Ida Mae. I'm sure I won't need to send him, but I'll be glad for his company." She smiled and rose to open the door and let her guardian in. Together they watched a nightdressed figure make her way back up the lane.

For two days, Lottie worked through twinges and backache. By Tuesday night she awoke with a severe jolt of pain and had to admit that her calculations were wrong and Ida Mae was right: babies did have minds of their own. She hobbled to the door and let Sparky out with the command to "find George." A short time later, she heard a scratch at the door and opened it to find Sparky back and Ida Mae not far behind carrying a bucket of water and an armful of clean rags.

The woman did not say, "I told you so" but placed her hands on Lottie's tummy and gently felt the activity inside through another contraction. "You gots a ways to go yet. If you get worried before I can get back here, send Sparky again." She stared at the dog, pointed toward the bed and shut the door as she left.

Lottie closed her eyelids and waited. She rolled to her side and opened them to the droopiest pair of hound dog eyes she had ever seen and a wet nose inching toward hers. She scratched behind his floppy black ears and said, "I'm glad you're here." Sparky blinked and scooted a little closer to the bed. He did not stir again until he detected footsteps padding toward the cabin.

Ida Mae let herself in, this time laden with another bucket of water and an empty one with more rags. She stoked the stove and put a bucket on to boil. They did not chit-chat while they waited. The woman felt Lottie's tummy through another contraction, then removed the bucket from the stove before she left saying, "You gots a ways to go yet. I be back soon."

"Isn't George suspicious with you leaving again in the middle of the night"

A slight chuckle escaped the woman's lips. "Soon as I tell him I'm going to the privy and grabs me a bucket, he don't want to hear no more 'bout it." She pointed toward the bed. "Sparky, you's on duty again." As soon as the door closed, the dog settled beside the bed, and Lottie felt his muzzle rooting beneath her pillow.

On her third trip to the tiny cabin at dawn, Ida Mae brought another bucket, empty but for a pair of scissors and a jar of hooch. She sat on the bed and felt Lottie's tummy as before. "I got to go get George his breakfast and ready him for his trip to the junction. I made up some extra errands along the way to get him out of here early. By the time he gets back, I think you'll have you a baby." She managed a comforting smile.

"Oh, I forgot. Today's Wednesday," Lottie said "See that packet of papers on the table? Give those to George to take with him for Mr. Tyrell. If that man doesn't get his papers from me, he'll know something's wrong and be back here in a flash. I can't handle two sudden arrivals in one day." She tried to manage a smile but a groan interrupted her.

Ida Mae smoothed the damp hair from around Lottie's face to pat her cheek. "Don't you worry, Dearie. As soon as he's gone, I'll come sit with you." She picked up the packet and left with no directions necessary for the dog.

The only memories Lottie had from that time forward were the heavy steam from boiling water, the warmth of a cloth to her forehead, the fire of hooch down her throat, periodic painful spasms that disappeared as swiftly as they came on, the snip of scissors soaked in alcoholic liquor, and Ida Mae's soft voice telling her, "You gots you a boy."

*

Less than forty-eight hours following the birth of her child, Lottie looked around the one room that had been her sanctuary for the past few months. She left a thank you and goodbye note on top of the documents she wrote up the previous day. Making sure the floor was swept and all her personal effects packed away in her carpetbag with Bible on the bottom and diapers on the top, she straightened the bed and stretched her shawl on it where she laid her baby in readiness to cradle him in a sling across her chest. She struggled under the snugness of her three dresses and started to pin on her hat for the cart ride into Troy to catch the train north.

Sudden shouting from the direction of the main house spurred Lottie to her baby's side. She flicked an end of the shawl over him and turned toward the door to investigate. It crashed open from a boot's hefty thrust and nearly threw her into the wall, bringing her face to outraged face with the attorney.

"What the Sam Hill do you think you're doing, running away without telling me!" he shouted with purple apoplexy. He clenched his jaw and raised his hand but did not use it. "If you were my daughter, I'd have you across my knee and take a switch to you for showing no regard for the folks who took you in when you needed help! The least we deserve is a word of thanks and an explanation." His wide-eyed stare bore into her demanding a response.

She backed away. "But I did. I left you a note…" She pointed to the stack of papers. "…and we hoped to pass you on our way into town to say goodbye."

"More likely you hoped *not* to pass me on the road so you wouldn't have to justify your sudden departure to my face!"

Lottie stood her ground against his furious bellowing. "Not true! My departure is not sudden! I told you when you hired me that I could not commit longer than a few months. Those months are gone, and the time for me to leave has come. I need to move north before winter."

He tilted his head back to run his fingers through his hair, causing his hat to fall into the dirt behind him. He stepped into the room without invitation and engaged her in a stare-down. He blinked first. "I told you once that judging character is my job. *You* don't do anything 'sudden.' You plan. You carry only what you need—none of the frills. You work hard and save your pennies to support yourself if needs be. But taking off today *is* sudden. Why not wait until we're together for Saturday or Sunday dinner to give us the news?" He glared at her hard and slammed his fist against the table. "What are you hiding from me, girl!"

Lottie did not have to answer. A squall came from the bed.

Mr. Tyrell leapt to attention and strode in the direction of the sound. He yanked the corner of the shawl away, stared in disbelief at the two-day old, glowered at its mother and stomped his way out of the cabin, trampling his white hat and kicking at the dusty path as he headed further into the red maple woods.

She picked up her baby to soothe him, but her rocking and humming could not drown out the heart-rending wails coming from outside. Was that the yowl of a wounded bobcat? The high-pitched squeal of a trapped razorback? She pressed her hands over the baby's ears, but her own vibrated with each shuddering whack of wood on wood as if a tree were being chopped down with one of its own branches. Then silence. She cuddled her child until he fell asleep again, then laid him down and cozied him in the folds of her shawl.

When she turned around, Mr. Tyrell was standing in her doorway looking as if he had been on the business end of a bullwhip. He dusted off his hat and blew his nose into a handkerchief. "I apologize for losing my temper and stomping out of here. May I come in?"

She nodded but kept her distance.

He pulled a chair out from the table and sat with his arms resting on his thighs and his hands folded. He had to look upward to catch her eye across the room. "Seeing your babe lying there so new sparked a pain in me that I thought was long buried." He removed his handkerchief again and wiped his eyes. "I'm going to share with you something very few folks know. And in return, I expect you to be straight with me. Deal?"

Lottie nodded, sat on the edge of her bed, and lifted her baby to her lap.

"My dear wife, rest her soul, expected a child five times in our life together. The first two miscarried. The next two were stills. And the last—a little girl—lived for just a week. She would be a couple of years younger than you are now. During all those months and years of hopeful waiting and then disappointment and sorrow, my precious wife never *ran away* from what the good Lord put on her plate. If I turned my back on you now, her spirit would haunt me for the rest of my days. 'Benjamin,' she'd whisper in my ear at night, 'you had a chance to save a child and you didn't. What kind of man does that make you?'

"Well, *this* man is *not* going to allow you to run away and drag that blessed gift along with you. Whatever it is that's got you spooked and thinking that safety lies somewhere in the north, we're going to root out and face up to. Did you lie to me? Are... were you married?"

She nodded. "Yes."

"Do you have any proof? In Alabama we do not record marriage certificates, and I assume Georgia is the same, but do you have anything that would prove when you married?"

She gestured toward her bag. "My Bible is at the bottom."

He got up, crossed the room and rummaged until he found it. "Hmmm. Italians. Carlotta? I wondered how you got that name. James Dickson. Married more than a year ago, so you weren't forced to because of the child. Did your husband know you were expecting?"

Lottie lowered her head and shook it.

"Why didn't you tell him?"

"I was on my way to give him the news when…."

"The truth, Lottie. Tell me the truth… please."

There was no avoiding his compelling appeal. She lifted her head and stared at him through misted eyes. "…when I saw him hanging from a tree!"

He dropped the Bible, turned on his heel and darted out the door. "Dear God, when will it stop!" he shouted to the trees. "Enough! Enough of this barbarity!" He stood stone still staring at the sky and searching for answers in the clouds before returning to the little cabin. "Let me see your child," he demanded.

She clutched her baby to her chest and set her jaw.

"Give me your child… please. I just want to examine him." He lifted the baby from her and cradled him in one arm. "Hmmm. What fraction is he?"

"My husband was a mulatto. His mother was white. I'm not sure about his father. Folks whispered he was black."

"That makes your baby one-quarter at most, but by law he is colored. He has your narrow European nose and head, and your eyes. No definite eye color yet. That's a good sign. High cheekbones from his father. Hair no darker than yours and not much of it, and he's only a slight shade darker than your olive skin." He smiled. "This little tyke has a chance of passing."

"Is that a good thing?"

"We'll see what the rest of the family says. In the meantime, take off a couple of those dresses, climb into bed and feed your infant son. You're not going anywhere today."

Lottie followed orders and even worked in a nap before she felt Sparky's nose nudge her shoulder. The dog raised his eyebrows alternately, looking from her to the baby as his muzzle inched toward the little bundle. At the sound of a shrill whistle, he hustled to take up guard by the door.

Moments later Mr. Tyrell appeared bearing one of the rockers upside down on his head, a comfy quilt across one arm, and a flour sack of edibles in the other. "Ida Mae insisted, now that we all know about your baby. George near dropped his teeth. We men are mighty upset that you women played secrets with us, and you need to know that!" He plopped the sack on the table, the chair on the floor near the bed, and folded the quilt to cushion its back and seat. He motioned for Lottie to take her place right there and right now.

She complied and rocked her baby in comfort for the first time.

He pulled a chair from the table and situated it to sit eyeball to eyeball as he had in their first serious conversations. "Time for you to have a social history lesson. I doubt customs are much different in Georgia, but here in the place we live, 'mixed' doesn't exist. Folks are either white or colored. The laws may define who is who now, but laws don't change how people feel. Our communities, cities and many states have their own minds and social conventions. Around here, folks are classified first by appearance and then by the ones they associate with, and if you think they're wrong, *you* have to prove different.

"So, is 'passing' a good thing? That depends. If your boy is legally colored and you want him to be white so he can fit in with the majority population, go to a good school, and have more opportunities... and if his appearance gives him that choice, then 'passing' can be a good thing. On the other hand, those who 'pass' spend their lives denying a part of their heritage, or they find that blood traits they thought lay hidden show up in a later generation.

"At the moment the problem is this: 'Mixed' have no place in our society at present. Neither color will claim them. *Your son* is not old enough to make a choice. *You* have to do it for him and *both* of you will live with the consequences."

Lottie stared down at the bundle in her arms.

"Babies are born into this world as innocent beings. They do not know race or religion or hatred or prejudice. They do not choose to be pigeonholed. That's our doing. Maybe the laws and the folks who make them in the next century will guide us to fairer, kinder attitudes toward all our neighbors. But right here, right now in Alabama in 1899, we have to live with the reality we've created. And *you* will choose that reality for your child."

Lottie sobered.

The attorney got up and helped himself to an apple from Ida Mae's sack. When Lottie waved off anything to eat, he returned to continue their one-sided discussion. "To be honest, George, Ida Mae and I are very hurt that you did not trust us enough to confide in us and ask for help. By intending to 'go it alone,' you risked your baby's life and your own needlessly. Your reason for leaving home and the support of family at a time when you needed them most is obvious now. But that was yesterday, and the situation you've dumped in our laps is about tomorrow. The three of us have put our heads together and come up with three options for moving forward."

He scratched his mustache, stood erect and paced, switching from his teacher-voice to his attorney-voice. "Number one: You spend the next week or two regaining your strength, then pack up your things—broken typewriter and all—and leave for who knows where in the north. You will be a single woman with good skills capable of finding adequate housing and a job. You will not look back. There are lots of families, both colored and white, who sharecrop my land. We will see that your son is placed with one of them—a loving one—and we will provide support and schooling for him and any other children in that family so he will not be thought of as 'different.' You will likely never see him again or won't recognize him if you do.

"Number two: You spend the next few months here with us raising your child with the intent of returning for him when you are settled up north far beyond Jim Crow land. Then you will leave to find and hold a job for at least six months, a job that will support *both* of you. That will give you a chance to investigate neighborhoods, housing, schooling and the restrictions that may apply to your little family. Can you handle single-motherhood there? Will you be able to take your child anywhere *you* can go? If, at the end of that time, you are satisfied that the two of you will have a good life together, send me a letter and I will travel there to see your situation for myself. If *I* approve, I will bring your son to you shortly thereafter.

"Number three: You give up your idea that all your problems will be solved if only you can settle in the 'north.' That means you will stay with us indefinitely, and your child will grow up in a white family. To that end, we will help you build records that declare him as white. We will not openly lie or break the law. We will use it. In return, you will not be allowed to take your child off this property without one of us accompanying you because frankly, we cannot trust you not to run away again. We will not allow you to endanger the life of that precious gift you hold in your arms. We *will* save *this* child." He wiped his eyes with his handkerchief.

Lottie shook her head. "You can't keep me here against my will. I know enough about the law to know that."

"You are right. *You* can leave anytime you want. But until *I* decide he's healthy enough and old enough for you to take him off *my* property, that baby of yours will *not* leave with you!"

He hesitated as he reached the doorway and signaled to Sparky to stay on guard. "All three of us agree on these conditions, and we'll expect an answer at Sunday dinner. We know this is difficult and that you must have loved your husband very much, but before you decide, ask yourself this. Where was your husband buried? Where will you be buried? Where do you want this son to be buried?"

The minute he was out of sight, Lottie wept harder and longer than she had since she left home. Sparky rested his muzzle on her lap next to the baby and licked at the salty tears pooling on his tiny fingers.

*

Mr. Tyrell was true to his word. After Lottie's agreement to option number three, she and her son did not leave the property together unaccompanied. She came to accept that reestablishing trustworthiness was much harder than telling the truth in the first instance.

Establishing a record for the boy involved his mother at every turn and the assistance of the other three adults. "Many who pass try to cover their tracks by leaving as little historical record as possible. We're going to do the opposite: establish a record for your child, beginning with a name," Mr. Tyrell informed her a week after her decision. "Where is that family Bible of yours?"

Lottie removed it from her bag, still packed and sitting by the crate, ready to leave on a moment's notice if evicted.

"Churches have a lot of power hereabouts, so the first public thing we'll do is have your boy baptized in the Banks church. To do that, he'll need a name. Have you given him one?"

"I wanted to call him James after his father, but that's probably not a good idea."

"That's the perfect idea," the attorney smiled. "Many families name their first boy after the father. Now for a middle...." He scanned the entries for her family. "Grandfather: Carlo Lombardi. Father: Charles?"

"An English translation for Carlo, to fit in here in America. I was supposed to be the first son, Charles, but wasn't, so Carlotta was the compromise."

He grinned broadly. "Perfect again—building on your Italian heritage, but adapting to American ways. That, along with your skin tone, gives the two of you a logical and factual background." He took the baby gently from his mother and cradled him. He patted the infant on the head and offered a finger for him to grasp. He wiggled the tiny fist as if shaking hands. "Welcome to the family, James Charles Dickson. Welcome!"

The attorney scheduled the baby's baptism for a couple of weeks following the Christmas holidays. "We'll have the preacher sign your Bible as well as the church's record book and certificate. As a white preacher from a white congregation, his signature carries with it the assumption that the child is white. Colored folks have their own churches. Let me see your Bible again." He studied the entries more carefully this time. "No preacher attested to your marriage." He gave Lottie that "something's fishy here" look. "No legitimate preacher would marry a colored and a white. That is illegal in most southern states and likely why he didn't sign below your names... if he even existed."

She flushed.

"No matter now. Preacher or no preacher, your marriage is not legal in Alabama, and there's nothing we can do to change that." He squeezed his eyes shut and pressed his thumbs into his forehead. "A Bible is not an official public record. It is merely accepted as such in the absence of or in support of other records. We'll go ahead as planned. We won't hand him your Bible until after I have the signed baptismal certificate in my pocket. Then, if he begins to question you about any of the entries or your past, we'll make polite excuse, take the Book with us, and leave."

The rites went off without a hitch. All four of them plus swaddled baby attended church that Sunday. Mr. Tyrell rode his horse in and arrived ahead of the others in the cart. He lingered outside gabbing with the regulars while the others took their seats inside. Lottie and baby sat between George and Ida Mae, giving the impression that this young woman whom the congregation had seen off and on over the months was likely related to the older couple rather than to the attorney.

All four adults went forward for the rites. All four waited after the service to collect the certificate that went straight into the attorney's chest pocket. Lottie presented her Bible. The preacher signed it with a big smile, hardly glancing at the entries. George, Ida Mae, Lottie and James left immediately. Mr. Tyrell lagged behind to gab casually a bit longer. The new family celebrated over Sunday dinner with pulled pork and pecan pie.

A birth record was next on the attorney's list. "In our state at present, registering a birth is not required. Many children are born on farms and their births are not questioned until time for school, *if* they go. If we voluntarily add James to the birth register as other fine families do, his case will be stronger. Next time I'm at the court house, I'll see how involved a process that is."

He returned at the end of the week with good news. "I had quite a chat with the County Recorder. When I told him I needed to register a birth for the son of a young woman who works for me, he fell all over himself to help. Said he would do anything for the person who makes my documents readable. Saves him time and frustration.

"Recording won't take but a couple of minutes. No name necessary, but we will list him as James Charles. Sometimes they list parents, but mostly just someone who witnessed the 'event.'"

He smiled. "And here's the kicker. He says he can give us a copy to keep right off. They've started using something called 'carbon paper' so they can make a copy of what he's writing in the record book as he does it. Then *you'll* have a record in case the county's books are lost or damaged. I guess courthouse fires are fairly commonplace. Anyway, I asked him where he got this 'carbon paper' and he gave me a sheet to use until he gets an order in and will sell me a package. Can you believe that? Now you can type two copies at once, and I'll have one for my files instead of a box full of chicken scratches!"

"Sounds great! When do we go?"

"Monday morning when I usually show up. *If* you've got your rent paid by then"

"Rent!"

He had that sly glint in his eye. "Yes, ma'am. If the County Recorder asks you where you live, I can't have you saying 'at Mr. Tyrell's place.' That would cause all kinds of talk. So you must be able to state truthfully, 'I rent a cabin from Mr. Tyrell.' Time to pay up." He extended an open right palm for the payment.

Lottie's eyes took a turn toward the ceiling. She swallowed hard and asked how much.

"One hundred per year."

"One *hundred*!" she cried. No one in her family had ever held that much cash in his hands at the same time. "You know I haven't earned that yet. Can I pay by the month?" She did not have that either, but it was worth a try.

The attorney shook his head. "All my rents begin on January 1 every year. Makes it easy for folks to remember. You're a lucky one. I won't charge you for the months you've been here."

Lottie stared him in the eye and stood firm against him. "You better not. Room and board were part of your offer."

He lifted his hand as if to scratch his nose but hid a smirk behind his palm. "I said, and I quote, '*You'll* have room and board.' Now I'm providing for two, and you *two* must be on my rent rolls to keep me honest."

"But you know I haven't earned near a hundred."

"I beg to differ. You've earned more than ten times a hundred." A chuckle was about to erupt.

Lottie threw up her hands in frustration and was nearly in tears. "There's no way I have a thousand dollars in the bottom of my bag. You... you... you're...."

"Who said anything about dollars? I collect all my rents in pennies, just like I pay you."

If there were an exotic description for embarrassment, Lottie was displaying it from top to toe. Despite being mortified, she joined her tormenter in eye-wiping laughter.

"I apologize, but you left yourself wide open for that one. Lesson for today: know the law, define your terms, and make no assumptions when dealing with important issues. Many of the folks who farm on my place have had little, if any, schooling. I require 100 pennies for rent and I require them to count it out for me and to sign two copies of a receipt. They'll have to be able to write their names in order to register to vote when granted that right.

"We gave each family a large jar with a band around it at the one hundred level. If they have more than enough, they keep that as a start on next year's rent. If they're a little short, we carry along some things that need doing—like mending or canning—and pay them for their work in pennies. We don't deal in IOUs or handouts. We deal in dignity. And a lesson or two in planning ahead, like when they need to pay poll tax too.

"Which gives me an idea. *You* could collect rents this year, and you could type up receipts with the carbon paper that's coming. Save me from handwriting two for each family." He stuffed his hands in his pockets and stared smugly at the floor. "I suppose I'll have to pay you for the extra work. Say, one hundred for collection and one hundred for receipts."

"Dollars?" she asked excitedly.

He threw back his head and laughed out loud. "Pennies! And you better be thankful for them. Now, you get started counting out your own rent and bring it with you to supper. Or do you need help?"

"Do you trust me to do my own or will you check my work?"

He left and strutted toward his house, raising a finger for each emphatic statement. "*Know* the law. *Define* your terms. And *make no assumptions* when dealing with important issues."

Monday morning would arrive all too quickly. Lottie had to wash and iron her best dress—the blue one with yellow flowers—and brush off her hat. Ida Mae's nimble fingers crocheted a tiny cap to match for the baby, and she searched her fabric scraps for a large enough piece of warm flannel to wrap him in. George readied the cart with extra blankets in case of inclement winter weather, and he grumbled at the "goings on that didn't set quite right" until he was sure that cute little thing winked at him. Mr. Tyrell recounted Lottie's pennies, entered her rental payment in his account book, wrote receipts for her to sign, locked his money and records in his safe, and went fishing.

"Stick to the plan," he reminded them all at Sunday dinner. "I'll go into the County Recorder's office first. You follow and sit on the bench by the door. I'll file the Land Agreement we finished over the weekend and give you its receipt on my way out. That will suggest to the Recorder that you are the woman who works for me. Then, it's your turn. You and Ida Mae go to his counter. She will carry your Bible. You hold James and fuss with him a little. That will encourage the Recorder to fill out the paperwork for you, as he often does.

"Either of you may give the baby's name and date of birth, but do not say 'white' if he asks for James' race. Lottie should merely tip the baby toward him and smile lovingly, allowing the recorder to judge for himself. If he is reluctant, show him the baptismal record in your Bible, but under no circumstances should you say the word 'white' or mark that box yourself. Do not break the law!"

"Isn't that lying?" Lottie asked.

The attorney shook his head. "Only if *you say* the word 'white.' There's the truth, and then there's the *whole* truth. If the recorder asks for a witness, nod to Ida Mae. Do not let your name, Lottie Dickson, be written down and do not sign your name that way. An illegal marriage does not entitle you to a legal name."

Lottie had never considered that aspect of her predicament. What would she do in the years to come if she could not prove that she was James's mother?

"If the situation becomes uncomfortable at any point, interrupt to ask if there is a fee involved. When he tells you how much, become embarrassed and say that you 'do not have money on you.' That will be true. Ida Mae will carry the money. Apologize and say you will return when you can to finish up. Then, leave. Do not rush; chatter with Ida Mae until you are through the door. If our plan *does* succeed, pay up, give gracious thanks and tuck the carbon copy into your Bible.

"If there's a hitch, we'll think of another way. If all goes well, I'll see you on Friday with smiles." He pushed back from the table to leave. "Oh, you might brush up on that southern drawl you've hidden away. We wouldn't want anyone taking you for a northerner."

A fresh baked peach pie greeted him when he rode in on Friday.

*

Six months later, Mr. Tyrell arrived with news. "The Enumerators are out to record the Twelfth Census of the United States. You all know what that means. Start baking now. Loads of cookies and bread that will keep until they get here. You'll have two extra hands to help this year, Ida Mae."

The kindly woman nodded with a gentle smile.

"Say, Lottie. Can you handle a cart?"

She gave a so-so nod. "I have done. On my family's farm, but it's been a while. If I have a choice, I'd rather ride a horse than drive a mule."

The attorney shook his head. "Sparky doesn't do so well on the hind end of a horse. He'll stay with you every minute."

Lottie shrugged her ascent. "Why horses and cookies for the census?"

"Good question. I like to keep the government workers who look us over very happy. If you and George travel ahead of the enumerator with meat sandwiches and cookies, and the farm family provides water and juice, those workers are mighty grateful for the kindness of our folk who are usually very suspicious of strangers riding in.

"I encourage them to have a couple of chairs ready outside on the porch or near their door so inviting a stranger inside won't be necessary. They can answer questions there and eat at the same time, leaving everyone feeling comfortable. No money changes hands and no signatures are asked for.

"The census is one of the reasons I insist my people pay rent. On the form, there are only two choices for where they live: own or rent. There is no option for a shrug of the shoulders and an 'I don't know.' Our folks can reply proudly, 'I rent this here house.' That also saves them answering questions about the farm.

"The forms are never exactly the same as the previous census. I looked at a blank one posted at the courthouse, and there are a couple of questions that will be difficult for our folks to figure out. No matter when the enumerator shows up, the applicable date for each family will be June 1 this year. Since you met some of our people when you collected rent, you'll know who was expecting at the time. A baby born before June 1 is counted. After June 1 it is not, even if the family doesn't get tallied until July or September. That's a hard concept for them to get their heads around. You'll be a big help there. Most adults know how old they are but can't remember the year they were born. You may have to figure that out for them. They can usually remember the season but not the month they were born. Just pick one.

"Then there's education. That's for children and asks for how many months they attended school. It must refer to 'in the last year' because if the answer were fifty-four, they might as well ask for six or nine years. Many schools are open for only five or six months a year around here.

"For you, your occupation is 'office clerk.' Don't try to explain what you do. It would never fit in the blank. In this case, your legal name is not important. You sign nothing. The enumerator fills in the form and frequently misspells names. For James's sake, Dickson might be someday, so check his spelling carefully. The census is not concerned with *who* you are but *what* you are: white or colored, male or female, adult or child, married or single, and your nationality/citizenship.

"The census taker decides race. When it comes to you and James, let him judge for himself as the recorder did. Don't you say 'white.' That would be a lie. If you and your parents were born in the US, then you don't answer the questions about when you immigrated or became a citizen. All of our folks are citizens. George, anything to add?"

"Don't drive your cart so fast that you tip it so the cookies fall off and git crushed. Folks will be real disappointed if they don't git their goodies."

"The census may not seem like a big deal to you, but once you have your family recorded, you will have a church record, a county/state record and a national record of James's birth and race. If you can copy down the two numbers in the upper right-hand corner of the form, his information can be easily found in Washington and sent wherever.

"The questions that bring me to tears every time are 'Mother of how many children' and 'Number of these children living.' Just a glance at any page of entries—as many as fifty per page—tells the tragic story of how many children don't live to adulthood."

If the mother was not allowed to take her child off the property unaccompanied, the same was *not* true for the child. Over the years, he left the property frequently with one of his three guardians but without the company of his mother. He learned to spot nesting places for foxes and flickers; listen for the sounds of chickadees and deer; bait a hook and scoop up its catch with a net; feed and care for the stock after rounds to the farms with George; play with other children while on those rounds; and interact with all adults with politeness, respect and a smile.

Jimmy, as he came to be called, stayed with Ida Mae when his mother traveled with George to collect rents. By the age of two, he began riding along with them. By three, he was counting too. By four, he suggested counting by stacks of ten, and by five he could figure out how much was lacking and what chore they had in the cart that could make up the difference.

When he turned six, Mr. Tyrell told his mother to stay home and concentrate on her own work; Jimmy could handle the counting and receive the one hundred pennies for the job. At the end of collection season, the boy counted out his own pay and put it in a jar.

"What are you saving for?" Lottie asked her son.

"I want to see the circus in Montgomery."

"What makes you think there's a circus in Montgomery?" the attorney asked.

"I read it in your newspaper a while ago. If George can find more chores for me, I might have enough by the time it comes in summer."

Mr. Tyrell turned to Lottie. "He can read?"

She nodded. "We spend time every night learning more and more words from the paper. I doubt he can spell 'elephant' for you, but he recognizes the word if there is a picture with it." Her eyes filled with appeal. "May I take Jimmy to Montgomery this summer?"

He eyed the boy up and down, then his mother, and shook his head. "Based on our agreement, Jimmy is *not* old enough yet for *you* to take him alone as far as Montgomery, especially when there's a train involved."

The boy's smile fell to a droop. His mother's rigid stare cut through the air.

"But," the attorney continued, "I'd love to take Jimmy to the circus. We'll make a day of it… and your mother can come with us if she agrees to abide by our rules."

The trio did travel to the circus, saw the elephants among other exciting exhibits, tried gooey food treats, and immortalized the event with a gadget the attorney brought along called a camera.

By the time Jimmy was eight, it was obvious that the boy needed more schooling than his mother could provide. During a Sunday dinner near the end of summer, Mr. Tyrell stood to make an announcement. "The courthouse is back up to full service after the '02 fire. Thanks to all of you, my business has increased several fold. There is now enough demand in the Troy area to keep me there for most of the time, with only an occasional sally along my usual rounds. I have, therefore, rented a small office space in the new county courthouse, and I intend to work there almost daily."

Shock and congratulations came from around the table.

"I did some investigating and found that a five-month school term in Troy begins in a couple of weeks. I propose that Jimmy be enrolled in third grade there."

The boy nearly fell off his seat.

"Do I have anything to say about your proposal?" Lottie asked.

"Say away."

"We don't know how Jimmy feels about going so far away to school each day. He'll spend more hours traveling back and forth than he will in a classroom."

"A problem already solved. I bought one of those Ford automobiles everyone talks about, so the two of us will ride in style. Jimmy may have to do his homework in my office or run some errands for me until I can leave, but I'll pay him for his time—for the running, not for the homework. What do you say, young man. Are you interested?"

Jimmy could hardly contain his excitement, then suddenly burst into giggles. "That means Mama will have to take up my old job of counting pennies while I get to ride in an automobile!"

Two years later, another announcement was made during Sunday dinner. "I have good news and bad news. I've been asked to serve as County Prosecutor."

Cheers circled the table.

"As such, I'm pretty much on call at all hours, so I've taken a room in a boarding house nearby."

Boos circled the table.

"How will I get to school then?" Jimmy asked.

"You'll have to walk. So will your mother… to her new job."

Lottie and her son traded glances of dismay.

"And I've found a nice little place for you two to rent not far from the courthouse. I don't want my secretary coming to work late."

George, Jimmy, and even Ida Mae cheered again.

Lottie grew very quiet and thoughtful, then asked, "What's the rent?"

"One hundred a month."

"Dollars?"

The attorney shook his head and grinned. "The new owner deals only in pennies."

Two years later, Sunday dinner was again the scene of an important announcement. "All votes are counted. You're looking at the new Magistrate Judge. I guess the time we've put in over the years to educate our neighbors and to show them some kindness and respect has come back to us."

George and Jimmy whooped. Ida Mae clapped softly. Lottie waited for the "but...."

"But... there are a couple of hitches. I can't come back to the farms every weekend. There's almost always trouble on Saturday nights, so the most I can manage is Sunday dinners. George can come in with the cart on Friday afternoons if you two want to spend the whole weekend here sometimes."

Mother and son exchanged a "how do we choose" look.

"The other problem is this. Magistrates don't have secretaries. They have sworn in clerks and there's a long line of brothers, uncles and sons waiting to be mine. Local office politics, they tell me. So, Lottie, you have a new position as assistant clerk to the County Recorder. He's tickled to death to get you. Said he campaigned for me on the side so he'd have a crack at you. He's still behind on replacing burned records from the '02 fire. What do you think of that?"

"Does he pay in pennies too?"

The attorney laughed and shook his head. "I guess you'll have to learn to count dollars."

Four years later, Judge Tyrell announced that he had won the election for District Judge. "My term doesn't begin until January, so that gives us time to find housing in Montgomery. You and Jimmy can wait to move until after school is out in the spring. Lottie, you may be my clerk if you want that job. Frankly, I can't do without you any longer. And Jimmy, there are some good colleges in that area and even a law school, so you'll have to decide whether you want to become a lawyer who helps folks who get themselves in trouble or a farmer who helps folks stay out of trouble. Lots of change ahead for all of us."

Jimmy received his diploma early.
Lottie followed Judge Tyrell to Montgomery.
Jimmy fell in love and joined the Navy.
The United States entered World War I.
Then the telegram arrived.

1978

I am lost. The road ahead forks into four, and I have no idea which prong points toward my destination. Buoyed with the confidence that I need only a ten-year-old memory to guide me, I followed the main route from my motel at the edge of Montgomery southeast through wiregrass country until I reached Troy. Now what? None of the forks looks familiar. I curse myself for not bringing a map. I need help. Which way do I turn?

I recall snippets of my conversation with a very nice man in the cemetery. He mentioned that this town boasted some of the best down-home cooking around, so I park my rental car and scan the main street for such a place. Three possibilities catch my eye. I walk to each and peer through its window to gauge the size of the breakfast crowd. Number two wins the "favorite" award. As soon as I open its door to enter, I understand why. Friendly faces and jovial chatter greet me. Inviting aromas of bacon, eggs, fried grits, and steaming coffee entice me. But the plate overflowing with chocolate gravy with bacon over biscuits that whisks past my nostrils convinces me that I have reached the mother lode.

I survey the crowd for the oldest employee and find her behind the counter.

"Can I he'p you, suga'."

"I'm looking for the cemetery."

Her laugh extends from her face to her ample belly. "You don't look near old enough to be needin' a cemetery yet. Which one you want? There be more than a dozen 'round here."

I turn as red as the strawberry-topped hot cakes whizzing by. "I thought there was only one, so I don't know its name. It's old and about ten to fifteen minutes from here."

"Good. Now we're down to half a dozen."

I fluster with the keys in my pocket. "Small with a sad wrought iron fence around it?"

She steps back to look me up and down. "Say, where y'all from?"

"California."

"Well, I'll be. You're that... *that* woman!" She turns toward the kitchen. "Lester, hurry y'self out here right now. She's real and she's here!"

Lester, I assume, appears wiping his hands on his apron. "Shush yur hollerin'. What woman?"

"The one your friend always asks about come fall, but she never shows up. Well, she's here now exactly like he said she would be, wantin' to know the way to the cemetery, exactly like he said."

The two stare at my face, now approaching beet red. Then at each other. "I'll gather some tins and the knife he left," the man says, "while you tell her how to git there." He hollers over his shoulder as he disappears into the kitchen, "Ask if she needs flowers. We still have some good ones out back."

I shake my head. "I did bring flowers, but not my wits apparently."

"Our friend told us as much. Said you might need some he'p cuz you tend to fluster about. Reminded us every now and again not to judge, just be prepared. Oh, you'll need a jug of water too. That place out there is bone dry." She giggles behind her hand at her own joke.

She motions to an empty stool. "You set y'self down right here while we git y'all fixed up. How 'bout some coffee?" A cup of tongue-scorching brew stares up at me before I can shake my head. "And sumpin to eat." Her eyes inform me that refusal is not an option.

I point to a tiered carousel of sweet treats. "One of those looks yummy."

"Pecan sticky buns. One of my specialties."

No fork accompanies the saucer-sized goody, so I pick it up and take a bite to confirm that both sticky and yummy describe it perfectly.

"Now," my hostess says, "to git where yur going, you go straight down the road about a mile." She points south. "When you come to a bright yellow house..." Her finger swings past my nose. "...turn right. The old road looks like an alleyway, but keep on it for six... seven miles. You'll recognize the place on yur left." Here comes her finger again.

A box appears on the corner of the counter. "Here you go, ma'am. Some empty quart tomato tins, a knife, and a coupl'a garden tools in case you find some weeds where you don't want 'em," the man says. "Jes' drop off what's left over when y'all come back through town. Oh! Water! Be right back." He hurries into the kitchen again.

I thank the hostess for helping me find my way and place a five-dollar bill on the counter. Her steely gaze implies that my money will not be accepted, so I say, "You've been so kind. Please allow me to treat the next person who comes in needing his day brightened." I gather the box and water and leave.

I find the bright yellow house with no problem and turn onto the rarely used road beside it. As I bump along, I realize how fortunate I am for the second time in this strange place, not only for the kindness of strangers but also for the confirmation that my cemetery acquaintance is *not* imaginary.

I confess to a hint of disappointment when I stop alongside the cemetery. The man is not here. My hope that our paths would converge again on this birthday anniversary remains unsatisfied, but there is no other car parked nearby. I do not hurry to carry two armloads into the graveyard. Perhaps he will come.

The graves appear well-tended requiring only a quick brush away of dried leaves, and I thank him for that. Green groundcover blankets my mother's plot. I cannot tell if it is natural or if he seeded it down, but I thank him for that just in case. I set out the three tin cans, fill them with water and thank him for anticipating my needs. I arrange three colorful bouquets and slip a freshly packaged handkerchief beneath his grandmother's in thanks for his loan that became a gift on my first visit.

When I step back to admire the colorful display, I sense that something is missing. I remove two flowers from my mother's bouquet and place one each at the bases of my grandparents' headstones—two people I never knew, but that kind man would have a wise explanation for my sudden impulse to honor them as well.

I rebox my scatter of clippings and tools and return them to my car. I pause before driving off. Did I come all this distance only to place a few flowers and then fly away? Or does proper visitation etiquette require expressing gratitude for the gift of life, as my caring acquaintance does?

I return to linger for just a few minutes longer. Think positive. Think positive, I remind myself. With so many happy memories to choose from that should not be a problem, but before long a familiar feeling rises from my chest into my head and behind my eyes. I came prepared. I reach for one of the two handkerchiefs I have in my pocket and, with no witnesses for miles around, I weep openly.

With no footsteps as warning, a familiar voice startles me. "I knew you'd be back one day, but I did not expect to find you unchanged after ten years. You cried when you left, and you cry now on your return. I'd recognize you anywhere. Welcome."

I appreciate his attempt at lightheartedness, but I am embarrassed to expose my blotchy red face.

"I'll just step over here and tend to my grandmother while you gather yourself. Take your time. I have lots to tell her." He turns his back to me and squats near her to carry on an inaudible conversation.

I am grateful for the space and do my best to pull myself together. Then I return his thoughtfulness by wandering away to "visit the neighbors" as he once put it. After a time, he catches up to me. "Mighty nice flowers you shared. Thank you."

"My pleasure. And my thanks to you for watching over Mom these last years."

We stroll as if we are long-time friends out for a daily constitutional. "Maxine at the café said you stopped by earlier this morning, so she hustled me away to catch you here before you left. All these years she and Lester thought you were an imaginary friend created to keep our conversations interesting. Would you be willing to share a harmless tidbit about yourself that I can pass along to keep them in the know?"

Harmless tidbits. Pleasant memories. A chance to divert my mind from recent events. Why not? "When I was a little girl, I loved Shirley Temple. I used to dress up and tap dance my way around the house from kitchen, to hallway, to bathroom and back, singing all the way. I even imitated her dance from the movie—you know, the one where she taps down the stairs—until I drove my mother crazy. My father loved it and egged me on."

He snickers. "How long did your 'entertainments' continue?"

"Until I outgrew my tap shoes and Mom said she couldn't find another pair in town. Will that tidbit do?"

He shakes his head and laughs. "I can hear it now. I share that and every time I walk through the café door, Maxine will holler loud enough to stop all conversation. 'Heard from your tap dancing woman friend lately?' But it'll be her eyes dancing when she does."

I laugh too, for the first time in a couple of years.

We wind our way back to our neighboring plots and gaze at them again. He breaks the silence. "Mind my asking what brought you here *this* year in particular?"

I do mind, but sharing with a barely friend far away from home might be easier than with curious mere acquaintances where I live. I take a deep breath and remind myself to stick to the facts. "My husband died two years ago."

I notice the shock in his eyes but plow straight forward before he can speak. "My husband was eleven years older than I and had a bad heart, so his death was not unexpected. I had not intended to return here for many years—if ever—but when we spoke of his desires, I realized how much consideration goes into final decisions. That led to my wondering again about my mother's choice to be buried here."

He has the politeness to remain silent, as if he were accustomed to listening.

"When we designed my husband's stone, and I finally ordered it and had it set, I also realized my mother did *not* have one. I tried contacting the funeral home in Montgomery, but they were no longer in business. No surprise there. Others that I contacted all needed the same information: cemetery name, location, and plot number. If I ever knew those details, I certainly can't remember them now." I start to well up. "So as soon as I leave here, I'm on a mission to knock on doors until I can find answers enough simply to order my mother a gravestone." And here come the tears.

He pulls the new handkerchief I left him from his sport coat, but I wave him off with my own number two of the day. He then pulls a notepad and pen from his breast pocket and begins to write, while I dab at my eyes and nose without embarrassment this time. He presses a ripped page into my hand. "All the information you need is right here. Mission accomplished," he says and walks off.

After all the exhaustion, emotion and frustration of this trip, I let go and allow the tears to flow. A full body-wrenching sob is exactly what I need. In a few minutes I pull myself together, secure that life-saving information in my handbag, and get ready to leave.

"Not yet!" he shouts from his car. He trots back carrying a container in his arms. "I have here the perfect medicine to bring you out of your glums today." He opens the small cooler to reveal two paper bowls, two spoons, a scoop and... "Maxine's hand packed, fresh churned peach ice cream!"

I cannot help but laugh. We sit on the ground facing our colorful array of remembrances and dig in. He explains that when I did not return the first year or two, he was left with a melty mess. Maxine suggested the cooler setup she used when folks ordered picnics. "If yur friend don't come, y'all can take it home to yur birthday party." He did just that the following year, and his family was delighted with the ice cream treat that soon became a party staple. He replaced the cooler he borrowed annually and gifted Maxine another half-dozen for folks who showed up unprepared for their outings, so long as she kept one back for him to use. "Let's leave all the dirty dishes and a little ice cream in the cooler as evidence that you came this year; otherwise, my family won't believe me."

"But your party...."

"Don't worry. I'll pick up another pint to take home on my way back through Troy. I'll return the garden tools too, if you like."

I nod my thanks to this kind, thoughtful man. "That would be great." We continue to make a dent in the ice cream, and with every spoonful I feel another layer of my anxiety slip down my gullet and disappear. A gentle breeze teases the hanging moss and sways our flowers, inviting me to relax. My voice speaks without my commanding it. "My husband was such a good and loving man. I give thanks every night for the time we shared."

My companion is as surprised as I, given my previous outburst. But he does not interrupt.

I point my spoon at him and use it to accentuate my words. "Now, here is a story that will really set Maxine back on her heels. My husband and I met onstage in Hollywood."

His blue eyes widen, but he does not respond, and I cannot stop myself from blurting out more than I have shared with most of my friends back home.

"He was cast as a doctor attending an aging patriarch. I played the role of the family's recalcitrant teenager and came to rehearsals dressed as and acting the part. One day called for an early start time, so I rushed straight from work in my dress, high heels, curls and lipstick. Our first scene together brought us face-to-face and nose-to-nose, and the rest is history. Here I sit, a widow, enjoying ice cream and still star-struck after thirty-plus years of marriage to a wonderful, handsome man."

He flashes an impish grin my way. "I see lots of pieces of pie coming my way for those stories. Got any more, like Oscars on the mantelpiece?"

"Hardly. The rest is pretty mundane. Theater kept body and soul together. Bit parts in movies paid for the frills. During World War II my husband's health deferment kept him from service, but the push was on in Hollywood to produce films that glorified our part in the war. Many bits were available for fighter pilots, jeep drivers, machine gunners, sailors, nurses and weeping wives until the war ended, the film industry went on strike, and we had a baby on the way. We gave up our aspirations for the big screen and worked in theater full time, my husband in scene design and construction and me in costuming. We moved out of the city, lived a modest but creative life, and raised two children with no complaints, no regrets. The most you'll get for that blasé story is a couple of day-old chicken wings."

He laughs heartily and wipes his eyes with his new handkerchief. "You're probably right, but there's nothing wrong with a simple, satisfying life. You are fortunate. Coincidentally, both my father and then I played our parts in the world wars as sailors, and that's when I met my wife, an army nurse, so you and I have more in common than just this date and place. That info ought to be worth at least a drumstick."

We share a good laugh, and I do... I really do feel so much better. "Yes, I am fortunate and so are my children who are now in their late twenties/early thirties. They made happy memories with their father as kids *and* as young adults. I lost my father at the age of sixteen, so only interacted with him as a child. My favorite memories of him are 'daddy/daughter days.'"

"Never heard of that."

"When my parents were first married and to maintain peace in the household, they adopted an 'arrangement' whereby each was granted freedom from the other for one day per week—the same day. My father was a true believer and regular church-goer; my mother turned ashen at the mention of either, so they settled on Sundays. He went his way; she, hers, and they recommenced late afternoon for supper together... until I came along. He eventually agreed with her that caring for a baby while being alone was not really 'freedom,' so he assumed all responsibility for me on Sundays—made animal pancakes for breakfast, slipped me into a pretty dress, learned to comb my hair, and off to church we'd go.

"He taught me to curtsy to the older ladies, shake hands with the gentlemen and not to color in the notes in the hymnals with my crayons. After, we'd go for a snack, to the movies or the local zoo, for a row on the lake, or read books under a shady tree. As a teenager, I was more interested in sodas and boys than I was in cotton candy and elephants, but I remember those 'daddy/daughter days' fondly."

Images of those sunny memories flash through my mind before I find words again. "When we returned home, my father always reminded me *not* to tell Mama what we'd done unless *she asked first*. She never did, probably because we would ask her the same right back and if she shared her private moments, they wouldn't be private any longer. I still wonder how she used those free days." I slip into silence and realize that every memory gives birth to a new question, and the more I remember, the more I will never know.

His raised eyebrows at my mother's strange behavior quickly find their proper place in his neutral expression.

"From my own experience, fathers are so important in young children's lives not only as caregivers and protectors, but also as role models of what good men can be. I can't imagine what it must have been like for you never to have known your father." As soon as I say it, I realize how hurtful that must be for this sensitive man to hear. "I'm so sorry. That was thoughtless of me to...."

"No. No. No offense taken." He clears his throat to take a serious turn. "In response I will say that from *my* own experience, you cannot miss what you've never had. You may wonder what it would be like to have a person or a thing, but that is not the same as forming an emotional attachment to and then losing it. Your more pertinent point is that of role models. Again from *my* own experience, blood relationship does not guarantee quality role modeling. I had many young friends whose fathers were lacking in that respect. Others, like myself, had none but were guided by exemplary uncles, family friends, teachers and so on.

"In fact, my grandmother Lottie's incessant stories about my father Jimmy and his mentor, a man she called 'the Judge,' provided models for honesty, morality and the Golden Rule. Every time I'd lift a foot to step across a line, she would ask, 'What would your father say about that?' and I'd pull it back and find an alternative—one of the Judge's lessons. I perceived the personalities of these two men from their writings. I've read all the judge's rulings over the years from his time as County Magistrate to District Judge and was impressed with how many aspects he could uncover in an otherwise two-sided conflict.

"My father's letters gave me a sense of the man he might have become. He was well educated for a young boy growing up in the rural south. At the judge's insistence, no doubt, he took classes in advanced math and even Latin in preparation for a career in the law. Grandmother trained him in every new office machine that came along so he could always find a good job. During his time in the Navy, he wrote to her almost daily, and she saved a few of his letters for me to keep as remembrances. I pull them out and read them every so often as a reminder of how fortunate I am to have survived my turn at war to raise a family of my own. She saved some letters for herself, I know, but I never found them after she died. Too personal, I guess."

"Ah! So there's a mystery in your family too—not only the *where* are those letters, but the *why* did she secrete them."

"You're right. We have one more thing in common: unanswered questions about our loved ones." He pauses to consider. "What I did not experience was the physicality of the two men in everyday situations—the change in their faces from a glare to a smile and the scent and strength of their hugs. My dog Harley was their surrogate in that respect. Doggy licks are some of the best kisses ever, but my wife reminds me frequently that human ones are preferable."

He pauses to let that image sink in. "I guarantee Maxine won't give me a cold cup of coffee for that lengthy dissertation!"

We laugh together again, and again it feels so liberating. This man I hardly know displays wit with his wisdom. He must be highly educated, perhaps a professional of some sort. "From *your* experience, how do you feel about *father*hood?" I had never asked my husband outright.

"Twice blessed, for sure, but the most challenging job I've ever had. I tried to put all I learned from my grandmother to practice, but those teenage years were really something. Combined with social unrest in the south during the Sixties, when it came to practicing what I preached... well... take the Children's Crusade of '63 for example, a planned peaceful demonstration for desegregation that took place in Birmingham. My son who was sixteen at the time followed the developments on television and when young blacks were sprayed with fire hoses, attacked by police dogs and even jailed, he informed me that he needed to go march too. 'You always tell us to stand up for what's right and to fight what's wrong, and this is definitely wrong!' How is a dad supposed to react to that?"

I did not offer an answer. My own children were conflicted by similar situations in southern California at that time.

"I agreed to take him to the march on the jail scheduled for the weekend, if he agreed to use brains instead of bodies to help. We followed alongside the marchers and, as white men, we were allowed to enter the jail. We persuaded authorities to grant us permission to speak with those being held and to judge conditions for ourselves. We wanted to confirm that those who were arrested knew their rights and where to call for help to speed up processing. We made lists of parents to call, and recommended that more food, water and a medical professional be available until the youngsters were released."

"Sounds like Dad participated too."

"More than I had planned for a Saturday, but my son got his first intimate exposure to the real world. That served him fairly well when the march from Selma to Montgomery took place a couple of years later. He was eighteen by then and about to enter university in pre-law. At least, that was his argument—practical experience. Multiple races of folks joined in the march, so I kept pace on the edge with an old hand cart filled with water and apples, but primarily as a witness to unlawful acts.

"That's where he met his wife, as I told you previously. He planned to gather information as before and pass that out to me to make phone calls and match young people with appropriate attorneys and medical help, but reaching the crest of the bridge to face police officers armed with tear gas and clubs tossed that plan over the edge. The girl jumped off him and ran to join her friends, and they returned bloodied and beaten. My son and I administered first aid to many, and he learned very quickly that not every situation he encounters will be straight out of a law book and that a classroom sometimes has no walls at all—no means of escape, no place to hide.

"By the time the government sanctioned a peaceful march to our state capital a couple of weeks later, the two were hand holders and walked the five-day, fifty-four mile route together without incident.

"That month I learned that a dad can pop his buttons with pride while shaking in his shoes for what the future might hold for his loved ones. I also understood my grandmother's reaction to her young grandson's enlistment in the Navy during the war and why it is important to express gratitude for your blessings whenever you can because there's no guarantee you'll have another opportunity."

I rise and dust myself off. "Well said. And that's why I know I will find you right here the next time I come. For the present, I thank you for the ice cream treat, for watching over my mom while I'm gone, and for a conversation that truly lifted my spirits."

"Stay a little longer?"

"I'd love to, but if I don't get on my way, I won't have time before my flight to make contact with the monument service you so kindly suggested. Besides, we have to reserve some untold stories for Maxine."

He smiles and gets to his feet. "Don't wait so long next time."

"I'll do my best, and happy birthday to you." I wave and drive off wondering still about my mother's freedom Sundays and why, for the second time, I forgot to ask that kind man his name.

Jimmy's Story

PASSED BY CENSOR

Norfolk, Va
May 26, 1916
Dear Mama,

As you can see, I am in Norfolk, Virginia, ready for what comes next. I will be put on board a ship in a Pay Office as a Yeoman since I tested good for office skills and math, thanks to you and George and the Judge. I do not know what kind of ship or where we will go. For the time being, write me at the address below.

Thank you for making me feel loved with all your good home cooking during my furlough. It really took me back to our days on the farm. I wish my girl would have come to Montgomery to visit as I asked her to in a letter, but she must still be off me. I will try again. I miss her so much.

I love you and miss your hugs.

Your son, Jimmy

Address: J. C. Dickson, Yeo., Pay Office, Training Station, Norfolk Va.

Goshen, Al
May 28, 1916
My dear friend,

Did you know that Jimmy joined the Navy right after you broke up with him? Well he has been in Newport R.I. ever since until about two weeks ago when he had a ten day leave and went home to see his mama in Montgomery. He had to go back to the Navy and is now in Norfolk Va. This is his address if you want to write to him. My husband Joe says all the boys appreciate letters. J. C. Dickson, Pay Office, Training Station, Norfolk Va.

Your friend from Troy (and now Goshen)
Bessie Pirdle (now Mrs. Joe Robertson)

Norfolk, Va
June 5, 1916
My dear girl,

Your letter just came a few moments ago and I was mighty glad to hear from you. I have written you three letters but I guess they ended up in other hands than yours. Does your Papa suspect anything now? Tell me, do your people know anything that has happened within the last few days? Your idea to address my letters for you to our school friend Bessie will have to do until we think of something better. Tell her that hereafter when I write you a letter there I will put a capital X on the envelope's upper left hand corner. That way she can tell which are for you and not be opening your mail.

Why do you cry when you get a letter from me? Last time we saw each other, you cried then too and told me not ever to come around again. Did you have to do that for your Papa's sake or was that just merely something you had to get rid of me with? I grieved greatly until I got your first letter. Yes, I cried too at our unhappy parting. I was ready to die, for I thought that life was not worth living without my girl. I did not want to come away up here by myself, but after that happened, I did not care what came.

I may leave here at anytime, and if you should get a letter from some place unknown don't be surprised, for if I get aboard our traveling will be secret altogether, and you would have to send my mail to New York and then I would get it about two weeks later, so you see how it will be on ship.

Write soon to the boy who loves you dearly. Tuus, Jimmy

PASSED BY CENSOR
June 22, 1916
My own dear Girl,

Well, you can tell by the envelope stamped as Passed by Censor that I am finally at sea. Came aboard yesterday afternoon. I knew nothing of it but about an hour before we left. Think that I am going to like everything alright.

Believe me, I did have a good time with that box of pralines, and if you care to send me more candy, you can be sure that it will be appreciated very, very much. You know I like the candy that you make fine, for I have tried it before. Do you remember that last box that you made for me? I do.

The U.S.S. ▇▇▇▇ is a ▇▇▇▇▇▇. We will ▇▇▇ ▇▇ to the ▇▇▇▇▇▇, but I can't tell you exactly where we are. Our biggest danger is from ▇▇▇▇▇. I mean to come back to you as soon as I can, that is if I am not killed by the ▇▇▇. Don't tell me your opinions on me being in the Navy and the dangers that may come to me when I am out on the high seas. If you was in my place, I would be scared half to death all the time for fear that I would never see you again. There is no telling when I cross the ocean with the ▇▇▇ looking for anything that belongs to Uncle Sam, and it would be my luck for them to see and then where would I go? I know. Do you?

In your last letter you spoke of slipping around writing to me that could not last long. Has there been anything said about it or has your mama gotten a little wise to it? Hope that all will go on well and that we won't have any trouble as we once had like what broke us up.

You spoke of writing with a pencil and how that didn't seem good enough for me. Well, I write on a typewriter and I will continue to do so as long as I can. The only thing why I use it is that I can get along much faster. I can't write as much with pen as I can on this. I will write you whenever I get the chance.

I suppose that you know that all the mail that I send out from the ship is censored but all that comes to the ship is not. They think that some one might give the location of the ship and that is why all the mail is censored. My boss, the Paymaster, censors all my mail, but that won't keep me from telling you how much I love you and think about you every day. He is standing behind my shoulder right now and smiling at what all he will cross out from this letter.

As you go about your daily duties remember that I am somewhere thinking of that Girl that is all my own. There is no telling but we may never see each other again, but I live in hopes. And if I do pull thru this all right and get home again, I will know that I did something that I will have to think of in years to come. Write to me often for I am farther away from you now than I have ever been.

Remember at all times my love for you, and that it will never fail.

As ever yours, Jimmy

From now on address me as J.C. Dickson, Yeo.

c/o Postmaster
Hudson Terminal Sta.
New York, N.Y.

New York, NY
July 20, 1916
Dear Mama,

After more than 25 days out, we are back in port here in the U.S. I don't know for how long, but once back on the high seas any letters I send through my ship's mail will be censored. That is why I have waited so long to write you. If I mail from a Post Office on shore it is not censored as long as the return address is not a ship. That's why I used our home address, so I can tell you what my boss the Paymaster crossed out of a letter I sent my girl and not break any military law. Remember what the Judge always said. Never break the law. Use it. Well, I will use it to tell you where I was and what I was doing the last 6 weeks since it is over and done and not really a secret anymore.

I am assigned to an armored cruiser that escorts supply ships to the European war. This last crossing was to France. Our biggest danger was from German SUBS. That is why we travel in packs or convoys of supply ships and protectors. No problems last trip. I won't be able to tell you where we are going next because we are never told until we are halfway there.

Boy, do I miss trees but the ocean is pretty too. I never saw so many shades of green and blue but sometimes there is not even a bird flying by. And watching waves for too long can make a boy feel sick so it is best to keep busy.

I was sorry to learn that the Judge feels poorly. I have a story that will cheer him up. We have been coaling ship and everything is full of coal and dirty. My, when the order comes to coal ship all hands below put on their dirty clothes and stay that way all the day and generally everybody is as dirty when night comes as they can be. We have had sickness here too and more hands were needed to take the places of some who could not make it through the day. We boys who work the offices were asked to help. I was one of the few who volunteered. I didn't mind. I worked alongside lots of coloreds on the farms over the years. But others had to be ordered until there was a boy on every shovel.

Well, at the end of the job you should have seen me. I was as dirty as I have ever been since I have been in the Navy. We wear white suits all the summer and it takes one suit a day. You can see how much washing we have to do. I know that you would like to see me washing my clothes. Ida Mae too if she was still with us for she used to make me wash my own clothes when I came home real muddy. But that is as regular here on the ship as it is for people to walk around there.

Anyway, I was up to my elbows in suds the next day when a boy came up to me and thanked me for being first to volunteer to take his place and could he pay me for the work since I lost a day off. I remembered what the Judge and George used to say that every man has his pride and that's why they made such a deal of paying rent. So I said, "Sure," and he asked how much and I said "Five." Those dark brown eyes of his filled his whole face and he asked, "Dollars?" I didn't laugh. I said, "Pennies" and watched him sigh with relief and then cast his eyes down. I guess he thought I was joking him and that made him feel bad. But I work with payroll and I know how much these boys earn and it isn't much. So I added, for dignity's sake, that I would be grateful if he could bring me some ice cream from town when he went ashore that afternoon since I'd be washing clothes until after dark. He agreed happily and sure enough brought me two scoops in a cup later on. It was a little melty but very fine. I thanked him and told him it was just about the best I ever ate. He went away feeling pretty good, and I finished my wash before any of the other white boys did.

So you see what a good upbringing you all gave me to find my way in unusual conditions. Thank you.

Well, I see that this letter is very long. I hope you did not fall asleep while reading it. I will write again when I return from another crossing that I can not tell you about until I get back. Please do not share the whats and wheres with others because they might not get such particular information from their own boys.

I love you as ever. Your sailor-boy, Jimmy

PASSED BY CENSOR
August 1, 1916
My dear Girl,

Your letter came just awhile ago and you have no idea how miserable it makes me feel. What did I tell you that made you feel that way? Was that the first letter that you had gotten from me since I came aboard the ship? Why did you pray that you may die that night? Why do you think that you will never see me again? I am coming back to you just as soon as I can. I am here. I am going to do my duty. It may cost me my life, but then I can say that I did it for a cause which I thought just, and I am here to do my part in protecting our country and protecting my country means that I am protecting the girl I love. Had you thought of it that way?

Now you can say these verses in the Bible over in the book of Ruth. As Ruth started to her own country, her two daughters-in-law started to go too, but only one went. You see what she said to Ruth and tell me in your next letter, and if you don't get it right I will tell you then, but these verses you can then say and say them truthfully I think.

You have not seen me now for several months and I have changed wonderfully. I am going to buy me a folding pocket camera the next time that I go to New York and make an album full of pictures and send to you to preserve memories for the days that are to come.

I wish that you would send me one of your pictures. It has been a long time since I have had one, altho the one that you sent me while you was in Troy is still with me. For some reason I did not destroy it when I burned your letters before I came to the Navy. Just before I left home I burned every letter that I had. Did not keep even one. Now I have another collection. I have very little space to keep things like that but I do manage to keep the ones that I want. And now I want another picture too.

No you can't write me too often. The more that you write the more I will love you. Write every time that you want to and I am sure that I will never object to it at any time. Do not forget my love for you at all times.

As ever, that boy. Sum tuus (you know), Jimmy

New York, N.Y.
Sept. 8, 1916
My dear Girl

I am certainly sorry that your people are having a few bad thoughts. I wish that things could go along well for once. I know that you are feeling bad. Wish that I could do something for you that would cheer you. If things get any worse for you at home, you may not be able to write but I hope that they won't. Should they, remember our promises to each other and that some day all will come our way.

I suppose that you have gotten the camera. I know that this is not what you want for your birthday but I wanted you to have one. There is a lot of pleasure in them most any time. It will preserve memories that nothing else will. Now about your present. You may have the camera and me too, if you want them both. But you can have my whole heart and life for sure. It is yours, yours alone. Will you accept it?

Remember all that you and I have promised each other. Though time may pass, let nothing change us. Trials are sure to come. Let us suppress them.

With lots of love from your boy, Big Jim

New York, N.Y.
Sept. 17, 1916
My dear Girl,

Your letter came to me today and I was somewhat surprised to get it the way that I did for I never once thought that you would think that I was at home by putting my home address on it, (the package). If I had I would not have done so. But dear, you must know that all our mail is censored and that I bought your present in the city and did not bring it back to the ship to send it off but rather had the dealer to send it for me. If I had put my ship's address on it, it would have given me away, for all postal authorities know that ship's mail ought to be censored, and then they could get me in court. You see, I am taking a risk in doing that, but there had to be a return address on it so thought that I would put my home address and then be sure that all went well. If I had once thought that it would have caused all that trouble with your people knowing I wrote to you, I would have brought it back to the ship and then sent it. Forgive me this time, will you?

When your papa returned the package to sender, my mama got it and wanted to know if I was planning to come home and was having my mail sent there. I have now set her straight and am happy she found a way to get the package to you.

I do hope that I can get off to go to see you soon, but dear you do not know the Navy. It is a hard matter to get off for any length of time. There is no telling when we would be called upon for some kind of duty that would require the whole crew. When I can't come to see you, I get a lot of consolation in knowing that I have a girl that loves me all the time and one that belongs to me alone.

Remember my love for you all the time, for I just love you heaps.

As ever your boy, Jimmy

Philadelphia, Pa
October 5, 1916
Dear Girl,

I wish that I had you here with me now. How I could talk to you as there is no one in the office but me. You have no idea how much I love you. You will never be able to realize my true love for you. Oh for the day to come when I can call you all my own. I know that that day alone can make me happy. Will it ever come?

I have thought several times about marrying if I can get the other party to consent. This all happened before I ever heard from you the last time. But if we were to marry now or a little later on, your people would never forgive me nor you as long as we both lived. There is the trouble. Why? There is not one thing that is wrong with me, that I know of, except that my papa died before he could raise me up. And your people know nothing of me at all, so why do they object to me going with you? Why don't they give me the chance of proving myself then pass their judgement on me? But they won't even give me a trial. But then why should we worry? If you don't care, I don't, so let us go on and not think of it.

Now don't let me give you the wrong idea. When I say that I wish you were here with me now I mean just for awhile. No it would be impossible for you to stay on the ship only long enough to look around. And anyhow I would not want you to stay here, for this is not the place for a woman. Yes the days are coming when we will be together, and all these days that we have been talking about will then be a reality.

If I can find it, I will send you a copy of the "Sailors Prayer." Everything that it says is true, so this will give you some idea of the life that we live, altho it is a happy life in one respect, it is nothing to compare with civilian life. I think that I will have been in the military life long enough when I get out of this that I am going to come straight to you and marry you and live with you for the rest of my days.

So good-by my girl, good-by. Good luck. God bless you. Jimmy

PASSED BY CENSOR
November 19, 1916
My dear Girl,

I am sorry that you have been sick. Glad tho that it just lasted as long as it did. Hope that you won't be sick any more. I am sorry too to know that Bessie and Joe are both sick. You do all that you can for them as I know you will. Now we know why you were worried about not hearing from me. There were five letters from me waiting for you at Bessie's when you went to look in on them. I was afraid we would have trouble with the mails but I believe in you as I hope you believe in me.

In that letter that I got today you spoke of your other correspondents and asked what to do with them. I thought I was the only one! But if your papa makes you write to the Goshen boys and talk to them when they are in town, you must do what you think best to keep the peace with him. If you think that you can do all of them and me justice, then go ahead. But if you can't well you are the only one to decide that. I think that if you really love a person you can't be writing to another and tell them all kind of things like you have me. I can't tell you what to do, but be careful what kind of a time that you have with those boys, for you know that some day you are to be my wife and I want a wife whose character is spotless. She must be that, or else I will not have her.

I must confess that I too have been tempted. Now it has been so long since I have been with a girl that I suspect that I have forgotten how to act, altho I could have been with lots of them for they fairly rave over sailors. No matter where a sailor goes, he can always get a girl there. But I do not care to be with them. Only you. Sometimes a fellow gets to that place where he thinks only of the one he wants to be with forever.

Yes I love you as I did in those days at Troy and more and more every day. But listen, Dear Girl, it is impossible for me to get a furlough now. You have no idea that we are ███████████████████ I may be near enough to come and then I might not. Yes there is always danger. But whatever happens to me, love me always. For if death should come to me, thoughts of you will be the last that I will think of. Oh for the day when I can be with you and the next time that I see you we will get married and then things will be different with us.

Remember the boy that loves you all the time and shall until time is no more. I am always yours, Jimmy

Norfolk, Va
December 3, 1916
Dear One,

Say, since writing to you last I was transferred to the Supply Office that is aboard this ship now. It will not stay here long and I may go with it, so if I do I will send you a telegram thru Bessie with nothing on it except the address of the place where I go, so whatever the address will be you write me there.

I think that I am going to like my new assignment fine. I have been having the pay work of the ship. Now I will take up the general store keeping. That is, the accounts of it. That is more of bookkeeping than the other and that is why I think that I will like it better and will learn some new skills. There are only two of us here and have an office to ourselves. The other was crowded very much with the paymaster, pay clerk, chief yeoman and two rated yeomen. The man that I am with now is a Chief. Fine man.   As ever your boy alone, Jimmy

Norfolk, Va
December 3, 1916
Dear Mama,

I suppose that you have noticed the change in print, that is I have changed ribbons and typewriters because I have a new job, one that you will appreciate from once working in a general store. Supply Office Clerk. I think I got the promotion for my office and math skills like before but also because of an observation I made that our Captain heard when we watched a ship that will travel with us be loaded. The boys had a heck of a time loading her. I told the sailor next to me that it was because the dimensions of the crates were different from the last ones they loaded so they could not do it the same and get all the supplies on.

The Captain called me over and asked me how I knew that and especially the word dimension. I guess boys who didn't go to military school aren't supposed to know such things. I told him I knew dimension from when I learned to read using newspapers and dictionaries and just by looking you could tell the crates were bigger and had to be turned a different way to fit the space best and get the most in. Geometry taught me that. Well, next morning I found myself in the Supply Office with a new friend to make.

We may leave port soon and have a different address. I will send you a telegram of what that address will be. Write me there.

Wherever I go you are always in my thoughts and prayers. The Judge too. Tell him thank you for making me stick with my lessons, especially math and Latin, and I tell him every time I write him. I find I understand more than most people think I do.

As ever your loving son, Jimmy

PASSED BY CENSOR
December 15, 1916
My own dear Girl,

I have been thinking of you all morning while on watch. Christmas is almost here and I know I won't he home or even near home to be with you so I made this little poem as your present so that you won't forget me. It is the first I ever tried in my life.

There's a girl in Alabam, boys
With a heart that belongs to me
And she knows that I am coming
(Someday) there with her to be.

How I wish that day was here, boys
But it seems to not be coming fast
But you can bet your boots, boys
When it comes it's going to last.

That Girl is mine forever, boys
And I'm hers I do suppose
How I do want to see her
Surely, there is no one that knows.

As I say, that day is coming, boys
In the town where I reside
For someday I will carry there
This Girl, as my bride.

There is a Girl in Alabam, boys
With a heart that belongs to me
And she knows that I am coming
(Someday) there with her to be.

Merry Christmas! Remember at all times my love for you for I'm loving you all the time and more than anyone can tell too.

I am as ever your boy, Jimmy

PASSED BY CENSOR
January 3, 1917
My dear Girl,

We have been out now ███████ and no telling how much in the coming. Here it is a brand new year and I have not received mail to know if you received my poem or if you had a good Christmas. I was on duty New Years Eve so spent time with my thoughts and remembering you and wondering what you were doing without me there to tell you that all will be well with us soon.

Do you remember the times that I used to go over to Flora Belle's place and cut wood and you would sit on the steps and talk to me while I worked? Or the time that I got sodas for all and we were there at the window, you all on the inside and me on the out, but who did we hear coming and how I got under the house but quick? Or the time that Flora Belle was sick? You remember that night don't you? The first night that she was so sick you came out on the porch and I came out to try to get you to quit crying and you asked me to stay there with you? I can recall most every instant that took place while I was at Troy. How about the time that I hid some fruit up near the steps at the school building for you and Annie?

I remember that time there under the tree at Troy. That time there by the door at Miss Morton's room was the time of my life and I thought I owned the whole world. You said in your last letter that those days at Troy were the sweetest of all and that you wish they could come again. Me too.

Say, do you remember the letter that I wrote you over a year ago that was twenty-three pages long? I did not try to put it in an envelope. Just rolled it and gave it to you the next time I saw you in Troy. We stood down on the path that led from the school building and you read it and we talked it all over. And do you remember the time that I came back from Fred's wedding and got that letter from you while we were out at Flora Belle's one Sunday morning? You were so cute and your blue eyes just sparkled. You were embarrassed and did not want me to read it out loud to you then. Oh they were all sweet times. I shall never forget them.

Isn't it all wonderful? I do believe that there has been something behind it all to cause things to happen this way, something that mankind has no power over, and that is God in His infinite goodness has seen fit that we should be together in this new year. Within ourselves we could not have kept loving each other thru all this separation. This is why I say that there is more to it than what man can do. Once the tiny fire of love was begun in our lives it never stops. It grows and grows until there is no limit. It is boundless and unbreakable.

I am your same old boy, the one that loves you most of all. Jimmy

PASSED BY CENSOR
February 9, 1917
My dear one,

Did you get the letter that I sent to you direct? I mailed it a day or so ago. Wish that I could send them all that way. Maybe your people will look at me differently now, and I hope they will, for you have no idea how I feel writing to you thru Bessie as I do, but then if that is the only way, I can do it.

If you could read it, I would write you on my Stenotype, then I know that no one could tell what was going on. Have you ever seen one? It is a little machine that looks more like a toy than it does a machine. I use it instead of shorthand and it prints words on a narrow roll of paper. I can write as high as 175 words a minute and take it from me, that is going some. My mama taught me how to use one and I picked it up real fast because she taught me how to type or read back with missing letters, and this has 10 missing letters! Sometimes I helped the Judge by substituting when his regular clerk got sick or when he wanted me to sit in the back of his courtroom and record all that was said to compare it to his clerk's record. In some tricky cases he wanted to make sure that all was absolutely correct. Some day you may see it. I hope that you will, that is if I am not killed by the ███████.

Now since I am a long ways off I hope that you won't forget me and let another boy come between us. Could that happen? There are just lots of girls that hang around when we come into port but I think more of my girl than I do of them. They will pass in other boats and just wave and wave. Some will throw kisses. That's nearly enough to make a fellow jump overboard, but if you will promise not to let another boy get you I will promise not to jump overboard after some of these girls, for you are the one and only for me.

Remember always what you are to me and what I am to you and don't let anything come between us.

As ever your boy that loves you dearly, Jimmy

PASSED BY CENSOR
March 23, 1917
My own dear Girl,

Your letter came to me yesterday and believe me I was so glad to get it. And I thank you for expressing your self as you did and that no one helped you on it. Your candy came too. I will never be able to express my thanks to you for it, for I think that it is mighty kind of you to remember your boy in that way. I am not the only one that passed their judgement on it. All that had a hand in it said it was the best that they ever ate. I know that it was for me, altho that at Troy was mighty good too.

You liked the poetry? Well I made that up one night that I was on watch. So you think that I am sweet, do you? I know that. Tell me something that I don't know.

No I have not got the letter that your mama wrote me while I was at Norfolk. I have not told you yet but your Mama wrote my Mama also when I was on furlough after I first joined the Navy. It was about that same thing but I happened to go to the Post Office that night and got the mail. That letter was in it and she put her return address on the envelope and I saw who it was from so I read it. Mama has not to this day known that there was ever a letter for her from your Mama and I don't think that she will know anytime soon, but the next time that I go home I think that I will tell her about it because I must always tell the truth. I did not want to tell her that time for things then wasn't like they are now.

I love you my girl. I do. Yes you are mine. Don't forget that for there is coming a day when you will prove it. Can you live up to what I said was my ideal of a wife? No I am not tired of hearing a certain thing and I will tell you so. Tell me that every time for I want to hear it. It does me so much good to know that you do. It is the same old story with me too. I love you.

Write me soon and think of that boy for he is all the time thinking of you.

As ever yours, Jimmy

PASSED BY CENSOR
April 8, 1917
My Dearest Girl,

I suppose that by the time you get this you will know that we are at War. Know that you have been wondering, but things will happen that we can't help at times. This is the time that I have written you about that I was expecting anytime, and now it is here. As I am writing this I am alive and well but very busy.

I think we will not land for some time yet, but as soon as I get to an American port I am going to call you over long distance. Makes no difference how much it costs, for I have just got to have a talk with you. When we go into the yard at ███ for minor repairs I will call you then.

I can't tell just when or what day it will be, for I don't know when we will land tho I know that we will land and take on coal, so that will give us a chance to call our families. I will call in the evening for that will be the only time I will be able to get liberty. I will call Bessie Pirdle first so she can go get you and then I will call again later so that when I call you will be there and won't be disturbed and can talk freely to me. I will tell you all I can about how our job will change now that we are at War and what I have planned for the two of us.

I have thought of you continuously this time while I have been out. It seems that you have meant more to me for the past few days that we have been out than you ever have before. I suppose that we have gone so far and that the possibilities have been so slim of us ever getting back. Oh you have not the least idea how I have worried away out here on the broad expanse of Gods waters, with the enemy always near, knowing not what moment we may be blown into atoms. It is terrible. You can't imagine, but still thru it all I know that I am doing my duty and not like some that are at their homes slacking, having a good time while we are here trying to do our duty as we see best. But thru it all I think that we will have the pleasure of saying we helped our country when we were needed and that we were not forced to.

Pray for me that I may see you soon, and that I may not meet with any dangers that would keep me from seeing you again. I will do the same for you. Love me girl, love me. Think of the boy that before long will be yours and I will think of the girl that will be mine.

As ever your boy, Jimmy

New York, N.Y.
April 8, 1917
Dear Mama,

I know you will not get this until long after you have heard the news. We are at War. I will wait until we get to the good old U.S. to mail this so that it will not be censored, but remember not to share too much with other mothers.

We were out in the middle of the seas heading home from Gibraltar when we got the word. We turned suddenly and started in the opposite direction and headed back. I never saw a big ship turn so fast. When we get there we will take on a load of depth charges to transport to southern Ireland for SUB patrols in the English Channel. Then we will guard supply ships on their way home. I have not slept for 2 days figuring out how and where we will stow safely as many charges as they want us to take on.

I have to say that the mood on ship changed as soon as we got the word about the War. We boys are all fine when we are working hard for that is what we are trained to do but at night it gets real quiet real fast. No joshing or fooling around. Everybody heads for their bunks to be with their own thoughts. Nobody admits they are scared but pretty much everyone is. I really need an old Sparky lick and hug like when I was a boy. He could always make me feel better. But I will try to be brave like you will expect of me.

I have not said much to my girl about how it is out here. I don't want her to worry about me but I know you will if I tell you or not, so I am glad I have you to tell.

I'll write again when I can. Must close up and go to chow. Remember at all times that your son loves you. Jimmy

PASSED BY CENSOR
May 5, 1917
My dear Girl,

Two letters came from you just a while ago. I hardly know where to start for you covered so much until there is very little for me to say. Do you know that we have been writing each other for a year without ever seeing each other but we still have lots to say? I am glad to know that you are still pleased with the camera and use it often. Now, send me more pictures for I want some mighty bad. I wonder what I will get you for your next birthday. Maybe a special something for your finger? Would you like that?

I suppose that I will be unable to write you now for a few days. If you don't hear from me for a while, think of that day girl when our lives will be bonded with God's Will, when we shall live for each other's happiness, for the joys and for the sorrows, for the comforts and for the pleasures and for all that will go toward making our home a home of peace and a God Fearing home, for we cannot live without God. He has brought us thus far and by His good will, He will give us what we desire.

I am still trying to serve Him even while I am in the Navy and out to sea. I will sing for the boys next Sunday. We have our own Chaplain aboard. He is an Alabama boy too and we have services every Sunday morning. I was asked to sing last Sunday but I did not have anything ready.

Do you still keep up with your music? You better for you are very good at it. Those times when we sang together at school programs were some of the greatest in my life. You was always so pretty when you sang.

Be good girlie. Remember who you belong to, and don't forget to pray.

Your boy alone, Jimmy

PASSED BY CENSOR
June 12, 1917
My dear sweet Girl,

Do you often think of this old boy of yours? Did you know that your life was his life and that your pleasures were his pleasures, that your joys were his joys, and that your sorrows were his too?

I suppose, girlie that we will leave here tomorrow. Where we go from here I do not know. We may go a long ways and then we may go to target practice. There are chances of us going across to ███ again tho. You may not know it but the ██████ are waiting for us to come back again and then they are going to put it to us for we are doing too much against them for them not to get something on us. You have never been in such places and you can't realize what it means to go. There are dangers that you never think of and that most people would never, but they are many.

Let me tell you something. I had my fortune told me last night and they told me several things that I asked about you. All was just as I wanted them to be. One thing was that I would marry the girl I was going with now. That is good, don't you think?

I am sending you a clipping of part of the last letter that Mama wrote me. She was talking of me getting a furlough and coming home. She thinks that it would be so nice for you to go there. "Tickled to have your little Lady visit us," she says. "We have much to catch up on and so much to talk about if this Lady is going to be your future." I had thought of that too.

Would you consider it? You could say that you were going to stay in Montgomery for the week end which is the truth. Then I would meet you there. I do not think that there is a thing wrong in this, that is if we two love each other as we should, and I think that my Mama would not ask a thing like that unless she thought that it was alright. You often hear of a young lady going to visit her to-be's people so that they can get to know each other well before the day. Let me know what you think about this. Tell me your honest opinion.

Remember me, sweetheart, as your boy, for I love you all the time and trust that you are still the same by your boy as you once were. I love my Girl. So good-night dear.

Your boy, Jimmy

PASSED BY CENSOR
June 14, 1917
Dear Mama,

I just wrote to my girl about visiting you in Montgomery the next time I am on furlough. I will let you know what she says but no such visit will take place for some time. When I am up on deck all I see is water everywhere. We could be sailing to Australia for all I know with no landmarks to point to.

All the boys are a little down with the sameness of things now with crossings of ███████ and barely an overnight in to pick up mail and supplies for the next crossing. I am always busy with loading supplies so I don't get to go ashore very often, even to mail a letter as you can see by the envelope.

They do keep us well fed and busy. The food is quite different from any that I have ever had, but it is good such as it is and lots of it to keep us healthy. But it is nothing like the heaven that you and Ida Mae used to make with a ham hock and butter beans from the garden. And peach cobbler after. Yum! I can't wait to sit down to your table again soon, and with my girl, but there's no telling when that will be.

Don't get me wrong and don't be sad or lonely for me. I really want to serve my country in this way. We want for nothing but our loved ones and a safe journey. These memories will be great for me in later life, if I live to see them thru.

As ever, your sailor-boy son, Jimmy

PASSED BY CENSOR
July 3, 1917
My dear Girl,

Tomorrow is July 4. You remember that we were together on one holiday, the best picnic ever, and I believe I know well what I did the last July 4. I did the same thing that I am doing now. Writing you. Altho then I did not think that I would be here just one year later. Just think what has taken place within that year.

Believe me it is certainly hot here. All hands are sun-burned bad. We have disregarded our jumpers and consequently our arms are blistered. I tan up well in the sun but this time I have really burned. My arms are mighty sore. Before we finish our trip we will be wearing our blues, for where we are going it will be cold. Then again we will take to our whites for awhile. This is as hot as I have ever felt. You can't be out in the sun no time until you are red and then it goes to stinging. I have been using mentholatum by the box.

I am glad to receive your honest opinion about visiting my mother with me. On thinking about it some more I believe you are right. This is not the right time if you are still having trouble with your people and they don't like you sneaking around to write to me. If your people know me and are still not friendly toward me, then if you went you would have to be quiet about it and they might find out anyway and that would not be a good thing for us. I wish that it could be so, but I am afraid that it will be impossible for you to visit with Mama and me just on general circumstances.

You don't know that I am nearer you today than I have been for a long time, now do you? Well I am. Expect that you would like to know where I am, but I can't tell.

Must go for this time. Remember your boy in all and he won't forget you.

As ever your boy, Jimmy

PASSED BY CENSOR
August 7, 1917
My dear Girl,

Your letter came this afternoon. You said that you love me and wish that you could see me this afternoon and that you have been dreaming about me. I am glad that you have, and you have seen me so plain you surely must have been thinking of me pretty strongly. I have seen you at times too, and I knew that you was thinking of me then. Perhaps I was thinking or dreaming of you too, for I very often dream of you.

Dear, you have no idea how glad I am to know that you are going to stay home this year. As well as I want you to go to school, I had rather that you stay at home. This is for reasons that I can't very well express just now. Do study hard on those things that I mentioned in an earlier letter and when I see you I will have you singing all the time, for I love good music. And to imagine that I had a girl that could master both music and voice would be great.

And you look at my pictures all the day? I am surprised, for you rarely say anything about them. I know that you think that you may never see me again for I am in the Navy and a War is on. Well I am about as safe here as I would be on the outside and I had lot rather be here than out just at present, for I do pity those that come in now. When we anchor in a U.S. port and go ashore, we see posters everywhere for "Uncle Sam Wants You" to join the Army. Well, I just laugh because I joined up more than a year ago but in the Navy and I'm a proud sailor. No one had to stare and point at me to make me volunteer to do my duty.

It won't be long until I will have to write you on cards, and I will only be able to tell you hello and how I am. But you still write me at the same old address all the time. For no matter where I am, you will have to send my mail there. Will you send me another picture so that I will have that to look at in the days that are to come? I will look at it all during the day and think of that girl that I left behind, the girl that is mine, the girl that I love, the girl that I am protecting maybe with my life. I love you dear girl. I do and I will always. Don't worry about me for my sake. I will take care of myself. I can tell which way the water flows and can float long enough to get back to you.

Your boy alone, Jimmy

Philadelphia, Pa
August 8, 1917
Dear Mama,

I only have a short time to go ashore and mail this. It won't be long until I will have to write you on cards only to be able to tell you hello and how I am. Cards with only a few words on them are much quicker and easier to censor which tells you how busy everyone is and how important it is to keep our secrets.

In my early months with the Navy our cruiser traveled in convoy with supply ships to protect them. Well, now some of those merchant ships are being converted to transport our troops heading to the front and we must protect them. When I see the boys load up I am surprised at how different they are from our crews. All the officers are fine, white, military school men as usual but the troops are all sorts. Coloreds of course but many others are immigrants who speak languages I've never heard before. I don't know how they understand orders or what is really going on. And they seem so young. I'm no oldie but I have some experience now and a good education behind me thanks to you and the Judge, so I can pretty well take care of myself if trouble should come. These boys we see loading up now have a look in their eyes like they don't really know what they signed up for. I complained before but now I am mighty grateful that my job keeps me on open water instead of in what they call trenches.

I think of you all the time and love you so much. Someday I will finally get a furlough and come give you a hug that will last a whole day long.

Say a prayer for your son who loves you like everything, Jimmy

PASSED BY CENSOR
September 25, 1917
My dear Girl

Well, that is really something! To get a present for someone else on your own birthday. I am mighty honored that you thought to buy some Liberty Bonds for your Navy boy and glad to know that you support what I do as it is important for our country.

I wrote you many letters sending you my love for your day and I have a present for you that I cannot send from here. It would be too dangerous. Besides I want to be there to give it to you and that means I have to wait for a furlough who knows how long. Will you be patient and wait for me to bring it? Can you guess what it is? I will give you a hint. When I place it on your finger that will be the happiest hour of my life, just to know that I have a girl that I can call my own and take as my ideal wife.

Dear girl, I won't be happy without you. I love you. My life is alone yours. Won't you promise to be my own dear wife? May the day soon come when I can take you and love you with a love that is unexpressable with words. Then 'twill be sweet to live. Look to God. He guides our destiny just as He guides that of nations and all mankind. He alone is the one that will make our future as we have planned it.

Your boy who loves you and misses you so much, Jimmy

New York, N.Y.
October 30, 1917
My dearest Girl,

I just received a letter from Bessie that has me very much worried. It is with regret that I hear from her how things are going on down there with you and your family. I am glad that she told me. Now I know better how to go about things. I am so sorry that my dear girl has been punished, tho I thought that something was against you more than just your mama's objection. Oh I only wish that I could be there. Is your love for me strong enough to hold regardless of your punishments?

We must see each other and soon, but here are the circumstances. If I were to leave my ship without being granted leave, at my return I'd be tried by general court-martial and the verdict would and could only be "imprisonment." I know that you would not care to know that I had been court-martialed for that would always go with me the remainder of my life and would take two or three years from it. So I have all planned what I'm going to do. You will have to help me too and do a risky thing for me.

I am going to ask for a furlough tomorrow. The Navy owes me one and my Chief knows it. I have raised my hand for every extra duty request for the last months. There has been so much sickness on ship that they are always looking for volunteers before ordering boys to do extra and I always step forward. Now it's time for payback and I can make a good case for it and I will ask my Chief to back me up.

I will ask for 10 days to attend to personal business. If I'm lucky they will only knock it down to 5 which is more than the 3 that we need. I will ask for any east coast port because "I can take a train from any of them." And here's where you come in. You will travel by train to where I am instead of my wasting days traveling to you. I send you the money now for a train ticket to the farthest away place, probably New York, so you will have more than enough for any other city. I will send a telegram to Bessie for you as soon as I know date and place. Then it's up to you to get yourself there. So pack a small bag and have it at the ready.

So what will we do when you meet me there? I will slip that birthday present on your finger. We will say our vows and walk out of the courthouse as husband and wife. I feel proud of myself for claiming you when so many others want you too. When we meet look out, for what you and I have been wanting to happen will then.

We will meet at the train station and decide where to go from there. We should have no problem because we are both of age but I will check with county clerks in all ports just to be sure. So what do you think of my plan? Are you in agreement? It all depends on getting a furlough in the middle of a War which may be impossible, but I am going to break a trace in trying.

Notice the postmark. I am mailing this from on shore so it will not be censored. No one will read this except for you and no one will know of our secret plans. Be patient. Soon you will be punished for loving me no more. It is time for this sailor boy of yours to be a man and stand up for what is right.

My dear sweet little girl, I love you every minute of every day and all the nights in between.   As ever, James Charles Dickson

PASSED BY CENSOR
November 3, 1917
My dear sweet little girl,

I got a load of letters from you this afternoon and was mighty glad. Some were from a few weeks ago and crossed with some of mine. You have no idea how blue I was feeling. Now I think I could fold a paper boat out of each one and float them back to you, one each day, and you could follow them out to sea to me.

Yes, I am going to call you my little girl again, for that is what you are to me until I can call you my wife.

So you don't think that you are worthy of wearing a ring from me? I already have the stone. It is one that you have never seen many like, and they are rarely found in this country. I am proud of it myself, tho you can hardly tell the difference with any other diamond. But when it comes to price, you will find that there is considerable difference. If you love me as you say you do, then you are worthy of my love, my rings and anything else that I have a mind to give you like the rest of my life.

You said that you dreamed of a home, when just last week I was sitting here in the office drawing the plans to one. Wonder if we were thinking of it at the same time. I drew one that I thought would just suit you. It was not very large, but plenty for us and the babies we will have.

I am glad that you are going to live up to my ideal. Do not forget your God. You know that it is He that has brought us thus far. I would give anything to be with you now, but we will have to wait until we meet soon I hope. I intend that we are going to be to ourselves there. We shall talk and talk and plan our life together to our hearts content. And also a certain thing will happen then that I intend that no one shall know anything about but you and I. You know what that is.

Oh for the day when I can take you and call you my own wife. Just to know that there was nothing that could possibly separate us, would be great I know. In our home there will be no madness, there will be no cross words, there will be no displeasure of any kind.

So with a kiss if you will allow it, I go, yours as ever and always, James Charles

TELEGRAM
November 23, 1917
Mrs. J. Robertson, Goshen, Alabama
    For Her 5 day furlough Dec 16 Portsmouth, Va JCD

PASSED BY CENSOR
December 23, 1917
Dear Mama,

    Sorry I couldn't make it back home for Christmas once again. We are at sea. The ship's Chaplain asked me to lead some singing for Christmas Eve service so I am getting organized for that. I will think of you and the Judge too when we pray together for an end to this War and Peace on Earth. Maybe all will come to pass by the time you receive this letter. I hope the New Year will find us all together again to share old memories and new surprises.

    As ever your loving son, James

PASSED BY CENSOR
December 25, 1917
My dearest bride,

    Today is the merriest Christmas of my entire life. Your "I Do" was the best present a man could ever get from the woman he loves. 5 days with you to cherish as my one and only is 100 times better than one day beside a decorated evergreen tree. Oh for the days we will sit together beside our own tree and watch our little ones play beneath it!

    We had a nice service last night. I sang some and then we all sang together. The boys seemed to enjoy the music. Soon we will have a big meal together. In between it has been work, work, work as the work on a ship never stops.

    I believe we did right to keep our marriage a secret from our families until I return and we can face them together. I agree that your people will be the hardest to get to come to our side and that is why I was happy to buy you a chain to wear your ring around your neck. For our bond to remain strong it must always be on you, not under your pillow or your bed. Hold it close to your heart every night and know that I am loving you.

    Now remember, if something should go wrong with your people and they start coming after you, you go to Bessie's right away. Don't stop for nothing. Send me a telegram from there and then go on to my mama's in Montgomery. She will take good care of you until I can help you decide what is best. You could stay there or go about from place to place as the ship moves. Some of the officer's wives go that way and are with theirs part of the time. But that way you would be alone when I am off on trips like this, and I would not like that. So think on it.

My dear, I go to bed at night with a vision of you getting off the train in your beautiful blue suit and smiling at me with your blue eyes shining. Then I knew that all would be well with us and that God will keep it so.

For this Christmas all I can give is my love to my wife. I love you more than anything in this world. Your husband, James

PASSED BY CENSOR
January 15, 1918
Dearest wife,

It seems that the time will never come when we can be in port again. We have been on seas for ███████ now with no mail and a lot of sick boys and I was one of them. I am some better and have lots of work to catch up on since I was transferred to a new job. I am studying for a new and additional position. My Chief noticed how fast I am on the typewriter and how accurate and also with the Stenotype. He brought the Captain in to watch me and I was very nervous but I guess I passed. So they moved me to the Flag Office and want me to learn communications also. That means listening to codes and changing it to type real fast. I wasn't sure about telling all those clicks apart but I'm getting pretty good at it. I think all that singing we did in school helps a lot. Anyway while all my friends went ashore last night, I had to stay aboard and practice.

I will write you as often as I can to let you know that I am not forgetting you, but my time to write is shorter these days with the new job. The one good thing is that I will have a raise in pay and can send you more money when I get it, so think of that when you are missing me as I hope you are.

With lots of love, I am forever yours, James

New York, NY
January 21, 1918
Dear Mama,

We finally reached New York after a month at sea so I will go ashore soon to mail this. I received your letters and am sorry to hear that the Judge still feels poorly and not any better. We have sickness on the ship as well but it is mostly flu where you either get better pretty soon or you don't get better at all. Because of our crew always shifting and boys not returning to their old jobs, I keep moving up. Now I work in the Flag Office where all the work of the ship happens. They call it administration here. That is something for your Yeoman son to be proud of.

Everything you taught me about office work and math is coming in real handy. My new job also includes communications so I study real hard on Morse Code. They want to see how fast I can go from clicks to words they can read over my shoulder. Now I need to not get sick again.

Tell the Judge that I pray for him every night. He is a good and fair man and the world can use more like him right now.

Always loving you, your son, James Charles

PASSED BY CENSOR
February 13, 1918
My dearest wife,

I remember so well the 5 days we spent in Virginia talking about the life ahead of us. I think on that almost every night before my thoughts of only you take over and carry me to sleep. Here is one of the questions I have. Where would you rather live? In the country or in a city? On a farm we can have anything that we want, as we want it and when we want it. But in the city we will have to take things as they come. Houses are mighty close and everything is dusty and smoke. All those are mighty bad but there a person can go where they want to and have a great many things that those in the country can't have.

I am thinking of two things that I could do when I come home to you and I don't know which I would like the most. The Judge said that I could take over some of his farm near Banks if I want to. There we could build the house I told you about before and have plenty of space to ourselves. I would raise stock. That is my long suit. Fruit also. If we choose the city, I have the office skills now to get a good job, for sure in Montgomery where both my mama and I are known around the courthouse. The Judge would tell me to go to school and become a lawyer and he would write a letter to help me do that. I could live with Mama until I was out of school. Of course, he didn't know that we would be married when I came back from the War.

But now I want you to say what you want me to do and don't you be afraid to say anything you want to. If you don't like what I have said I want, I am going to expect that you say so. I want you to be perfectly satisfied for it is your pleasure that I will do anything. I am going to live for you alone, work for you and your pleasure and try as best I can to make you happy. Then when I can sit with you and know that no one can separate us, that will be the happiest moments of my life. So tell me what you want. I want to know and let us work for one great end.

I sent you a beautiful valentine decorated with ribbons and lace, but I doubt you will get it by tomorrow or even in a few weeks. The ribbons are long blue ones and you can wear them in your hair anytime we are together, for you are my wife now and your husband says that it is fine if you want ribbons to help you feel pretty. But for me you are in all ways beautiful at all times, ribbons or lace or no. I don't need a special day to tell you how much I love you. I'll send it in a thought.

Your loving husband who can't wait to hold you again, James

PASSED BY CENSOR
March 4, 1918
Dear Judge,

Mama writes that you are still not feeling well. I am sorry to hear that and hope you will be fit enough for a day of fishing soon. Those were the best days of my early life at your place. Besides being a very good judge, you were a very patient teacher and I want to thank you for that. Also for the many things you have done for me and my mama over the years. You always provided everything we needed very generously, but when I wanted something you told me to work hard for it. You had me saving pennies in a jar from an early age. Boy was that a good lesson. I worked hard in school and that got me a good job in the Navy. I work hard at my job on the ship and I get lots of praise and promotions. And it comes to me now that every time I wanted something pretty important a job opened up that took care of it. I bet you had something to do with that. Thank you.

Whether I decide to farm or get a courthouse job when I get home, I want you to know that I will always make use of your most important lesson to never break the law but to use it wisely. And I will always look out for the people around me like you did.

Thank you for all you have done for Mama and me.

With love and admiration, James Charles Dickson

PASSED BY CENSOR
March 18, 1918
My Dearest Wife,

Just before we left NY they threw on a bag of mail and inside were a whole bunch of letters for yours truly. More from you than anybody else. Boy did that make me a happy sailor. I was worried that something had gone wrong with you when almost nothing was waiting for me when we first got there. But now that I've read through them all to know you have had very little problem with your people, even I am glad. The best of all was your valentine. The best of any the other boys got. And I'm grateful that you liked my valentine to you. That I am dear to you as you are to me is important for us as we look to a life together.

I mailed a fat letter to you from on shore. It cost me 4 cents! I've never paid so much but you are worth every penny and more. I tried not to complain about being apart from you. Instead I talked about many of the times we spent together and there were so many special ones that it took lots of pages to tell you. Here is more I forgot about.

The time that we was down at Miz Beckham's on the day we didn't go to the circus and we were out in the swing. Do you remember what happened there and then? And the afternoon that you got on the train going to Newton to school almost 3 years ago. You never had had no idea that things would be as they are with us today. You were crying when we got off at Newton, and you and Ruby wanted to go back home. I knew even then that you were the girl for me. I knew from when we first met in third grade but we were not old enough yet to decide such things.

And do you remember that the next day we all went to ride and you stayed at Mr. Tate's crying to beat all things? And the next day we all went to the depot together to put me on the train to home and that was my first time to be with you alone for a long time. The last time until we met in Virginia to be married. They are all happy moments. I shall never forget them.

You say that you have a surprise for me but you don't want to tell me just yet. Now that you have my curiosity up when will you tell me? Please don't wait until this War is over for there is no telling when that will be and this sailor is not patient when it comes to secrets!

I have more letters from you than I know where to put now. We have very little space to ourselves on ship. And you say you have too many letters from me now to hide away from your people. Why don't you read through them all one more time and then choose only a few special ones that you can keep safe and burn the others? More important than letters is to keep you safe until I can come home to you. Then we won't need to write words anymore. We can speak how we feel to each other every day. But I will always make you a special valentine.

All my love to my wife from across the seas, your devoted husband, James

PASSED BY CENSOR
April 6, 1918
Dear Mama,

I just received your telegram by wireless that the Judge passed. It came straight to me since I was on duty then, so I delivered it to myself. I am so sad that I couldn't be with you and with him when it happened. I would have asked for leave to come to you but he would be long buried before I ever got there, and the Navy would say no because we were at sea and still at War.

I'm sure his funeral was well attended as so many people from all the small towns around admired him. You said he was buried in Banks with his wife and all the children he never got to enjoy. Well, now he can be with them for Eternity for we know God would have it so.

Thank you for writing me that he got my letter and read it over and over. I'm glad it gave him some comfort in his last days. I am finding that we never tell people enough how much they mean to us. Well, I'm telling you now that I love you more than any mama in the world. And when this War is over and I come home I will hug you and tell you every day.

God bless you, Mama. Don't be too lonesome. I will be home soon I hope.

Your loving son, James

PASSED BY CENSOR
April 6, 1918
My dear sweet wife,

I do not want to make you sad, but I must tell you that the Judge has passed. I got a letter from Mama telling me so. We have been at War for just over a year now and there is always talk of death and we have even seen some when ██████████████████████ but his hit me real hard. Oh how I wished I had you to hug to make me feel better.

He was the most important person to me after you and Mama. My Papa passed before I was born as I told you and when I was little and needed a man to look up to I always looked to him. He was more like a grampa I guess because he had a big gray mustache and gray hair by the time I noticed such things. But he was always very good to me and Mama. You would have liked him very much and he would have liked you too. Maybe what I am most sad about is that you two will never know each other.

I will stop for now and write more when I feel better. I have just learned that when someone you love dies it just makes you love the other people you love even more. I don't know how I could love you any more than I already do but I do. Can you believe me?

I am as ever your husband that loves you with his whole heart.
Yours forever, James

Portsmouth, Va
April 15, 1918
Dear Mama,

I know that I promised to never break the law and to always be truthful. Well, I have to break that promise now but it is for a good reason. In other letters I mailed from on shore I told you information that would have been censored if I mailed from the ship. I said it should not be a problem because that excursion was over. Well, the time has come for me to tell you what we are about to do and to take the consequences for my action.

We are at Norfolk. Our ship is being converted to a minelayer and then we will go north to help lay a minefield from Scotland to Norway to keep the German SUBS from leaving the North Sea. I know this because I work communications in the Flag Office where the officers talk about this mission and I take the messages sent to them over the wireless. I have security clearance to do this but not to share the information. That is illegal so keep this as secret as ever you can. I don't want to end up in court-martial.

There is a good reason for me to take this chance and hope I'm never found out. My dearest girl and I were married last December in Portsmouth. We promised each other not to tell you or her family because we wanted to do it together in person and there was not enough time for us to travel home then. I am sorry that you and the Judge missed our big day but that is how it is for many soldiers these days. We will come to you together as soon as we can. Please be happy for us.

This mission is very dangerous. I know this to be true because the officers decided to encourage all the boys to write letters home. Usually they give us only cards to cut down on the time it takes to censor, but this time they say to write nice long letters because it may be some time before we get to mail again and we shouldn't worry our families.

Another reason I know this time will be dangerous is that my Captain asked me if when we get to mid seas I would bunk in the office. There are only two of us who can work the wireless and Stenotype and I am fastest, so the minute they go on in the night he wants me up and at it. I said "Aye, Aye" and have a double bedroll ready to store under my desk. I hope I never hear those clicks in the middle of the night for that is a bad sign.

If the mission should go bad for me, please take care of my wife. As you know, her people have given her many problems so I can not count on them to support her like I know you can. I will not tell her of this mission until I come home safe. Until then I count on you to keep it secret. You invited us to visit you once and said you had much to talk about. I'm sorry we couldn't have that conversation before. We will for sure when I come home.

God bless you and keep you, Mama.

Your loving son, James

PASSED BY CENSOR
April 20, 1918
Dear love of my life,

Oh how sweet it was to hear your voice over the telephone last week! I was only ashore for a short while before we left port again and just took the chance that Bessie would be home and that she could run get you for when I called back long distance a few minutes later. How lucky that the plan worked!

Now I am the happiest man in the world, War or not! Your surprise gives me the courage to go forward and do my duty the best I can so I can return to you as fast as ever. Then oh what a happy family we will be!

Now remember what I have said before. If your people give you any trouble over this or anything else, you go to my Mama in Montgomery. She helped you once before and she will take care of you again.

Once we leave here, if you don't get mail from me for weeks at a time don't you give up. You must remember that I am in the Navy and that things are not like they are on the outside. We won't stop except ■

███████████████ so you keep writing me and let me know how you are getting on.

Remember my love for you at all times, and if you should not hear from me for some long intervals do not worry. Keep your ring close to your heart so I will always know that you are thinking about me and never take it off until we are together again. I live in hopes for the day to come when I can be with you and ours. If I could be with you now for awhile I would go on and do what is just ahead of me without hesitation, but it is hard to do now after your happy news. Pray for me that I may come back to you soon and there live in blessed solitude where joys of this life will abound. If God permits I will return to you and then our dreams will be a reality. I will come back to you the same as the man who took you as his bride.

I do not know what I would do without your love for it helps wonderfully in times like we are about to go thru. I love you, you have no idea how much. What you are doing for us makes me love you that much more, tho I do not see how that can be possible. For as time passes I can realize more and more what you really mean to me.

Love me, dear wife, for there is no telling what there is before me. Only God knows. Love me, think of me and live for me and ours, as I do the same for you.

Your loving husband, James

1988

I hurry through Troy without stopping for one of Maxine's pecan sticky buns. I am anxious to see if the headstone I ordered for my mother is in place. I contacted the Montgomery monument company suggested by my acquaintance on my way home last trip. They were most accommodating when I told them what I wanted, but not yet. I paid a deposit and assured them I would forward the inscription and date for installation as soon as I decided—maybe a year or so. No problem, they told me. Ten years passed. I lost track of time, and before I knew it Mom's birthday loomed only weeks away. I contacted the company again. No problem, they told me again. I wonder.

Secretly inside, I want to arrive before the man does, if he does. I want to be first to see the stone before anyone else has the chance to pass judgement. Surely he will show up as usual unless a sudden something prevents him. I have lucked out twice already, but this time I *must* be first and *he* must come.

My hopes are dashed. He is at my car door and grinning the moment I pull up. "Beautiful!" he shouts through the window. "Go see." He helps me from the car, then reaches in the back for my flowers. "I'll bring these along for you."

The gravestone exceeds my expectations in tone and simplicity— exactly what I imagined, with an engraved mother and child centered above Mom's name. I notice the kind man hang back to give me crying time—over-anxious, but still thoughtful. I oblige by finding my handkerchief and using it a time or two, then inviting him to join me.

"What do you think? Are you pleased?" he asks.

"Very," I reply. "What do you think?"

"That modern, minimalist representation of a loving mother with her child moves me greatly. I'm about to ask to borrow your handkerchief."

We both chuckle and shed a tear each, then we combine our colorful bunches of flowers and begin to arrange them in the three tins he brought from Maxine's.

"She must have been a very loving mother," he said, placing a bright blue blossom in her tin.

"Very. Sometimes, as a teenager, I wondered if she loved me too much. She anticipated my every desire and need despite the Depression. I never wanted for any of the basics. I had a closet full of frilly dresses, shiny shoes and ribbons—the most beautiful hair ribbons of every color and design imaginable. And she loved doing my hair in curls or waves or braids, whatever I wanted. Sometimes she put lipstick on and then gave me a quick kiss on the mouth 'to pink me up' she said. I almost felt guilty for receiving so much attention, but she told me often that every young girl deserves to grow up feeling good about herself. After my father died and she moved us to California and worked in a bakery, we still did not want for anything except, as she put it, 'more people in our lives for us to love.' She smothered my children with her hugs and kisses too, and they did love her greatly. We all miss her, even after twenty years."

"And you will for the rest of your days, but that is as it should be. Her name—Lila—is a pretty one, a strong one. Is it a family name?"

I shrug. "Not that I know of, but I really know nothing about her early life or her family. Could be. I worried over whether to include her maiden name—Larson, but I decided that if she wanted to be buried next to other Larsons for whatever reason, that name should be included."

"My daughter's name is similar—Delilah. My grandmother suggested it. She said Delilah Dickson sounded distinctive. My daughter goes by Dee. My son goes by Skip. His official name is James Charles Dickson, the Third, but about the time he reached adolescence he asked if we could just skip the number part because it was kind of embarrassing. So we call him Skip."

"Then, you must be James Charles Dickson, Jr."

"Just Charlie to my friends. That's the way I like it. And you are?"

"Officially, Penelope Jane Tolbert Simon. Most folks call me Penny, but my dad would have none of that. He said I was worth more than one copper. At least two bits, and he wasn't going to call me Bitty Bitty either. Penelope was too long to shout to get me out the road before I was squashed by a truck, so he settled on Janie."

"A man after my heart. Janie it is." He extends his hand. "Janie, pleased to meet you. I'm Charlie."

I take his hand and shake it. We exchanged names properly. We are official friends now. As friends, we stand back and admire our colorful display. Suddenly, Charlie reaches forward to make a correction. He removes two flowers from my mother's arrangement and places one each on her parents' tombstones, my mysterious grandparents.

"Recognize them or not, you wouldn't be here if it weren't for those two. And I, for one, am mighty glad you are." He pats my hand. "Now, I have a surprise for you. Hang on for just a minute."

I notice that Charlie does not trot to his car this year. He ambles. Are we really getting older? Seems like only yesterday we met. He returns loaded down with a blanket on top of a huge cooler. He drops the one to the ground and shakes out the other to spread before his father's waiting place.

"That is a gorgeous quilt! Wherever did you find it?"

"Grandmother made it. Stitching was one of her many talents. Lottie couldn't keep her magic fingers still. She was partial to this one. That's why it's so worn."

I run my fingers over the still brilliant colors. "The design is charming. Is it significant in some way?"

"Yes, as a matter of fact. She combined two of her favorites from underground railroad times. Each pattern gives a specific direction to help slaves find their way north. Those escaping were told that help—food, clothing, a place to sleep during the day—would be given by folks displaying a quilt with one of the designs hanging over a fence or from drying lines. In Grandmother's, the eight blocks around the center tell them to follow the flying geese, and the center one is the North Star above Canada indicating that they have arrived. She repeated the other designs that comprise the route in the two-by-twos that form the border, except for this one in the lower right corner. LD. Grandmother's initials. Lottie Dickson. She signed every one of her quilts that way. Now sit down on some of those geese and close your eyes."

I do as I am told and hear the clink of plates and utensils, the pop of plastic container lids, and the gurgle of pouring liquid. The aromas are too many and varied to pinpoint other than the heavenly fried chicken.

"Open!"

I do, and a veritable feast lies before us.

"I brought us a picnic today! I asked Maxine to fix us up with the best of everything she has, so we'd both be surprised."

He takes his time getting seated comfortably, passes me a plate, and points to each delectable dish. "We have here buttermilk fried chicken, of course. No one fries it up like Maxine. She sent some succotash salad, macaroni salad, potato salad, and coleslaw along with dilly snap beans and pickled carrots for vegetables. This here is her special smoked sausage with peas and rice. This one is some pork loin with baked beans and deviled eggs, for those who don't favor chicken. Buttermilk biscuits for sopper-uppers. Marinated melon and ambrosia salad for fruits. Ooh, yum. Her pecan pralines and peach hand pies for sweets. For drink, sweet iced tea. And of course, for dessert, some fresh peach ice cream. Dig in!"

"I don't know where to start." I really do not. "We can't possibly eat all of this. The waste...."

"Try a bite of everything. Go back for what you like best until you're full, and don't worry about the leftovers. I'll take them home for my birthday dinner, and they won't even make it from the car to the table, guaranteed."

I take his advice and spoon a little bit of everything onto my plate. I have never seen such a mountain of food before. Partway through, I start to giggle. "I feel like such a glutton. I want to stop, but I can't. This is sooo good!"

Charlie giggles too, and then laughs out loud. We reach for napkins to wipe our eyes at how ridiculous we must look—two older adults spread out in the middle of a graveyard, laughing loud enough to wake those resting below, while sharing what looks to be our "last meal" together. If we were the kids we used to be, we would roll onto our backs and kick our feet in the air and not care about what anyone else thought.

Soon we gasp for breath, exhausted. We calm ourselves and each other, then dig in again. I go back for seconds of succotash salad and marinated melon—dishes new to me. We save the peach hand pies for last, and as he reaches for the ice cream to go with them, I shout, "Wait! I have a surprise too!"

Out of my purse I pull a small packet of seven birthday candles and matches. "Surprise!"

Charlie chuckles again and dishes out the ice cream.

I decorate his scoops with the candles and light them. We sing the traditional birthday song, and I encourage him to make a wish. His face turns very serious. He pauses for a deep breath and blows, displaying satisfaction when the candles all go out at once.

"Your wish?"

"I can't tell you because then it won't come true."

"Is it truly possible?"

"A man can hope. Everyone leaves a trail—a letter, a picture, a trinket."

We enjoy our dessert and chat casually. Then there is nothing left to do but lick the bowls, clean up and leave. I do have a plane to catch. I am about to toss the candles and matches into the trash sack, when Charlie stops me.

"Janie, don't! I need those. My family humors me, but they don't believe a word of my stories about you. The sole reason my wife is sure you're not my mistress is because we only meet once every 10 years! Now that you have a name, and I have burnt candles and matches as evidence, they'll have to believe me. I'd never pack that stuff along and sit by the side of the road singing to myself."

I chuckle and thank him again for the great picnic—a blue ribbon surprise, no contest.

"And I thank you for the 'party' to go with the picnic. That was very thoughtful. One falls into the routine of the same old, same old and tends to forget how delightful a simple gift can be. Please say that you still have time for our usual walk around the grounds to check in on the neighbors."

I smile, note the appeal in his eyes, and glance at my watch. "Maybe a short one."

We take the opposite route this time, "for variety" he says. We walk and talk, and the conversation turns to his children. Both Skip and Delilah have young ones themselves now and are dealing with keeping them in line.

"When I was a kid, besides the 'what would your father say?' line, my grandmother punished me by denying me access to one of my two favorite things for a specified amount of time—my bicycle or my dog. Pretty simple. But today, there are too many options for take-aways: car keys, music, earphones, the latest have-to-have shoes like everybody else, and if you deny the kid one, they still have the others. Delilah doesn't have the same problem, but Skip is real sensitive to his kids being mixed race, and they have learned to use it. 'We're already different from everybody else. Why do we have to be more different when you won't let us...?'

"I agree that you, Janie, and I and his sister don't have that same problem. Mixed race kids come with their own set of challenges, for sure, but Skip can't let them use that line of reasoning. 'But, Pops,' he says. 'You don't know what it's like for them.' And I tell him, 'No, I don't and you don't either, but none of us has a choice in when, where or to whom we are born. We all have challenges, but we all have to learn to live in this world together by the rules, whether that's at home or at school or in the workplace. And if they don't like the rules, then they should work to change them.' Or as the old judge would say, 'Don't break the law. Use it.'"

He stops, pauses, and turns to me. "Granted you are a little emotional at times, but otherwise you are such a kind, thoughtful person that I can't imagine you've ever been punished."

I scrunch up my face trying to think of a good example. I do not have one. "The warning in my house was, 'Wait 'til your father gets home' because he was the disciplinarian. When I was little, he would pull me onto his lap and wrap one arm around me. Then he'd ask a series of questions like 'what did you do today,' 'anything else you want to tell me,' 'what can you do to fix that,' and so on until we came up with an acceptable resolution together. He always ended with, 'I like your idea. You're a very smart little girl, Janie. Now, give Daddy a kiss, climb down and get busy.' I don't remember ever being *given* a punishment; I always *chose* one."

"That's right! I remember now. I used a similar tactic during the war. I'll have to tell Skip about that. Maybe he can...."

"Stop! Wait. I do remember being punished by my mother once. A bunch of neighbor kids and I were in the yard choosing sides for a game with 'eeny, meeny, miney, mo....'" I stop, embarrassed. This is not appropriate for a conversation in the south, but forging ahead beats explaining why my face just turned red. "Anyway, Mama heard me, ran out to us and washed my mouth out with soap right in front of my friends. She had never done anything like that before. I was so startled that she was the one who ended up crying and running back into the house. Her reaction to punishing me hurt more than the embarrassment or the scrubbing."

"She was a sensitive woman before her time where race relations are concerned, especially for a woman who grew up in Alabama when she did."

"I suppose so. Did you ever make your grandmother cry?"

He smiles. "Lottie? Lottie and I cried together many times—whenever we got the glums or witnessed a horrible occurrence in the city—but I only *caused* her to cry once that I remember. I finished university and congratulated myself by buying a record player for my bedroom and a few of the latest have-to-haves, among them one by Billie Holiday—a haunting, veiled protest to lynching, I learned later. When Grandmother came home from work one day and heard that song playing, she came straight to my room, grabbed the disc from the turntable, and broke it over her knee. Then she ran to her room, slammed the door and cried. No, she sobbed like nothing I'd heard before. By morning, the house was quiet again. She came home from work with a different popular tune of the day to replace mine and said not another word about her reaction. And I never asked."

I sense him struggling in his mind with the why, even after all these years, and understand how much he seeks answers to unanswered questions just as I do.

"Now, it's only fair," he says. "I can't imagine you ever making your mother cry like that. Did you?"

For this, I have a very good example, one that is hurtful to repeat now that I am a mother too. "When I was almost two, Dad took Mom to the hospital to bring home a baby brother or sister for my birthday. When they returned empty-handed, I asked where my baby present was. Mom went straight to their bedroom and cried and cried. Sobbed, like you said. Dad told me there would be no baby, and I shouldn't ask unless she asked first, like on Sundays, because it would make her cry again and we wouldn't want that, would we. The next year at birthday time, Mom *asked* me what I wanted for my birthday, so I told her to go back to the hospital and come home with a baby brother this time."

We reach our starting point and pack the rest of the picnic away. "Did your mother cry again?"

"No. A couple of weeks later a package arrived from the catalogue company. 'Not all babies look alike,' she said. 'Not all babies come from the hospital. This one came in the mail, special for you. Happy birthday.' I opened the box to find a little black baby doll inside. 'This doll is as precious as a baby. You love him like a brother, and he'll love you. We're all the same, you know,' she said and taught me a lullaby to sing to him every night. And I did, love him and sing to him. Mom sang with me at night, too, in her soft, soothing voice. For years that little guy and I were inseparable. No need for an imaginary friend.

"Perhaps Mom realized that I had expected a doll all along. When I was old enough to understand why she didn't bring home a baby from the hospital, I was too frightened to tell her how sorry I was for fear that would bring back a painful memory."

"You can tell her now… here… today. I'm sure she'll hear you." He pats my shoulder and turns to carry the cooler to his car, leaving me space to say my goodbyes as he so kindly has learned to do.

I meet him back at the cars, and we say proper farewells this time, with proper names. "Thanks again, Charlie, for the picnic and pleasant conversation. Today has been a very fine one. Thank Maxine, too, for her wonderful cooking. But don't you dare tell embarrassing stories on me."

He laughs. "Not more than a biscuit's worth, anyway. You take care of yourself, Janie, and the next time you come, I'll be waiting."

We share a lingering handshake and part ways, leaving me to wonder what other sorrows Mom had in her life that she never revealed to me, or perhaps even to my father.

Lila's Story

LITTLE BLACK BABY DOLL

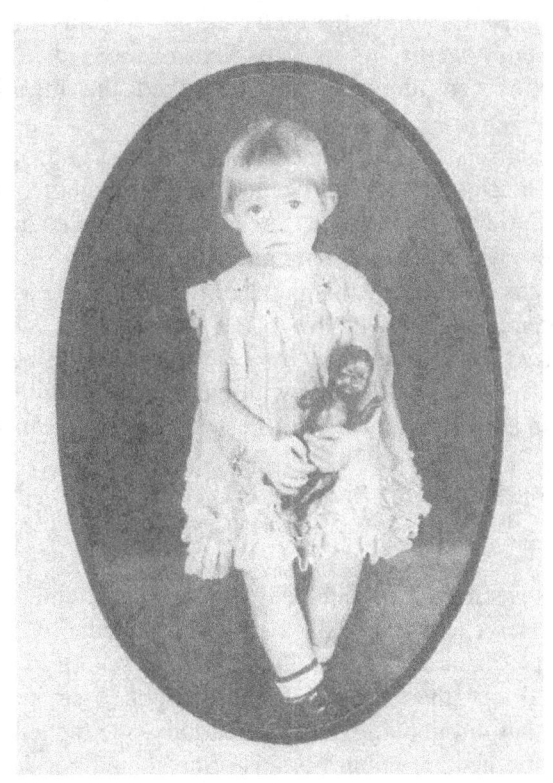

Lila was a sinner, or at least that was what she had been told for as long as she could remember. Her first sin was being born. She had trouble with that one. If being born was bad, why be born at all?

So she could be saved, her papa said.

Her second sin was being born a girl. That was really puzzling. She could not remember choosing to be a girl, and if girls were so sinful why would her parents pick one for their family? They did not choose to feed her rotten peaches. And what was wrong about being a girl anyway?

A woman brought sin onto humankind, and now we must *all* seek deliverance from it, her papa said.

Lila knew what sin was—breaking one of God's laws. But apparently she did not know all of them—her third sin—for she was constantly being told not to do: Do not speak at the table. Do not leave anything on her plate. Do not disturb her father. Do not bother her mother. Do not squirm during prayers. Where could she find a list of all the sins so she would not commit any?

In the Good Book, her papa said.

That required her to admit a fourth sin. She could not read. She recognized letters from learning the alphabet, but she was stumped when they were scrunched together into groups that made words. She and her five-year-old brain were doomed, so she asked the meaning of the deliverance part.

When the Lord sets us free from our sins, her papa said.

How could she come by this deliverance, she wanted to know.

Follow God's laws all the time. Accept His punishments, and pray for His forgiveness when you stray, her papa told her.

"What happens if I can't be that good all the time?" she asked.

Her papa glared at her with his cold, gray eyes. "When the End Times come, all who are saved will fly away to join with believers who came before us. Together we'll meet with our Lord among the clouds for everlasting life in His glory. *You* will be left behind... *alone*... on this bleak earth!"

Lila was not just doomed. She was damned!

*

Contrary to her teachings, Lila bubbled over with excitement. Her blue eyes glistened. Her cheeks pinked. Her heart-shaped lips pursed in an effort to hold in the thrill of her first day at a white school in a new town. Her papa warned her that eagerness and delight were sins requiring punishment, but that did not stop her anticipation. She tugged at her flour sack shift and smoothed her auburn braids. She should not do that either, she knew, but with no mirror at home, she wanted to make sure she looked nice for her new teacher.

When a kindly young woman appeared at the door, Lila followed the line of other students through it into a large room set in rows with long tables and benches numbered from one through six along the one aisle between them. Her papa had told her to look for the number three. Since her mama already taught her numbers and letters, she would be in third grade. By the time she arrived at that table there was barely space left at the aisle's edge on the girl's side. She inched her way onto the bench and sat with her hands folded in her lap and her eyes lowered.

She had never been in such a large room with only children separate from their parents. When she went to church all children sat between their parents and were reminded to remain silent and listen carefully to God's word. She tried to obey her papa at all times, but Sundays were difficult because he always stood in front so she could not sit between her parents as instructed. She wondered if God would notice when she wedged herself between her mama and the wall and if He would add disobedience once again to the list of sins she committed.

Because her mama was soon to bring a new child into the family, they moved from Goshen to Troy for weekdays during the five-month school term so Lila could attend classes while her mama took care of the new family member. When she asked where her mama would get this child, she was told to be quiet. Her papa intended to expand his sect's conservative influence to Troy once his community in Goshen remained stable and their petition to incorporate that small town became a reality. On weekends they would all take the cart together to worship with his Goshen congregation for as long as her mama could travel safely.

The new student felt out of place in this strange environment. The girls in front of her giggled. The boys across the aisle from them pushed and shoved. The girls behind her whispered. The boys behind spoke in loud voices and acted out. Such behavior would not be permitted in her circle except maybe on a summer picnic. Lila squirmed in her seat and waited for order.

All commotion halted the minute the teacher raised her voice to welcome her students to a new school year in the fall of 1907. Then she directed them to take out a pencil and paper. Her papa did not tell Lila to carry such supplies with her to school. She gulped to hold back a spurt of tears, but one escaped the corner of her eye. Just before it dropped to the table, a sheet of tablet paper slid in front of her and a pencil with a whittled tip rolled alongside. She glanced across the aisle at the boy who smiled at her. He had a kind face and neck-length wavy dark brown hair that tucked easily behind his ears. She was not supposed to smile at boys, especially strange ones, but she could not help an embarrassed upturn of her lips.

Midmorning the teacher released her students for a run in the schoolyard. The boys whooped and roughhoused. The girls skipped around the one tree in the yard. Lila sat on the ground and picked at the sparse grass. She did not know anyone and was not sure she wanted to.

After a time she noticed a pair of legs standing nearby. "Hi," their owner said. "My name's Jimmy. You new here too?"

She glanced upward at the boy from across the aisle and nodded.

"I already know a few of the kids from seeing them at Saturday markets and a couple from church out near where I live. Come on and I'll introduce you around. A person can't have too many friends, you know." He tilted his head toward a group of girls who stopped to rest from all that skipping under the tall oak and hopping over its roots.

She hesitated. If she met other children properly, then they would not be strangers anymore and she could talk to them without disobeying her papa. She nodded and rose, wiping the dust from her behind. "My name is Lila. Thanks for sharing your paper with me this morning."

"Glad to. Everybody needs a hand now and again. One time when I drove the mule cart...."

As they strolled toward the others she thought, *Jimmy is my very first friend in the whole world.*

*

The day began with a light drizzle. By midday a torrent rained down on the town and its little schoolhouse. Inside a tornado raged as youthful bodies caromed around the room and the teacher at wits end with no way to let the mob out for a runaround. Storm season had arrived.

The disobedience surrounding her dismayed Lila. If her papa happened to walk through the door at that moment, he would yank her out and to home immediately. He did not cotton to such behavior and might even pull her out of school altogether—a dreadful thought. She had accustomed herself quickly to the daily routine and the friendly students.

She glanced across the aisle at Jimmy who appeared to be engrossed in memorizing his three times tables with an elbow on the desk and his chin resting in his palm. He knew them already. She could tell by the way his lips moved beyond the three times twenties into the thirties and forties and beyond. She was still on the teens. Everyone else seemed to disregard arithmetic completely in favor of physical exercise.

Suddenly Jimmy stood on his bench and shouted, "Hey you rowdies, listen here! I have a penny in my pocket for the lion who sleeps longest."

Silence. Then from the sixth grade row, "Where'd ya get that kind of money? Steal it?" Titters sounded from around the room.

Jimmy shrugged. "I earned it. I run errands and clean an office at the courthouse every day after school before I start my lessons. Do *you* have a job?" That remark quieted the herd. "Then I suggest we play a game for a penny prize."

"You gonna rig it so Lila will win cuz you're sweet on her?"

Lila felt her face pink. Jimmy noticed her embarrassment and countered with, "Sure I'm sweet on Lila. She's a nice girl. I'm sweet on

94

Annie too. And Mable. And I can be sweet on you too, Tommy, if you feel left out."

Gales of laughter and jeers erupted. Now it was Tommy's face that pinked as the teacher brought the classroom back to order. "A game we can all play together is a good idea. Tell us about the sleeping lions, Jimmy. Where did you learn it?"

"From a book. It's real easy and better for outside on grass, but we can do it here with our heads down on the tables. All the lions make one big roar and then yawn and fall asleep. The hunter comes along. That's you. And he... she tries to wake them up by telling jokes and stuff that will make them laugh and move about. No touching allowed except when you spot someone wiggling you can tap them on the shoulder and they can sit up and watch until everybody's up but one and that's the winner."

"Sounds perfect," she said and clapped her hands. "Now everyone in your seats. Let out a last loud roar.... Now a big yawn.... Front paws and heads on the table.... Hind feet flat on the floor, and close your eyes. I'm... going... hunting!"

The young teacher glanced at the clock, did some quick division, and calculated how many minutes between taps should get her class through what was left of the afternoon. She hummed as she strolled up and down the aisle and between tables. When almost all heads were up and trying not to giggle at the last sleeping lion, she gave a signal and they all let out a loud roar to wake him up, for smart-aleck Tommy had actually fallen asleep.

Jimmy reached into his pocket, pulled out the penny and handed it over. "You won, fair and square." The mortified boy grabbed it and ran through the door into the pouring rain after the others.

Almost all of the others, that is. Lila stood to the side as if waiting for the rain to cease miraculously and provide a dry path for her to run home.

"You have far to go?" Jimmy asked.

She nodded. "Four streets to the edge of town, and I'll be in trouble if I get wet and muddy."

"Not much chance you can stay clean and dry today. I get wet and muddy even when there's no rain." He waited for a laugh or even a smile, but she did not. "Here's what I do. First I take off my outside shirt to use on my head. I tie it under my chin by the sleeves. That leaves my hands free to take my shoes off and cover them with my arms across my chest. You could do that and put your stockings in your pocket and I'll lend you my flannel shirt for your head."

Lila shook her auburn braids.. "I couldn't. Then you'd be all wet, and Mama would ask where I got a boy's shirt."

"My people are used to me dragging in damp and dirty. I'll only be in trouble if I don't clean up the mess I drag in with me. Here, take it and get ready to run. I'll go with you and you can give the shirt back just before we get to your house. Okay?"

She sucked in her lips and stared at the floor, thinking. "I guess so."

Their teacher watched the two eight-year-olds ready themselves for their dash through the rain and marveled at the ingenuity of young minds faced with a problem. Just as they opened the door to leave, a familiar horn tooted not far away. Jimmy shouted and waved. "That's Mr. Tyrell! He's come to take me home. Come on! We'll give you a ride."

Lila balked and shook her head. "My papa says I can't go with strangers. If I do, he'll punish me." She tugged at the shirt to untie it.

"But he's not a stranger. He's my boss."

She shook her head. "But that man is a stranger to me."

"Hold on. I'll go talk to Mr. Tyrell. He always knows what to do." He raced to the car and jumped in.

Lila watched the ensuing conversation complete with hand gestures and Jimmy's toppling over the seat into the back and popping up with a smile and a hunk of something.

He raced back out of breath. "You're right. Mr. Tyrell says that you should always try to obey your father. He says to use this piece of torn canvas like a tent to cover us while I walk you to your house. He'll come behind with the car and pick me up when we're sure you're home safe. How does that sound?"

This time Lila's eyes widened along with her pretty smile. The two tented up and scampered out much to the delight of their teacher. They waved as they passed by the car. "How can I thank Mr. Tyrell for helping us?" she asked from under a flap of canvas.

"No problem. I'll be cleaning up the mud inside the car as soon as the rain stops and give up my pay for today."

The muddy road home to Banks was slower than usual, providing the attorney and Jimmy an opportunity for a heart-to-heart talk. The man did not want to overstep the authority or advice of the boy's mother, but the prickly issue presented itself that afternoon during the storm so best to tackle it head on. "That was a fine thing you did today for your friend, not running off like the others to leave her alone in the rain. Has her family lived in Troy long?"

"I don't think so. Her family is kind of like ours where they spend the week in Troy so she can go to school and weekends at their place near Goshen where her father leads a congregation. She doesn't talk much except to be polite and to say what she can't do cuz her father would be mad and punish her if she did. Why?"

"Do you know her last name?"

"Lawson, maybe? No. Larson. That's it. I'm sure glad I don't live in that family. I try to be a good boy, but sometimes I'm like every other kid and slip a little. I'd a lot rather do more chores than get a whuppin'. Why?"

The attorney scratched at his bushy mustache and tried to recall the name. Then it came to him. Larson was the leader of a religious sect that moved into the Goshen area a few years back. Mr. Tyrell learned from his regular rounds through that area that the group believed in the strict authority of the Bible as written, especially the New Testament, and conducted their lives accordingly. They were intolerant of those who did not share their beliefs, and anyone unknown to them was suspect because he might bring sin onto them. Members' moral conduct was monitored and expulsion was threatened for those who did not conform. Wives submitted themselves as servants to the authority of their husbands, and children were subjected to punishment for whatever act or behavior the father deemed as a sin, including everything pleasurable—a tall order for youngsters. He suspected, now, that the group had expanded enough to warrant a second affiliated congregation near Troy and that Larson's move with his family was the first step. How could the attorney explain to this innocent boy sitting next to him that his kindness to a new friend was a threat to her safety?

"My papa was a man chock-full of life lessons, and what you did today was a perfect example of one of the most important: 'Never break the law. Use it.' Can you guess what that means?"

Jimmy crinkled up his nose and shook his head.

"I feel very blessed to have grown up in this part of the state. I know most of the folks. Don't necessarily like them all, but I respect how they feel differently from what I do. We all pretty much agree on what's right and what's wrong, but the further we get from home the harder it is to find agreement with all those new folks in that bigger circle. We pass laws— like rules—to help us find the best ways that the most of us can get along. Sometimes they don't work and we have to change them, but most folks agree that killing somebody is not right. That injuring someone on purpose is not right. That stealing is not right, and so on. Someday when more people have cars, there will be laws to tell us how fast we can drive and when to stop to keep everybody safe. That's the big picture, and we— even kids your age—should try very hard never to break those laws.

"But when we get back down to our own families and churches, we might need more help or guidance for the people we live close with to get along. Instead of laws, we call them rules and they may not be the same in every house or church. There's probably not a big law for the whole state that says it's not okay to eat dinner with your elbows on the table, but some families make a rule that in their house it is not polite so don't do it. There's probably not a big law for the whole state that says it's not okay to kick the dog because he tore down the fort you were building, but some families might make a rule that you will be punished if you hurt the family dog or cat or mule."

"You don't have to make a rule like that for me. I'd never hurt Sparky. He's my best friend."

"Right. You don't have to worry. I trust you. And there's probably not a big law that says a person can't talk to strangers. That wouldn't make sense for going into a store with a new clerk or going into a store in a different town where you didn't know anyone. How would any business get done? But for a family with children it makes good sense to have that rule. If a child sees his parents talking to a strange adult at church or at market, then that person is probably not a stranger and it's okay to be polite and say hello or accept a glass of lemonade on the walk home. But if a child has never seen that adult with his parents, he might be dangerous. Parents don't want their children to get hurt, so they make a rule that helps to keep them safe.

"That's the first part. Never break the law... or rule. So, what do you do when you are faced with a rule you don't agree with? You think hard about the consequences... the result if you break it. First you have to know what the words in the rule mean. When your friend said, 'I can't *go* with strangers', did that mean ride or walk or talk? You could have tried to convince her that since they didn't have a car 'go' probably meant 'walk' or that maybe the rule was really 'talk' and if she kept her mouth shut, she wouldn't actually 'talk' or any other crazy reason you could think of to make her riding with us okay. But that's not the point. When her parents found out—and they would—*she* would have to convince *them* of *your* reasoning. That's not fair to her and she might be punished anyway for arguing with them.

"Second, you think about why you want to break the rule. What was the reason you wanted her to ride with us—to have a ride in our car when she probably never had before or to keep from getting wet?"

"The second one. That's the one we did."

"But how did you come up with that solution?"

"You kinda helped me, probably because I never had to think this way before."

"Right. And in the end, a good solution to keep dry had nothing to do with her problem of not breaking the family's strangers rule. That's what 'use it' means. Come up with a solution that doesn't break the rule but helps you get same result."

"Does that work for robbing banks too if you get someone to grab the money for you?"

The attorney shook his head and chuckled. "No, it does *not*. There is also a law that says anyone who helps a person rob a bank can be punished too. So if you're thinking of robbing a bank, you have to know all the laws about doing such a thing and that means going to law school when you are old enough, and that takes lots of pennies!"

Jimmy rolled his eyes. "I'll never have enough for that."

Mr. Tyrell mulled over the term Jimmy used earlier—whuppin'—and expelled a deep breath. "There's one more piece that we have to talk about. The word 'punishment.' If you break a law, you will be punished—with jail, county work, a fine or some other thing that a judge decides so you'll never do that again. The punishment for breaking family rules is usually decided by one of the parents or both. Most penalties are okay, like more chores or no dessert for a week, but some break the *big* laws. If any of your friends talk about being punished often and come to school with a black eye, lots of bruises or an injury they can't explain, like a fight with a brother or a fall from a tree that took a doctor to fix, or if they are embarrassed and don't want to talk about it or try to hide it, the kindest thing you can do for that friend is to tell an adult. Me, your teacher, or your mother. We know the big laws and can help. To be a good friend to someone in trouble, you must be a person they can trust not to convince them to break their family's rules. Got it?"

Jimmy nodded his lowered head. "Got it."

Mr. Tyrell clapped him on the knee. "How's that for a lesson on life? I'll bet you thought school was over for the day. Any questions?"

The boy perked up. "Only one. Why do you carry around a no good, ripped piece of canvas in your car?"

The attorney laughed and thought to himself, *In one ear and out.* "Here's another life lesson: Always be prepared in case you don't want your clothes to get wet or dirty if you have to repair a wagon wheel or now, a tire."

The boy sat quietly pondering for a minute. "When I'm old enough to have a car, my first rule will be always to carry an extra large piece of canvas too."

"To repair a tire?"

"No, as a kindness toward those you meet along the road who didn't leave home prepared."

A life lesson well learned, the man smiled to himself as he side-skidded across the last bridge to home.

*

Now in the fifth grade, Lila had a best friend. Bessie Pirdle. And two other girl friends, Annie and Flora Belle. The four of them sat together, skipped at recess together, walked home together, and saw each other at church. Sometimes they whispered, but most of her secrets were saved for her special friend Jimmy. She could tell him things she did not want to share with the other girls because they would tell their mamas and their mamas would tell her mama and then she would be in trouble with her papa. But Jimmy never told her secrets to anyone. He always helped her work out what she could do not to be punished again.

On a sweet-smelling early May day, the four girls huddled near the school's entrance with the rest of the students pushing from behind. Just before they left for lunch their teacher told them that the mysterious large object draped in brown cloth at the front of the room would be unveiled when they returned. The door opened and the horde rushed in. Some whistled in amazement. Some gaped at the sight. Others looked puzzled at what the thing was for. And Lila spoke volumes with her eyes. They dilated to the size of saucepans, then focused on a spider skittering between the students' dancing feet.

Their teacher had hinted that come the school year's end, the students would be responsible for a special program to honor their parents. No one expected a *piano* to be a part of that celebration, least of all Lila. It was old and scratched, to be sure, and slightly out of tune as demonstrated by the teacher's playing a familiar melody, but that did not change the fact that it was a musical instrument.

Lila clapped her hands over her ears, whispered to Bessie that she felt sick and needed to go home right away, walked quietly to the rear of the room and ran all the way home. Her papa had said many times that musical instruments were not allowed in his houses of worship; the human voice was God's only true instrument. A school was not a church, Lila reasoned, but at the beginning of every school year her teacher repeated the story of how the structure became available when a church vacated it after building a larger one for its growing congregation. That was the reason for its sloped ceiling in front. Before she disobeyed her papa by singing with a piano at school, she wanted to tell him so he would not find out from others and give her a whupping.

She sat quietly on the steps waiting for her papa to return from Goshen. Her mama was napping with her little brother so she dared not make a sound. Bessie passed by on her way home from school and found her friend with a finger to her lips cautioning silence.

"Do you feel better now, Lila?" she whispered as she settled down next to her friend. "Too bad you had to leave. We had great fun singing to the music Teacher played. She said the piano was a hand-me-down from the church on Mills Street cuz they bought a new one."

Oh dear, Lila thought. *I will have to tell Papa about that too.*

"She said we're going to have song practice every day after lunch for three weeks until our program. Isn't that exciting!"

Lila nodded politely. "Excited" was not an emotion she was allowed to exhibit. Nor were her friends but as recent converts to her papa's church, their families probably did not understand yet that displays of joy and pleasure were frowned upon. She shuddered at the thought of how her papa would react if she showed delight at singing with piano accompaniment. "Thanks for stopping, Bessie. See you tomorrow," she said and turned her thoughts to what to do. What to do?

Mr. Larson returned late afternoon to find his daughter waiting for him on the front steps. "Girl, what have you done?' he asked gruffly.

"Nothing bad, Papa. I swear. But I seek your guidance for a problem at school." When she spotted the skin around his eyes begin to tighten, she hastened to add, "I'm not in any trouble. Truly. I'm up on my lessons and my reading. But today our teacher brought a piano into the school and told us we would be singing with it every day until the end of this year. You probably know that our school was a church before, so I wanted to make sure I had your permission to sing with the rest of the students. May I?"

"Hmm. Hmm." Her papa scratched his whiskered chin. "What did you do when it came time to sing?"

"I left and came home."

"The others?"

"They stayed. They might not understand."

"Hmmm. You did right, Girl, but don't you be prideful about doin' what the Lord expects of you. I'll think on it. Parley with some of the others. Let you know." He stomped past her and into the house. "Wife, where's my supper?"

At breakfast Lila asked, "May I sing today, Papa?"

"Not today, Girl. I gathered with the other men last eve. Explained our position. Pirdle said that if we could find out who owns the building now, that could solve the problem right there. So until we know for sure, you young people will leave before the singing starts. Understood?"

"Yes, Papa." Lila was crushed but could not allow her disappointment to show or she would be in trouble for that. But she was sad. Singing was her favorite, and her teacher had told her several times that she had a very nice voice. Of course, she could not seem pleased when given a compliment or she would be in trouble for that too. What to do?

Obey. When the teacher announced time to practice, one by one, Lila and the others from her congregation put a hand over their mouths, the other on their stomachs and left.

At breakfast the following morning Lila asked, "May I sing today, Papa?"

The ill-tempered man shook his head. "Still thinking on it," he said.

Disappointed once again, she realized that "thinking on it" might take a really long time, maybe until she graduated from school altogether. She reconciled herself to three weeks without singing and wondered how to explain her predicament to her teacher. She could not get sick every day at lunch; that was unbelievable even though she started feeling nauseous just walking toward the school. She could not say that she must go home to care for her little brother because her mama was sick. That would be a lie, and lying was one of the worst sins of all and it would be easy for her parents and her teacher to find her out and her punishment would be a dandy. What to do?

Obey. As soon as the teacher announced time to practice, the little band of congregants feigned illness and left. A minute later, Jimmy followed.

"Lila, wait up," he called once they were well away from the school. He caught up, caught his breath, and caught sight of the explosion of tears from her bright blue eyes. "What's the matter? Has this got anything to do with your papa?"

She wiped a sniffle on her sleeve and nodded. "He forbid singing. Not with a piano. Not any of us. It's a religion thing with him, and I don't know what to do." She sniffled again, proceeded to share the particulars, and appealed to him for an answer.

Jimmy did not have one. Not right that minute, but he told her he would figure something out. When she was out of sight, he hustled back to school and sneaked to his seat when the teacher had her back turned. He joined in singing, but his mind churned on other matters until he heard....

"James Dickson! The rest of us have put our song sheets away and are beginning the arithmetic assignment. Will you join us, please?"

He pinked. He had never been called out before. "Yes, ma'am. Sorry, ma'am."

"And you will stay after school to explain yourself. Understand?"

"Yes, ma'am." He was humiliated, and now he had two things clanging around in his brain: how to help Lila and how to save his own skin.

At day's end he presented himself to his teacher. "I apologize for disturbing class today, ma'am."

"I accept your apology, thank you. But I do want to know about the strange behavior from you and some of your friends. Sit down right here..." She drew a chair near her desk. "...and let's talk."

He did as instructed and felt every bone in his body shake inside his skin. He hoped she would not notice.

"For the past three days I've watched a small group of students walk out of school after lunch for no apparent reason and not return. Today you joined them. What can you tell me about this strange behavior?"

Jimmy squirmed until he was sitting on his hands. "My mama and I have a good friend. Mr. Tyrell. An attorney. He eats supper with us almost every night, and I've learned a lot from him about what is right and what is wrong. I know that I must not lie and that I must not share a secret that's not mine to share or I won't be that person's friend anymore. If I tell somebody about someone else and that somebody tells another somebody or word gets around to that someone else's family and that causes trouble for that someone then I won't be a very good friend. So, no, I can't tell you exactly about this strange behavior. I'm trying to work out how to tell without naming names or giving exact details, and I need to talk to Mr. Tyrell before I say anything because he's really good at keeping secrets. That's part of his job."

The teacher hid a smile behind her palm. After three years with this young boy she was not surprised that he could spin his way out of trouble. "Do you know the difference between general and specific?"

He nodded. "General is like it's nice outside and specific is like it's seventy-five degrees and the flowers are blooming."

"Very good. Could you try to give me a general idea of the problem? If it is tainted food or the like, we should try to find a way to fix that."

Jimmy squirmed again and his elbow found its way to the edge of her desk. "You know how we're all the same but all different? Most of my friends are ten and in the fifth grade but some of us are better at arithmetic and some better at reading. Most of us go to church on Sundays but we don't all go the same place. Families are that way too. Some let you eat with elbows on the table and some have a rule that you can't. Some say it's okay to play on Sunday afternoon and some have a rule that you should read the Bible instead." He paused and studied his knees. "And some say it's okay to sing whenever and wherever the spirit moves you and some have a rule that singing is okay but not with musical instruments." There. He said it without saying it.

His teacher immediately recognized how she had put a number of her students in a quandary. Some families did expect strict obedience to their religious teachings, and she would never win an argument over religion. "Well, we can't always change what other people think, but we can change how we react to that." She tapped her pencil on the desk. "You know, I've been thinking about a problem *I* have. I've noticed that when we sing right after lunch, you students don't settle down for lessons after. Maybe you can help me come up with a plan that will solve both problems."

The young boy beside her broke into a face-wide grin.

The next morning at breakfast, Lila did not even bother to ask if she could sing. She knew the answer and readied herself for the half-day ahead, for she would be leaving at noon… again. And as days and weeks passed she would miss not only music but other lessons too. Then she would not do well on her exams and that would anger her papa and she would be punished… again.

The school day unfolded not at all as Lila expected. The first clue was the piano. It had been moved from its position front and center to a far corner, shrouded again by brown cloth. The second clue was change of seating: the boys and girls were switched to opposite sides of the center aisle. The third clue was a change in the order of daily lessons: arithmetic, language and geography in the mornings, then spelling and reading in the afternoons. Music ended the school day.

Music last! Lila was thrilled. She could be present for all of her lessons and not get behind. But that was not the end of the surprises. The teacher had determined that there were too many students to maintain control of one singing group, so she was dividing them into two groups:

Act I, *a cappella* with voices only and Act II, with piano accompaniment. Both would perform at the year-end program and their composition was as follows:

Gasps and whispers crept around the room. Girls wanted to be with their friends. Boys did not want to be there at all. Lila prayed to be in the voices only group. And Jimmy did not seem to be surprised by any of the day's shocking developments. The teacher read out the boys' voice only group first. There were eight from grades four through six including Fred, Joe and Jimmy who had all left class the day before. Ten girls were named from grades three through six including Bessie, Flora Belle, Annie and... Lila! Her sigh reached every corner of the room.

Jeers erupted from the remaining students. "Ha! Ha! We get the piano!" they sing-songed while jabbing their seatmates.

"Where are your manners? Your impolite behavior calls for another change. Everybody stand. *A cappella* on the left side of the aisle and piano on the right. Move!"

There was a scramble for seats and vociferous commotion. "I want to sit by Eddy." "Save me a seat, Julie. I don't wanna sit in the first grade row." "Hey, move over. It's too crowded on this side."

"Silence! *A cappella* has more room. You others have the piano. Be grateful." The teacher passed out papers to the right. "Mixed arithmetic review. You have thirty minutes to impress me while I explain their program to *a cappella*." She turned to the left and passed out a second sheaf of very crisp sheets of music. "I've been saving these for some time, hoping I would have a group of students who could do justice to this beautiful music. You are that group."

She explained that they would sing in parts—high and low—in twos, threes and fours—with not all of them on the same notes at the same time. "This is very difficult music and it requires fine vocal instruments to showcase its beauty." She sang through the basic melody one time, then as they went through the music again together she had them note where the girls would sing the melody and then the boys. Once their short session ended, the voice students were excused to go outside under the tree where they could not hear the piano. "Begin to memorize the lyrics, for you will have another difficult song to learn next week. You may not leave for home until I dismiss the rest of the students. I will come out to make sure you are right where you are supposed to be. Do you understand?"

"Yes, ma'am," they chorused, gathered their papers and departed.

Lila flashed Jimmy the slightest sinful smile. "Thanks," she whispered.

The two singing groups practiced daily, but separately. One language class was spent writing a proper invitation to invite families to the year-end musical program. They outlined date, time and place, listed Act I with voice only and Act II with piano accompaniment, and announced refreshments between the two acts. On program evening, lots of families attended, even Lila's. Her papa threatened to yank her out in front of everybody if he found that she had not told him true. She was very nervous, but when it came time for her solo, she did not make one mistake. Everyone clapped... except her parents, and she knew her family would take her home at refreshment time. She did not care. She sang beautiful music and detected no gleam of punishment in her papa's eyes.

*

Most of Lila's friends liked spring best because spring meant summer was right around the corner with no school or lessons, just time to be outside. Some moved back to Goshen or other small towns around; others remained in Troy. Everybody had chores or worked in the fields, of course, but many found time for fishing or squirrel trapping or berry picking or skipping stones across the lake. A few had bicycles or a pony or mule and could meet up with friends in nearby towns. A very few were confined to home most of the time and did not enjoy summer at all. Lila was one of those.

The summer before seventh grade was particularly hard for the young girl. Her mama was soon to bring another new child into the family, so the bulk of the cleaning, washing and cooking became her responsibility. She did not mind doing the chores. She sang or hummed while washing clothes or kneading bread and the music always made her feel calm inside. What she did mind was her little brother. He was four and a troublemaker for his sister. She cleaned up; he messed up right behind. She hung the washing; he threw dirt at the dripping clothes. She chopped the vegetables; he scraped them onto the floor. She tried to be kind and gentle with him as she knew the Lord would expect of her, but sometimes she could not stifle her anger and called out to him to pick up his own mess. Then he bawled and her mama or papa came running to scold *her* or worse. No matter what the offense—and her papa did not listen to any excuses—it was *her* fault.

Even on a day when she held her tongue, her papa found something that was not as he thought it should be: dirt tracks near the door, soup not hot enough, his shirt not pressed properly. "My appearance before the congregation is important, Girl!" Her brother soon learned to mimic his papa. When she asked him to pick up his clothes or clean off his shoes, he stared at her with a look too stern for a youngster his age. "Don't you tell me what to do. You're just a *girl!*" Criticism and punishment were her thanks all summer long.

Fall was her favorite season. Fall meant beautiful colors and harvest smells. Fall meant school and friends and time to herself. Lila had hardly seen any of her friends during the summer. Fred, Joe and Bessie lived in Goshen during the summer too and she saw them every week at church, but there was never more than a minute to talk before she was hustled home. Jimmy rode over on his bicycle one Saturday. Her papa met him at the gate and told him to go back home because Lila was working in the house. She was not working in the house. She was peeking out the window and so happy to see him. Jimmy spotted her, got the message and flicked her a wave on his way back up the lane.

Fall this year was even more special. She was in a different school with no more little kids, just seventh and eighth graders. Most of her best friends were in the same classes, and some of the subjects were new ones: arithmetic was now called math, and history and writing were added to the schedule. She looked forward to every day.

Lila's birthday was in mid-September, a bright fall day. She was twelve now and soon to be baptized with some of her friends because they were considered "spiritually mature." When she told Jimmy, he seemed surprised. "You mean you haven't been baptized yet? I was when I was a baby."

"My papa's church does it when you're old enough to understand the responsibilities of membership. I'm a little scared, though, of being under water. I've never done that before."

"You could practice holding your breath. Only a little at first and then longer and longer. Try counting to yourself and see if you can finally make it to 100. That should be plenty of time for a good dunking. I wouldn't know. My mama held me in her arms for my baptism. You'll be fine. Good luck!"

Lila was fine. She only had to count to forty-seven before she was on her feet again. She remained speechless for a very long time waiting to feel differently inside. Maybe a tingle? Mostly she felt relieved that her papa called her a "believer" and a member of his flock. Now maybe she was more than "just a girl."

Fall also brought change, the growth of seeds to maturity. Lila experienced change too. Her clothes tightened. Her body ripened. She awoke one morning with a sour stomach and messy bedclothes. She stifled a scream but not the sobs that followed. When she did not show up for breakfast, her mama found her—still sobbing—in her room.

"God is punishing me!" she cried. "He's punishing me, and I don't even know what sins I've committed for this to happen!" She pointed to her bedclothes.

Her mama sat beside her and took her hands. "*You* have *not* sinned. The Lord has sent a sign that you have reached physical maturity. You are a young woman now." She helped Lila tidy herself and hustle to school so she would not be late and have to explain her tardiness.

Lila felt very self-conscious, as if being grown up now were obvious to everyone who looked at her. After a few days the feeling subsided because no one had treated her differently. She wanted to know if any of her friends had changed also or if she was the only one so blessed, but every time she broached the subject, Bessie and Annie blushed. Flora Belle seemed not to understand what was going on. Lila did notice that those two friends wore ribbons in their hair from time to time. Not to church after her papa frowned on them once when they did, but to school. She asked her mama if most mature girls wore ribbons, but her mama did not respond.

Then it happened. One morning as she dressed for school, her mama came to her with a surprise. Blue ribbons. Two skinny blue ribbons. "You're a young lady now, Lila. These are for you. To tie 'round your braids, but don't...."

Lila could not believe her eyes. Ribbons! Shiny ones! She wanted to throw her arms around her mama in thanks, but such exuberance would not have been appropriate. "Thank you, Mama," she said. "I promise to take very good care of them. You'll see."

She tried not to flush when her brother noticed them at breakfast. "Lila's wearing ribbons!" he shouted.

Her papa stomped into the room and jerked her from her chair, spilling biscuits and gravy down the front of her sack dress. "Ribbons? You better not be fancying yurse'f up to go to school. Vanity is a sin!"

"But Mama ga...."

"Don't you go looking to yur mama for he'p. She knows better."

Mama stood rigid at the wood stove, her back to her husband's outrage.

Papa's eyes narrowed as he shouted at his daughter. "Don't you dare give in to the temptation of lookin' pretty. God did not create woman to be pretty. He made her to birth her husband's children. *Boy* children! It's woman brought sin into this world and yur not goin' t' bring more on *us*! Git those ribbons outta yur hair now!"

Tears cascaded down Lila's cheeks as she reached for a braid and struggled to untie the fabric, but she only succeeded in knotting and tangling it more.

"Git on with it! Yur mama told me yur a young woman now. Well, yur not! Yur nothin' but a sappy, good-for-nothin' girl. Can't even untie a ribbon. So worthless there's not a boy within miles who'd ask to marry you and birth his babies. Probly birth him nothin' but more no good girl babies like you."

In words barely audible, Mama turned toward him. "Husband, please. Calm yourself. I didn't make your rules clear to Lila about when...."

"*My* rules? The Lord's rules! And don't you put yurse'f in the middle of this. This *girl* is gonna pay for her sin right here and right now." He yanked a braid away from her with his left hand, the kitchen knife from the table with his right, and hacked away. "I'll show you, Girl, how to git rid of a ribbon!"

"Husband, no!" his wife screeched and ran to protect her daughter.

"Wife! Quiet! You grab that girl's wrists and hold her arms behind her back until I'm finished teaching her what shame looks like." He whacked and sawed at her hair with the frenzy of a man desperate to free himself from a thick rope around his neck.

Every slash to the end of her braid sent a sharp pain into Lila's scalp as her head lurched to one side. She wailed with every tug until he stopped long enough for her to catch her breath. *Finally*, she thought, but no. Her papa grabbed the other braid and hacked away at it. Her mama still held Lila's hands tight behind her back letting her own warm tears fall onto both pairs of them as if she could share her daughter's pain and humiliation.

At last the mutilation ended. Lila's neck was sore and her head throbbed, but it was over. Her papa forced the two, eight-inch hanks of thick auburn hair and blue ribbon into her hands, opened the wood stove's pot belly, and ordered her to throw them into the fire. He left the door open for the hiss and stench to fill the kitchen. She wiped her tears on her sleeves and head down, turned toward her room.

"Not so fast. You git yurse'f to school."

Lila stared at her soiled dress and ran her thumbs along the stubs of braids barely drooping onto her shoulder. *I am not fit to be seen by anyone. I cannot go to school like this. Everyone will laugh at me.*

"And when you git there, you stand in front of ever'body and show them what shame looks like and tell them what happens when you disobey yur papa and commit a sin. And when you git home you go straight to yur room and prostrate yurse'f and pray to God to be forgiven for the sinful being you are. And don't you git up 'til mornin'!"

When Mama emitted the slightest whimper, Papa turned on her. "Wife, if I hear one more sound out of you, baby in yur belly or no, yu'll be on that floor next to her! Now both of you, git!"

Lila did not dare wait to be told twice. She burst out the door and ran faster than ever before. She wanted to run away, far away, but where she did not know. She ran past the school and beyond, then pulled up short. She had no idea which road to take, and she trembled at the thought of how her papa would punish her when he caught her... because he would. No. She must stay... and obey. She tried to make herself invisible by huddling within a small stand of young loblolly pines until she built up the courage to go to school.

That is where Jimmy found here. "Lila? I thought it was you darted in here. What's the matter?" He walked in closer until she stopped him and shook her head. "Looks like you better tell me what went on with you this morning. And don't leave anything out."

Her halting description of traumatic events expressed her anger and humiliation through another flood of tears. Jimmy tried to move closer to comfort her, but she waved him away and covered her head with her hands.

"Lila, this is not the kind of problem where we think about what to say and how to say it. This problem takes cleaning you up and fixing things. I'll be back as fast as I can. Don't you move." He ran away the direction he had come.

The wait for Jimmy's return seemed an eternity, and she could not think of any way *he* could help "fix" her up. She cringed at the sound of whispers nearing the trees.

"She's in there, Mama. Be kind. She's really scared."

"I see her. Now, you go on to school and make your apologies for being late. But remember, tell the truth. 'Problems at home' should do."

Lila heard Jimmy's footsteps whiz off and his mother's draw nearer. She shivered at the thought of anyone looking at her, but the woman's voice seemed calm and friendly, and the frightened girl had nowhere else to turn for help.

"My name is Lottie and I'm Jimmy's mother. He told me about your difficulties with your parents this morning, and I'm here to help you clean up. I brought a scarf for your head. May I bring it to you?" After a long silence, she heard a "Yes, ma'am" and approached the girl. She placed the scarf over Lila's tangled hair and tied it gently beneath her chin. "Come home with me and we'll see what magic we can work to get you ready for school by lunchtime so you can tell your papa that yes, you did go to school today." Lottie wrapped an arm around Lila's shoulders, and the two came out from the trees headed away from the school toward town.

Lila inspected the tiny room that had been fixed for washing up near a back door of Jimmy's house. A stack of fluffy towels and washcloths sat on a crate on one side of a large galvanized tin wash basin held to the wall with metal brackets. An arrangement of soaps, creams, brushes and combs occupied the other side. Layers of old towels, neatly folded, lay on the floor in front to keep feet warm. Three hooks on the inside of the door were for clothing that would be put back on and one hook outside the door was for items that needed a wash. An empty peg above the basin could have held a mirror.

Lottie sent her to that washing room with an old bathrobe, clean brush and comb, and directions to stay until she felt squeaky clean and relaxed inside and out. "But hang your dress outside first thing so I can give it a good scrub. I'll bring you some water as soon as it warms."

Lila peeked behind a curtain on the far wall and found a wooden-framed and seated bucket toilet—an inside dry toilet with a lid and all the necessaries stacked neatly within a hands-reach—the first she'd ever seen! Her home was more of a scatter than an arrangement, so Lila took her time to enjoy the fresh scents and order around her. And the privacy, with no one spying over her shoulder to criticize. She felt comfortable here, at ease enough to use the facility and to remove her stained dress and hang it outside.

Two buckets waited for her as promised with a note explaining how to drain them. She soaked and lathered and rinsed; lathered and rinsed again wondering whether it was sinful to be too clean. She tried to run her fingers through her tangled hair, took a comb to it, and finally gave up and just plunged her head into the basin for a good scrub too. She toweled off as well as she could, drained and cleaned the small room as well as she could, slipped into the bathrobe, put the comb and brush into its pocket and picked up her shoes.

She glanced around the welcoming room one last time, sighed, and opened the door to leave when she heard voices. Two of them. A man and a woman. The man's was deep and strong but not angry, so it was not her papa. The woman's was soft and kind, definitely Lottie's.

"I came as soon as the Recorder told me you left because of a problem at home. Are you ill? Jimmy?"

"No. We're both fine. Jimmy's at school. A friend of his needed some help, but all is under control now."

"That's a relief. You never walk out of work early, so I imagined the worst."

"Again, we're both fine. You may tell Mr. County Recorder that I will be in shortly after noon and will come early for the next couple of mornings to make up the time."

"He's so tickled to have you working in his office that he won't expect you to."

"Perhaps not, but I'll be there just the same. You know I like to keep accounts up to date. Will you come for supper?"

"You know I will."

"See you then. Thanks for checking on us."

Lila heard the door close and waited a minute before padding up the hallway to the kitchen in her bare feet. She watched Lottie busy at the kitchen's wash basin—busy but calm, with all the tins and jars and utensils arranged just so. So unlike the kitchen at home with this and that everywhere there was an empty space for a this or a that. She felt comfortable in this room too.

"Oh, Lila. You're finished? Have a seat and I'll be with you in a minute. I'm just peeling some potatoes for supper tonight. The Judge will join us."

"Jimmy talks about the Judge a lot. Was he the man I heard you talking to? He seems nice."

"He is. Very. He helped me once when I had a big problem." Lottie turned and smiled at the young girl. "Now I have a chance to thank him by helping someone else." She dried her hands on her apron. "I'll bet you're starving. I fixed applesauce and toast with cheese. Would you like some before we get started?"

Lila nodded and helped herself. She had not realized how hungry she was with all the fluster of the morning.

Lottie joined her at the table and sipped at a cup of coffee. She pointed to a small hand pump in the corner. "Yes, the Judge is very good to us. He convinced Jimmy and me to move to Troy a few years ago by claiming to know a guy who could run a line from the pump outside for a small one inside and another man who could build a dry toilet inside. 'But', he added with a twinkle, 'you two will have to find a man who will dump and clean it every day.' Jimmy loved the farms so much, and especially Sparky the dog, that he was the hardest to convince but as soon as he heard the words 'toilet inside' he was sold. His hand flew up in the air and he volunteered to be 'that man.' So I have water to clean the kitchen and Jimmy cleans the bathroom every day."

Lila smiled softly and nodded. "Jimmy works hard with all the jobs he tells me about, but he never complains. He's pretty clever too."

"That he is. He's the one who set up the drain water system in the wash room. The Judge finds lots of projects to keep him out of trouble."

Lila dropped her hands to her lap. She could not imagine Jimmy ever being in trouble or punished. She wondered what it would be like to live in a safe place instead of a fearful one.

Lottie caught the girl's gaze and held it. "I will help you, Lila, but I hope you can understand that I cannot put my hands on you to change you. Only your parents have that right. But I've come up with a way to guide *you* to fix whatever you want. Do you use scissors at home?"

Lila nodded. "Sometimes when I do mending."

"Have you or your mother ever cut your hair?"

"Sometimes when she thinks it's getting too long in back, Mama comes along with the scissors and cuts straight across the bottom."

"Well, I believe you can do a better job than that. Do you know it is healthy for your hair to have a trim every now and again?"

Lila shook her head. She had never thought about hair being healthy or not.

"You can learn to take care of that chore anytime you want. Ready?"

The young girl nodded, unsure of what she should be ready for.

"Good," Lottie said brightly. "Back in a flash. She disappeared down the hallway and returned with two old towels and two pairs of scissors. She sat again and put a towel across her shoulders. "You do the same, then lift all of your hair up and over onto your towel."

Lila was careful to follow directions and, finally satisfied that every last strand of hair was where it should be, looked to Jimmy's mother for the next step. To her surprise, Lottie was a half-step ahead removing hair pins from her workplace bun to let her long dark brown hair fall to her mid shoulders. Lila noticed that it was not quite as dark as Jimmy's, or as wavy, but shiny with soft curls on the ends.

"Remove any pins or other things that might be stuck in your hair and run your fingers through it to make sure." She found a couple more pins. Lila found mostly pine needles from hiding in the trees.

"Now, pick up your comb and we'll both work out our tangles. Are you pretty good at that?"

Lila shook her head. She was not good at all, and her mama was even worse trying to force a comb through where it had no intention of going. She usually gave up and left her daughter to it. The girl had no idea that there was a special way to reduce the frustration until she watched Lottie methodically work through her own hair and quickly learned to copy her technique. Done.

"The abuse you suffered this morning was horrible. May you never experience such a dreadful assault again. But I'm here to warn you that you will find yourself in a similar pickle—accidental or not of your own making—many times during your adult life. For instance..." Lottie separated a penny's-width of strands of her own hair from behind her left ear, pulled it forward and slid her fingers down near the ends. "...you may have a child someday who's playing with his molasses-covered mush and, when you turn your head to reach for a cloth to clean his hands, he grabs a hank of your hair with his sticky fingers and you have a mess to deal with. Or maybe you're walking in the woods with your child who has been investigating wonderful things on the ground. You pick her up, and she grabs a hank of your hair with her pitchy hand."

Lila giggled at the thought.

"Will getting angry or upset solve the problem of goo in your hair?"

Lila shook her head. Lottie was sounding like Jimmy when he worked through finding an answer to many of her difficulties.

"So what do you do? You have kids to clean up, chores.... You can't stop everything to clean sticky stuff out of your hair. So you get rid of the muck as quick as you can by..." Lottie picked up her scissors and snipped a good inch right from the bottom of the strand she was holding. "...and save the fixing up for later."

Lila clapped her hands to her mouth to stifle a very surprised "oh no!" Who would cut off a hunk of her hair just to help someone else?

"Don't worry. This won't be noticeable at all once I've finished with it. How can you learn if I don't *show* you as well as tell you how to solve such a problem?"

Lila nodded slightly and emitted a very deep breath.

"Start with the shortest bit and work toward your face, like this." She demonstrated, and a few more short strands fell to the table. "Now that you've combed your hair, it seems that one of your short pieces is longer than the other. Do you want to use a mirror to see?"

Lila shook her head. "I'm not allowed to use a mirror. It's sinful."

Remembering what Jimmy had told her once about a friend's restrictions, Lottie took her turn to nod and emit a very deep breath. "Then you'll have to feel your way through this lesson. Find the shortest part and begin, just a little bit at a time."

Lila's hands trembled so violently that she expected to see a confetti of hair all over the table and the floor. But snip by tiny snip she relaxed and fell into a rhythm, keeping the scissors beneath the two fingers that held her target.

"Well done! Now use your fingers to find where on your chest the done side stops and find that same place on your other side. Snip the tiniest bit and measure again. Watch me first, then do the same as before."

The two snipped in unison until each had two even sides.

"Well done again! Now for the hardest part, the back. Do you know, Lila, that your hair is still quite long in back, only a little shorter than mine? You'll have no problem weaving braids if you comb your hair just right first. You won't cut straight across like your mama does. You'll make a nice curve by angling your fingers and the scissors. Follow me."

The young girl paid close attention to her model, then put the scissors aside and looked to her for approval.

"Lila, you have done a wonderful job. Are you sure you don't want to see how lovely you look?"

She shook her head. "I want to, but I can't. It's prideful to look at myself in a mirror, and vanity is a sin requiring punishment."

Lottie thought for a long, hard minute. "Tell me exactly what your papa's rule is about looking at yourself."

"Looking in a mirror is a sin. Don't do it or you will be punished for being vain."

"That seems pretty clear to me. Does he ever say, 'Do not look at your image'?"

Lila shook her head. "I've never heard him say anything about an image."

Lottie could not imagine going through twelve years of life without seeing what she looked like. "Have you ever seen yourself in the lake or in a puddle?"

Lila shrugged. "Once or twice maybe."

"Were you punished for that?"

"Not that I remember. Why?"

"I think I have a solution. Back in a flash." Lottie rummaged through a cupboard and turned up a tray, a silvery tray for carrying food to a table. "Let's try this. Would you call this a mirror?"

Lila giggled. "No. It's a tray."

The woman placed the tray on the table in front of the girl. "I'm going to put my cup on this tray, way over near the edge. What do you see when you look at the tray?"

Lila thought that was a silly question. "The cup, of course."

"Stand up and look down very carefully. Now what do you see?"

Lila stood and studied the large, rectangular object carefully. "Handles?"

"Keep looking...."

Her eyes sparkled with a flash of amazement. "Is that... is that me?"

Lottie just smiled.

Lila gazed down at the tray again, taking in all the details. Tears dropped slowly onto the image, distorting it bit by bit. "I look the same as everybody else," she wept. "I always thought that my parents don't like me because I'm different and that's why they punish me so much. Because I embarrass them. They don't even remember my name."

"I can't speak to why your parents treat you as they do, but I can tell you that you are a perfectly lovely young woman. You're strong and healthy, bright and talented, and your deep blue eyes are far more fascinating than any blue ribbons will ever be. The only things you lack are confidence and a handkerchief."

Lottie handed the girl one of hers across the table and moved the tray aside. "I would never criticize how your parents teach you what they believe, but I will tell you what I teach my own child about pride and vanity and sin. Each has an inside part and an outside part. For example, when Jimmy cleans the stinky toilet buckets, he can resent the job or he can feel good about the job he does. That's the inside part. If he feels good about the way he completes his task, proud even, he can brag to me about what a fine job he did, or he can thank the good Lord for blessing him with the energy and ability to create his clever cleaning system and then go on about the business of getting ready for school. That's the outside part.

"Take me for example. I have a job in an office where I am expected to look appropriate and tidy. Every morning before I leave for the court house, I check myself in the mirror to make sure I look nice and do not have pins sticking out of my bun because that would be a distraction for anyone I serve. That's the inside part. If all is in order, I can admire myself and say how fine I look and hope everybody notices, or I can thank the good Lord for blessing me with the ability to do my hair up right so I won't be late, and then I go about my business. That's the outside part.

"Now let's think about you. You have a very nice voice. I've heard you sing solos at school programs. When you sing well and make no mistakes, you feel good inside, proud even. That's the inside part. You can brag about what a beautiful voice you have, the best of anyone else in the choir, or you can thank the good Lord for blessing you with a talent that brings joy to other people. That's the outside part.

"Not every good feeling you have about yourself is sinful, Lila. How you express that feeling can be and it's up to you to decide. If someone claps for you or tells you what a fine voice you have or tells you how nice you look, saying "Thank you" is *not* showing pride. It's being kind to someone who has been kind to you."

Lila attempted to take to heart the lessons Jimmy's mother had given.

"You didn't come here to have me yatter at you, did you? You came for help, so let's get on with it. I'll show you different ways to style your hair so when you have permission to make changes, you'll know what you like best."

Lila watched intently as Lottie braided her own hair tightly on one side and loosely on the other, noting that the loose braid appeared longer. The woman then demonstrated pigtails above the ears and below, one long braid or ponytail down her center back, and completely combed out and tucked behind her ears or not.

"Now it's your turn, Lila. Play a little, then fix your hair for school. Since you don't use ribbons, what should we find to tie your hair?"

"At home I use thin strips of leather like boot or shoe laces."

"I'll see what I can dig up in Jimmy's room."

Lila shook her head. "I might be asked where I got them, and I can't lie. I'll use the ones from my shoes."

"Whatever you think best. I'm going to my room to put myself back together for work. Then I'll fix us a bite of lunch and you a snack for after school in case dinner at home is a problem. Your dress is just outside the back door. We have about half an hour."

Just short of that time, Lottie reappeared to find Lila in the kitchen fixing food. Her hair was in loose braids, neatly tied with half a lace each. Her shoes were adequately tied with the other half a lace each. Her dress showed a little discoloration intentionally left from the morning's spill so it would not attract a "Who cleaned your clothes?" All the clippings, both auburn and dark brown, were swept away, the towels folded and the scissors cleaned. The silver tray remained on the table but scooted closer to the place Lila had sat.

The two walked together back toward the school. Lottie interrupted their conversation to ask, "Who fixed your hair?"

Startled, Lila replied, "You know I did."

"But I'm not Lottie. I'm one of your girl friends, so 'Who fixed your hair?'"

"I did."

"It looks really nice."

"Thank you."

"Why weren't you at school this morning?"

A shrug, "You know. Stuff at home."

"Good job, Lila!"

"Thank you."

Lila crossed the road to school without looking back, one pocket filled with a snack and the other with a pinch of confidence.

"I'm home," Lila hollered as she walked through the doorway into an environment completely different from where she had spent her morning. She proceeded straight to her sleeping room without stopping, closed the door and prostrated herself on the cold, uneven floorboards. Her nose and chin rubbed against the grit. She dared not open her eyes or they would fill with dust and she would not be able to wipe them. She was ordered to pray to God to be forgiven for her sins, and her discomfort was an intentional part of the process.

She collected her thoughts for a long time before she began. What should have been the most horrible day of her life, ended with a new feeling inside. Maybe that was the tingle she expected following baptism when she was told she was now "spiritually mature" or what it felt like to be a "young woman." She wondered if it was a sin for parents to hurt or shame their children and if so, how *they* were punished. Both parents abused her with their harsh action or inaction when a reprimand would have been enough to change her behavior immediately, but she accepted that she did deserve some blame for her punishment.

First, Lila asked the Lord's forgiveness for being so hasty to assume that because she was given ribbons meant that she could wear them. She promised always to ask permission before trying something new.

Second, she asked His forgiveness for creating a conflict that forced her mama to choose between her husband and her child. No mother should be faced with such a decision. She promised never to place her mama in such a position again.

Third, she asked God to forgive her for her lack of trust in His plan for her salvation. She promised to look to Him for guidance and not to question how He chose to reveal it.

Then she continued her prayers by asking blessings for others:

For her mama and papa, who really needed His guidance to be good parents. She would help by being as obedient and invisible as she could.

For Jimmy, who was a good friend and a good example of how to work hard to earn what you want. And who taught her never to tell a lie.

For the Judge, who showed love and caring for people who were not of his blood and who was a good model for Jimmy of how a boy becomes a man.

For Lottie, who was kind and treated even kids with dignity. She taught how to turn something bad into something good without wasting too much time crying. Every child deserved a perfect mother like Lottie.

Yes, for a bad day, it ended as just about the best one ever. Lila fell asleep content with her place on the floor.

*

Many of Lila's schoolmates quit after eighth grade. They were needed to help at home or in the fields and had acquired enough math and reading to support them in the few opportunities available in 1913 southeastern Alabama. She hoped against hope that she would not be kept home or worse, that the family would move back to Goshen for good. Perhaps she had sealed her own fate by offering to take on more and more chores over the last couple of years to convince her papa that she was not just a "sappy, good-for-nothin' girl."

Her friend Jimmy helped her work out how to ask permission before trying something new by introducing her to compromise. "That means two people give a little bit of what they don't agree on to get something else each wants. For example, you might want to wear your hair a different way but are afraid to ask in case that causes trouble again. But what if you thought of a reason why that would be a good idea? Like 'if I could do this with my hair, then I would have time in the mornings to help....'"

Lila thought for several days before she acted. She chose a morning when she felt brave and her papa had been in a good mood for several days. She arose the minute she heard noise from the kitchen and met him coming in with buckets of water. "Papa, I could do that for you each morning if I didn't spend so much time braiding my hair. Maybe wear it in loose tails like this." She gathered a tail below each ear and let them fall onto her chest. "The water would be warm by the time you and mama get up. Would that help you?"

He muttered the usual "Hrmmph. I'll think on it," dashing her hopes. But two days later her papa woke her early telling her to get up and fetch the water. "I have to leave now for Goshen today and yur mama don't feel so good."

Reminding herself not to assume but to ask permission first, she gathered her hair below each ear as before and asked, "May I save time by doing this?"

He nodded. "That'll do." And walked out.

Lila's feet carried her to the pump behind the house as fast as a freight train. In minutes she had the fire stoked, water warming and another bucket waiting nearby. She dressed quickly, then brushed and fixed her hair, noting how the two tails were thick and wavy with natural curls on the ends. She did feel older, and was about to leave for school when her mother stopped her at the door with frightened animal eyes. "Don't worry, Mama. Papa gave me permission."

When she arrived at school, Jimmy told her how nice she looked. "Thank *you*," she said.

Lila continued to trade more chores for small privileges like staying late at school to work on a project or visiting friends to study. Sometimes the girls took a break to cook a snack, ones she never fixed at home, like pralines or tiny cakes, because they required ingredients her family did not store.

She tried to remain obedient and invisible at home while doing her tasks, but sometimes her younger brother goaded her to speak sharply at him. Her mama did not call out her misbehavior, but if her papa was around she was in for a switching. He did not force her to bare her bottom any longer; he used a fatter stick to whack through her clothes or the traditional one to strike the palms of her hands until they burned red.

Shaming or humiliating punishments occurred rarely once Lila learned to check her reactions to her papa's outbursts. Those eruptions seemed to accompany his bad moods on a regular schedule, so she stayed as far away from him as she could when she recognized the signs that troubles were worming their way to his surface. But sometimes she was taken by surprise.

A fall rain came on with a vengeance. The road through town turned to thick red mud. Vehicles chugged through the muck. Horses slogged, and children took off their shoes to slosh home.

Lila's papa met her at the door. "You too good to dirty your shoes like the rest of us?"

She did not know how to respond. Ordinarily she would be punished for soiling her clothes or shoes. This day, it seemed to be the opposite. "Aren't we to keep ourselves clean at all times?"

"Look 't yurse'f! Mud up to yur knees and the bottom of yur dress. Is that bein' clean for a meetin' with our Lord, Girl? You know we're goin' for a foot-washin' and sharin' of the Lord's Supper with our congregation this eve, and you ain't fit to have any believer clean those dirty feet of yurs."

Lila fumbled for words. "I'll... I'll wash up quick, and... "

He pinned her against the door jamb, tight enough for his warm breath and spittle to reach her cheek as he shouted, "Yu'll do no such thing! Yu'll show up just as you are and humble yurse'f before every woman there by doin' all the washin' and none of the receivin', stupid girl that you are! You will *not* partake of the Lord's Supper this eve, and when you git home yu'll ask His forgiveness for thinkin' yur better than ever'body else by intendin' to go fancier than the rest of us. And for the next week yu'll have no shoes to wear at all, school or no. Give 'em here!"

Lila obeyed. She sat on the dirty floor in her dirty clothes and bare feet while the rest of the family ate supper. She followed behind them to the congregation's meeting, knelt before every mother and daughter there, and as she washed each pair of feet she said, "I committed the sin of vanity today. I, therefore, humble myself before you and am your servant as we all are to Our Lord." When she came to her mama's feet, she did not look into her eyes but felt the tremble of her body trying to hold in sobs.

She followed her family home, went to her bed, and puzzled over the events of the day. Since her previous confrontation with her papa in seventh grade, she had studied her Bible almost daily and attempted to understand the meaning of every story and every sin mentioned in it. She knew that Jesus and his disciples lived in a hot, desert kind of place. They probably wore sandals or went barefoot most of the time, so most everybody's feet were probably dirty most of the time. She also knew the story about the Last Supper from the Book of John where Jesus tells Simon Peter that if you have already bathed, you only need to have your feet washed to be clean, and then he washed Simon Peter's feet. That was why her papa's congregation practiced foot-washing before celebrating the Lord's Supper. No mention of *sin* was written for which parts were clean and which were dirty. As she understood it, then, sharing His table was a kind of come-as-you-are deal and was more about performing service for other people than it was about who you were and how you showed up to do that.

What she did not understand was how her papa read the written words in a different way. Where did he learn the stories that he preached to others? How was she ever to know what was right and what was wrong in the eyes of her papa and of their God? She prayed for forgiveness for committing a sin she could not figure out; then she fell asleep before an answer to her questions was revealed.

*

With Jimmy's good advice and her own attention to her many chores and to her papa's shifting moods, Lila survived the seventh and eighth grade years with fewer punishments for sins that must be written between the lines of the Good Book in words only her papa could see—sins like breaking a plate or spilling soup or for general disobedience. By end of summer it was clear to all of her classmates who would go on to school and who would stay at home to work. After a long summer in Goshen, Lila dreaded what her future held. She wanted to be like Lottie, an educated woman who found a good job in a pleasant place, but her papa gave no hint of what he had planned for her. Until autumn. Her papa ordered the family to pack up for the move back to Troy for the school term.

Lila was overjoyed. She was going to school! Or not. Maybe she was destined to stay home to take care of the house while her mama watched over her two-year-old brother and the pesky one would start school early. Now she was heartbroken. At least she might see some of her friends from time to time.

Her fortunes changed with a pronouncement by her papa at a meeting of his congregation. "We men decided that the time has come to spread our reach 'round the county, so we need to train up some of our young folk to he'p with schoolin', buildin' and attractin' converts to us. We pooled what we could from 'round our places to come up with an old wagon and a coupl'a old horses that kin carry ten kids down the road to the white high school in Brundidge that's lookin' to expand to a six-month term real soon. Got a strong program too.

"Two of our boys, Fred and Joe, will drive the wagon. Other boys, Frank, Abel and Ralph, will he'p keep it in good runnin' order and hobble the horses in a field near the school. They'll take classes mostly in buildin' skills and repair. Bessie, Annie and Flora Belle, you study up on basic subjects so you can teach 'em to the young kids once we have enough converts to start our own school. Ruby and Lila, yu'll spend more time on singin'. We 'spect bigger crowds at our revival meetin' once we git goin' and yu'll need to teach 'em and lead 'em in the good songs.

"Now, y'all be ready early on Monday two weeks and you won't git back 'til later than yur used to. Meetin' is over."

Lila could not wait to tell Jimmy. Maybe they would end up at the same school. She knew he was going because he told her that the Judge insisted. The Judge always insisted that he spend part of every 365 days in a year studying; a five-month term was not adequate for young minds. Jimmy was to double-time with lessons in Latin and history too so he could test out of school and into university early. Plus he was supposed to learn more office skills than typing to help out at the courthouse. With all this learning he could get a good job and more education to become an attorney someday, if he wanted. At least he would have more choices than most boys his age.

Early on the appointed Monday, Lila hurried down the road to the schoolhouse where the wagon loaded for Brundidge. As they got underway, the eight in back chattered about what to expect—new faces, new subjects, new teachers, and time to visit with one another every day as the horses plodded along. She knew she was not supposed to be having fun, but she could not help enjoying the ride and wondered where Jimmy was headed and what he was thinking on this first day of a new school term.

She did not wonder for long. Jimmy rode up behind the wagon on his bike and hollered and waved to them. He peddled up by the drivers to exchange a few words with Fred and Joe, then he sped away, too impatient for their slower pace. They found him sitting on the high school steps studying while waiting for classes to begin.

They did not have any classes together, but at day's end Jimmy was waiting on the steps to exchange stories with all of them about their first day—what classes they liked, which ones were way too hard, new friends they had made. Lila noticed how he had grown over the summer. He was taller and lean except for his broad chest and shoulders and muscled arms. She wondered if he noticed changes in her too. When the wagon was ready and loaded, Jimmy sped off with a wave to all.

The students followed the same routine morning and afternoon. Jimmy always showed up early, and Lila began to do the same. A few minutes alone to visit started her day off just right. When the wagon returned to Troy in the afternoon, there Jimmy would be studying while he waited for his friends before going to his job at the courthouse. Most went on home after a short while, all but Lila. The two hung around together under the tree where they first learned to sing *a cappella* together. If the weather was too cold or windy, they sneaked into the school near Miss Morton's room, the closest to the door, so they could escape quickly if spotted.

The rains came on early that year. Lila arrived at the wagon's pickup point to find Jimmy huddled under a piece of canvas that he offered to share. Gladly she stepped underneath beside him. The wagon arrived a few minutes later, also dressed with a canvas cover. The students climbed aboard and held the tarpaulin in place. Jimmy asked Fred if he could hitch a ride; his bike was not making much progress in the mud.

Fred scratched his chin. "Don't think we can take friends. This wagon's s'posed to be for our own kind."

"What if I paid for the ride? Then I'd be a customer and not a friend."

Fred scratched his chin again and felt Joe's poke to his ribs and whisper in his ear. "Might be okay. How much yuh figure?"

"Ten pennies each way. I'll tie my bike to the rear, and if the sun's out by afternoon, I won't bother you to haul me back. If the season's short this year, I won't ask often. Deal?"

Fred and Joe nodded and smiled. "We're hopin' the wet season's a long one, long enough fer ever'body some ice cream now and ag'in. There's a new parlor comin' to town soon, you know. Hop aboard."

Jimmy hitched his bike to the rear of the wagon and scooted underneath the tarp beside Lila. As dripping wet as they all were, she thought that this wagon ride was just about the best one ever.

*

A blast of cold weather followed the rains, and a wallop of envy struck Lila in the chest one Saturday when she arrived at Flora Belle's for a study session and found her in back with a very familiar figure—Jimmy! The two were chatting and smiling and laughing with an ease Lila had not experienced. Flora Belle played coy, egging him on to show her how to hold an ax properly.

Lila marched toward them. "Don't let me break in on you two. I just came over to tell Flora Belle that I can't study with her today. Maybe next week." She disappeared as quickly as she had appeared and fought against the whirling dread in her gut. Maybe this was what sin felt like, she reasoned—feeling jealous of her girl friend and speaking to her unkindly. Maybe this is how you recognized sin, not from the words in a book but from the sensation aroused when you did something wrong. She did not need to tell her mama or papa and ask to be punished. She was old enough now to decide on proper penance including a heartfelt prayer for forgiveness.

The following Monday, Lila sat next to Flora Belle on the school wagon and apologized for her bad behavior. Her friend seemed to have forgotten completely about the incident and suggested they try for a study session on next Saturday if Lila stayed in Troy for the weekend again. She hoped she would. Most of her friends remained in Troy during the full school term. Now that the Troy congregation required so much of her papa's attention, her family frequently stayed in town too.

Lila showed up the following Saturday, books in hand, to find Flora Belle and Jimmy chatting in back as before. This time she sauntered toward them in a friendly way, sat on the steps and joined the conversation.

Flora Belle excused herself. "I'm going to check on papa, peek in the oven and heat some juice for a break when you're ready."

"Great!" said Jimmy. "I work up a sweat real fast when it comes to cutting wood." He took off his jacket and laid it on the steps next to Lila. "Better get to work while the wind's down." He took up the ax and chopped away.

Lila now realized where he got those strong arms that caught her eye on the first day of school, for he made quick work of the pile of logs waiting for him. He sat beside her to take that break before Flora Belle reappeared with refreshment. "What brings you here today?" he asked, shoving his muscled arms back into his jacket.

"School work. I learn better when I can talk over our studies with somebody. And you? Since when do you cut wood for folks?"

Jimmy wiped his face with a handkerchief and his hands on his pants. "Since the Judge told me to... or rather, suggested that I help Flora Belle's papa out. The Judge met him hobbling into the courthouse to pay his taxes a few weeks ago and asked what the problem was. I guess he let the ax slip and cut deep into his leg, and he couldn't get around well enough to keep up with the outside chores. And with cold weather coming on...."

"'The man has plenty of girls to help around the house, but no boys to do the hard work, so I told him that I knew a boy who was perfect for the job,' the Judge told me. I must've had that look in my eye that asked 'how much' because the Judge added right away that no money would change hands between the man and me. 'Remember, a man needs his dignity, so when Mr. Colby asked how much, I told him that you about eat your mama out of house and home, and a snack on work days would do just fine.'"

Jimmy continued, "So ever since I started chopping, I go home with sandwiches, a cake, cookies, fruit preserves, a big hunk of roast, or whatever Flora Belle puts into my hands. I always take at least one bite and tell her how great it tastes and thank her and her papa for the work." He chuckled to himself before adding, "The Judge is a pretty smart guy. When he comes for supper on cutting days, he wants to know right away what good stuff I got for my work. He sets aside a slice or a handful or a hunk of whatever takes his fancy saying, 'That looks worth about fifty pennies.' He'll put the money on the table, wrap what he wants to take with him in a napkin or dish, and not another word is said about it. We all come out of the deal with some of what we want and some dignity to boot."

Lila smiled and thought to herself how every boy should have a grampa like the Judge. She did not know one man in her family—old, middle aged or young—who understood how to show kindness and understanding to others.

*

Early spring. Heat and humidity increasing. The earth greening. The school term ending soon. Projects due.

Projects due! Lila had never done a project before. Sure, she had written reports on famous people, battles and heroes of the War, and why cotton was important to Alabama, but never a project that required doing something over time, then showing the finished product and writing about it. She would never pass science class and that would make her papa angry and he would punish her. She was doomed.

The science teacher distributed packets of twelve seeds to each student—three seeds each of four varieties—with the following directions: First, separate the seeds into the four different kinds and plant each kind a foot away from every other, water them, give each group a number and begin a chart for their plants' growth. Lila felt confident about this step. She and her mama started regular garden work a couple of weeks earlier, so planting her seeds in a corner would not be unusual.

Second, note the day the tiny seedlings first emerge and make a sketch of what each looks like. Days and sketches should differ. Remember to keep the soil around them damp. Not a problem for Lila. She was good at spotting details and okay at sketching.

Third, when the seedlings are two inches tall, note the day and sketch again. Days and sketches should differ. All three plants in each group should be the same. If they are not, the seeds were mixed up at planting. If any of your groups have a mix, remove the plant or plants that are not the same. Remember to water. Be honest. No problem for Lila. All four groups were correct.

Finally, in five more days, note the day and sketch for the last time. Identify each plant. Pull all plants left and dry them by group to submit with your report in one week. Grades will depend in part on how many dry plants are submitted and identified correctly.

Lila had already identified three of her plants. Corn was easy because the seed looked just like what they ate. Cotton was easy because she had picked before and noticed the dark seeds inside the bolls. Number three should be peas. They popped up real fast and their leaves looked like the ones in the family garden. But number four was a puzzle. Everything about the plants was tinier and daintier, as were their seeds, so she supposed they might be flowers. Each had a couple of buds that she checked every day for a hint of their color.

Day Five was the day! Lila dropped to her hands and knees to examine the bright yellow flowers more closely. "Oh, you beautiful little things! Such a pretty shade of…" The next sound out of her mouth was an agonizing scream as a heavy weight landed on her left hand and crushed it into the ground. A massive fist pushed her away and yanked the flowers out of the soil. A second heavy boot ground them into the dirt.

"What you doin' plantin' flowers in our garden? You know that's forbidden!"

Lila wanted to shout, "It's for school!" but knew that would anger her papa more.

"And admirin' 'em, callin' 'em 'beautiful' 'n 'purty'. It's a *sin* to talk of purty things. They tempt your adoration of other than the Lord! If you haven't learned that lesson yet, yull learn it now. Git in that house and open that Bible of yurs and memorize every word of *Genesis I – III*. Bread and water only fur you until you can recite every word. Now, git!"

Lila did not wait to be told twice. She cradled her wounded hand and ran for the house. Tears streamed down her face, not just from the pain but also from the fear of failing science class. Her papa would really be angry then. Probably crush her good hand or worse.

A severe spring thunderstorm came on late afternoon and buffeted the wagon about. The nine students in its bed held onto their protective tarp with both hands, anxious to get home. All but Lila. She used only her right hand and kept the other in a pocket. No one really noticed until the wagon hit a bump, jostling the students against one another. Lila let out a faint cry and grabbed her left pocket.

Jimmy sat next to her and recognized immediately that she was in pain. "What's wrong?" He reached toward her arm, but she shied away.

"Nothing. I'm fine." She turned away from him and lowered her eyes.

"Lila? The truth?"

She could not lie to Jimmy. That was one of the first rules he taught her years ago. She shrugged and gave her stock answer. "You know. Stuff at home."

He reached for her again. She moved away again, shaking her head. "I can't let anyone see."

"I'm your friend. You have to let me help you."

A few tears slipped from her eyes as she opened her pocket gingerly. Her fingers were bandaged and her entire hand was a blackish purple.

Appalled, Jimmy clenched his jaw to ask, "Is that the same kind of 'stuff at home' that's caused trouble before?"

She nodded.

"Then you have to tell me everything, just like before, so we can figure out how to help you. We'll find a dry place to talk as soon as we get back to Troy."

They rode the rest of the way in silence, their friends unaware of Lila's personal horror.

The next morning, a sunny one, Jimmy caught up to the wagon to hitch a ride. He scooted in beside Lila and was allowed a glance at her hand—still discolored but not as swollen. He had felt of it the previous afternoon. The best he could tell, nothing was broken. He reached inside his rucksack and pulled out a pouch. "There's a towel soaked in vinegar inside. Mama said that should help the swelling. If you can keep it damp, the cold should help and maybe with the pain too. She sent along some herbs that are better for that, but I wasn't sure if you were allowed...."

Lila shook her head.

"Okay. Then Mama says to get back to kneading dough as soon as you can bear it. That will make the pain go away faster." He tossed the small packet into his rucksack and came out with a large mysterious bundle. "I've come up with a way for you to finish your project by tomorrow. I'll tell you all about it after school, but don't worry yourself when you should be tending to your lessons. If you can live for one extra day on only bread and water, you'll have tonight to finish your report on time and the next one for memorizing. By the way, is there any chance your papa will be gone this evening?"

Lila nodded. "He has a men's meeting every Thursday after supper."

"Perfect." Jimmy opened the sack to reveal a large loaf of bread cut in thick slices with all sorts of goodies baked in. "This is my mama's specialty. Bread with nuts and dried fruits and carrots and applesauce and a few chunks of chocolate at one end. Eat as much as you can today, and if it's safe, save a piece for tonight. This will keep you healthy and full, guaranteed. And here's a jar of water from what we call the 'medicinal well.' Nothing forbidden, but it'll perk you right up."

Jimmy was true to his word. By the time the school wagon returned to Troy, he had a work area spread out under the tree with paper, pencils, a small set of paints, scissors and a straightedge. "I won't touch a pencil, but I can hold the paper and straightedge still while you do all the writing. I brought lots of paper so you'll have enough for a separate page for each type of plant. If you set each page up to like a chart, it will look neater and be easier for your teacher to read. Teachers like that. That's why I brought the straightedge."

Lila made a column for days and measures, one for sketches and a third for what Jimmy called conclusions. "That's where you put what the facts and your observations mean together. You can glue your pressed plants and the name of each at the top of the page or the bottom. You decide."

She decided to put them at the top. "But I won't have any flowers for the last page."

"Then you'll draw them, very detailed. That's why I brought the paints. And in your conclusion you will also tell what happened to the plants and why—only the truth."

That suggestion made Lila very uncomfortable. She would have to think long and hard about what to write, but she also had another problem. "How do I press the plants that are still in the garden? They'll never dry in one night."

Jimmy grinned. "That's why I brought lots of paper and this." He pointed to a small jar with a grainy substance inside. "Cornmeal. Put a piece of paper on the floor and the plants on top of it. Sprinkle some of this on and then another piece of paper. Slide it under your bed and put heavy books on top. The cornmeal will soak up some of the damp from the plants. At least that's what Mama says. And if your papa's going to a meeting, you can go right out and pull up your plants as soon as he leaves instead of waiting until everyone is asleep. You may even have time left to do a little more memorizing."

Lila worked using her notes. Jimmy watched and held. When they were both satisfied that she had done as much as possible until she could pull her plants, he placed all the pages and extra paper into a large envelope to keep them neat. They agreed to meet earlier than usual before the school wagon arrived so he could hold while she glued her dried plants in place.

All went as planned. The next morning he held. She glued. And before he slid her completed project back into the envelope, he sneaked a peek at what she wrote about the missing flowers.

Some families have different rules than other families. In my family it is forbidden to plant anything in the garden, especially flowers, that cannot be used as food or to make something useful. I planted all my seeds as you can see from this report. It was not until the very end when they bloomed that I knew they were flowers. They were all pulled from the soil and destroyed, so I could not dry them. That is why I painted a picture instead.

I have seen these flowers before down by the lake. I think they are called buttercups, but I'm not sure because my family doesn't recognize flowers. If you don't believe me, I can show you where they grow and tell you how they are alike and how different from the ones I planted. The ones by the lake are smaller, not as bright and creep along the ground. They must be a different variety because the leaves are the same, maybe a kind of weed. Maybe that is part of the lesson. That not all plants are useful and you don't want to mix the troublesome ones with the useful ones or that could cost you money or time or both. The end.

Lila did finish memorizing the first three books of *Genesis* and was allowed back to the family dinner table. Jimmy listened to her practice and corrected her when she made a mistake. She waited nervously for the reports to be returned. So did he. When they were, she had received a very good grade. Not perfect, but very good—good enough to satisfy her papa. She also received a separate, short note from her teacher.

Thank you for telling me about the problem you had with your report. In the future I will take more care in selecting seeds for this project so other students will not have a similar problem.

She could not wait to show Jimmy the note. Her papa would never see it.

One evening two weeks later a stranger came to the house at suppertime when both parents were home. He said he was a deputy sheriff and was handing out updated information to all the families in town since so many new folks had moved to Troy in the last few years.

"There's a short list here of new laws, like 'pedestrians have the right of way' now that automobile traffic in town has picked up, and a few of the old ones that folks might have forgotten, like it's 'illegal to injure or cause harm to another person or child,'" he emphasized, then grinned. "Next thing you know, we'll have to be putting up stop signs if folks start driving too fast near the town center, and I'll have to come 'round again. Thanks, and y'all have a good evening." He tipped his hat and left.

Lila was pretty sure that Jimmy and the Judge had a hand in that deputy's visit. She asked blessings that night for people who cared for her. They made the pain go away faster.

*

Spring 1915 was decision time again. Many high school students left after tenth grade because they reached the age of sixteen. Some went to trade schools for their last two years of high school. Some continued to finish out their four years toward a diploma. Of the ten sponsored by the Troy congregation, Frank, Abel and Ralph had places at a trade school. Fred, Joe, Bessie, Annie, and Flora Belle would continue in the Brundidge school. Ruby and Lila would be sent to Newton to live in during the weeks with a member of the sect there, a music teacher who would instruct the two girls not only in voice but also in sight-reading sheet music. Ninth grade brothers and sisters would fill the five empty places in the school wagon. Friend Jimmy busied himself studying for exams that would allow him to graduate high school early and gain entry to a college in Montgomery.

Newton for five days each week! Elation did not describe Lila's feeling inside. A chance at a new beginning. To be welcomed. To be noticed for other than misbehavior. To not be afraid of doing something wrong for reasons she did not understand. She promised herself to stay far away from her papa's heavy hand so he would not change his mind about sending her away.

As before, her family moved back to Goshen until school resumed in the late fall. When she was not busy doing chores or watching after her two brothers, she found a sunny spot to daydream about singing every day, learning clerical skills, and someday getting a real job in a city.

Her family, however, had different plans for her. One day she found two dresses on her bed. Both were of neutral color, moderate styling, no frills—definitely not flour sack shifts, not meant for chores or garden work. When she questioned her mama, the response was, "You'll need those when you travel with your papa this summer."

Travel with her papa! She did not want to sit across the table from the man, let alone travel with him. And where would they go? What would they do?

Next came the shoes—brown lace-ups, the kind someone like Lottie wore to work, definitely not meant for gardening. Shortly thereafter, Lila found a bonnet on her bed, neutral color, no frills but it did tie under the chin with ribbons. When she questioned her mama again, the response was the same with a surprise on the end. "Time to learn to bun up yur hair."

Bun up her hair? None of her friends did that yet. What new world was she living in? She soon found out.

Her papa woke her early one Saturday morning. "Git dressed in one of them new outfits and all. We're settin' up for a revival tent meetin' tonight in Sanders Hill and yu'll be singin' for us."

She just finished her hair and donned her bonnet when Joe and Fred rolled in with the school wagon loaded with long poles and a huge bundle of canvas. Both boys did a double-take when she walked out, and they hurried to help her into the wagon. Her papa brought a carpetbag with him and took a seat up front where Joe drove, leaving Lila and Fred in the back. "Please tell me what a tent meeting is. I don't know what I'm supposed to do."

"I've never been to one, but your papa says we'll pitch this big tent and call to folks passing by to come on in and listen to some preachin' of the Lord's message. Yu'll prob'ly sing while Joe and I collect coins to start up a new meetin' center there. Your papa bought us nice jackets to wear too."

Sanders Hill was not too far away from Goshen, but no direct road took them there. They arrived by noon, and the boys and her papa spent the rest of the afternoon erecting a large tent while Lila passed out notices of the evening meeting to passersby. Doing such a blatant thing made her uncomfortable. Later, seeing her papa and the two boys emerge from inside the tent all smartened up for the meeting made her even more uncomfortable. The two boys wore the nice jackets that Fred mentioned along with new caps and clean pants. Her papa was unrecognizable in the white linen shirt Lila had pressed a couple of days earlier, a dark sateen vest, and white sport coat and trousers. A golden watch chain looped from his vest pocket. Such a slick appearance and polished speech seemed sinful for a man who preached temperance in all things.

A whirling dread arose in her gut when her papa introduced her as "my purty little girl with a voice like an angel." Comparing her to anything divine was bad enough but to announce to a crowd of strangers that she was pretty? She had been punished time after time for appearing, admiring or saying that word. Was this another case of opposites where only her papa could see words between lines in the Good Book? Another case of sins applying to everybody else but her papa when it suited his needs? Or maybe this was planned public humiliation as punishment for sins she had not owned up to. Her own fault—the reason for her internal trepidation.

Evening brought on unbearable heat, humidity, and the air thick with dust created by a shuffling crowd in a dirt-floored tent. Her papa selected the three hymns she sang: "Onward, Christian Soldiers" to welcome, "Abide with Me" during the collection, and "God Be with You Till We Meet Again" at the closing. After all the curious revivalists departed, she was expected to hold and haul for the tent's breakdown.

The ride home in the dark was interminable. By the end of the evening, her dress was unwearable until she could give it a good cleaning. The minute they arrived home, she stripped and threw it in a corner. She scrubbed the grit and sweat from her body until she could stand to be in the same room with herself, then climbed into bed. She dwelled on the content of her prayers for forgiveness, and finally settled on:

Forgive my lack of appreciation for the shelter, food and clothing provided by my papa. Forgive me for being so slow to understand the path You've laid out for my redemption.

As the evangelist repeated his circuits, many folks returned and their faces became familiar, particularly the same boys competing for space in the front row. Her papa noticed and talked with them, then allowed a select few time with her. After numerous such "friendly conversations," she realized that all plans for music school in the fall were just a dream; her papa was in the market for a marriage partner for his "purty little girl." She remembered his words clearly from the dreadful morning when he chopped off her braids. "...there's not a boy within miles who'd ask to marry you...." Apparently there were a spunky few lining up for her favor, now encouraged by her papa.

Travel to revival meeting sites continued biweekly for the next couple of months. Once summer hit, her papa scheduled twice-weekly outings, and Lila dreaded every one. The only variation to that schedule was the week in mid June when the circus came to Montgomery. So many folks had mentioned traveling north for the spectacle that her papa decided best not fight that inclination. A sparse crowd on meeting nights would look bad. As devoted as he was to sharing the Lord's message at all times, common folk did not feel the same. They looked forward to the distraction of the elephants and calliope, so he gave his little band that whole week off.

Everyone Lila knew was going to the circus. They saved their pocket money for the train ride, treats and attractions. Lila had pocket money too. When she did chores or cleaned house or spruced up the garden for some of the widow ladies in town, she never asked for payment but they always dropped a few coins in her pocket anyway.

She could not wait for the big day, and when it arrived she jumped out of bed, tossed her floursack shift aside and slipped into her simplest dress. She spotted her friends waiting for the train that would take them to Troy to pick up the rest of the pack. She gave them a wave, then felt a harsh jerk to her arm.

"Jus' where do you think yur goin' t'day?" her papa shouted loud enough for all her friends to hear.

She turned at the shock of his harsh voice and his face twisted in anger beneath his fiery eyes.

"No child of mine's goin' to that den of unbridled excess and sin!" He scowled at the group of young people. "I'm not ever'body's parent. I'm yours! If others want to send good children into Satan's lair, I can warn but I can't stop 'em from keepin' unrighteous enjoyment out of their lives, short of threatenin' expulsion. But I'm telling you, *you* do *not* have permission to get on that train and spend your day in that cesspit of temptation!"

He dragged her away from the station toward home while her friends watched in horror. "Git out of yur meetin' clothes and do somethin' useful with yur free day. Read the Bible. Go for a walk. But yur *not* goin' to that circus!"

Lila had shed so many tears over disappointment at her papa's hand that she could not summon any more. Maybe marrying her off to some oaf from the backwoods would be a blessing. She stepped out of her dress and into her shift, resigned to work in the garden. She did not wave to her papa as he rode out to some insignificant Podunk of unsuspecting sinners to entice them to set up a "comin' together to praise the Lord."

Midmorning Jimmy rode up on his bike and found Lila working out her anger and disappointment on every clod she could find in the garden. "Need some help?" he smiled.

She nearly screamed with delight and ran over to him. "I thought you were going to the circus with the others."

"Ah... I changed my mind. I've been a few times over the years. When Joe told us what happened here this morning, I decided I'd better check on the caged animals down here in Goshen. Are you okay? Were you hurt?"

She shook her head. "Just humiliated, as usual. I assumed if Papa told the boys that he was giving everybody the week off, I had permission to go too. Wrong, as usual. I just wish he'd warn me calmly when I'm not part of 'everybody' before he makes a fool of me."

"Tell me exactly what he told you to do today. *Exactly.*"

"He said, 'Read the Bible. Go for a walk.'"

"I vote for the walk. I suppose riding on my handlebars isn't walking, is it?"

She laughed and shook her head.

"Then find me a place to stash my bicycle out of sight, and we'll go for a walk. I was thinking, we might just find our own circus down by the river."

The two almost sixteen-year-olds gabbed as they ambled along a pathway through shady, thick slash pine and oak forest toward the Conecuh River. She told him of the circuits she, Fred and Joe made in the school wagon with her roving evangelist papa. How lately they had all slept in the wagon some nights underneath the old tarp because they were scheduled for another nearby spot in the road the next day. How embarrassed she was to stand up in front of a crowd of strangers like chattel waiting to be auctioned off. And how her papa was looking to pawn her off on one of the "good boys."

"I don't know anything about being married except that I don't want to end up with someone like him. How can he do that to me when I haven't had a real boyfriend yet?"

Jimmy feigned surprise. "You haven't? Why, I've had a special girl for... oh... since about third grade."

Lila flushed as red as bee balm on a bright summer's day.

Jimmy turned silent and thoughtful until the "peto, peto" of an angry tufted titmouse complained of their intrusion into its territory. A flurry of its friends joined in a discordance that followed the couple until they turned through the trees in search of the river. "This is a beautiful place. Do you come here much?"

"Not really."

"Do you swim here? The water's pretty calm."

She shook her head.

"Wade?"

She shook her head.

"Well then, that's where we'll start. We worked up quite a sweat walking all this way on a hot summer day. We need a good cool off." He slipped out of his rucksack, sat on the riverbank and wiggled his toes in the water. "Come on." He patted the ground. "Right here beside me. There's nothing going to nibble your toes…"

She slipped her feet gingerly into the refreshing water.

"…except maybe an alligator!"

She almost fell in head first trying to get out fast.

He pulled her down again. "I'm just joking. I'd never put you in harm's way."

They discovered their own circus in the forest. River otters delighted them with their clown-like antics. Wild animals such as foxes and stinging ants kept them on guard, and birdsong filled the air with the musical sounds of a calliope. Jimmy provided a yummy picnic with caramel cake in place of popcorn and cotton candy. Real fishing for real fish challenged them like a game of chance.

They meandered the home path slowly, not ready for the afternoon to end.

"I've thought hard about what you said earlier, about your papa having an eye toward marrying you off. This is the one time I can't figure how to help you out of this fix. Until we're of age, our parents pretty much do the deciding for us. You can try to find something wrong with every boy he pushes you toward, but I don't know how long you can hold him off. You can try to make the case for going to more school, like that music school in Newton, or… or I…."

He reached for her hand and squeezed it. "I know my mama and the Judge won't let me have a thought about something as big as marriage until I've finished college and am on my way to a job, and I won't be sixteen 'til December, so I hardly have a say at all about what I'm gonna do next. Eighteen seems years away. I wish I could think of some way to help you, Lila, but I'm just a blank. So, short of running away, I don't know what you can do to stop your papa if that's what he's set on."

She breathed a deep sigh. "I know. I can't expect someone else to solve all my problems for me." She brightened. "I have some news! Bessie Pirdle and Joe Robertson are getting hitched the end of summer. She doesn't want to move away from her home in Troy to Goshen, but Joe has to stay here for his job with my papa. Her papa is going to get them a telephone so she and her mama can talk anytime they want to. I've never even seen one."

"We have one at the Troy house so the Judge can call us anytime he wants. He's gone on to Montgomery now, and Mama's set to follow pretty soon. Guess I'll be going with her once summer's over. Say, maybe I can use the Judge's phone to call you up over at Bessie's once in a while. Wouldn't that be something?"

She barely nodded.

"And I'll bike over here as much as I can this summer to make sure everything's okay with you… or as good as it can be." He noticed a tear puddle on the lip of her eyelid. "Don't worry, Lila. We won't lose touch. And if I come up with a plan, I'll send a telegram. Wouldn't that be something?"

She managed a smile and squeezed his hand back.

They took their time until the first house came into view. "Where did you say we'd drop this fish off?" Jimmy asked.

Lila pointed toward a tiny cottage tucked in the trees away from the road. "Miz Beckham is a nice older lady who asks for help with opening jars now and again when she sees me walking by. Your fish will be a welcome change in her regular diet." She waved at the curly, gray-haired woman who was talking to her flowers. "Miz Beckham. We brought you a surprise for your supper."

The woman dropped her trowel, removed her gloves, and labored to rise to her feet. "Well, Lila. Nice to see you, dearie. And who is that nice-looking boy?"

"A friend from school. Jimmy Dickson. We've been down to the river, and he caught a couple of catfish just your size."

Jimmy reached into his rucksack and pulled out the gilled gift.

"Oh Lordy! Them's beauties. I do thank you." She took the fish in one hand and pointed with the other. "You two younguns set a minute in the swing. I'll just take these inside and bring us back some lemonade. Won't take a minute." The screen door banged behind her as she disappeared into the house.

The young couple took a seat, side by side, hand in hand, feet finding a gentle to-and-fro cadence against the grass. In a stolen moment hidden from view by camellia shrubs and surrounded by garden flowers in full flush, they found one another and shared a common experience etched in memories throughout time—their first kiss.

Try as she might, Lila could not remember one time she had seen her parents kiss. In her prayers that night, she asked forgiveness for that brief moment of intimacy with a boy who was not her husband but who, she imagined, would be in her future in some significant way. Surely such an enjoyable occurrence must be a sin demanding punishment. She fell asleep on her knees beside her bed awaiting His word.

*

Once again, Jimmy was true to his word. He peddled south to Goshen twice a week if he could find time in the middle of a day when Lila's papa was not likely to be about. The man's circuit schedule left her free on

Mondays and Thursdays to freshen her clothes and his shirts for the next rounds. The two young people worked out a signal. If Lila's papa were home, she would hang his washed shirts closest to the house. If not and it was safe, she hung the shirts farthest away and if she was gone contrary to schedule, no clothing would be on the line. Jimmy could spot the laundry from a ways down the road and could stop to see her or turn around for home depending on the signal.

Their system worked fine through many weeks of a hot humid summer. Jimmy could never stay very long because his diploma exams were just around the corner, and he maintained his jobs at the courthouse for as long as his mother worked there. Reluctant to let her go, the County Recorder continued to find tasks that only she was capable of completing; she continued to insist that she would depart in September, tasks or no, Jimmy included.

During those summer weeks, Lila unloaded her frustrations with her current plight onto Jimmy. Her papa was never kind to her until there was a crowd of followers around—especially young men—especially Samuel Dean. "He's terrible!"

"Try telling your papa that when one boy hangs around all the time, like this Samuel, the others get discouraged and will fall away and his meeting numbers will decrease," Jimmy suggested.

In a brave moment, Lila did. Problem solved.

A few visits on, she worried over her papa's fixation for choosing a marriageable young man. "I can't! I can't be forced into making those vows with some guy I don't know or like, let alone love!"

"Why not plant the idea that when you are married, you will have so much to do keeping your own house that you won't have time to travel to your papa's revival meetings."

In a brave moment, Lila did. Problem solved. "Even better, when I offered to help find a replacement singer (Ruby was not as great as he hoped), he told me that as soon as the fall rains came, he would stop the revival circuit for the winter. I'm going to music school in Newton! Even better than that, in a week Ruby and I will take the train there to meet our teacher, see where we'll live, and find out about our classes. Then we'll come back here until the rains begin."

"I'm so happy for you, Lila. I'm sad we'll be so far apart after my move to Montgomery, but better Newton than here."

That conversation took place on a Monday. Thursday was Lila's next free day, but her papa told her he had business in Troy and would be home early. "Make sure supper's ready when I git here."

She hurried to finish the wash and hang her papa's shirts closest to the house to warn Jimmy off. When he arrived mid afternoon, the boy was surprised at how surprised she was at seeing him. As she stood there speechless, he pointed to the shirts hanging at the far end of the line. "What's up? You look ghostly."

"You're not supposed to be here. Papa's home today! I hung them next to the house. I know I did." At the sound of a giggle coming from the doorway, Lila turned to spy her pesky eight-year-old brother duck back inside. "You've got to go. Now. If papa finds you here, there'll be trouble."

Jimmy grabbed her hands. "Calm down. Nothing's going to happen. I'll get out of here as soon as you tell me when you're going to Newton for that visit."

"A week from tomorrow. Now go!" she cried through tears.

In the chaos of the moment, neither one heard a second giggle from her brother or the clip-clop of her papa's horse turning the corner. "Hey, you! Git yur hands off my girl! Who do you think you are comin' 'round with no invite?" He jumped from his horse and strode toward the couple with clenched fists.

Jimmy grabbed his bike from the ground and pushed it in front of the oncoming man. "A friend... A friend from school," he shouted over his shoulder as he sped away.

"If I don't know you, you ain't no friend. Git on home!" he shouted to the dust trail left by the disappearing cyclist. "And you, girl! You git in that house. No supper for you tonight."

*

After the trouble and punishments from her papa, Lila looked forward to a couple of weeks away from home. She had never been separate from both of her parents before and she had never ridden on a train, so she was a little nervous about traveling far away for such a long time. She and Ruby boarded together in Troy, sat together and giggled when a train whizzed past heading north before they could count all its cars on their southbound journey to Newton.

Their train stopped at small towns along the way to take on farm produce and a few passengers. As they left Brundidge, a voice from behind surprised them. "Hi, girls. How are you likin' this ride?"

Both girls screamed and turned to find Jimmy grinning at them. "What are you doing here?" Lila asked.

"Making a short trip to Newton to visit with a good friend."

Lila flushed. Jimmy jabbered. Ruby listened. By the time they reached Newton, both girls were in tears at the prospect of being alone in a strange place for so long.

"Don't you girls worry yourselves. I know a boy who will be happy to watch over you for a few days," he grinned.

Jimmy and Lila did spend a lot of time together over that weekend, usually with Ruby along too. When they carved out some time to be alone on his last day there, he tried to talk about their future; she found more tears than words to express her emotions.

Lila's papa watched her closely after her return from Newton. At times he saw a faraway look in her eyes; at others, a soft impermissible smile. Armed with tattles from her brother, he stayed home on the next free day and watched that strange boy bicycle as close as the corner, then turn and leave. His suspicions confirmed, he confronted his daughter outside.

"*I know* you been seein' that boy when I'm not around. *You know* that is forbidden. I done some checkin' and that boy with no papa and no religion is not fit for my girl! *You* don't do the choosin'. *I* do."

Stunned at being found out, Lila summoned the courage to fight back. "Jimmy is a fine young man! He can't help it if his papa died. He knows his Bible real good and goes to church regular, just not the same as ours."

"There *is* no church but ours! Don't you cross me, girl. I do the decidin' in this family, and I'm tellin' you, that boy is not fer you and yur gonna tell him so."

"But, Papa, I love him!"

"You can't *love* him! You honor your parents. You show kindness to your family and neighbors. But you *love* the Lord, and *only* the Lord. Pleasure in carnal acts is not love. It is the work of Satan, and you'll pay mightily for it."

Lila's cries turned to sobs—huge body-shaking, convulsive sobs—but not extreme enough to deter her papa from his rant.

"Look't me, girl. Whuppins don't do no good with you no more. Yur gonna punish yurse'f this time." He shook his finger right between her eyes. "When that boy comes 'round agin—I'm thinkin' that'll be on Thursday—you welcome him with my flappin' shirtsleeves at the end of the line. Motion him on up here by the steps and tell him straight out that you don't love him, like him, or ever want to see his sorry face 'round here agin! Tell him to go away and never come back. And if you start stumblin' on your words, I'll step through that doorway, shotgun in hand, and make sure he gits the message. There'll be nothin' left of him but bloody bits for you to sob over!"

He paused long enough to assure that Lila accepted her fate. "Now git in that house and help yur mama put supper on. I swear, purty voice or no, yur not worth the trouble it takes to set you straight!" He stomped back into the house, pushing aside his gleeful eight-year-old son.

As hard as Lila prayed for time to stop, Thursday arrived on schedule hot and heavy with humidity. When Jimmy showed up early afternoon and noticed how upset she looked, she blurted out almost word for word the commands of her papa. She thanked him silently for being grown-up enough not to challenge her with "why" questions even though his humiliation was clearly visible. She held her tears until he turned his bike around and rode slowly away.

Lying on the floor by her bed that night, Lila asked forgiveness for treating her best friend so cruelly. Jimmy was the only person in the world who really cared for her, the only person she could count on, and now she had driven him away. She wondered if she would ever see him again.

Her papa told her to love the Lord, which she did. The Bible told her to love her neighbors and her enemies, which she tried to. But nowhere could she remember reading that it was a *sin* to love a good person, a sin she would "pay mightily for." She prayed for understanding of His word.

*

Eight months passed before Lila received a letter from her friend Bessie Pirdle telling her about Jimmy joining the Navy. She could not believe her eyes. What happened to school? To Montgomery? Was his drastic change of plans her fault? At the first opportunity, she secreted herself behind a tree down the road and wrote to him. Her papa would punish her if he knew she actually mailed it, but she did—and asked forgiveness later.

Jimmy's friendly response emboldened her. They corresponded secretly for another year and a half discussing everything about life and their futures, and she grew to love him more and more. When he finally asked her to travel to Virginia for a long weekend to get married, she did not hesitate. If she could make it past her papa, she would be there.

The marriage went off without a hitch. She was overwhelmed by the emotion of sharing herself so intimately with another person and knew at that moment that the two of them were destined to spend their lives together *'til death do ye part.* She knew the hardships. She knew the risks. She knew she could not survive without him.

When she realized that a child was soon to join their family, she prayed every night for Jimmy to come home soon, to come home safely from the War. She tried not to worry when his letters arrived further and further apart. He had warned her there would be such times until his duty to country was done. But, Jimmy did not warn her about the knock on her door that would change her life forever.

*

Early July, 1918. Sultry Alabama summer. Wilty flowers tried their best to perk up and show their colors. Even the birds were too miserable to sing. Lila had been successful in hiding her condition beneath an apron or an armload of dirty clothes, and she managed to adjust her revival meeting dresses, but that would not continue much longer. She wiped her brow with a dishtowel and sat for just a minute to catch her breath when she heard a knock at the door. Strange, she thought, because her papa's friends walked right in and her mama's friends did not visit at all.

She pulled herself up from the chair and walked slowly to the door. She opened it to a nice but simply dressed professional woman in suit, hat, gloves and purse. Dark circles rimmed the woman's eyes, her rigid lips clenched tight and straight as a pencil. "Is this the home of Lila Larson?" she asked.

A voice from behind Lila's shoulder replied, "Who's askin'?"

The woman stretched out a gloved hand to the mother. "I'm from Tyrell Farms Inc. in Banks. Lila has been recommended for a job, and I've come to interview her. Are you Lila?' she asked with a stare into the girl's eyes that warned, *Do not let on that we know each other.*

The young woman nodded. She got the message.

"Would it be convenient for you to come with me for a few minutes now to hear my offer? I'm anxious to return to Banks as soon as possible."

Lila stepped forward. "Of course."

"I don't know, girl. Your papa's not home to ask."

"This is my business, Mama. I'll deal with Papa later." She stuffed the dishtowel into her mama's hands and followed the woman to the road and an automobile she recognized as the Judge's from many years ago.

Lottie drove down the familiar dirt road through the woods toward the river. She scanned the area carefully for other autos or foot traffic. When satisfied that she and Lila were alone, she pulled off the side of the road and parked. She removed her hat and gloves with a "Too hot for these!" She slipped out of her suit jacket and hung it carefully over the car seat, and dug in her purse for some handkerchiefs to tuck into her waistband.

Lila fingered her chest, feeling for her wedding ring on the chain hidden beneath her shift. The woman had not offered one word of explanation for her unexpected appearance. Good news would have brought at least a smile or liveliness to her eyes, but there was no sign of either. That whirling dread routed its way through Lila's gut again.

Lottie exited the auto and motioned for Lila to do the same. She grabbed the girl's hand and led her through the broadleaf forest toward the water. "Three years ago, Jimmy came home one afternoon with a story about the two of you discovering a circus in the forest. You picnicked, waded in the river, fished and collected snails to lure the otters out. He said over and over again that the day was one of the best in his whole life and he would remember it forever."

She took a stance behind the girl, interlaced their fingers and wrapped their arms tightly around Lila's chest. "I want you to look out at the river here, remember that day as fondly as Jimmy did and drink in its peace, for what I am about to tell you will burn in your memory for the rest of your living days."

Lottie rested her chin on the girl's shoulder and whispered into her ear. "Jimmy is not coming home. His ship sank. After several days of searching, the Navy found no survivors. Because of treacherous waters and depth of the ocean at that location, very few bodies were recovered. Jimmy's was not one of them. Our dear boy is not coming home."

When Lila's rigid body succumbed to collapse, Lottie turned her face-to-face and cradled her. She did not mark the duration of the girl's sobs, for she knew well that sorrow knows no limit.

Back in the auto, the time came to address the unspoken question, "What next?"

"I don't know what to do. My parents don't know about our marriage or the baby and are likely to expel me from the family and the church when they find out. My papa will punish me for hiding such secrets. He may even kick the life out of me and the baby. I can't imagine bringing an innocent child into their world—not Jimmy's child."

"You have another choice. I've sworn to take care of you and the baby, whether you go home to your family or come to Montgomery with me. You need time to make that decision, but not on the heels of this terrible shock."

Lottie proceeded to explain to the girl what life held for them in Montgomery or how she would support the baby financially through its education should Lila decide to stay in Goshen with her family. Of course, she would appreciate visiting privileges. "Send me a letter when you make your decision." She withdrew a stamped, self-addressed envelope and pressed it into the girl's hand.

Lila gave it back. "I don't need more time. I want to leave today… right now… before my papa returns. I don't want to take the chance that he'll hurt us."

"You're sure? If you leave like this with no explanation, your parents will probably not welcome you back anytime soon. I speak from experience."

Lila nodded. "I'm sure."

Lottie turned the auto around. "We'll stop by your house for just a minute so you can pick up your personal items and tell your mother that you have a new job."

Lila shook her head. "There's nothing at home that I want."

"Surely you have some remembrance."

"Only Jimmy's letters. And the money he sent me from his pay."

"Where are they?"

"Hidden beneath a tree not too far from the house."

"Then I say we go dig a hole."

Lila found a slight smile for the first time that horrible afternoon.

The transition to becoming housemates was not an easy one for either woman, not because they did not get along; they did. But because neither one felt free to grieve in front of the other. Two broken hearts in one small household were too many. Every time she felt her baby kick, Lila wept. Every time she passed by Jimmy's bedroom, Lottie grew weak in the knees and had to hold herself up. Every time they sat across the table from one another, they remained rigid and silent. The mere whisper of Jimmy's name opened the floodgates.

Ready or not, the time arrived for Lottie to return to work, and Lila needed privacy and her own space. Camping on the sofa was not a long-term solution if she were to remain with Lottie for weeks, months, maybe even years. Lila was sent to town with a long list, including suitable clothes for herself and her baby, and an envelope of money. She was told to take her time; Lottie had work to do. That work consisted of taking *her* time to strip and pack away all the love and care it took to raise her boy.

When Lila returned, the two women spent the afternoon refashioning the room for a young mother. The only remnant that remained of its previous occupant was the well-loved stuffed bear Lottie had given to Lila on her first night away from home to press against her chest and calm her uncontrollable sobs.

Through several weeks Lottie gauged the girl's competence in the kitchen and with other household chores and found her to be willing and able to tackle any task—good qualities in a single mother. Best of all was her baking. The girl had a real flair for experimenting with a pinch of this or that; she had never used spices before except at her friend's house. After several unsuccessful attempts with the old typewriter, Lottie gave Lila accounting lessons instead and left work for her each day. The girl was quick with figures and enjoyed keeping the house's accounts but wondered why she was learning an office skill.

"In this house the Judge's rules were: Do not break the law. Use it. And do not lie. Remember, I told your mother I was interviewing you for a job. Now you have a proper one for which you will be paid. You work for Tyrell Farms, Inc. should anyone ask. If or when the time comes for you to strike out on your own, your skills can support you and your child."

Lottie recognized Lila's acceptance of her future without Jimmy when her nighttime sobs turned to song—a signal that she was ready to focus on a future with their child. The expectant grandmother prepared herself for the difficult conversation that would bring to light the darkness in that future—one that could not be avoided with only a couple of weeks until the child was due.

She chose a Sunday—time enough for lengthy conversation, questions and contemplation—with Monday following for Lila to be alone to digest the implications of their discussion. Lottie set a tray of lemonade and baked snacks near the sofa and motioned Lila to join her. She took the girl's hand and fixed her eyes on Lila's beautiful blue ones.

"I hope you know by now how much you are loved, how thankful I am to celebrate this most joyous event in your life, and how happy I will be to have you and my grandchild live here for as long as it suits you."

Lila smiled. She was lucky to have someone so generous with her hugs and support as Jimmy's mother.

"Do you remember over a year ago when Jimmy asked you to visit us in Montgomery the next time he had a furlough? I had written him several times about how important it was that the two of you *together* see me before you made future plans. That did not happen, or we would have discussed then what I am about to tell you now. You two deserved to know the consequences of your choices *before* you made them. But the War got in the way, so here you are with fewer options open to you."

Lila gave no sign that she suspected what Lottie might reveal.

"Jimmy's grandfather was a colored man. I knew that when I married Jimmy's father and had his child. What I didn't know was how cruelly my husband would meet his end as do many of mixed heritage. At a difficult time in my life with nowhere to turn, the Judge rescued me. He helped me establish a record for Jimmy that shows him as white—not by breaking the law but by using it. I can do the same for you, that is if none of the typical traits show up in your child. They shouldn't, but nature has a way of playing wicked tricks whenever it suits her. If your child is unable to 'pass' easily, we'll discuss your options then."

Lottie tried to measure Lila's reaction to the news, but the girl remained stone-faced. "One more important factor you should know. Like mine, your marriage to Jimmy was illegal. In Virginia, as in Alabama, it doesn't matter what a person looks like, the one-drop rule applies. Technically, interracial marriages are against the law."

That revelation had immediate impact. If her marriage was not legal, Lila's child would be illegitimate—a bastard, with no hope of salvation—and it was her fault.

When Lila's time grew closer, Lottie asked, "Do you want me to contact a friend? Your mother? Anyone else in your family?"

She would love to have a friend like Bessie nearby. Bessie had a baby now and would be good support. But Bessie was steeped in the church and would tell her mama. Her mama would tell Lila's mama and she would tell her papa. Her mother had never defended Lila against her father. No! She shook her head.

Lila's baby arrived without complication on September 19, her own nineteenth birthday. "You have a son. A beautiful baby boy."

"But is he...?"

"He's perfect. He looks much like Jimmy did, but I think he'll have your beautiful blue eyes."

Lila cradled her new son. He *was* perfect. Pure and innocent. If only she could keep him that way.

Two nights later, with her baby well fed and lulled to sleep by his mother's song, Lila lay prostrate on the floor beside his cradle. She thought seriously about how her families shaped her—the one she was born into and the one with her newborn son and Lottie. Before she began her prayers to ask forgiveness, she tried to reconcile the two.

In the first family, she was constantly referred to as good-for-nothing, worthless, stupid, vain, disobedient and sinful by virtue of her birth as a female. In the other, she was bright, competent, lovable, huggable, kind, trusted and valued for bringing new life into a grieving family with so much love to share. How could she be two completely opposite people? Which was the real Lila?

Her own words returned to her: her plea to God to forgive her for her lack of trust in His plan for her salvation; her promise to look to Him for guidance and not to question how He chose to reveal it; her appeal to understand the path that the Lord laid out for her redemption; and her asking a blessing for every child to have a perfect mother like Lottie.

Perhaps this was the Lord's way of revealing her path—that she could not accept blame and be blameless; she could not serve two masters. She was either a sinner who must be punished in order to be redeemed or she was a sinner who was willing to trade fleeting pleasures for condemnation of future generations.

A cloud of sin followed Lila throughout her life, and she had suffered many punishments for her errant ways. All those lies she screamed at Jimmy to make him go away. Sins. It was her fault he joined the Navy. Now, she had committed the gravest, most unforgivable sins of God and man. Her love was dead. Punishment! Her marriage was illegal! Punishment! Her son was illegitimate. Punishment!

That now familiar whirling dread in her gut returned. This time it would not go away with penance and prayer. The only way to redeem herself was "to pay mightily for her sins," to sacrifice what she loved most to save who she loved most. Her baby was perfect. Of course, he would be. His father was. She was the imperfect one. She was the sinner. She could not ask her son—that pure, innocent new being—to bear the sins of his mother. She knew what she had to do.

She prayed to God to forgive her for the sins she had committed and for the one she was about to. Teardrops of sorrow puddled around her. She pressed her body harder into the floor to make her final appeal. "Please punish *me* mightily... but save my boy from *my* sins."

*

Hungry baby cries from Lila's bedroom awoke Lottie. Unless the new mother was using the bathroom, she would tend to his needs immediately, but the cries continued. Finally, Lottie decided to intrude and knocked on the door. No answer. She knocked again, then turned the knob and entered. No Lila. Her bed was neatly made. Her baby was safely in his cradle squalling. A note lay on the nightstand with her wedding ring and chain.

My Preshus Boy,

It breaks my heart to leave you, but I must.

I can not be the kind of mama you deserve.

I must make the hardest choice of my life between being with you now or for eternity.

Your Gramma Lottie will love you and take good care of you and you will grow up to be a smart, loving and caring man like your Papa.

At all times remember that your Mama loves you more than anything in this world.

Until the next one,

May the Lord keep you safe.

1998

I so hope I will run into Charlie again at the graveyard. I am a little behind schedule, so he might have come and gone before I arrive. I should have started out earlier. I do not drive as fast as I used to, and the traffic is much heavier than I remember. Then there is the house that marks the turn. After thirty years it may be dressed in a new coat of paint, from bright yellow to everyday gray. If I miss the turn, I am done for.

Ah, relief! The no longer yellow house bears a striking blue that attracts my attention to the dirt roadway next to it. Relief again! A car sits near the gate to the cemetery. Despair! A man opens the car door. Please do not leave yet, Charlie. I speed up. My honk disquiets the surroundings just enough for the man to notice, pause and flash a familiar smile. Relief!

"Janie! Good to see you!"

"Charlie! Good to see *you!*"

"I was afraid you couldn't come this year," we both say in unison, then laugh together.

He peeks into my car and spots the mess on the passenger side's floor. "Did you drive all the way this year?"

"No," I reply. "That is my latest discovery. Did you know that soda comes in huge paper cups now? Almost as large as Maxine's tin cans? I thought that if... well... I thought they might be useful this year. Gallon jugs of water are also available, so I brought one of those too."

"Thoughtful, but as you see I'm still above ground." He peers into the back seat. "Hefty bunch of flowers you brought along. Very fragrant."

"They nearly put me to sleep. Why don't you help me with these, then I'll help you with yours."

We unload my car and return to collect his offering—also a multitude of bunches. "Charlie, you've lost faith in me. If you're still walking around, what made you imagine I wouldn't be?"

He gazes into the distance. "Events. No guarantees in this life."

I recall my Dad's admonition not to ask first and decide to save the "what events" for another time. He loads me up with a huge armload of flowers and carries the tins and water himself. When we arrive at the plots, there is a moment of confusion when he has difficulty bending toward the ground. I set my armload down and relieve him of his before he can protest. I then gather the two armloads of flowers and place them both in his waiting arms.

"My knees are still in pretty good shape, so why don't you stand and pass to me and I'll sit and place in the tins like an assembly line. We'll have arrangements fit for a magazine cover in no time."

He casts me a skeptical glance until I get down onto my knees easily and raise my hand for him to fill it. We do make good time in creating three generous bouquets and still have a bevy of blossoms to deal with. I stand and take half.

"Why don't we share with the neighbors now and return for private time when we're finished. That way, my hands will be free to find my handkerchief."

We begin our tour of the grounds, and Charlie smiles at me. "You surprise me every time we meet. You originally appeared so unsure and on guard, but you are really a very independent, take charge kind of woman."

"I get that from Mom… and from twenty-two years as a single."

"Really? I would have thought from your dad."

"I only had Dad for sixteen years. Mom for forty-four, so her influence has had the greatest impact on how I live my single life."

"Hmm." His mind grinds away. "That makes you seventy-four. I wouldn't have guessed that either."

"Why? Do I look older than you?"

"Not a day over fifty, I swear."

"Then you need to have your eighty-year-old eyes checked."

"What more can you tell me about your mother's independence streak that you apparently inherited?"

"From my childhood perspective, there was a mom with dad and a mom without dad. I never imagined a mom before that time because she never shared details of her earlier life. With Dad, I got the impression that she did not have much experience in decision-making or taking control of her life. I doubt she had ever held a real job before. Without Dad, those were her only options.

"As soon as I graduated from high school, we moved to California. She found a place for us to live in an apartment complex, a job, and an opportunity to fashion a new history. She made lots of friends—all kinds and colors. She rediscovered old talents for computation and baking. And her singing voice took on a joyful quality.

"She worked in a bakery for a couple of years. When the company expanded to selling its product in a new chain of grocery stores, she was offered her own 'counter' position in a store near home because she smiled all the time and her eyes sparkled when she did. She had 'a way with customers' they said.

"Mom took great pride in her new position and her new uniform—a bright blue one that matched her eyes. Neighborhood kids flocked around her as soon as they spotted that blue uniform turn the corner toward home. She shared hugs with them all and day-old baked goodies from her store.

"She developed a self-confidence that served her well when her company proposed to sell out to a big name. All of her duties and benefits would remain the same, she was told, but the new company was a union one that required membership for a price. She and her store friends objected to that requirement and gathered quite a block of 'No' votes.

Before the vote was taken, she and others were harassed at work by the yessers, intimidated on entering and leaving the store, and hustled on the way to and from work. Once she came home with bruises on her arm and another time, was robbed of her handbag."

"What did she do? Cal the police?"

"No. I tried to persuade her to give in, but she said that she'd suffered worse and survived. These were minor incidents. Bullies had no power over her anymore. She certainly didn't mean my father because he was the kindest, most considerate man I've ever known. Anyway, vote taken, union membership required, dues required, and not previously disclosed, attendance at quarterly meetings required.

"She and her friends really balked at that one. They remained compliant for a year or so, then conned some of their male associates to propose that all votes taken on future propositions be by secret ballot. 'After all, that's how we elect a president,' they contended. Their block of 'yes' votes helped win the day, and thereafter they attended meetings as required, voted 'negative' when it suited them knowing the union had no proof of their vote, and went to dinner afterwards to celebrate how clever they were."

"That is a Maxine-worthy story with a great lesson. As the judge would say, 'if you don't like a rule, work to change it.'"

"I was really proud of how she stood up for her convictions, and her example served *me* well when my husband and I experienced similar union conflicts. She converted the pain that lingered in her life into positive action—a truly transformed woman."

We reach our starting point and still have plenty of flowers left. We make a joint decision to introduce ourselves to some of the strangers here, particularly anyone who died during the Civil War era, and begin a second round. After a time, Charlie is relaxed enough to share more of his own story.

"Grandmother Lottie never retired. She couldn't. She had a blueprint of that dark, skudgy basement burned into her brain, and was the only one in the courthouse who knew the location of every record and legal file from the beginning of time. She probably decided that dying on the job was preferable to training someone to do her job, so she worked until they had to carry her out.

"I may have told you that we passed in the courthouse halls every day, so it was easy business to keep our eyes on one another. Not all folks like to have their relatives nearby all the time, but we thrived with that constant contact. When it came time to retire a few years ago, it was hard for me to give up work too. Skip keeps our family name alive in the justice system, and I put a word in when I can. I'm always available to lend a hand if needed.

"During hard times, my grandmother reminded me almost daily that we owed our security and good fortune to the judge and were obligated to give back in a way he would. She taught me to help those who couldn't help themselves by dedicating our every extra dollar toward food and shelter security for the poor—black, white, red, green yellow. 'If you help folks, all folks, they'll support you when *you* need help,' she said.

"For the most part, that was true, but our philosophy of helping folks on both sides of the color line was not appreciated by everyone. In my adult life, there were those who took issue with how I...." He pauses to search for just the right word. "...how I interceded to give misguided youth a fair shake in the justice system. My experience taught me that color and troublemaking were not necessarily related, that harsh punishment was not always called for, and that many troublesome youngsters were simply parroting their parents in both attitude and behavior. Take my cross burning incident, for example."

My eyebrows shoot up. Cross burning is a light-year away from union activities. Charlie enthralls me with the tale of discovering his front yard ablaze on his return from ferrying his family up north to spend a weekend with the grandparents.

"After listening to their parents' dinner table discussions that were critical of me, some neighbor boys decided to take justice into their own hands. They fashioned a cross out of small broken branches tied together with twine, wrapped themselves in sheets, and paraded to my front lawn. Apparently they had a heck of a time igniting their creation because they had not planted the cross in the ground, and they couldn't hold it up long enough for it to catch fire. I found the remnants of a burning sheet, a partially charred, lopsided cross, and one very expensive sneaker abandoned by a fleeing princess imitator."

"What did you do? Call the police?"

"No. They were just kids following in their parents' tracks, never given the opportunity to make wise choices for themselves. Remember, I make it my business to know my neighbors, so I knew exactly who could afford sneakers like the one I held in my hand when I showed up at his house the next morning. I told his father that he and his friends were 'volunteering' to do some landscaping for me, and I would bring him back when they finished. We collected the rest of the perpetrators, stopped by a garden shop, and soon they were digging up the ruined portion of my lawn. The boys planted all the flowers I purchased while I shared persuasive arguments regarding dignity and respect for differences to my captive audience. When they finished to my satisfaction, I thanked them, drove them back home and returned the shoe. Lesson learned, I hoped."

"What a creative solution. Are you always so clever?"

"Clever enough to keep you around here until lunchtime so I won't be alone on my birthday. I'm eighty today and getting too old to sit on the ground for long. How about we go to my favorite café in Troy? Surely you trust me by now."

We have spent barely six hours together over thirty years, but yes I do trust him. "If it's your birthday, it's my treat. I'll follow you in my rental, but first...."

He finishes... "Let's spend some private time with our loved ones."

We turn in opposite directions to express our love and gratefulness for their companionship and guidance over the years, handkerchiefs at the ready. After a time, we gather ourselves and head out for a birthday lunch.

We arrive at a place that has aged over the years just as we have, but the enticing aromas are as inviting as they have always been. Charlie is welcomed heartily. I receive stares and pointed fingers until a middle-aged man mouths "*that* woman?"

Charlie nods. "The grandkids run the place now. Same recipes but not quite the same product. Or maybe my taster is not up to snuff anymore. Keep a lookout. Maxine may come back from the dead just to see this day with the two of us here together."

We sip iced tea and mull over the menu. Our lunch is more than satisfactory, and we agree that having someone to share it with enhances its value. Grandchild number one brings us a "birthday special"—pie with peach ice cream, on the house. "Grandma's orders." We chuckle and wonder where we are going to put all that.

Charlie begins with a forkful pointed in my direction. "I have a notion there's more to your story than you're telling." He locks me in a stern but understanding gaze. "The time has come for the *whole* truth."

"Mine or yours?" I ask.

Taken aback, Charlie bursts into a hearty guffaw.

"Agreed," I say. "We'll start with yours."

With no way out, he begins with the facts that answer my 'what events' question. "My wife died. Three years ago."

"Oh, Charlie, I'm so sorry. Why didn't you say something when we were...?"

"I honor her on a different day, in a different place, and in a different way."

"My heartfelt condolences. It seems we are connected by a constant sense of loss. Is she near here?"

He shakes his head. "Far away in the northeast corner of the state with her family. When the time came for *that* discussion, she said she had little emotional attachment to the city and none down here, but she was related to a whole village-worth of folks up there, and they were all together. Her wish was to join the clan.

"I thought about your dilemma, and mine too, in adhering to our loved ones' burial wishes even though we didn't understand them. My wife's, I understood very well and told her I would pick us out a couple of nice shady plots up there. But she had a better idea, she said, like she always did.

"She would be buried up north, no argument. I was to have a choice. If my father's remains were returned before I died, he would get the plot next to his mother, and I would be buried next to my wife. If near the time of my demise, my father's remains had not been found and returned, I had a choice of keeping my family together here or joining her. No hard feelings; she understood my pull to this place and my desire to keep my grandmother company. 'Lottie shouldn't be left alone,' she said. If I could not, or failed to, make that choice, it was up to the kids to decide based on the imminence or probability of my father's discovery and return, given scientific advances at the time. Even if I remarried, I would be bound by our agreement in order to save our children a fight with another family. I belonged to my grandmother or to her. End of discussion.

"She made me promise to follow through. Then she said my promise wasn't good enough; she wanted a binding legal agreement. We wrote one up together, had Skip look it over, signed it in front of unrelated witnesses and done. Skip is bound by attorney/client privilege not to reveal this agreement to his sister until absolutely necessary. Delilah would spend every day worrying about what to do with me, and that is not how I want her or me to spend the rest of our days together."

He studies the table for a moment. "So if there's no stone on my father's grave and I'm not here a couple of times in a row, you'll know what the kids decided. I'll count on you to leave a posy for the Dicksons."

I nod. "Of course I will." Although the chances of either one of us sitting here twenty, or even ten years from now are pretty slim. The thought sobers me.

He faces me again and perks up. "You've stalled long enough, Janie. Your turn. The *whole* truth."

I do not know how to explain what I do not understand myself. "I told you how Mom transformed once she was forced into independence. That lasted for..." I bend over to inspect my grandmother's headstone. "...over twenty years until she received a visit from a brother I never knew she had. 'How did you find me?' she asked. 'Bessie Pirdle,' the man answered. At that point I was asked to go to the kitchen and fix tea. No introductions.

"The two tried to keep their voices low, but every now and again their conversation got out of hand and I'd hear words... phrases... that made no sense to me since they talked about people I didn't know. The tea was ready, but their heated conversation indicated that they were not. I couldn't help listening. I'd never heard Mom raise her voice like that before.

"Her brother told her, 'Mama's dying. You gotta come home.' Mom answered him very sharply, 'I will not! Not now. Not ever again will I put myself within five states of that man.' 'Papa's long passed and can't hurt you anymore,' he replied. 'Mama needs you home now to forgive her.'

"Mom got really upset. 'She never took my side—not once. Why should I sit by her side now?'

"Her brother was angry too. 'You know Mama can't rest until you forgive her. She's begging you. Her redemption depends on....'

"Mom stopped him and shouted, 'Hers? What about mine!'

"They tossed the word 'forgiveness' back and forth several times before her brother said, 'I won't leave without you. I'll tell that girl of yours....'

"Next thing I knew, she packed an overnight bag and left with him, informing me not to worry. Family business. She'd be home soon. When she returned a few days later, it was as if... this sounds silly... as if she had left a part of her soul behind. I didn't ask of course. Dad taught me well."

I stop for a sip of iced tea to camouflage how much recalling that event has upset me. I scrape the last of the pie's sugary syrup into my spoon and spend many moments licking it. I do not want our visit to end this way. Today is Charlie's day, and should be a happy and positive one. How do I turn this around?

"I can't imagine why Mom's forgiveness was so important to her mother and brother. She hadn't seen any family for years, as far as I know. But I do recall Dad giving me advice once when I was a young teenager and came home crying after a tiff with my best friend. 'Janie,' he said, 'I've told your mama many a time, and now I'm telling you. You cannot be happy until you forgive people who have caused you pain, whether your falling out was their fault or yours. When you learn to forgive fully—not just say the words—the Lord's mercy will lift your sins away.'

"Once she returned, she drifted between mom-with-dad and the transformed-after-dad mom. Sometimes when we were sharing a particularly good time, her face would cloud over and her eyes grow blank and faraway. A year later she made me promise to bury her here with her parents. In a way, that discordant event has turned into a blessing."

Charlie does a double take and his spoon drops to his plate.

"If she had not decided to rest here and if I had not followed through, you and I never would have met. Yet here we are, celebrating your birthday, wondering who or what engineered this very agreeable coincidence. And now you know as much as I do."

Charlie nods and smiles. "You're right. I do wonder, and I also wonder if I'm old enough to lick my pie plate without asking."

We both chuckle. I nod... and he does.

"You know," he says, smacking his lips, "your stories today of both your mother and your father remind me of similar experiences. During the war, I wrote many letters for young soldiers who faced the reality that they might not return home, and for others I bore witness to their last thoughts and prayers. The words most frequently used in those situations were 'love' and 'forgive.'"

He pushes his plate aside and folds his napkin. "I too must confess the whole truth… about Lottie's death. She collapsed at her desk—true. Died at the courthouse before the ambulance arrived—true. But we shared precious moments in between while I clung to her. The last words I could make out of her mumbles were, 'Great joy. Love you. Forgive me. Your mother.'"

He pauses, and his eyes take on that same faraway look I remember in my mother. "I suppose all of us are guilty of at least one forgiveness-worthy transgression in our lives, but I cannot fathom what that good woman might have done."

On that note, we thank our host for the wonderful meal. I pay the bill, and we return to our cars. We express mutual wishes for good health and assurances that we will meet again soon. Our short visit ends… with a hug that feels so right.

Charlie's Story

LEARNIN' GRATITUDE

As a young boy growing up in Montgomery, Alabama, Charlie Dickson never thought of himself as an orphan. He knew lots of kids who lost parents in the War or from the Spanish flu—both took young adults in large numbers in 1918. A few children lost brothers, sisters and grandparents too. He lived with his granny and saw her every day, so she was not lost. He had no brothers or sisters. He never knew, saw, heard, kissed or hugged his parents, so he could not lose someone he never had; therefore, he was not an orphan.

Charlie spent his early years in a box. The daytime hours, that is. He went to the courthouse every day with Nana. (Lottie told him to call her Nana because she was too young to be a granny.) As soon as he "came into this world" as she put it, she asked to be moved from the current Judge's service to the County Recorder's. She needed regular hours with a new baby in her house. The Recorder was happy to snatch her away given her vast legal knowledge and training from the renowned Judge Tyrell. That's when baby Charlie got his box.

Actually, it was more of a crate. Lidless, a soft quilt covered its bottom. Spaces between the side slats allowed the baby to poke his fingers and toes through once he was old enough to discover them. Its place was beneath Nana's desk, out of sight and sound of those who came to her, but perfectly arranged for their daylong conversations. Her soft, soothing voice was a constant in the tiny baby's world. She explained everything she was doing, every motion she made, every observation of the beauty outside her window.

The other constant in the baby's world was Nana's touch. He was never separate from it. As soon as he was arranged comfortably in his box at work, she removed a shoe and stocking and placed her bare foot beside the baby so he never felt alone. She tickled him with her toes and rubbed him with the ball of her foot. When he awoke from a nap, he could reach out for her soft flesh and know he was safe.

By the time he was one and could pull himself to standing, he needed a taller box. By the time he was two and toddling, he needed a tether... and a taller box. By the time he was three and all over the place, Nana tried to discard the box altogether, but the little boy protested in the most blaring manner and would not let go of his safe place. Nana relented, tipped the box on an end and delivered the child's first lesson—Obey the rules. Thereafter when a patron or superior entered her office, she snapped her fingers and sent the tiny person scampering to his box to sit and look at picture books until he heard a soft clap signaling it was okay to move about again.

*

On his fourth birthday, Nana and Charlie went box shopping. They drove the car to a large Saturday market place and scoured the stalls for the perfect box. Charlie spotted it first—an old wardrobe that was taller than the growing boy, wider than his wingspan and roomy enough to curl up for a nap. Perfect. The two carted it home, removed its two doors, sterilized it inside and out, painted it and added a curtain in front for privacy.

Monday, the two appealed for the janitor's help to lug the "birthday box" up the stairs and into Nana's office. He shifted a file cabinet to make space for it along the wall nearest her desk. As he turned to leave, Nana asked her boy, "What do you say to this kind man who helped you?"

"Thank you for helping me bring my birthday box up here. I never could do it by myself, so I'm grateful for your strong muscles." He reached out a tiny hand to shake the man's larger dark brown one.

"You welcome, Charlie. Anytime you need a han' jus' call on me."

A year later on his fifth birthday, Charlie did just that. To his mind, his box needed remodeling. He wanted to ditch the curtain and rehang the doors for more privacy. He and Nana had an adequate number of hands and a good screwdriver but between the two of them could not balance a door, line it up and fasten it properly in place. After several frustrating minutes, Charlie rushed out and returned with the janitor in tow. "Our friend is going to help us," he announced.

Sure enough, two more strong hands made the difference, and the job was completed in no time. As the man turned to leave, Nana asked her boy, "What do you say to this kind friend who helped you?"

Charlie scratched his head and thought for a moment. "Would you like some of my birthday cake, Gabe? We brought it to celebrate my new box!"

"Thank you, Charlie, but I dunno if I...."

"Of course, you'll join us. Charlie helped make it, and he'll be disappointed if he can't share with you," Lottie said.

The man nodded and accepted with a smile. "Thank you, Miz Dickson. Charlie. This do look mighty good."

The three sat on the floor in front of the birthday box and chatted about all the things the boy could do now that he had doors on his safe place. Finally, Gabe got up to leave. "I best get back to work. Thanks again for the cake. It be mighty good."

"Do you have any children at home?" Charlie asked.

The man nodded. "Three."

"Why don't you take the rest of this cake home to them? Nana and I are pretty full of it." He folded a sheet of paper over the half-cake that was left and handed it to the man.

"I dunno..."

"Of course, you'll take this. It's Charlie's birthday wish to share, so you must honor it."

"Well then, thank you, Ma'am. Charlie." And the man left.

"That was generous of you to share your cake with Gabe's family. What gave you that idea?"

"You said once to repay kindness with kindness. I guess my head forgot to forget."

Lesson 2: Repay kindness with kindness.

*

During that fifth year, Charlie expanded his borders. He explored every nook and cranny of the courthouse upstairs and down and introduced himself to all its regular inhabitants. He was not permitted to go to the basement or outside the building without Nana.

Lesson 1, repeat: Obey the rules.

As he made his rounds, he came to recognize when a worker was busy and should not be disturbed and when an interruption was welcome. He looked at fingers. Were they tapping on a desk or busy on a machine? Soon he became a welcome visitor and sometimes errand-runner. He could be counted on to bring a smile and take away papers or documents for other offices. Nana stitched an over-the-shoulder bag for him so he would not lose important stuff. "You must treat every piece of paper like a secret that's to be shared with only the addressee," she warned.

"What's an addressee?"

"The person who is supposed to get it."

"Oh. Then who gets this piece of butterscotch candy in the bottom of my bag?"

Lottie examined it carefully, sure that it came from the Court Clerk. "With no proper address, it must be meant for you from a secret person who appreciates the time you save him from walking up and down stairs all day."

"How do I say thank you?"

"We'll think of something."

After several other instances of finding sweets in his bag, Charlie announced, "We're getting behind on thinking of thank yous."

That weekend Nana and he drove to the Tyrell farms near Banks to "check up" on the harvest. They returned with several pecks of pecans—one for each office and one for themselves. To his disgruntlement, she helped him deliver to prevent spilling all over the stairsteps. That would be dangerous. He presented the nuts to each group with a, "These are for you all to share. I helped pick them to say thank you for letting me help you with your important job."

At home that evening, Charlie said, "Everybody seemed real grateful for our surprise."

"Gratitude for small treats is as important as for big ones."

Lesson 3.

Throughout the autumn and spring months, Nana and Charlie made other trips to the farms and brought back squash, pumpkins, lettuces and peas to share. From comments he heard, he learned that with movement from surrounding farms into the city for better jobs, working folks really appreciated fresh produce. He made a note to remember to be grateful for the farms that provided enough good food to share.

*

By spring, Charlie knew everyone's name and how to spell it, and how many children each had and how to spell those names too. In fact, he was quite capable of operating in a grownup world as long as he was in a building. Outside was another story.

In order to familiarize him with the hustle and bustle of a big city, Nana decided on a game of "Find the Courthouse." The two left their home located only three blocks from her work a little early each morning and walked a different route of eight or more streets. When they were a good distance from the building, she said, "Charlie, find the Courthouse," and he took the lead. He soon learned to spot landmarks and corners where they turned.

Sometimes they walked right past the courthouse into another part of the city before they turned around and tried to find the building. Soon Charlie asked to play a game after work too called "Find our House." On weekends they really challenged themselves. They drove to unfamiliar parts of the city and tried to find their way home. Then they had to retrace their steps to find the car. That is when learning store and street names came in handy. They spent a few afternoons scouting for safe places to enter to ask for help if needed and discovered a treasure trove of soda fountains that served fresh peach ice cream. From then on the game was called "Let's go for peach ice cream!"

Communication with adults. Check. Orientation to surroundings. Check. Socialization with other young children? Charlie was enrolled in first grade at a white school come the fall term beginning in October. Lottie was terrified. Her beautiful, innocent grandson functioned perfectly well in an adult world. He knew nothing about navigating the social realities of 1920s America. Her panic inspired another game: Explore the Neighborhood.

Many spring evenings the slight, mature woman, led by her active almost six-year-old grandson, wandered the neighborhood streets of Montgomery. They took off in a different direction each time and discovered that not all neighborhoods were alike. They passed through some with homes like their own—small but trim one-story buildings with tidy yards. Further on the homes grew to two stories with picket-fenced yards. Further on, to three stories with fancy trim, ornate wrought-iron fencing and expansive, tended grounds.

In another direction, houses were in disrepair with cloth hanging behind broken windows and porch railings missing pieces. They discovered sections of row houses, some apartment buildings, and another where people lived above the shops where they worked. Charlie absorbed every detail and bombarded Nana with questions. How do people decide where to live? What kind of house to live in? Do all houses have electricity? Water? How many people can live in one house? And on... and on....

Nana tried to keep her responses simple—family, friends, jobs, sometimes—and let her grandson put the puzzle pieces together. She realized he had completed the task when he included blessings for their modest home in his prayers.

"...and may I always be grateful for the house where we live. It has everything a boy could ask for except... maybe... a dog. Amen."

In early summer their tours took on a different objective—people watching. Grandmother and grandson meandered through various neighborhoods again and focused on children playing and adults engaging in conversation. Charlie drew his own conclusions—that most kids liked to play and grownups would rather watch and talk. Some yards had balls and bikes; others, sticks to draw in the dirt. Those with no yards used the streets and the grownups used apartment steps to sit on. Some wore nice clothes, some were dressed in clean, well-mended clothes, and some were in dirty, ragged clothing.

He also noticed that most of the people they saw were either children or older grownups—not many young parents. Nana explained that at the time he was born, many young men were across the ocean fighting a war and many of them were killed, like his papa Jimmy. At the same time a horrible disease—the Spanish flu—spread to some countries and to many cities in America by troops traveling on ships and trains. After a year of war and disease, the flu had killed more people than fighting had. Most of those people were in their twenties, the healthiest part of the population, leaving a lack of young men to produce children or to support families. For some unknown reason, many older folks were spared.

"Those were terrible times here, Charlie. The flu came on quickly and killed just as fast. Folks put dead bodies out on their porches for death carts to carry off to mass graves. When you came along in the middle of this horrid epidemic, I still had to work, but I couldn't trust precious you to be safe in anyone else's house. That's when I settled on your box to keep you with me night and day."

He squeezed her hand. "Gosh. That makes me pretty lucky. I bet not many kids have a granny smart enough to save a baby with a box."

"One more thing you should know before you start making neighborhood friends. It is not polite to ask other children about their parents. Some live with grandparents like you. Some, with aunts or uncles. Some, with cousins, and some, with kindly friends who took them in. Who they live with is not as important as whether the people they live with love them, so don't ask. They'll share their family stories when they want to."

Once he had the age thing figured out, Charlie focused on the biggest differences between him and other children. Some chattered in words he did not understand, and some were different colors. In his mind he put together that where children lived and how they played were connected, but he did not understand the why of not mixing. To his way of thinking, if a boy needed a friend to kick a ball around with, all he needed to do was find a boy with a ball. But that did not seem to be the case in the farthest away neighborhoods.

Charlie urged a return to the troubling districts. Nana opposed it. *She* was not ready. When her son Jimmy was growing up on the Tyrell farms, he interacted with animals, grownups and their children daily. When a job needed doing, all hands were called on to help, even Jimmy's, no matter the colors of those hands. Those practices served him well throughout school and even in the Navy. But the social realities of big city life were different. Unmarked lines and unspoken norms were too many for a young boy to master.

Her grandson's persistence signaled more than a child's curiosity. Observation was not enough to satisfy his need for peer interaction. He craved companionship beyond what his loving grandmother had to give. She had no choice. One Saturday, Nana took Charlie firmly by the hand and headed for the immigrant section of the city.

On their first two trips through those neighborhoods, they skirted the edges in route to the next area. This time they meandered, up one road and down another, focusing not on physical things like people and buildings but on sounds and smells—no pointing or staring allowed.

Charlie pricked up his ears to the odd vowel combinations and guttural consonants and tried to mimic them. "I sound like I'm about to spit." He picked out the sounds for "papa" and "mama" easily because they sounded similar. "Why do people have different words for the same thing?"

"Because they learned their words, their language, in different places. Some families have come from way across the ocean to live in America, and they brought their common words with them. Children learn from their parents and grandparents, so they learn the words their families teach them. Here in America, the children also learn English once they start school."

"Will any of these children go to my school?"
"Probably."
"Will they know English words?"
"Probably?"

"What if they don't?"

"Then you must help them understand. Take 'ball' for instance. Another child might call it a *balle*, *bola* or *lopta*. If you ask him to kick a ball around, he might not understand, but if you show him one or draw a picture, he'll know right away and learn a new word. You might learn new words too. Maybe it's time for you to learn to type so you can make a list of all the new words you learn."

"I'd like that, but what about the words I teach?" Charlie thought for a minute. "I better always carry pencil and paper with me and brush up on my drawing."

"Or?"

"I could draw them ahead of time or cut them out of the newspaper, put them in an envelope and carry that around in my pocket to share. Not talking isn't very much fun."

Smells excited Charlie most. He was a good sniffer. He could come from outside when Nana was cooking supper and tell her what was on their menu. As they walked the streets that day, he recognized garlic and onions, cinnamon, cloves and vinegar right away. With hints, he identified stewed tomatoes and sweet peppers with oregano, leek and potato soup, and rye bread. But he was absolutely stumped by stewed apricots and prunes, apfelkuchen, gingersnap meatballs, sauerkraut, bratwurst, cardamom buns, and chicken curry. "I won't ever taste something that smells like that!" he warned her.

He also hinted that all those good smells made him hungry, so they made their way to a small café with food they could select from a case rather than from a menu they could not read. Nana chose sausage in a roll and red cabbage. Charlie pointed to something that looked like a pancake but it came with a sour cream sauce instead of syrup. "I think this will taste much better when I'm older," he decided after cleaning his plate. They both ordered apfelstrudel for dessert.

On the trek back home Charlie asked why different people cook different foods.

"For the same reasons they speak different languages. People learn from their parents and grandparents before them. Not all people from faraway places use the same words or cook the same foods. When people leave their homes for a new place, they can't take very many objects with them. Trunks fill up fast with clothes and linens and books. But they can take memories of what 'home' was like for them. Favorite recipes, songs and family stories don't take up any space at all. Once here, it makes them feel good to share what they like best from their old country."

"Like building a café so we can come and taste new foods?"

"Yes. If we moved to a new city way out west, we might want to share recipes from our lives here, like fried dill pickles and crab cakes."

Charlie shook his head. "I don't think we'd sell very much of those, but your caramel cake could make us rich!"

Lesson 4: Sharing feels good.

*

On a different Saturday, they headed for the colored section of the city. Lottie knew many of the folks who lived there; it was her job to know them and to serve them. At times, she was the only clerk who would. Her oath and her husband's, son's and grandson's ancestry compelled her to treat all patrons with dignity and fairness. She also knew that a mature white woman with a little boy in tow would be an oddity. But they would not be in danger, for she had armed herself with secret weapons—an address and a plan.

Nana did not meander. She steered her grandson directly for a small, well kept white house closely bounded by others. Her firm knock brought a tall, strongly-built black man to the door with surprise in his eyes that sprang to his lips. "Miz Dickson!"

"Good morning, Gabe. I hope you don't mind my stopping by, but I have a project in mind for my home and am hoping you can point me to someone who can help."

The janitor stepped onto the small porch, wiping his hands on his overalls. Three young stair-stepped black faces peered through the doorway. Charlie waved at them and smiled. They waved back cautiously.

"No, Ma'am. I be happy to he'p if I can. What you need?"

"I need to build a picket fence around my yard—about four feet high. I'll need two gates in it—one in front and one in back. It will need paint too. The job can be done after work hours or on weekends. I pay a good wage for a job well done. I'd like the fence completed before school starts. I thought you might know a man or two who would like that job and could give me their names and addresses so I can talk to them while I'm here in your neighborhood."

He tilted his head and shook it. "I dunno, Ma'am. Folks don't us'ly come 'round askin' to hire."

"Well, I'm always looking for honest, hard-working help around my place—at least until Charlie is older. How about we walk around a few blocks while you think about it? We'll stop back before we leave." She smiled, took her grandson by the hand again and walked toward the street. Three pairs of curious eyes watched them go.

When they rounded a corner, Charlie made an observation. "There are lots of kids around here. Bunches more than where we live. Why's that?"

"We live in an older section of the city that lost a lot of our young people. Remember my telling you about the war and the flu? Here, lots of young folks left nearby farms to find jobs in the city after the war and brought their children with them."

"Will any of these children go to my school?"

"No."

Charlie was jolted by her abrupt and negative response. "Why not?"

"Colored children have their own schools."

"Why would they want that?"

"It's not about what children want. It's about the rules grownups make."

"Could I go to their school sometime? Just to visit?"

"Not until the grownups change their minds."

They continued walking through the activity of a warm Saturday morning. "Nana, how do you know so much stuff."

She chuckled. "I've lived longer and seen more than you. But when I was your age, I studied real hard at school and learned as much as I could. If you do that, you'll know enough to be just about anything you want to be."

The boy thought for a moment. "Could I grow up to be a teacher and build a school where anybody could come?"

"Possibly."

"Maybe I could be like your friend the judge and help to change the rules."

She leaned down to hug him. "Oh, my dear boy. I do hope so. Maybe by the time you're a grownup the rules will be different. Until then, we just have to do our part each day to help folks change their minds about those who seem different."

They rounded the last corner to find Gabe talking to a lanky black man. "Miz Dickson, this here's Nate from across the road and three houses down. He's real good at buildin' and will do the job fer you if I'd he'p him. I'm better at motors but can carry and hold steady jus' fine. An' I have a truck to haul boards with. If that be okay with you...."

As the three grownups discussed particulars, Charlie slipped away to talk to the children sitting on their steps, two boys and a girl. "Hi. My name's Charlie." He reached out a hand, but the kids did not seem to know what to do, so he stuffed it back in his pocket. "I'm starting first grade this year. Do you go to school?"

All three nodded.

"My favorite treat is ice cream. Do you like ice cream?"

Three heads nodded. One face smiled.

"My favorite flavor is fresh peach. What's yours?"

Without thinking, the kids blurted out, "Chocolate!" "Strawberry!" "Chocolate!"

"I like those flavors a lot too. If the soda fountain doesn't have peach, I choose one of those." He pointed to Nana. "That lady over there is my granny. She's real nice but not so good at playing kid games. We don't have many kids my age live near us, so sometimes I play with my imaginary friend Harley. He's okay for rainy days but not so good to kick a ball around with. I have to loan him my left foot, and I do my kicks with my right one."

The little girl giggled behind her hands. The boys shook their heads.

"I bet you two kick balls around all the time."

"Nah," said the oldest one. "We us'ly kick cans."

"That's a great idea! I never thought of that. Harley and I will give it a try next time." Hearing his name called in Nana's "come here" voice, he said his goodbyes. "Nice to meet you. Maybe next time we can kick a can around together and I'll get to use both feet!" He ran to Nana's side and stood perfectly still just like he should have been doing the whole time.

She handed each man a card. "These have my name, address and phone number. Carry them with you anytime you come to my house and you will not have a problem. Gabe can let me know when you want to begin. Thank you so much. You've taken a load off my mind." She smiled, took her grandson by the hand, and led him directly toward the street dividing black from white.

"That was quite a conversation you carried on with Gabe's children."

Charlie nodded. "They seemed real nice."

"What do you suppose would happen if we gathered one child from every neighborhood we've explored and put you all on a playground together?"

He did not hesitate for a second. "After all the grownups left, we'd play together just fine!"

Out of the mouths of babes she thought as she smiled and started to cross the street. He tugged her back. "Can we go down there?" he pointed. "I see a soda fountain sign and I've worked up a real appetite for ice cream."

"We'll cross the street and find another one further on."

"But why? Why can't we go there?"

"The truth? Because they might have a rule that we can't go in there."

"You mean kids can't go to the same school and they can't go to the same ice cream shop either?"

"That's correct. It may not seem right, but you are correct."

"But can we at least try? You said it yourself this morning. You said, 'We have to do our part every day to help folks change their minds.' Ice cream could be our part for today."

Nana tousled his hair. "You do make a point. Tell you what. We'll try. We'll walk to the shop and read all the signs on the outside. If there is a "NO" or an "ONLY," we must leave and cross the street to find someplace else. If the signs are okay, we may enter and ask. But if we are refused, we'll say 'thank you' politely and leave. No argument. Got it?"

"Yes, Ma'am."

On their way back out the door, Charlie licked all the way around two scoops of peach ice cream. "This is just about the best I ever ate. I can't wait 'til we come here again."

Nana's eyebrows shot up to her hatband, but she did not have the heart to discourage her hopeful grandson. She took a big lick of her vanilla praline and decided to change her mind to "maybe someday."

Charlie continued to enjoy his drippy treat. "Nana, can I ask you a question?"

"Of course."

"Why do we need Gabe and his friend to build us a fence? Are we just being nice to him because he has another baby coming?"

She laughed. "Not at all. We need a fence because I've never seen a hedge that could keep a dog in."

The boy's bright blue eyes bugged out of their sockets and he nearly plopped his ice cream on the ground.

*

Two weeks had passed since the fence was completed and Charlie still had not found the perfect puppy. He and Nana checked out several shops and markets and even answered ads in the newspaper with no luck. She was about to give up thinking the boy had lost interest, but he assured her that he would know the right dog as soon as he saw it.

One day Charlie did. The sorriest excuse for an animal friend that Nana had ever laid eyes on peered out at them from the corner of a kennel outside the city. He was a dusty tan color with streaks of dark gray and small splotches of black and white all over his runt-sized body. Small black triangle ears flopped near his droopy eyes, and his tail wavered between a wag and dread.

"He's the one, Nana! He's perfect," Charlie shouted and ran toward the mutt, skidding across the grass on his knees. He poked a finger through the wire to scratch the dog's shoulder. "Can we take him home now? Can we, please?"

She was mortified and tried to reason with her grandson. "Are you sure? Several of the others are very nice looking and friendly," she said as she sat beside him. "How about that brown one over there? He seems frisky."

Charlie shook his head. "No. I want this one. Please!"

Suddenly she was struck by a memory—a memory of old Sparky and how wonderful a companion and guardian that unsightly hound dog was for her son Jimmy. "I'll say yes if... IF... you can give me a really good reason why this puppy is the perfect one."

"Because he's *different*. Look." He pointed toward a mound of frolicking fur. "All the other puppies are playing but they don't want to play with him because he's different. That's not right. He's got all the

163

same parts as the others. His colors are just mixed up on the outside. But that's not a good reason not to play with him… whether he's a puppy or a person."

Nana could not argue with her grandson's reasoning and went in search of the owner.

"You want that runt? Heck, I'll *give* him to yuh fer takin' him off my hands."

She passed him ten dollars. "I'll take the dog and two days' of food, and I assure you, I got the better end of the deal." She packed up food, dog, and boy and hit the road for the city. "Have you thought of a name yet?"

Charlie nodded. "This here is Harley." He patted the pup on the head. "My imaginary friend is named Harley too, but I won't be playing with him so much now that I have new Harley, but I don't want old Harley to feel bad if he hears me playing with new Harley, so maybe if he hears me call his name now and again he'll know that I remember him."

That evening, the two, exhausted, new friends turned in early, the four-footed one settling on a ragged quilt in Charlie's first box and the two-footed one kneeling beside it for his prayers. Nana caught the tail end of his pleas:

"…and thanks for bringing me and Harley together. You'll hear his name lots from now on. And a special blessing for my granny. For an old grownup, she's real good at knowing what a little boy needs. Amen."

Lesson 5: Difference is good.

*

By Charlie's eighth birthday, both boy and canine grew to be hefty companions. With no competition for food or attention, Harley filled out, his coat became thick and glistening, and his tail wagged his whole rear half anytime his boy came near. The boy outgrew clothes as fast as Nana could sew them. Harley outgrew boxes at the same pace.

Both learned how to mope if they could not go out to play. Nana found that frequent weekend trips to the farms where the two were free to run the fields, explore the woods and splash in the streams provided an immediate cure for the grumps. The lack of color lines and rules was a bonus… until she noticed rules being bent. At the farms, the two frequently managed to share the porch swing to sleep, but at home the rule was "no dog on your bed!" When she entered Charlie's room to change the linens after such a weekend, a nest of dog hair covered the quilt. She used her stern, "come here *now*" voice to call him.

When he appeared at the doorway and saw her pointing to the bed, he knew the jig was up and started to protest.

"None of that!" she exclaimed and then asked, "Do you shed?"

He shook his head.

"Then explain to me how this got on your bed."

Charlie knew there was only one true explanation. "Harley slept there."

"You know the rule. How should he be punished?"

Shock rendered the boy speechless.

"Well… What is a reasonable punishment for a dog?"

Charlie's eyes welled with tears. "I don't know. I don't think Harley should be punished. He's only a dog."

"Did you teach him not to get on your bed?"

"Yes."

"Then he knew that he shouldn't and did anyway. That calls for a penalty."

"But *I* called him up onto my bed."

"You coaxed him to disobey? This is serious, Charlie. If you are out with a friend and go into a shop for a candy bar that neither one of you has the money to pay for, and your friend coaxes you to steal one, does that make it okay for you to break the 'no stealing' rule—because someone else told you to do it?"

He lowered his shaking head. "No.…"

"What do you suppose a judge would say?"

Charlie thought about the judges he knew. They were all pretty nice but strict too. "He'd prob'ly say that anyone who gets you in trouble is not a friend and if you're trying to blame each other… well… it takes too much time to figure out whose was the most fault so you should both go to jail."

Nana could barely keep herself from chuckling. "So, how do you suggest we solve our problem?"

"Both Harley and I did a bad thing so we should both be punished. But please, Nana, I want him to stay my friend, so don't make it too awful. I'll do extra chores or…"

"I have something else in mind. First, no playing outside today for either one of you. Second, no sleeping in the same room tonight. You figure out how to make that happen." She left the boy to think and said no more about it.

Charlie was crushed. Staying inside on a sunny day with school only a week away was bad enough, but being apart at night was the worst. Since they first brought Harley home, the two had never been separate at night. He dreaded trying to explain to a dog what was expected of both of them.

They survived a very boring day, but bedtime arrived all too quickly. Harley cocked his head to one side and then the other as Charlie gave him his instructions.

"You have to sleep out here tonight," he said, patting the floor outside his bedroom door. "I made you break the rule about not getting on my bed, and you know what happens when we break Nana's rules. We have to pay for it. Don't worry. I'm going to fix you a nice bed right here so you'll never know we're apart. Now, stay."

The dog started to follow the boy into his room but was ordered back to the hallway. Charlie patted him on the head and held his muzzle. "You stay here. Stay! We have to show Nana that we can mind her rules. Stay!"

The dog started to follow again. "No!" Charlie led him back to a spot outside the door. "Sit and stay! Don't pretend you don't know what 'stay' means. You're real good at that command and Nana says that not knowing is not a good excuse. You stay, and I'll make you the best bed ever."

Harley's eyes drooped, but he remained where he was told. Soon Charlie dragged out a pile of quilts and layered them for a cushy bed. Then he hauled out a lumpy bundle and set it at one end. He moved the dog onto the bedding and placed its head on the bumpy heap. He rested his hand over the dog's eyes and whispered, "You stay just like this with your eyes closed all night and pretty soon you'll think I'm right here beside you. Do not whimper. Do not scratch at the door. Nana needs to know that we mean to follow her rules."

He hugged the dog gently. "I love you, Harley, and I want us to be best friends forever, but sometimes we have to do something we don't want to if we want to get something that we do want. That's going to be our lesson two after 'obey the rules.' Now, think your prayers and go to sleep. Morning will be here before we know it. Stay!" He closed his door, leaving the dog outside it.

Nana awoke in the middle of the night and tiptoed out to check on the offenders. Both were sound asleep on their separate beds where she had last seen them. In the morning she asked Charlie about the lumpy bundle.

"Oh, that. I stuffed all my dirty clothes and even my shoes into my pillowcase so it would smell like me, and Harley would think we were together. He got along okay, but I was pretty chilly without my jammies."

Lesson 6: Take responsibility for your misdeeds.

*

Midmorning on Charlie's first day in third grade, a short get-to- know-you Friday, Lottie returned to her desk after a quick run to the Tax Collector's office. She sat down, picked up a pencil and stared across the room wondering how her grandson was faring with a new group of students and a new teacher when she noticed something amiss. The doors on the old wardrobe were ajar. An intruder had prowled around her office!

She rose and tiptoed toward the cupboard when a voice from inside it said, "Leave me alone! I'm punishing myself."

"Charlie? Why aren't you at school?" she asked, opening the wardrobe. A hunched ball of boy rolled onto the floor in front of her, his face and shirt covered in blood.

"My teacher s'pended me for the rest of the day, so I'm getting a head start on my punishment from you."

She pulled him up to sitting and leaned him against a cupboard door. "Oh my dear boy, are you badly hurt?" At a shake of his head she asked, "What did you get yourself into? Let's get you cleaned up; then you can tell me about it." She left and quickly returned with a warm, damp cloth. After a wipe-up it appeared that all the blood was the result of a blow to his nose. "Did you throw the first punch?" He shook his head. "Good boy. The second?" He nodded sheepishly.

"Oh my dear boy. I'm sorry you had to learn this lesson the hard way. I tried to tell you, but you must have been too young to understand. Now maybe you will. Any first punch may be accidental, so duck if you can and let the other kid throw it. Any second punch is intentional and becomes your fault if you throw it. Any third punch is self-defense. Make it a good one and flatten the other kid, and I will defend you to the end."

"I tried not to, but Billy the bully really made me mad. He called me a liar and when our teacher came out, he said I started the fight and she s'pended me. I'm sorry, Nana. I just couldn't wait long enough for it not to be my fault."

"Why did he call you a liar?"

"Because my teacher said I was an orphan and I said no I'm not and she said it's not right to lie. So Billy called me a liar."

"Why would your teacher call you an orphan?"

"She was making a list and asked us to raise our hands if we lived with two parents or one parent or no parents. I didn't raise my hand for any of those because I live with you, my granny, and that's a different kind of a parent. She said, 'That's not right. You are an orphan then. It's also not right to lie.' Then when we went out to play, Billy called me an orphan and a liar, and you know the rest."

Nana folded her arms around her miserable grandson and told him to wrap himself in her shawl and rest in his wardrobe until she returned. She dreaded the day Charlie's parentage would become an issue, but she could not avoid it now. The whole truth, that he had a living mother who abandoned her newborn, would be incomprehensible to a young boy who had adjusted so well to life with a granny. But someday.... She reached years back in her memory for advice then attorney Tyrell had given her about her own son Jimmy. Then she left on a mission to right the wrongs that had been done to her grandson and to every other child in his class.

Nana returned shortly after noon with a fat book in her hands. She rustled the boy from a snooze, took him by the hand and marched out the door.

"Nana. Where are we going so fast?"

"To school, to teach your teacher a lesson."

They arrived just at the moment of early dismissal, as Lottie had planned. She led her grandson to the principal's office and announced that they would await his return from seeing the students off. When the man entered his own office, she stood and greeted him, and then requested that he invite Charlie's teacher to join them. When the two arrived, she jumped right in.

"Thank you for meeting me on such short notice. I know this is a particularly busy day for you both. I'm here regarding my grandson's suspension this morning."

"He fo...."

"Charlie informed me that he and another boy fought in the play yard. I assume that *both* boys received the same suspension."

"Billy said...."

"I'm not here to question your disciplinary action regarding Charlie. I agree with it and will add to it when we get home this afternoon."

"I didn't mean to...."

"But I am concerned about what caused the fight in the first place. Charlie tells me that Billy, is it? That Billy called him an 'orphan' and a 'liar,' parroting *your* words about him earlier this morning."

The principal perked up his ears and finally showed interest in the conversation.

"I'm here to correct your assumptions about my grandson because he is neither." She passed the thick book to the teacher. "Will you humor me, please, and tell me what that book is?"

The puzzled teacher replied with the obvious. "It's a dictionary."

"Would you say it is a reputable one? One whose definitions most people would accept?"

"Yes, Ma'am."

"Please open it to the page I have marked and tell us where we are in that book."

The young woman did as she was asked. "We're in the Os."

"Good. Find the word 'orphan' and read the first definition please."

"Orphan—a child whose parents are dead."

"Do you agree with that definition?"

"Why, yes. That's common knowledge."

"Good. We agree. By that definition, Charlie is *not* an orphan, and therefore cannot be referred to as a *liar* for denying that he is."

Both the teacher and the principal seemed confused and uncomfortable.

"Let me explain. For a person to be 'legally dead,' a bona fide witness must attest to the identity of a dead body; a mortuary or cemetery will have a record of place of burial; or a Death Certificate for the deceased will be recorded in county records... or all three. I have spent the morning on the phone with officials in a third of Alabama's sixty-seven counties surrounding Montgomery and none of these records exist for Charlie's parents; therefore, they are not 'legally dead.' James Charles Dickson, Jr. is *not* an *orphan*... or a *liar*."

Beads of sweat broke out on the principal's balding pate. If Lottie Dickson, a woman well known and respected throughout the city as well as the county, chose to take her issue to the school board, the teacher would be the one suspended for using such derogatory language toward a pupil.

"For anyone who has not lost a child or for any child who has not lost a parent, such reasoning may seem illogical. But I can assure you that until you see or touch physical evidence of the death of a loved one, there is always hope that someday that someone will return to you in some form."

Lottie paused for a moment to dab her eye with her handkerchief. "To assign a child a hurtful label is insensitive. Children are not born into this world by their own choosing. They do not choose their parents. They do not choose to be black or white or brown or green. They do not choose their place of birth or nationality. They do not choose their language or traditions. They do not choose the labels we pin on them. They come into this world as innocent sponges that soak up every word, every action, every opinion they come in contact with. Our obligation as the adults in their lives, whether blood related or not, is to arm them with the most positive self-images we can and the greatest acceptance of others possible in this day and age."

Now it was the teacher who flushed and lowered her eyes.

"How do you propose we resolve this unfortunate incident with your grandson?" the principal asked, fearing her answer.

"An apology to Charlie for not believing him and embarrassing him in front of others would make a good start. And Charlie, do you have any suggestions?"

The young boy, mute throughout the adults' conversation about him, thought for a moment. "Maybe when you want to know personal stuff about a kid, you should ask him in private or call his parents or even visit his house. And kids are not so great about being told they've done something bad in front of their friends. But if you just want to get to know kids, ask them fun stuff like... who likes ice cream or what they like to do at free time or what books they like to read. Kids can talk all day about those things."

"Is that everything?" Nana asked.

"Um. I really liked the way you said hello to each of us when we came into the room even though you didn't know us yet, and you already had our names on our desks to help you learn them faster."

The principal nudged the flustered young woman. "May I apologize now or in class on Monday?" she asked, hoping he would not choose the latter.

Charlie looked at Nana who shrugged her shoulders. "An apology is kind of a private thing between two people, so now would be best," he said. After his teacher expressed her sincere regrets for the events of the morning, he accepted and turned again to his granny. "Can we go now, Nana? I'm worried about how to keep our dog from licking my sore nose to make it better."

His remark brought smiles to everyone's face, breaking the tension in the room. Lottie stood and reclaimed the dictionary. "Thank you for your time. We'll chat again soon." She ushered Charlie out the door but paused long enough to overhear the conversation between principal and teacher.

"I'm so sorry, sir. I didn't mean to cause such a fuss over a few remarks. We sure dodged a ticklish problem."

"You are mistaken. *You* did not dodge anything. That woman gave you a free pass from an appearance before the Board. She knew that there are accusatory words a teacher is not allowed to say to a student in public. She also knew that you did not treat her grandson fairly or respectfully because Billy was not given any punishment. She saw him in the schoolyard when she first arrived, as did I."

"But Billy said that Charlie started the fight."

"And you believed one boy over the other because he shouted louder or first? Did you even ask Charlie who started the fight or why? Did you ask other students what they saw or heard? Did you take the two boys inside to settle the argument privately?"

The young woman lowered her eyes. "No, sir."

"A teacher's first year is difficult, in any case. You will learn as much as your students. But those two could have made your life miserable, or at the worst, ended your career in this city. Instead, they chose to give a new teacher a break. Remember that the next time you rush to judge your students."

On their brisk walk back to the courthouse, Charlie asked, "Why can't I just go home?"

"Because you are suspended from school. Suspension does not mean go home and play with your dog. It means think long and hard about what you did that got you in trouble, why you did it, and how you can keep yourself from doing that again. So, you will join me in my office and do lots of thinking this afternoon. No dogs allowed!"

"Oh.... Will I get anything to eat or drink?"

"I'll share my lunch with you. It's already late, so the afternoon will be over before you know it."

"Oh.... Nana, you said a lot of words today. Which one of Judge Tyrell's lessons did you teach my teacher?"

She smiled. "Lots of them. 'Don't make assumptions'—don't think you know before you check the facts. 'Know the law'—I tracked it down while you rested. 'Define your terms'—know exactly what the words you are going to use mean. 'Use the law'—we found one that said we were right. The judge would say that a different way. He'd say, 'Don't break the law. Use it.' At your age that means, 'Do not disobey a rule. Use it.' If you don't agree with a rule, think of why you don't and how you can change what you want enough not to disobey. That's called a compromise. You get some of what you want but not quite all of it."

She gave him a firm pat on the back. "Keep learning his lessons, and you'll be an attorney before you know it. But that's enough legal talk for one day. Rest and think about how to stick to the rules—at home and at school."

Charlie's unusual silence throughout the rest of the afternoon and evening worried Nana. Perhaps he had been physically hurt worse than he let on. She checked on him again and found him lying quietly on his bed with his legs crossed, staring at the ceiling with Harley on the floor near him. "How do you feel, my boy? Do you have any aches you've not told me about?"

He shook his head. "But I have a question. I've thought all afternoon about your rules. You said if I don't like one, think of a way to do the same thing only different that makes it okay. Right?"

Uh oh, Lottie thought. *Here it comes.* "Yes, more or less."

"I know your rule about Harley is 'no dog on my bed', but I don't remember a rule about me that says 'no boy on the dog's bed.' I'm on Harley's bed all the time—to pet him and read to him and say my prayers, so why can't *I* sleep on *his* bed too?"

And there it lands, she thought. *Now what?* "You make a good point, but I would not be a good parent if I let my grandson sleep on the floor all the time. Sleeping in a draft is not healthy and there's school to think about. You must be fresh in the mornings. I don't see...."

"What about weekends? Like Fridays? Like tonight? There's no school tomorrow. And I sure could use a good snuggle tonight after all I've been through today."

She gave him a hug. "You certainly have had a day of it. Okay. For tonight. But that is not a promise for every other Friday. We'll take them one by one. Can I help you comfy up Harley's bed enough for a boy?"

He gave her a big hug. "Thank you, Nana. You'd make a good attorney too. Harley and I can handle the bed, only I won't let him have my pillow tonight. He can use my tummy.

Lesson 7: Do not make assumptions.
Lesson 8: Know the law.
Lesson 9: Define your terms.
Lesson 10: Do not disobey a rule. Use it.

*

January 1, 1930. Rents due. As owner/manager of Tyrell Farms since the judge's death and with more than thirty years of experience as rent collector behind her, the bleakness of this year's picture troubled Lottie. Farm prices fell throughout the last half of the twenties leaving many farmers unable to pay rent or mortgages. All of her land was free and clear now, so mortgage was not a problem, nor was rent payable to her which had not changed one penny during those years—one hundred pennies per farm per year. The difficulty was continued declining prices, leaving each farmer's share of crop insufficient to support a family. With every sector of the economy now pitched into depression, friends and neighbors were hurting. What to do?

"Nana, I'm only in sixth grade, but I can tell something's wrong. Folks don't smile as much—even my teacher—and kids act out more and most of them can't come over and play after school like they used to. And some are moving away. What's happening? Is the flu coming again?"

Lottie took her eyes from the road to Banks long enough to glance at her rapidly maturing grandson. He had the general build and look of her son Jimmy but was heftier. What fascinated her most, though, was his ability to relate to others with a sense of fair play like his father. "No. This is not a health epidemic. It's more of a business one—too complicated to explain."

Charlie rolled his eyes in pre-teen fashion. "I'm almost in junior high school. Try me."

She heaved a sigh and tried. "Take our farmer's corn, for example. He grows and harvests a good crop and takes it to the mill to sell. To make the arithmetic easy we'll say he's used to selling it for one dollar a bushel, but when he gets to the mill he's told they will only pay fifty cents a bushel this year because too many folks are growing corn and not enough are buying it. To sell all of what he has, he has to lower his price. The farmer can agree to the fifty cents or take his crop home and dump it on the ground." She glanced at the boy. "Are you still awake?"

"Yeah," he replied lazily and reached to the seat behind to scratch the dog's ear. "Harley's listening too."

"Glad of that. Maybe he'll have a good idea. So, supposing the farmer sells one hundred bushels and takes home only fifty dollars. He makes a long list of everything he needs to buy before he sells the next crop—seed, harnessing for the plow horses, a couple of shovels, shoes for the kids, boots for himself, a doctor's bill, medicine, food he doesn't grow and so on. Then he puts dollars next to each item and there aren't enough, so he makes choices. Seed and harness—yes or he can't grow another crop. Shovels—no, he'll repair the handles himself. Shoes—only for the oldest girl and boy; the others can wear hand-me-downs. Boots—no, he'll make do for another year. Doctor—half what he owes. Medicine—no. Food—half, and so on."

"That doesn't sound good at all. I can't imagine wearing another guy's shoes."

"And that's not the worst of it. The shovel factory has to lay off some workers because not as many shovels are sold. The shoe factory lays off workers because not as many shoes are sold. Same for the boot factory workers, and so on down to the soda fountain that may have to close because not enough people have money left over to buy ice cream."

That realization brought Charlie up to full attention. "No ice cream! How did we get from corn to no ice cream?"

"The way of the world these days. We're all connected, so we'll all have to work together to find a way out of these hard times." She crossed the last bridge before the farms. "We're almost there. Ready to work?"

He nodded less enthusiastically than usual. Charlie had a lot on his mind.

The two assumed their traditional roles. Charlie helped the farmers count pennies and Lottie wrote out the two receipts. When she handed over a farmer's copy, she reminded him to keep the receipt safe in his pennies jar so he could say, "I rent this here house" when the census taker visited late spring. At the same time, she gauged the well-being of the household and heard bits and pieces of gossip—Smiths a mile east were going under; they could not make their mortgage. Frandsen's cousin and family were moving in with him. The bank over in Tulle closed. No matter which way she looked, the landscape was grim.

She stopped at the big house to give it a security check before heading back to Montgomery. Charlie did not feel like going in. He sat on the porch with his elbows on his knees and chin resting on his fists. Harley stretched out by his feet. When she closed and locked the door on her way out, Harley had wandered but her grandson had not moved an inch. She sat beside him and felt his forehead. "You're not getting sick, are you?"

He shook his head. "Nah. Just thinking." He turned his worried eyes toward her. "Nana, you aren't going to get laid off, are you?"

She folded an arm around him to draw him close and rested her head atop his. "I hope not. It could happen. Gabe has been reduced to part-time as well as a couple of others from the offices downstairs. I might be too, but *you* don't have to worry. We'll never have to stand in food lines downtown like some folks we've seen. Judge Tyrell provided for us before he died."

"Why would he do that?"

"Because he wanted to know that we would always have a roof over our heads and food to eat from the farms… and that your papa would have an education and maybe grow up to be a fine attorney like he was. That schooling goes to you now when you're old enough to need or want it."

"That seems like an awful lot to give people you're not even related to. Did you pay him back some way?"

"Every day. He provided our essential needs and we satisfied his emotional ones. We thought of him as the father and grandfather we didn't have near us and he thought of us as the family that did not live long enough for him to enjoy. Your papa idolized that man and practiced all his lessons including 'Help others when they need it, and they will help you.' So you don't have to worry about my job. As long as we can pay the taxes on the farms with our share of the crops, we can always move back here and survive. Would you like that?"

"I like it here just fine except... all my friends are in the city and there's no one near here my age to hang around with. There's Harley, of course, but a boy needs kid friends too." He looked down at his feet. "Where is Harley?"

Right on cue, barking sounded from behind the house. The two followed the dog's cries and found him digging excitedly at the sagging door of an old shed. "Grab your dog, Charlie, and let's be on our way."

"We have to go in and see what he found."

"Probably a cat or maybe a skunk. Let's go."

The boy was persistent. "We have to see what he found. Please."

Nana relented and unlatched the padlock. "You'll do the scrubbing if your dog gets sprayed," she warned and pulled the door open. Harley scrambled in after a white cat's tail that disappeared underneath a canvas in a back corner. Charlie followed close behind and stubbed his toe on the heap. He pulled the canvas away and gulped. "Look, Nana. It's a bicycle!"

Her eyes teared up when she recognized Jimmy's two-wheeler. He must have left it here to be safe and out of the way until he returned from the war. Memories of her son riding in all flushed with excitement from his days' adventures swirled through her mind until she felt a pat on her shoulder.

"Are you okay, Nana. All of a sudden you look sad."

"Happy-sad," she tried to smile and dabbed at her eyes. "That bike was your papa's, and oh how he loved it. I think he rode it more miles than we've driven the car."

"Wow! Can this be mine now? I can fix it up and learn how to ride it and Harley can run along beside me. And... and maybe I can think of a way to use it to help us if you get laid off."

She chuckled at his ability to make solutions seem so simple, but the thought of her dear grandchild turned loose in the big city scared her to death. What could she say? "If you can get this old thing in the car, we'll take it back with us."

Charlie carried the bike to the car and struggled to get it in the trunk. He went back to the shed for an old piece of rope and, when satisfied that his found treasure would not fall out on the way home, he broke out in a big smile so reminiscent of his papa. "I guess you were right, Nana. You said Harley would have a good idea, and he did!"

Lottie took a short detour just outside of Banks and pulled up near an old cemetery. At Charlie's quizzical look, she said, "I think you are old enough now to meet the man who made the lives we live possible. Every now and again we should pay him a visit to express our gratitude for the gifts he's given us—our home, the farms, and your future." She led him to Judge Tyrell's grave where they sat near his headstone while she recounted stories of the saintly man and his shadow, Jimmy.

That night, Charlie's prayers were followed by a list of gratitudes that lasted longer than he did. He slumped to the floor before his "Amen" where Nana found him. She rolled him onto Harley's bed, covered him with a quilt and tiptoed out. *Yes*, she thought. *We'll get through these hard times together just fine.*

Lesson 3, revised: Express gratitude for blessings large and small.

A few nights later, Charlie put down his fork after dessert and did not leave to take Harley outside as usual. He stared hard at his grandmother. "Nana, we have important matters to discuss."

At that mature statement, she sat up to pay attention.

"You want me to grow up slower than I want to. Lots of kids don't have a childhood anymore. They are *forced* to grow up fast because their families are hurting. I can see it in their eyes. I am *not* one of those kids. I've had a great childhood and am one of the luckiest boys I know. But I want to know more—the bad and the good—so I can help *us* decide how to get through these hard times. I can't help if I don't know all the facts. You are holding some back."

Ah, she thought. *The difference between telling* a *truth and the* whole *truth, a lesson straight out of the judge's book. How could Charlie channel the man so quickly?* "What do you want to know?"

"When we were at the farms, you said something that puzzles me now. You said, 'As long as we can pay the taxes on the farms with our share of the crops....' I know we pay taxes on the farms because you manage them now, but what does 'our share of the crops' mean? I thought the farmers got the crops."

Oh dear, she thought. *Speak as if to a young adult. Charlie seeks that respect more than the answer.* "Our farms are run like a business between two people. We, the landowners, supply the ground. The farmer supplies his labor. We share the profits—the money we get for the crops."

"What is that share?"

"Right now, we share fifty-fifty."

"Is that a good deal for the farmer?"

"Right now, it is better than most. Judge Tyrell always believed that a good deal for the farmer guaranteed an honest and loyal partner, so he was willing to give up some of his profit for those qualities. Many families have worked our ground for several generations because we treat them fairly."

"Then the example we worked with corn wasn't quite right because the farmer got all fifty dollars. First on his list should have been half that amount to you, leaving him only twenty-five for all he needed. There go the harness, any shoes, the doctor and more food—barely enough to live on."

"Congratulations. You now understand the problems that face many of our people today. Do you have a suggestion for a solution?"

"Could we take a smaller percent and give our farmers more money?"

"If we still banked what we needed, we could. But we will not just *give* them more money. As the judge used to say, 'We don't deal in handouts. We deal in dignity.' Our farmers know what their labor is worth. If we just give them more, they will feel like they haven't earned it and will be embarrassed that they can't support their families."

"There must be some way to help them."

"If we came up with an idea that gave them *extra* work for more money, that would be okay. For example, when one of our families comes up short a few pennies for rent, we could just put those pennies in ourselves, but that would embarrass them. Instead, we take along mending for them to do. When I pick up the finished work, I pay them in pennies and they pay me what they still owe for rent. I usually make sure they have a few extra for a start on next year's jar. That usually brings a big smile to their faces. They feel like they earned their rent just like all their neighbors. Dignity."

Charlie considered the more money for more labor idea and asked, "How much money do we have to spare from our share? What is the most percent that we need?"

"I have no idea." She left the table and rummaged in her desk. "Here is my accounts book. You're good at arithmetic. If you can figure out whether we can get by on thirty or forty percent, then we'll both know. The total amounts for crops in this column are one hundred percent for last year. The mills and warehouses pay me, and I make sure their accounting is correct before I pay the farmers their fifty percents. This assures that all parties are treated honestly and fairly."

Charlie's eyes danced over all those numbers. He had definitely entered grownup territory. He closed the account book and headed for his room.

"What about Harley?" Nana reminded him.

"Oh yeah." He made for the door where his dog awaited with urgency in his eyes. "Better make it quick, Harl. I've got lots of work ahead of me tonight."

Lesson 11: A man's dignity is priceless.

*

A few weeks after his first grownup conversation, Charlie embarked on his second. He found Nana working in her flower garden and approached her with his we-have-important-matters-to-discuss eyes fixed on hers. "I have an idea. I'm not going to fix up Papa's bike."

Lottie nearly turned her foot under with the spade. "What! I thought you wanted to …."

"I hired Gabe to do it for me. He said he had some free time now that his hours have been cut. Shouldn't take him too long."

"Define 'hire.'"

"'To pay for the use of a thing or the work or services of a person.'" He winked at her. "I knew you'd ask."

"How do you expect to pay him?"

"I knew you'd ask that too. I'll use some of my savings."

Shock filled Lottie's eyes, "You have savings?"

"Yeah. You forced me into it."

She chuckled and parked her spade. "Tell me how."

"Remember a couple of years back when I wanted some new blue jeans and you gave me your 'want or need' lecture? You asked me if I had a roof over my head, food to eat, clean clothes, shoes and love in my life. I said yes, and you asked me if I really *needed* those new pants. I said no, but I sure did *want* them real bad. You said that the judge would tell me to be grateful that my needs were met and if I really wanted those jeans, to go out and work for them."

Charlie cast a wary glance at his grandmother. "By a strange coincidence, a neighbor lady asked me to help her weed her garden. After I did that a couple of times I had enough to pay for the jeans. She and other neighbor ladies asked me to do more and more odd jobs because they didn't have young family to help them. I saved every penny, nickel, dime and dollar they gave me, and now I have enough to pay Gabe to fix the bike. I can watch him real careful so I'll learn to do it myself. Then I'll hire someone else without a job to teach me to ride the thing."

"That sounds like quite a plan."

"That's just the first part of it. You wait and see." Now he was the one chuckling as he and Harley went in search of a snack.

Lesson 12: *Work* for what you want.

*

Scorching midsummer heat brought the worst out in everyone. On this particular day, an anticipatory frenzy filled the atmosphere at the courthouse. Everyone was on edge. Lottie recognized the signs and was not surprised to see all off-duty deputies show up to the sheriff's office. The Chief of Police stopped by and hunkered down with them until they all caravaned out of town heading away from the river. No employee met the gaze of another. Sometime before three o'clock, everyone cleared out. Everyone but Lottie.

She was paid for a full day's work, so that is what she intended to do. Work. Someone had to watch over the center of government for the county, especially its official records. That was her job and she aimed to fulfill it, no matter the sickness she felt inside. But her resolve was sidelined by worry. She spent the rest of the afternoon alternately flipping through certificates and praying. "Please, Charlie, don't follow your friends down to the old docks today. Don't do it. If they ask, go straight home and stay there. Remember. I made you promise... Promise!.. Promise!! NEVER to walk, bike, or hitch a ride down to the docks in summer. Dear Lord, please keep my innocent boy safe at home today."

As soon as fellow employees began to return flush-faced—some smiling and chattering and others with handkerchiefs squeezed tightly in their hands—Lottie knew that the spectacle was over and she packed up for home. She had no stomach for the conversations that would fill the offices until closing.

When she rushed through her gate and spied the bike on the ground, she knew her prayers had *not* been answered. Charlie never left his papa's bike lying on the ground; it had a special place to lean against the house, near the back door out of the sight of passers by. Her trembling hands barely had the strength to turn the knob on the door. She entered and listened.... Deep, guttural sobs led her to the bedroom where her grandson lay on his bed, curled into a tight ball like a baby.

"Nana's here, love. Nana's here," she whispered as she sat next to him and massaged his back.

Charlie rolled over and lunged for her arms, gripping her in a hug so strong she could barely breathe. "Oh, Nana. I'll never be able to unsee what I saw today. It was horrible!" He bawled big growing-boy tears that would not stop. Soon she wept with him. They were wrapped so tightly together that poor Harley could not find a face or a hand for him to lick away the hurt. He finally settled for wriggling his nose in between their tummies.

"I know, love. I know. Nana will keep you safe. You cry all you want. I'll keep you safe," she said while rocking their bodies side-to-side. But she was not sure she could anymore. Her innocent boy left his childhood by the old docks that afternoon when he witnessed man's inhumanity to his fellow man. How could she ever reveal the whole truth about his grampa's death and his own ancestry now that such a ghastly image was burned into his mind? No, not now. Not anytime soon. But someday....

"Why, Nana? Why?" Charlie wailed. "Why are people so vicious and cruel to each other?"

"I have no answer that makes good sense except that some people never learn to appreciate difference. Only to fear it."

"But he was just a young man, not that much older than Gabe's boy. Someone said that he wrote a note to a white girl and her mama found it, and that was that. No arrest. No trial. Only a rope, and the crowd cheered. A man hollered out to burn him, and the crowd cheered louder. I couldn't stand it!"

He snuffled against her shoulder. "I pedaled home as fast as I could. You warned me not to go to the old docks in summer, but I didn't listen hard enough. My friends dared me to go with them. Now I'll never be able to face them again... or any of my colored friends either."

The boy's wailing went on and on until Nana finally coaxed him into a warm bath and to sip some hot chicken soup. Then she took him by the hand and led him up the road with Harley trailing close behind.

"Where are we going?' he asked

"To church. We have lots to discuss with our Dear Lord tonight, particularly to ask a special blessing for that young man's soul."

"Do you think He listens on Tuesdays?"

"He listens to us every night, but especially on Tuesdays when we go to Him with terrible troubles."

By the end of the evening, Charlie's fledgling plan to save the farms and to help his friends and neighbors survive the Depression became a crusade. A call to action. A commitment to study hard and become a judge who would assure that folks take responsibility for their actions. Judge Tyrell's lessons would be his guidebook.

Lesson 5, revised: Respect differences.

Lesson 6, revised: Take responsibility for your actions.

*

Charlie experienced an unforeseen repercussion from the recent lynching. After school one day he went to the courthouse in search of Gabe. He wanted to hire the man, or his friend Nate, to build a shelf big enough to hold a crate or two securely on the back of his bicycle. He thought that his offer of a side job would be most welcome. He was surprised by the man's reply.

"I be happy to he'p you, Charlie. But best we not be too frien'ly for a time. We don't wan' no trouble comin' to us." Gabe did not seem angry, just resigned and apologetic.

Charlie flushed with embarrassment. "Thanks anyway. If you change your mind, let my gramma know."

Two weeks later, Lottie called Charlie from work. "Can you meet me here at five? I need help with a contraption I found in the wardrobe this morning. Bring your savings."

He arrived on the dot, anxious to see what strange device turned up there, of all places. He was not disappointed. His eyes frolicked over the double-crate-sized apparatus with a four-inch lip and stays for mounting from the seat to the rear wheel axle. "This is exactly what I imagined!"

He upended the contrivance and noticed a rude sketch of how to attach the thing to his bike. The number three was written to the side. "Do you think that's how much I owe Gabe?" he asked.

"Well, a chair costs about $1 to $1.50 and a whole dresser, about $3.50. Gabe probably makes less than that for a ten-hour day's work, so $3 is reasonable for labor and supplies. Did you bring that much with you?"

"Yup," he said. "But how will we get it to him. He won't want us to go to his house."

"Absolutely correct! Let's put the bills in an envelope, and I'll make sure I bump into him in the hall tomorrow. Write a short note of thanks if you want to, but do not write his name, or yours, anywhere. Got it?"

The boy nodded with no enthusiasm. "Yeah. Gabe is such a nice guy. I wish we could help him."

"I'm sure you'll think of a way."

A few days later, Charlie returned from the market with a couple of old crates secured in the contraption on his bike. He found Nana in the back working in her garden. He slumped to the ground and put an arm around Harley. "You won't believe what I saw in the city. People... men... lined up for food at the mission house. Their heads hung so low that I couldn't see their eyes. I didn't want to. They seemed miserable and discouraged." He tossed what was left of a rag ball next to the fence for Harley to fetch.

"I had this grand plan to peddle apples from my bike and use the money to help our friends and farmers. But one boy with a bike is not going to solve this city's problems. Will you help me think of a better plan?"

"Of course," she said and entered the house to return with a pitcher of lemonade. She sat beside him so the two could put their heads together— with Harley in between—and come up with a broad scheme that would touch as many people as possible. Two evenings of pencil to paper resulted in a proposal.

First: Keep the farms solvent. Without the farms, they would not have the wherewithal to help themselves or anyone else. Lottie and grandson together calculated that they could get by with a thirty-five percent share if they gave up a few frills. In keeping with extra work for more money, the farmers would be made an offer: to convert a minimum of two acres of farming ground into all-season vegetable and fruit garden, the produce guaranteed for purchase by Tyrell Farms. Chickens and eggs, extra.

Second: The farm produce would be separated into four parts: the offices at the courthouse, Gabe's black neighborhood, their church family, and Charlie's bike.

Courthouse—a large box or bag for each office to share.

Gabe—a couple of large boxes to take home and share with family and neighbors. Lottie would leave her dictionary on her desk when goodies were in the cupboard for him to take home and distribute as he saw fit.

Church family—a few boxes labeled "for those in need."

Charlie's bike—specialties of the season at the bargain price of one penny. A penny an apple. A penny a peach. A penny a tomato. A penny a handful of berries. Two carrots for a penny. A head of lettuce, a fat bunch of spinach or okra for a penny. A penny an orange, a lemon, a hard-boiled egg, a bunch of green onions, a turnip or potato or beet or squash, two handfuls of peas or beans—fresh or dried.

Earnings—gasoline for trips to Banks to pick up produce and for bike maintenance and repair.

On paper, their plan seemed to cover all bases and to be workable with extra time and effort on both their parts. In reality, it was a slow-starter. September harvest was a time of plenty, but no new gardens would be put in until after the crops sold. The farmers were delighted at the prospect of pay for produce and were willing to sell some of their surplus—mostly squash. Near Christmas, they would have more squash, sweet potatoes and some greens. Maybe some fryers.

Lottie and Charlie made do and picked apples and peaches from the farmhouse orchard to add to their collection. On the drive back to Montgomery they decided to rotate recipients weekly but to save a little of this and that for free in the shantytowns.

On one of their weekly runs, they combined fruit and nut picking with pre-census consultations. The enumerators would hit the farms the following week. Charlie begged to be the explainer. After all, if he wanted to be an attorney he had to know about such things, and there would not be another census until he was in his twenties. Might as well learn now.

Lottie was jarred by how swiftly time passed. Jimmy never lived into his twenties and his son was already planning for them. She agreed and suggested he make a list of everyone in each household now and check spellings carefully. Census takers tended to spell names phonetically if they were unsure, and later this caused problems in tracking records. "You might be a Dixon today if I hadn't watched carefully."

Official date was April 1 even though it was currently October. Each family was to include every person living on that date even if they had died a month later and not include any babies born after that date. "Draw a line through each name on your list for a later birth. Add names of deceased that qualify to be counted. Confusing for some folks to understand," she said.

"This time around, they'll be asked not only if they own or rent, but also how much rent they pay by *month*. We collect by the year, so the answer will be 'eight.' If they *do not say* 'pennies,' the census taker will assume 'dollars' and write it down that way. Interestingly, they'll be asked if the home has a 'radio set.'"

"We can say 'yes' on that one," Charlie grinned.

"We sure can. The biggest change for many people is the question about employment and whether the head of family is actually at work. If the answer is 'no,' he will have or be given an 'unemployed' number. That won't apply to our folks. They can all say 'yes.' But imagine the humiliation of the hundreds—thousands, even—who must say 'no.'"

The weekend before the enumerator was scheduled to go to the farms, Lottie baked cookies and made caramel cake. Charlie finished his lists— one to explain and then leave with each family. They were prepared! Somewhere between the gingersnaps and caramel cake, the boy conned his way into another concession. He asked to drive the car during the rounds to the farms.

"What!" Nana exclaimed. "You're barely twelve and riding a bike!"

"But I'm tall enough now to see out the front and strong enough to change a tire and I watch you all the time and I know the roads. Just around the farms. Please?"

How could she say no? They had a merry time that Sunday delivering cookies and lists with Charlie behind the wheel, gathering surplus veggies, picking apples and nuts, and singing all the way home. They even treated themselves to some peach ice cream.

By late spring of 1931, their plan was in full swing. The well-tended farm gardens produced enough for hefty donations to the courthouse, Gabe's neighborhood, and their church family. The farm wives smiled with cash in their hands. Charlie became known as the "penny peddler" who cruised the poorer neighborhoods for four days a week. On the fifth day, he frequented shantytowns on the edge of the city and gave away what was left, one piece per person, children first.

By fall his fledgling business had grown wings. He was amazed at how quickly the pennies added up. And how quickly they disappeared. On his rounds near the edge of town, he spotted an old pickup with a For Sale sign on it. The man had lost his job and had to sell the truck to pay his mortgage of $30 a month. For $400 cash he could pay the full year ahead plus taxes—enough to keep a roof over his family's head until he could find another job. But only for cash.

Charlie pedaled home at lightening speed for a heart-to-heart with Nana. Yes, they could afford the truck if Charlie would contribute some of his savings. But why did they need one? "Because once school starts in a month, I won't have time to do both. I will need to study sometime, and that time is probably weekends if I try to keep up with my rounds after school each day. I hate to let down my regular customers. So that means fewer trips to the farms and bringing more food back each time."

Lottie agreed to check out the particulars with folks at the courthouse. She was willing to pay a fair price for the vehicle, but no more. Her first thought was Gabe. She sent him a note that a drawer needed fixing, and he came by near the end of a workday. Yes. That was a fair price, but don't pay 'til someone checks out how much work it needs. Yes. He could do that if they could get the vehicle to him without crossing a "colored" line. "We don' want no troubles comin' on us." Yes. He could fix most things wrong with a motor if nothing's broken bad. No. Things were not especially good at home. Rudy finished school and could not find a job, and on half-time wages it took two weeks to pay the rent. "But I be lucky fo' da job. Most don' have it so good."

As it turned out, the courthouse and surrounding premises were the safest place to transact business. The facility was a public one open to serve all county citizens even though some may have to enter through a separate door, use a separate rest room or swear on a separate Bible. When a small group gathered around an old truck in a parking area beside the building, there was no reason to "tut tut." Both Gabe and Lottie Dickson were known and respected, and Charlie was their friendly samaritan.

The curious watched from their office windows as Gabe opened the hood of the truck, jiggled here, poked there, listened carefully to the running motor and nodded. Lottie handed the stranger a wad of bills. He handed her the keys and walked away. She gave Gabe the keys and an official-looking document. Charlie fixed a sign to the side of the truck—Tyrell Farms—and smiled and waved as Gabe drove away. The onlookers smiled too. There was only one reason for an older white woman to buy a truck and hand it over to a colored man to drive. More food!

After her first day behind the wheel of a truck, Lottie swore there would never be a second. Through jarring teeth she complained about the pickup being heavy, sluggish and hard to turn.

"Maybe you should hand this vehicle over to a man like me to drive," Charlie joked. Harley, squeezed between his two people, chimed in with a yip.

"Both of you. Quiet! I'm trying to keep this overloaded monster on the right side of the road." She grumbled and stared straight ahead. "I'm not sure that two weeks of produce at a time is such a good idea after all. I'm dead beat after so much hauling and loading, and I don't look forward to finding more space in the house to unload it all."

"Does Nana need a tune-up?" he teased.

"No sir. Not for five bucks. Nana needs a new plan!"

The following weekend—not a produce run, under the new schedule—Nana, Charlie and Harley took a casual drive to the farms to investigate the status of the home properties. Since the judge's death, she had not set foot in any of them except to unearth the bicycle. She had the cabins, sheds and stables locked or boarded up long ago, but perhaps they could be useful—if not profitable—in some way.

Harley loved the freedom to roam the woods surrounding the properties and quickly disappeared. The two-footed inspectors trod carefully over fallen limbs obstructing pathways, broken and missing steps, and through creaking doorways. Lottie found that much worth remained, but an equal amount of work would be required to make the places functional. For Charlie, the ramshackle buildings held nothing but possibilities.

He observed his grandmother lingering inside a little cabin a ways behind the main house with the tiniest tear in the corner of her eye. "What's so special about this place?" he asked.

"Your papa was born right here," she answered with a sniff.

"Here! Where's the bedroom? The bathroom!"

"No bedroom. The privy is thataway down the path."

"I can't believe you lived in a place like this. It's no better than a lot of the...."

"I know. And we thought it was heaven. Those were the happiest ten years of my life." She noticed his head droop slightly and gave him a squeeze. "Until *you* came along, that is."

He perked up. "We could make it a happy place again."

That night, in a cozy little house, in separate bedrooms, with a bathroom just down the hall and food in the cupboard, grandmother and grandson each expressed to their Dear Lord gratitude for their good fortune in a time of such trials and prayed that others too might find happiness in the simple gifts of life.

*

The next weekend—a produce run—Nana, Charlie and Harley took a casual drive to the farms again. Gabe and his oldest son Rudy followed behind in the truck to help Charlie with the heavy lifting and loading. She planned to sit in the sun and work on quilt blocks while they made the rounds of the farms.

At first, Gabe was not too sure about the plan she proposed. "We don' wan' no troubles," he said. But when she explained that the offer included $3 per trip for loading and transporting the produce every other week plus building repairs on his days off that might total as much as $12 to $15 dollars a month, it did not take him long to figure out that he and his boy could make enough for rent. "I jus' don' wan' no troubles."

"I assure you, there won't be any," she said. "Charlie will lead the way to the farms on Saturday and introduce you to our farmers so they'll be ready for you when you go back in another two weeks. They are from all different backgrounds but very friendly."

When the menfolk returned loaded and ready to return to Montgomery, Lottie took a few minutes to preview some of the building repairs she had in mind. "I will pay by the job, not by the hour. That way we'll both know what to expect, and you can come and go as fits your schedule. The document I gave you and the sign on the truck will identify you as employees of Tyrell Farms. What do you think?"

"Me an' Rudy be mighty grateful fo' da work, Miz Dickson. We jus' don' wan' no troubles."

No troubles came to them. Any of them. Most everyone in the city kept to the proper side of the line. With the extra work, Gabe and his family remained in their home. His friend Nate was not so fortunate. When he lost his job, he moved his family north to Huntsville to live with relatives while he looked for work near a cousin in Chicago.

Gabe and Rudy mastered the finer points of repair and restore by tackling the worst cabin first, figuring they could not hurt it too much. When finished, it was a trim and tidy one-roomer suitable for overnighting when they wanted to work two days in a row without making two round trips.

*

Charlie maintained his peddling schedule until nasty weather set in. He and Nana rigged up a canvas cover to protect both him and his produce until tornado winds and rains forced him and his bike inside. Spring was bleak, but summer and fall overflowed with the rich earth's bounty. They were paying for more produce than they could possibly sell. Time to expand.

"We need another phone line," Charlie announced at breakfast.

"What on earth for? We hardly use the one we have now."

"I'm planning to buy another bike and hire a rider for it."

"What on earth for?"

"I'm way too busy now and fall term begins in a month. There's plenty of work for another boy and plenty of boys who need it."

"Sounds reasonable, but the phone?"

"If I'm going into business and will have an employee, I need to be able to communicate over schedules and pick-ups and such. I want to buy another bike, hire Gabe to fix it and hire Rudy to ride it."

"Why Rudy? Why not one of your school friends?"

"Because we aren't treating both sides of the line equal. You made me promise not to cross 'the line' for anything... even for the best ice cream ever... and I know you're right even if lines aren't right. There are loads of people over there besides Gabe's neighborhood who'd love to get a melon or a pumpkin for a penny, and they deserve it as much as anyone else."

"You're right about that. There's plenty of need all over the city."

"And we can't keep meeting in the basement or the parking lot of the courthouse. It's dangerous for you and Gabe, so we need another way to communicate."

Charlie put his plan in motion. He bought the bike, hired Gabe to fix it and Rudy to ride it. Gabe got a phone for "work." (His wife loved that.) A produce run to the farms was rescheduled to occur weekly. The two boys became partners, sharing the work and the profits. In a small way, life was good.

Early the following summer when berries started coming on, Charlie discovered another moneymaker. Church. Or rather, after church. He still donated a great deal to the food program there and was unloading one Sunday as church ended. A few of the womenfolk stopped on the way out to look and to smell. They asked if they could buy some of his beautiful strawberries for Sunday dinner. He thought, *why not?* He offered them at two cups for five pennies, more than twice his regular price. The women were tickled to get such a bargain; less than at the markets that were closed on Sunday, and his were soooo fresh.

"Nana, was that sinful of me to charge those ladies more?"

"Hmm... No... Think of it this way. You provided an opportunity for them to spread their generosity to the less fortunate. Lots of folks want to help those who are desperate, but many of them don't know how. They believe that the extra money you make will go toward more food to share, as it will. I'm sure the Good Lord will see it that way."

The following year, the farm garden harvests were bountiful again. During a phone meeting, Rudy suggested another bike and rider.

"Nope," Charlie replied. "We'll only ever expand by twos—one black and one white. We have to be fair to both sides of the line."

They agreed to pool enough of their profits to make that happen. New riders would not become partners. They would be paid by the load. Every load would be inventoried on the way out and all pennies accounted for on the way in.

Employees must adhere to three rules: 1)Never cross the color line; stay in your own territory. 2)No fingers in the till or you will lose your job. 3)Always carry a small pad of paper, a pencil and a damp rag. "If a parent urges a child to beg for a piece of food, direct them to the nearest church. If a child asks for *work* in exchange for food, have him... or her... clean your handlebars or fenders, wipe down your spokes, arrange the fruit in neat rows, draw a picture for your bedroom or a map to somewhere close by, anything. Pay the child two pennies and tell him to buy one piece for himself and another piece to share. Thank him for his business and move on. We don't deal in handouts. We deal in dignity."

During Charlie's high school years, the business took on two more peddlers while he kept his nose to the books. He studied hard in an effort to graduate early just like his papa had. He learned to type and take shorthand just like his papa did. So he could always get a job at the courthouse like his papa planned. Growing up in a household with only a grandmother and a dog, his papa and the judge were his only male role models. Nana was always willing to tell him stories about his papa's imaginative solutions to problems, but figuring out the judge was another matter.

At least one afternoon a week, Charlie reviewed Judge Tyrell's old court cases and judgements—even from the Troy days—to understand his reasoning. "They are better than a legal text," he concluded. "But I have a question. He often says, 'You've told me a truth. Now tell me the whole truth.' What does that mean?"

Lottie thought for a long minute about how to explain the complexity of the judge's favorite phrase. "Supposing a man stops me and Gabe in the parking lot near the truck at the end of a produce run. He says, 'This boy tells me that he works for you. Is that right?' I would say, 'Yes,' and leave it there unless he asks, 'What does he do?' Remember, these are dangerous times, and knowing how people feel about coloreds having good jobs while many whites are unemployed, I would say, 'He works part-time as needed transporting produce from the farms to me here'—not much of a job, but a truth. I am not obliged to tell him every job that we pay Gabe to do for us—a fair amount of money, and the whole truth. To keep us all safe, I choose only what is pertinent to his question. Understand?"

"I think so." But Charlie was not sure he would ever learn when to say what.

Once he entered college, Charlie had little time left for peddling. The city was still in the throes of the Depression, and there was as much need as ever for the business. In a phone meeting with Rudy, the two agreed to replace Charlie with another rider and that he would retain all accounting responsibilities—a task he could keep up with on his bus rides to and from campus. He did continue his Sunday passes by the church.

Law school presented more complications for Charlie's participation in the business. He had no time left for it. Lottie agreed to do the accounting. He and Rudy hired two more riders, and he promoted one of the current ones—Billie, his nemesis from grade school—to manage territory designation and inventory. Shown a little bit of respect for the quality of his work, the boy was turning into a fine fellow. Charlie retired his bike and removed its crate-holder to be used as a replacement if needed. He fixed a secure place to suspend it just inside the back door. That bike belonged to his papa, and he would not dare entrust its use to anyone else.

*

With two and a half years of law school under his belt and the United States' entry into World War II a grim reality, Charlie's holiday tidings were not joyful. In early January, 1942, he announced over dinner that he had enlisted in the Navy, like his papa, before he was drafted. "I have more leverage to use my legal training by volunteering now."

Fearing this day would come, Lottie had done her homework. She gazed across the table at the young man who grew to be so much like his father. He was taller and heftier than Jimmy with broad shoulders, the same thick, wavy brown hair, high cheekbones, set of his jaw when serious, gentle and considerate manner, and her narrow nose and olive skin. Their eyes were a different story. Jimmy's were a misty, indefinite blue. Charlie's were the brilliant blue of his mother Lila, and Lottie stared hard into them now. "You do not have to do this. You should qualify for a deferment as a surviving son."

He had done his homework too. "*May* qualify. Likely because Papa lost his life fighting in the first war. More likely that I would qualify to be retained in the U.S., unless I have a nonhazardous duty overseas."

Her jaw was firm. "Will you? Request to be retained?"

He shook his head. "I made the recruiter an offer: to spare him from the paperwork if he could guarantee me assignment to nonhazardous duty using my legal training. I leave for Norfolk in a couple of weeks for a crash course in military law and the Uniform Code of Military Justice. I should ship out late spring, for where I don't know. I requested Europe since that's where Papa served."

Lottie could not stop herself. Tears rained down and pooled like melting butter on her sweet potatoes. "I love you so much. I can't bear to see you go."

Charlie came around the table to hug her spare sixty-five-year-old frame. "Don't worry, Nana. I'll be just fine. If I can manage a crew of bike peddlers all these years, I ought to be able to handle four guys six years younger than me who get themselves into a bar brawl. You can come visit me soon in Norfolk on weekends and quiz me to see if I'm keeping up with my lessons."

His attempt at humor and his muscular hold did not stem her quaking shoulders. "I love you too, Nana, and I promise I'll stay safe and be home before you know it."

The echo of those words from across the years thundered in her ears.

Within months, Charlie said his goodbyes to his grandmother and waved to the Statue of Liberty from a ship loaded with combat troops and medical units bound for Liverpool, England. As the war stepped up in the European theater, troop and supply ships were at a premium leaving none available for convoy protection from German subs scouring the sea for targets. Safe passage to the British Isles required evasive zig and zag tactics through rough North Atlantic waters. Unlike most of his companions, Charlie spent this time on deck inviting the turbulence to recreate his papa's last days and nights for his own memory.

Thick Liverpool fog provided a ghostly welcome for the sea-weary troops. As an augmentee attached to the Auxiliary Security Force responsible for order and disciple of troops onshore, Charlie felt obliged to follow the revelry of boys far away from home for the first time. They had reason to celebrate; their passage had been a safe one. Not all transport ships were so lucky. For Charlie, the festivities foretold his future duties—to discourage the whites, blacks, browns and any other group that was different from killing one another long before they met the enemy on the battlefield. He was not so far away from home after all.

Much later, he found his quarters and unpacked his footlocker, his wardrobe for the next months and maybe years. At the very bottom he found an item he had not packed, barely the size of a sheet of paper. One colorful quilt block, completed with a single layer of flannel inside, bore the intricately embroidered images of a boy and his faithful furry friend asleep together on a pile of blankets on the floor, with every detail of his bedroom just so. He pressed the square to his face and inhaled the scent of his dear departed Harley and home... and wept.

Armed with the philosophy that prevention was preferable to correction, Charlie became known as the guy who applied homestyle persuasion to keep boys out of the brig long enough to travel to the front with his mates. He frequented the popular pubs nearby as soon as a troop ship docked and greeted some with "Welcome. Welcome. Don't do anything you can't write your mama about." He scanned the groups for troublemakers and enlisted their friends to, "Keep your buddy out of trouble tonight, or he won't be around to have your back tomorrow."

If he ended up with combatants in his office, he sat them down on a bench barely big enough for two, allowed them time to become uncomfortable, and then passed a plate of snacks to one. If that boy grabbed an edible first, he reminded him that "At home we have manners enough to pass to our friends before we feed ourselves." Invariably the reply was, "He ain't no friend of mine!" to which Charlie said, "He better become one if you want to get out of here before morning."

Then he took the eats away and ordered, "Get acquainted. Find things you have in common. Talk about ice cream, baseball, I don't care. When I hear a civil conversation between two adults, *maybe* I'll let you go without turning you in to the higher powers for a longer stay in beautiful Liverpool."

For a long time the only sound in the room would be the turning of pages in the book Charlie read. In most cases, one of the boys would eventually break the ice with a question and a real conversation would ensue. When their penance was satisfied, he offered snacks again. Each enlistee deferred to the other. "Shake hands and get out of here," he smiled. Lesson complete.

Many times over the following months when Charlie waited for an incoming ship to dock, he crossed paths again with some of the same boys now on stretchers waiting to board a different ship for the trip back home. A few hailed him over for a moment of "civil conversation" with a friendly face. He made a point to leave them smiling.

These incidents sparked his curiosity. Where were these wounded coming from? The front, obviously. But where in Liverpool? Inquiries unearthed the 157th General Hospital just across the River Mersey. One off-duty afternoon he turned up to case the place and found a large building with multiple floors and dozens of wounded on each. Just as the reality of need in the depths of the Depression was more than one boy could satisfy, the sheer numbers of soldiers hurting was more than one man could attend to. He made a decision on the spot to confine his ministrations to Alabama boys from Pike and Montgomery counties first and then to others as his time allowed.

Charlie approached the first nurses station he could find to request a list of soldiers from Alabama and came face-to-face, eye-to-eye and smile-to-smile with the prettiest little lady he had seen since college. "Who's askin'?" she replied in the softest southern drawl he had heard since leaving home.

"Just Charlie. I don't have any flowers, but I'd like to give some of the home boys a little company and cheer."

"Black or white?"

"No matter. They're all the same to me."

"Are you a chaplain or somethin'?"

"More like a behavior counselor." He watched her bronze curls bounce as she flipped through admittance records.

"Well, Just Charlie. Looks like we have two on the third floor, east wing, and two on third west, for you to go behave with." There was that honeyed smile again.

Charlie thanked the young nurse and headed for the stairs. Smitten was never a word he would choose to describe himself, but at that moment it was the perfect one.

Over many months Charlie visited the General Hospital as often as he could. This required shelling out for a second-hand bicycle—one he fine-tuned from years of experience—to speed along back streets of the city and across the river, his trench coat flapping in the breeze. "His boys" perked up when he ambled toward them with goodies in his pocket straight from his gramma's kitchen. Her caramel cake and pralines were the favorites. Together Charlie and the boys shared memories of home, told stories of childish pranks, laughed a little, shed a tear now and then, and finished off with his reading to them from the free paperbacks the government shipped to troops overseas.

The soldiers liked mysteries, westerns and romantic relationships best from noted authors such as Agatha Christie, Raymond Chandler, Zane Grey, Steinbeck, and Fitzgerald. If a patient were in particularly bad shape, Charlie finished off with some soothing poetry. By the end of his tour, he lost track of how many times he had read *A Tree Grows in Brooklyn* to his boys.

He frequently met up with them again at the docks when they were well enough to travel home. He waved to the ones who were able to wave back and saluted respectfully to the Alabama boys traveling in a box. When he took on this personal mission to bring a little "home" to lonesome, wounded boys, he quickly realized the importance of bringing a little bit of the boy back to his home. As the numbers of dying soldiers increased, so did his visits to them. In their final hours he sat with them, held their hands, soothed them with songs of home, recited poetry or passages from the Good Book, and bore witness to their passing.

He accompanied the bodies to the temporary mortuary in the dock's warehouse complex and their coffins, to the docks for shipping home. Not all the fallen were so lucky to return to home soil, but for those who were, Charlie vowed to contact the families of his Alabama boys personally to share with them any details, words or wishes their loved one voiced during his final days—a solace his grandmother never had since her son's body never returned home.

After his experiences with the wounded and dying, Charlie understood at gut-level Judge Tyrell's lesson regarding the facets of truth: Do not lie, but consider truth carefully. There's the right time for *a* truth and a right time for the *whole* truth. Choose your truths wisely.

Charlie agonized over such choices. When his grandmother wrote to ask about his leave in Scotland, should he tell her that it included hiring a boat to take him to the area where his papa's ship was lost at sea because he longed to peer down through the clear, icy waters to imagine his papa's final resting place? How does he reply to a colored soldier who has experienced some freedoms during his tour when he asks if conditions have changed at home? What should he say to a dying soldier who asks if he will be home for Christmas?

When Charlie was discharged from the Navy, besides his official documents he carried with him two certainties:

His legal specialty would focus on helping adolescents and young men to stay on the right side of the law.

That pretty little nurse from the 157th would be his wedded wife until death parted them.

*

Lottie gazed down the aisle at the young couple so well suited for one another and so obviously in lasting love. Remembering the tragic result of her inability to reveal to her son Jimmy the truth of his ancestry at an appropriate time, she vowed not to keep her secret any longer. But every opportunity she found to broach that truth with her grandson and his fiancée evaporated in their happiness.

She considered her options carefully, her last chance to save this perfect match from a lifetime of illegitimacy. According to state law, the one-drop rule was still in effect and interracial marriage was illegal. Happiness or truth?

When the preacher bid the congregation, "If any man here has just cause why this couple may not be joined in Holy Matrimony, may he speak now or forever hold his peace," Lottie hesitated. She knew the law. She chose to define terms literally. She was a woman, not a man, and therefore not obliged to answer this command. She bit her tongue and chose happiness *and a* truth.

*

On this beautiful spring day, Charlie reset the wooden stake that bore his father's name. Until James Charles Dickson's body was buried there, his grandmother was not allowed to set a stone next to her own future grave. She died holding onto the hope that someday he would be found and returned to her. She made her grandson promise that he would maintain and replace a name stake until that expectation was fulfilled.

As manager of Tyrell Farms now that his grandmother was ten years passed, Charlie made frequent trips to the Banks area to touch base with the farmers there. He always found time on his way home to stop by the judge's grave near Banks and Lottie's here to show his gratitude for the lessons he learned from them, the gifts they gave him and the opportunities they made possible.

He leaned down to plant a kiss on the headstone and a flower at its base. "I love you, Nana," he said, and returned to his car. He was about to get in when a small party of a hearse and two vehicles passed him and pulled to the side of the roadway in front of him. The mourners appeared unremarkable except for the woman with her face pressed against the rear side window. Her pallor was in stark contrast to her brilliant, yet forlorn, blue eyes. For one gooseflesh moment they stared deeply into his. The cortege came to a standstill. Charlie got into his car and pulled out to head for Montgomery and home.

192

2008

Apprehension. I feel it in every finger gripping the steering wheel and every toe pushing on the gas pedal. I feel it in my gut and the pounding of my heart. Is Charlie still alive? Will he meet me at the cemetery? If not, how will I handle his absence? Why am I so fraught over the condition of a man I barely know but whose acquaintance I value so greatly?

Negotiating security at the LA airport was a major obstacle in my previously effortless flights east—all that crazy business with plastic bags for liquids and removing this and that near down to my underwear. Really? Does an eighty-four year old, white-haired woman with arthritis look like a threat? The "carryon-compatible, canvas-seated, collapsible walking stick" the kids gave me to keep me from tiring or falling and breaking a bone caused all kinds of hassle when four agents could not collapse that nudnick stick to inspect its empty tubings.

I scold myself. If I have learned one thing from Charlie, it is to be grateful for simple things in life like this sunny day—not too hot, not too humid—light traffic, relative mobility, my children's best intentions, and the expectation of peach ice cream at my visit's end.

I find the once yellow, then blue, and now a shocking shade of violet house marking the turn to the cemetery. The road appears unused since my last visit. The graveyard, too, seems a forgotten place. No other cars are parked along the road. I approach the gravesites slowly. No new headstone sits between my mother's and Charlie's grandmother's plots. Only a faded name stake slants toward Lottie, signaling that her son has not yet been found. I stoop to brush away dried leaves and tidy her spot. "Where is your grandson, Lottie?" I ask her. "Where is Charlie? If this is the end to our abridged acquaintance, I want, at least, to pay my respects."

No rustle of leaves or chirp of feathered friend whispers in my ear, but the low hum of buzzing insects is interrupted by the sudden sound of a slamming car door and the crunch of hurried steps along the far end of the gravel path. I turn quickly in hopes that I will see… but I do not. The man is younger than Charlie—late fifties/early sixties—with a full head of wavy, dark brown hair barely showing a distinguished gray through the temples. His overly broad shoulders seem out of proportion to his otherwise tall, slim build.

I follow his frantic progress up one path and down another until he stops abruptly, beats his forehead with his fists, and calls out in frustration, "Where are you!"

I approach him but maintain a safe distance. "Can I help you? I know most of the folks here." I do—their names, at least, and some of their stories—from strolls around the grounds with Charlie.

"I know where I'm supposed to be, but I can't find the place. Everything looks different. The last time I was here years ago...."

"Yes. Trees grow taller and extend their branches. Bushes swell to block the paths and cover nearby graves. New perennials spread their roots to add color to neglected places. But stones generally don't move by themselves. Who are you looking for? The name."

"Dickson. Lottie Dickson."

My heart stops. I cannot catch my breath. My limbs freeze in place, like a tree's, with my feet rooted to the ground. My greatest fear is on the verge of becoming reality, and I am not prepared. My voice wants to ask but my ears do not want to hear the answer. My mind chooses an alternate route. "Skip?"

The man startles at hearing his nickname. "Do I know you?"

"No. But I know many stories about you. Your father...."

He instantly displays the look of someone who just swallowed a gnat. "You... You couldn't be! Are you that... *that* woman?" he asks, stepping toward me.

"I don't know. What woman were you expecting? Not an advanced senior citizen, I gather. Your father...."

"Pops made me promise to meet up with the woman who comes to decorate graves with him."

"Your father....?"

"All these years the family thought he told stories about some woman and her children so that we wouldn't bother him about going to the graveyard on his birthday. But you are real!"

"Your father...?"

"Wait 'til I tell my sister. She probably won't believe me either."

I am the one who is agitated now. I must hear the words I hoped I never would. I shout out like a frustrated parent. "Skip! Stop! Tell me about your father. Is he...?"

Taken aback by my sudden outburst, he straightens quickly to apologize. "I'm sorry. Pops would have my head for not greeting you properly. Welcome. I am his designated stand-in for today. My orders are to secure your promise to return for his 100th birthday."

At last, I can breathe again. Charlie is still alive! But the chances of our reuniting here in ten more years are next to zero. "I will, if he will too," I smile. "I'm disappointed he couldn't make it today. Can you tell me where he is?"

"In the hospital."

My face drains to the color of the gravel path. "Oh dear. Serious?"

"Yes and no. He broke his hip. A few days ago, he received a letter from the Department of Defense informing him that the wreckage of his father's ship had been discovered in the North Atlantic. Pops was so excited to telephone us that he slipped running up the porch steps, fell and crashed back down. Prognosis for recovery from surgery is fair. Toll on his overall physical well being, guarded. He is ninety, you know."

"Yes, I am well aware of our ages. Your father is such a kind and considerate man that it saddens me to imagine him suffering in any way. What can I do to help?"

"Promise... sincerely... that you will come for his 100th. He wants so much to see you again."

I take a minute to consider my response, then dig in my bag for a pen. I reach for his hand. "May I?"

He nods with a we-aren't-teenagers-but-oh-well-humor-the-old-lady look.

I write in his palm: *3652 days. Here. Janie* "Will that do?"

Skip laughs, like his father. "He'll believe me for sure now. I couldn't fake such a clever reply. Is that your name? Janie? Pops always referred to you as 'my friend.'"

"It's an old nickname, and only he knows it and uses it. You have your proof positive. Let's go find your great grandmother's grave. I'm sure it's right where you left it the last time you were here."

Skip chuckles under his breath and dutifully follows me along the path. We arrive at the very familiar plots where I reintroduce him to his relatives. "The one on the far right is your great grandmother Lottie, as you may remember. The empty space next to her is for your grandfather Jimmy. I'm glad to see a name stake still here. I brought one just in case it was missing. Guess that won't be a problem now that he'll have a headstone soon."

"Soon? Not likely. The Defense Department's letter indicated that it may take years to recover and identify remains. Yesterday Pops provided a DNA sample for forensic analysis, and we all have our fingers crossed that they'll find a match sooner rather than later."

"I'm sure they will," I say with as much conviction as I can muster, and hope for Charlie's sake that they do. "In front of me is my mother Lila, and next to her lie her parents. All I know about them is what's written on their headstones, so don't bother asking. Why don't you take a few minutes to reacquaint while I begin unloading the car."

Skip thrusts one hand into his pocket and the other claps his forehead in frustration. "I can't believe it! Pops'll kill me! I forgot to pick up flowers!"

"Not to worry. I brought plenty to share in case... just in case." I take my time loading up with super large soda cups and jugs of water, then tiptoe back along the path and set them down before reaching the sites to avoid disturbing Skip's private thoughts, as his father so kindly did for me.

I return to the car, clutch my nuisance stick under an arm and juggle bunches of flowers the best I can. When I turn back toward the graveyard, I find myself nose-to-chest with a younger Charlie.

"Let me help, please. It's the least I can do after forgetting everything else today."

He obviously needs to feel useful, so I hand him the whole armload and thank him. We return to the sites, and it becomes obvious that he is new to the decoration business, so I set out the cups, fill them with water and begin to fashion bouquets. "Many nurseries sell potted flowering plants around Memorial Day, but they are difficult to find this time of year. I favor the old fashioned do-it-yourself arrangements. They seem more personal somehow, like you've put thought into what might please your loved ones."

I take up a handful of blossoms and begin. He watches and then follows my lead. "Your father prefers rosy red and lilac for Lottie. He has never told me why. I always choose bright blue ones to match my mother's eyes. Jimmy gets whatever looks like a guy. Suit yourself. There's plenty to choose from. Whatever is left over we usually share with the neighbors, as your father calls them."

Charlie used walk-and-talk therapy on me when I seemed upset, so I try the same on his son and suggest we take a turn around the grounds. "Tell me something about yourself, Skip. Do you work at the courthouse too?"

He nods. "I followed in Pops' footsteps. He always told me and trained me to help those who can't do for themselves and good will come back to us. I didn't realize that "good" equated to "votes" sometimes. He served as a juvenile court judge for several years before he was elected as District Judge. He was reelected several times until well into his seventies when he retired and passed his good name and voter support on to me."

"Charlie is a judge? He never told me." My quivering hands can barely cover my scarlet-splotched face. "I'm so embarrassed to have wasted his time with tears and trivialities when he undoubtedly had more important affairs to tend to."

"Don't be. Your visits energized him and entertained the rest of our family with stories he could share. Once you are a guardian of the law, about the only safe conversational topics are sports and the weather. A tap dancing friend made a pleasant digression."

I flush again. "He said once that he worked at the courthouse, but I assumed he was a clerk of some sort."

"That's the way he wanted it. He learned more about a person when he was 'just Charlie.' He never wanted to be judged as a judge first, but as ordinary folk with ordinary thoughts and ordinary problems like everybody else. The 'Charlie' bit was his way to tell the truth, without revealing the whole truth."

We continue our walkabout, placing a dash of color here and there, with me pointing out inhabitants his father found particularly interesting. We stop by the oldest grave from the 1850s for a young boy of four, his name scratched into a large stone. No other family members lie near him.

Further along, the most recently interred in 1971, a young serviceman of twenty rests near grandparents. An unspoken "Vietnam" passes between us.

I turn us away to say, "Charlie shared how you and your wife met, but by the time I returned we moved on to other topics."

"Yes, ma'am. That was quite a time. We wanted to get married, but the law and society were not on our side. When the Vietnam draft lottery loomed before us, Pops stepped in with a very heavy foot. 'Given who you love, these troubled times, and where you live,' he said, 'the most judicious course of action for you right now is to study to become a civil rights attorney. Finish your pre law with stellar grades and secure a place in law school until we know the outcome of the first lottery.'

"I asked about football. Pops shook his head. 'No stadium. Choose operating room or courtroom.' He surmised that a background in medicine or law would keep me closer to home and out of war zones as expertise in those fields was in demand. 'But my duty to country....'"

Skip notices me lagging behind and slows his pace, but he seems to enjoy recounting old memories and mimicking his father. "'Remember. Don't break the law. Use it,' Pops said. 'If called, you jump the gun and enlist so you can choose your branch and duty, but you can also serve your country equally as well from your community and your state in the battles for equality right here at home, and there will be many. My advice? Be smart. Stay a step ahead. Prepare for both possible outcomes with one major preferred concentration—the old "two birds" adage. But of course, the final decision is yours.' I remember there being a long silence while Mom looked on. Then Pops said, 'Tell you what. If this country needs another James Charles Dickson in uniform, I'll take your place. But you better hurry up. I'm not getting any younger.'"

I recognize so much of his father in Skip, the manner and tone I have enjoyed over the last forty years.

Skip continues his remembrance of those times. "I asked him how we could possibly afford law school then, and he said he would tap into Judge Tyrell's beneficence fund, as he called it. The man probably never imagined there would be a James Charles Dickson, I, II, and Skip III to educate, but the way it was set up, we all qualified."

"Did your father really follow through? Sign up again? I don't remember any stories about his recent time in the military."

"His word is his bond—always. The day I was accepted into law school, he took me with him to sign up for a two-year stint. Highly irregular, he was told, because of his age but his expertise in the law was in high demand, so they would figure out a way to approve his request."

I shake my head. "I can hear Charlie now charming his way into any position he has a mind to."

Skip chuckles. "Of course he did. He practically dictated his own terms, but boy, did my pops work his tail off. He had to cut back on about half of his cases and keep his bags packed for those two years. Pops became a Selective Service adjunct assigned to the southeastern district to review claims for exemptions, deferments, and postponements from military service. As such, he investigated irregularities in appeal boards' approvals and denials in an effort to reduce the number of appeals submitted and granted. That involved a lot of paperwork, a lot of travel, and a lot of uncomfortable conversations with upset parents, boys, and draft board members playing favorites or not doing their jobs."

Skip's face breaks into an admiring smile. "Pops had a real knack for spotting forged Guard and Reserve papers that showed a boy 'already enlisted' when he wasn't, and his blue-eyed stare could read a person's mind before he ever had the thought. In the end, his gift for creative persuasion swayed many young men to choose voluntary enlistment or alternative service to our country rather than evasion or prison."

I smile too. Charlie does have a special ability to read people... me in particular. "Do you remember your lottery number? My son's was 315 with initial S#17."

"Wow! That was something. I don't think anyone above 300 was called, at least not around here. I was a 283 with initial D#21, and they didn't call close to me either. I guess we both lucked out. Pops survived his two years, but as soon as he was released, Mom volunteered at the VA Medical Center near home. She wasn't about to let him do her one better. A few years later their service turned into votes, and a crackerjack juvenile court judge became District Judge Dickson."

We continue our stroll and come upon a cluster of graves for only one or two generations in each family, all within a similar range of ages. I try to explain Charlie's theory to his son—that they were all part of a strict evangelical sect that centered their proselytizing in the surrounding area in the early 1900s. Pirdle is the only name I recognize, but I cannot remember why. Then I point just beyond to our own small cluster and the end of our tour. I place my last two flowers on my grandparents' graves.

"We do have a history of extremist groups causing trouble in parts of the state," Skip admits.

"How did your family react to the cross burning on your lawn?" I ask.

Skip's face turns chalk-white. "What cross burning? The truth. Remember, I'm a judge too."

Under orders, I give him my best rendition of Charlie's storytelling but fall a little short in facial expression and delightfulness.

"You're kidding. Pops never told us. I remember coming home to a flower garden in the middle of the front yard. Mom was exasperated with him. 'Why would you put such a crazy fool thing in the middle of my beautiful lawn?' she scolded. Come to think of it, I do remember Pops' reply. 'Some secrets aren't for you or the children to know.' She passed several years ago."

I nod. "Your father told me. When I last saw him, the depth of his loss was very evident."

"Still is." He gazes at the empty plot awaiting either his father or grandfather.

To divert Skip's attention from his worries, I expand on my previous tale. Charlie attributed the adolescents' shenanigans to remarks they overheard at their parents' dinner tables criticizing his response to the year-long bus boycott following Rosa Parks's brave refusal to move. None of them knew for certain, but they suspected that he was behind a group that purchased second-hand cars, tuned them up and sold them for $1 to both black and white drivers who agreed to chauffeur workers to jobs for the standard bus fare so they did not have to ride a bus. "That peaceful protest was one of the opening salvos of the civil rights movement, your father told me, and he hinted that he might have one of those cars stashed in a shed at the farms, along with a charred piece of crossbeam and other souvenirs from his projects."

Skip is stunned. "How is it that you know more about Pops than we do?"

"Probably because I'm no threat. His words won't come back to haunt him when he's just Charlie and I'm just folks from far away."

"Come to think of it, Pops often used unconventional means to obtain his objectives for whatever catastrophe befell the community that supported him, as well as during his draft board service. I remember handing out pencils near voter registrations to those who would have been turned away if they didn't provide their own. He attended every peace march and demonstration I did peddling a dinosaur of a bicycle with an old handcart rigged up to its rear carrying first aid supplies, water and usually a bushel of apples. 'Gotta remain neutral,' he'd say, but he sure kept his eyes on us."

Skip checks the note written on his hand and traces the numbers. "Hurricanes and floods were the worst. As soon as it was safe, he'd show up with a small trailer, or later an old dump of a motor home, and load the whole family to visit the hardest-hit towns around here. He'd set up an aid station and folks would flock to us for help with replacing lost documentation, interpreting federal forms and filling out paperwork. He didn't want any of 'his folks' signing papers they didn't understand."

He shakes his head slowly. "Katrina in '05 was a real disaster. The devastation and the lines of folks needing help and comfort never ended... and Mom wasn't there by his side. That's what wore him out—the weather and the work, and then pneumonia. We've seen a steady decline in him since. He keeps referring to 'shuffling off, and then it will be up to your sister and you.'"

"Ah. The grand bargain he and your mother made before she died."

"You know about that too?"

"Yes. He told me the last time I was here."

"So, you understand my problem... our problem. If my grandfather is not found soon... What would you do?"

"You're asking me, a perfect stranger, for advice? I have no right to give it."

"Please. You know Pops in ways we don't."

I hate to admit that I am tiring, but I open the canvas seat on my walking stick to try it out. "Your father's love is with your mother. His loyalty lies with Lottie. And he cannot choose between them. He won't. He is afraid he will dishonor his grandmother—and the only history he has—if he leaves her. So... the obvious solution to me is that you show him... demonstrate that she will not be forgotten... that she plays an important role in how you have been raised and how you raise your own children."

"Demonstrate?"

"You are obviously a learned man. Have you not considered other options? As Lottie's friend Judge Tyrell would say, 'Don't break the law. Use it.' Find out if the old 'You can't erect a headstone if there's no dead body' is still being enforced. If it is, apply for an exemption. If not, place a stone and problem solved."

Skip actually seems interested in what I am suggesting. He sits on the ground facing me and borrows one of Jimmy's daisies to sniff, but begins to pluck its petals.

"If that doesn't work, try going the memorial route," I offer. "Apply to place a stone on property you own within the cemetery 'in remembrance of James Charles Dickson and his service to his country in the Great War' with no dates or mention of 'dead and buried' since the fact that there is no body seems to be the hang-up. A memorial can always be taken down or moved to another location later when remains are finally returned. Your father's yard. Tyrell Farms where Jimmy was born. Once you come up with an approved workaround, *then* involve your father. Knowing what will come to pass at a time of *his* choosing—either before or after his death—may give him the freedom to make the choice he doesn't want to face now."

"Why is being here with Lottie such a big deal? Dee will never understand."

I teeter on my seat. "How often do you two come here with your father?"

"Not since we were kids."

"There's the heart of the problem. You drew up a legal agreement for disposition of remains. I'm guessing it did not include the whys, *why* there was an issue to be resolved in the first place. Your mother was very sensitive to your father's needs. Your parents' agreement was her way of giving him permission to choose between the past and the present."

He reaches for another daisy. "How so?"

"Charlie's conundrum is a question of legacy—Lottie's, Jimmy's, his own and yours. A person's heritage is not only money, property and sometimes debts, but also his ancestry—physical traits, family history, belief systems and talents, as you know.

"There is an old saying that a person is not truly dead until no one living has memory of him. Your father doesn't want his grandmother to be forgotten. He owes his life and the man he has become to her. Frankly, you and your sister do too. And to the father he never knew. If he felt that you had an interest in his history and would keep it alive, he would feel free to follow his heart and you wouldn't be saddled with that decision."

"But how? Do we gather around his hospital bed and ask him to 'tell us the whole truth?'" He tucks a half-denuded stem behind his ear.

I smile at his attempt to lighten up. "Not the best plan. Baby steps. For example, suppose that in a month you and your sister suggest driving him down here to do his 'gratituding' since he missed his birthday trip. Bring folding chairs and flowers, cup cakes and ice cream, and ask him questions about when he was a kid. Get him talking about Lottie. Sometime later in the fall, you, Dee and a couple of your grandchildren might invite him along for a drive to the farms for some contrived purpose and inspect that shed I told you about. That's got to be a treasure trove of stories. Pick some fruit to take home and rave over how much better it is than what you find in the stores these days. He'll have stories to share about that too."

Skip folds his arms and studies the ground, but his head nods as the wheels begin to turn.

"Recognize how important these birthday rituals are for him. Encourage him to continue and include more family. Move his birthday picnics here. Maybe visit this cemetery three or four times a year with different children and grandchildren. Stop at Maxine's for a meal. Ask him questions. Take an interest. Make this roundtrip a regular outing. Include more youngsters as time goes on. Let him hear you say to your grandchildren 'When Pops was your age, do you know what he did?' so he understands that his and Lottie's histories are in good hands."

We both stand up and stretch. Skip brushes off his pants and diffuses the pile of plant matter mounded at his feet. "How can you see so many solutions to *our* problem?"

"I've had lots of practice. Since my mother's death forty years ago, I've had so many questions I wish I'd asked about her life. So much about her is a mystery to me. I'm haunted almost daily by the thought that if, as an adult, I had taken more time.... Charlie wants to leave this earth knowing that his presence on it was worth the efforts of those who came before him, even if he never felt their hugs. You need to show him that it was... very much so... and that Lottie's legacy and his 'gratitudes' are as important to you as they are to him."

I take a deep breath before closing with, "My opinion, with all due respect, Your Honor."

Skip tries to summon a smile but is obviously shaken and wipes his eyes with the palms of his hands. His quavering voice emits an almost inaudible "I'm sure gonna miss that man."

I stroke his back gently. "Sounds like you need a hug. I'll be your surrogate auntie if you'd like."

Instantly he grabs me in a teddy bear hold so tight that I can barely breathe, with my feet dangling above the ground and my arms flapping at his sides. The emotions of the last few days, and the uncertainty to come, breach the dam in a flood of sobs, drenching both of us.

It seems natural for me to join him, so I do. When he begins to calm, I try to assure him that Charlie will be fine. He will rally now that he has a reason. He has to be here when his father returns home. Jimmy would expect to find him waiting.

Finally, I'm released and my feet touch ground again. We both dig for handkerchiefs and attempt to right ourselves.

"I'm so sorry," Skip blubbers. "I don't know what got into me. I'm acting like a child."

"Because you are one today. You are your father's son and you are afraid you will lose him. You will... one day... but not today or tomorrow. Not for another ten years at least. Keeping his hope alive will keep *him* alive."

Skip nods and tries to smile. "Thank you for being here today. I can't tell you how much I needed your company. And counsel for the counselor."

"My pleasure," I say, and try to fold my seat back into its stick and collapse it, but I am all gnarled thumbs.

Skip gives it a try with about as much success. Pretty soon we are engulfed in giggles and give up, each of us taking an end of my carryon-compatible contraption to haul to my car. "I have to admit that I'm a little jealous of Pops," he says. "I wish I had an imaginary friend like you. I'd adopt you and take you home with me if I could."

I wait for the upper half of my face to unstartle. "An interesting idea, but I have a more pragmatic one. Let's choose a few flowers from each of these arrangements to make a small bouquet for your father as evidence that you followed through with your obligation. Call him now and tell him you'll be a little late getting back because the *two of us* are going to Maxine's for some peach ice cream."

"Lottie's secret remedy to chase the glums away!" we laugh in unison.

DEEP SECRETS

Nicholas Bray, a lanky guy who wore his sandy hair with the windswept look of a dust storm survivor, filled his lungs with invigorating sea air. The many months that the Kansas farmboy had spent on digs in Wyoming, Colorado and the Southwest did not do his light skin any favors, so armed with his crisp, new Ph.D and a crate of sunscreen, the eager young man in his late twenties headed for Hawaii and his first real job as a forensic anthropologist.

He entered the nondescript building that he assumed would be his home base for the next couple of years—long enough for him to learn to surf and maybe do some deep sea fishing. For the moment he was anxious to meet his supervisor, checkout the lab, and don white coat, safety glasses and gloves to solve mysteries for American families missing their loved ones from previous wars and conflicts.

Nick followed the signs and peered through the office window at Donald Rouse, a man in his late fifties and well-regarded in the profession, who had worked for the Central Identification Laboratory almost from its establishment. The man sported graying brown hair, barely there on top exposing a rosy scalp to match his ample cheeks. His ears stuck out from his face like single quotes to emphasize his expression, and his glasses rested below the bridge of his nose as he perused a thick file.

At a tap on the window, the man looked up and beckoned the rapper in. "Welcome. Welcome," Don said to the young man whose head nearly reached the top of the doorframe. "You must be Mr. Bray. Been expecting you. Have a seat. Have a seat." He motioned to the one guest chair currently loaded with papers.

Nick glanced at the pile, at the man, and at the pile again.

"No bother. Just stack that on the floor with the rest. I'm getting a head start on research for our newest project."

"Research?" Nick asked. "I thought we'd look *forward* to reuniting families, not backward."

"We do. We do. But every recovery site comes with its own story and this one's a doozy. Forty-five officers and 338 enlisted men minus thirty-seven bodies recovered at the time leaves us 346 missing to identify or list as not recovered/not identified. The latter outcome is not acceptable as far as this department is concerned. If we've identified soldiers as far back as the Civil War, we can surely handle a few hundred from World War I. It'll just take us a while—a long while."

Nick tried to appear attentive but with that potential workload, he was anxious to get started. "How long do you figure?"

"Hard to tell. The wreckage was authenticated only last year. Recovery has begun, but with 400 feet by 60 feet and multiple decks of twisted metal to sift through, that alone will take time. Add to that the strict procedures to ensure the chain of custody in 150 fathoms of rough seas and… well… hard to tell. The new generation of Navy undersea remotely operated vehicles might speed that up some. They'll send us what they can when they can. I hope we'll put a bow on this one before I'm due to retire."

Nick did not dare ask when that might be. Judging from the man's looks, his own two-year plan was out the window.

"Once recovery gets underway, it's our turn. We here are the identification and closure brigade. I've already hired a genealogist to find relatives who might be candidates for DNA comparisons. So far we've located a dozen who provided samples. No parents of course, because we're talking almost 100 years ago. Children, only a few likely for the same reason. We might find a sibling or two who were born later into the family and are still living. Other than that we'll have to make do with grandchildren or greats and cousins a few times removed. A real challenge for us, but doable. The more samples we have will narrow the possibilities for those whose remains are still to be recovered. That'll give us a good start." Don paused. "Want a soda or water?"

Nick shook his head and squirmed a little in his seat.

Don removed a bottle of water from a drawer and thumbed backward through the file on his desk. "How's your history?"

"Okay, I guess. Why?"

"Spanish-American War?"

"Umm. Teddy Roosevelt?"

"Good. Good. This ship whose history we're uncovering was built in the 1890s as a protected cruiser and patrolled the Atlantic coast and Caribbean during the Spanish-American War. Think of that! Just think of that! This lady and her crews defended this country of ours for about twenty-five years with none of the modern instrumentation that our Navy has now. Why, they didn't even have radio communication until after the turn of the century. Come the Great War, she was assigned as a convoy escort, protecting men and supplies from German subs while crossing the Atlantic, and…"

Nick struggled to keep his eyes open. He crossed and uncrossed his legs. This guy was really caught up in his own history lesson.

"…That's where *our* tale begins." Don rose and paced a trail through a maze of file boxes, then turned abruptly to face the young man, his heavy eyebrows arched in amazement. "With geography!" he blurted in a loud whisper.

"Geography?" Nick swallowed a moan.

"That's right. Geography. Think about it. If you're England and France, what do your soldiers need most? That's right. Food. Medicine. Weapons. And where can you find those supplies? That's right. North America. Shipping across the Atlantic is your lifeline. If you're Germany, what do you need most? To *prevent* shipping across all that open water. And how do you accomplish that? Right. *Submarines!*"

"Is that what happened to our ship? Was she torpedoed in the Atlantic by an enemy sub?"

Don chuckled. That reference to *our ship* hinted at Nick's initial buy in to the story. "Nope. Now, to get back to the point. Geography. With submarines, what did Germany need most? Access. Access to the Atlantic, and that she did not have. That country had minimal coastline and few ports along the Baltic and North Seas and only two access routes from there: the English Channel or far north between Scotland and Norway. A third option through the Strait of Gibraltar required a friendly port like Pula across the Adriatic from Venice and navigating the Mediterranean—more risky."

Nick watched the human wind-up toy carom off boxes and slip on files as he navigated the obstacle course on the office floor.

"At the height of the war, before our country was in it," Don continued, "Germany took a bold step to attempt to crush Great Britain's war effort and disrupt her supply chain. Germany declared the Atlantic a *war zone* subject to unrestricted submarine warfare where any and all vessels, including passenger ships, would be *sunk without warning.* Devastating losses of men, material and innocents were suffered before we adopted the 'convoy system' to decrease our own losses. Our ship served admirably and without damage as a convoy escort. She caused a fair amount of destruction to those pesky, swift little U-boats that had to come up for air every few hours, and she didn't lose one of our big ships in the process."

Don felt his way back to his desk to exchange one floppy file for another while Nick struggled to remain alert.

"The British surface-blockaded both the English Channel and the Strait of Gibraltar by intercepting all ships trying to pass through those areas—twenty miles wide each, give or take. Other anti-submarine measures included arming the merchant vessels, forming submarine hunter squadrons, and supplying ship, seaplane and blimp patrols with a *new* weapon—*depth charges!*" Don slapped the file against his desk to bring the young man back to attention. "So the Germans turned to the north route and a deep, 250 mile-wide gap between northern *Scotland and Norway*—too expansive to blockade with the Royal Navy ships and air support available for that purpose. Geography!"

Nick made a valiant attempt to feign interest. "Geography and weather. Cold, stormy seas, I imagine."

"And you would be correct," Don said with a smile. "Now listen up. Listen up. This is where our story gets interesting."

Finally, Nick thought.

"The British devised a new tactic to combat German use of the North Sea passage—not a blockade, but a barricade or a *barrage* as they called it—and they needed our U.S. of A. to help implement an effective *mine-field* scheme. Successful naval mine warfare depends on knowledge of the sea bottom, local tides and currents, and precise navigation, none of which were top-rate ninety years ago. The one thing that tipped the scale in this tactic's favor was *American ingenuity*."

"Mines," Nick interjected. "Was our ship's demise caused by mines?"

"That's what we'll try to figure out. Examination of the wreckage will tell part of the story, and our tests, backed up by our research, should fill in the blanks."

Nick's impatience started to show, so Don activated his wagging finger in the young man's direction.

"When pressed, our boys can develop a better ship, a better tank, a better torpedo. In this case, it was a better mine. Up to that time, mines were activated by contact only. Either a depth charge hit a sub, or a sub ran into a mine. Our boys developed an *antenna mine*, one with a gadget on top that activated when a sub or any vessel came within 100 feet of it, greatly expanding its sphere of destruction. The plan was to lay these *never combat-tested mines* in three horizontal and parallel paths spanning the passage to open sea—one set's depth was for surface traffic, one targeted for submarine traffic, and another even deeper just in case."

"Lay mines at different but specific depths?" Nick asked. "How does that work with the sea floor uneven and subs near the surface?"

"Stick with me here. Stick with me. 'Laid' is a confusing term when it comes to mining the sea. Makes it sound like the *mines* are planted on the seabed, but that is not so. The water is too deep. Maximum submarine depth at that time was about 200 feet and the seas were 900. The barrage mines were anchored to the sea floor by 800 pound cube-shaped steel boxes with wheels for loading and unloading transport ships. A mine was attached to its anchor box by a steel cable set for a desired depth. Once laid, the mine floated above its anchor, and its sensitive antenna was released. There was a safety feature—salt pellets that dissolved more slowly in seawater, allowing a twenty-minute window for the mine-laying vessel to move out of range before the antenna system was operational."

Don's ears entered the conversation, wiggling to accentuate the exasperation on his face. "Salt pellets. Can you imagine that? *Salt pellets!* The only thing between a boatload of boys and the briny deep! Of course, there were other hazards as well. Rough seas. Strong winds. Dangerous currents in frigid water. Poor visibility due to thick fog that could slip in when a guy blinked. Frequent, sudden storms that caused a ship to pitch or roll beyond its tipping point. Mine-laying at night to avoid detection by enemy reconnaissance subs or planes. And the obvious— premature explosions of mines loaded with 300 pounds of TNT that triggered unexpectedly from 1) breaking free of their mooring cables, 2) malfunctioning of those 'fancy' safety switches, or 3) being set too close to one another causing a chain reaction and Fourth of July fireworks twenty fathoms down."

"So, what was it? Why did she go down?" Nick asked, now truly interested.

Don shook his head and shrugged. "Long story short, by completion of the blockade with more than 70,000 of those antenna mines laid, the 'Northern Barrage' was hailed post-war as one of our Navy's largest operations in World War I, now barely mentioned in the history books. And that's where our lady sails in… and out. She was the *first* minelayer to go down. It's our job to help solve the mystery of *why* and return as many of those boys to their families as possible."

Long story short? Nick thought. *There's more?*

"That's enough background for today. Take some of these files with you to look over tonight. We have lots of research ahead of us before we get to the real work." Don picked up an empty cardboard box, tossed files willy-nilly into it until it was nearly full, and handed it over to the young man.

"Thanks," Nick said. "I will." *There goes my walk on the beach tonight,* he thought and turned toward the door.

"Not so fast, my boy. We want a schematic of the ship on this wall." Don marched to a position opposite the window that framed a coastal view and spanned his arms across the blank wall. "Right here. A big one. We want to know where every man should have been at the time of the initial incident. That will help identify remains when documentation tells us where they were found. We'll study every man's record, military and otherwise, to get to know these guys as well as they knew themselves. By the end of our vicarious voyage with these fellows, we'll have revealed secrets like an uncle who's really a father or a wife who's really a first cousin once-removed. Deep secrets. The ones below the surface where you can't see them, whether they're buried in the ground or at the bottom of the sea. The ones that were meant never to be discovered. But we're sure gonna try."

Don gave the young man another pat on the back and ushered him out the door with his box of homework. He grinned. He would discover sooner rather than later if his new partner's passion was for science or the surf.

*

Nick burst through the office door out of breath and dropped his box of files to the floor. His eyes betrayed his excitement before his words could. "When you talked 'deep secrets' yesterday, I assumed you meant the family hanky-panky kind, not the military kind. I turned every page last night and did not find one redacted or stamped 'classified.' I also did not find one public news reference to our ship's sinking. Only a directive to send notification to families that their loved ones had lost their lives at sea in service to their country… weeks *after* the event."

Don tried to hide a smile. "Really?" He continued to mumble an occasional "Hmm" or "You don't say" throughout the young man's animated discourse.

"Did you know that each part for those antenna mines was manufactured in a different plant around the US—more than 400 hundred of them—so no one could identify the end product? And that the mines weren't assembled until they reached Inverness, Scotland, by ship and then rail, to prevent development of this new device from leaking to the enemy? That radio transmissions were forbidden during nighttime mine-laying? That *after* our ship went down, the Navy halted mine-laying until it performed more tests with antenna mines for sphere of impact in… can you believe it… Loch Ness? And *then* readjusted the plan for depth and distance apart? Must have blown that monster to pieces."

I did. I did. I did. I did. I did.

"If all that doesn't point to a 'secret operation', then I don't know what does. Seems like our boys were the trial subjects, and we got the PG version of the test results."

Don gave his new partner a hearty pat on the back. "Well done. Well done. What say we take a break to check out that lab you're so anxious to get into? Then I'll walk you to a 'secret' eatery down the way. After lunch we'll get started downloading all the enlistment and operation files available and set up our own 'Recovered' spreadsheets. How does that sound?"

"Great!" He hesitated. "But dare I ask how soon we can expect the first remains to arrive?"

"You can ask, but I can't tell. Could be a few weeks, months… longer."

"What do we do in the meantime? Research?"

Don chuckled. "I know you're anxious to get to the 'real' work, so tomorrow we'll make our way through a simple case that should be here by then. Korean War. Crash site in China. One jet fighter. Human remains. One dog tag. Family DNA already on file. Should be a straightforward verification. You'll perform all the tests and prepare our forensic analysis while I reorganize this mess. I can't stand the darn clutter!" He kicked a couple of boxes. "I'll restack them in a section of the storage room that I've labeled and dedicated to this 'barrage' case."

Nick flushed at his new boss's successful ploy to size him up.

"Expect me to check and double-check your work. Old habit. Then I'll tell you the *whole* jet fighter's story. How does that sound?"

"I can't wait!" Nick said and threw his long arms wide to push open the double doors to a sparkling lab and his life for the foreseeable future.

2010

"Hey, Nick. I just got notice that the salvage crew is moving to a site in the south for the winter. The North Atlantic is too rough and cold now to make much progress, so recovery will resume in spring. Why don't you tally up our numbers so far, and we'll go over the totals before we shut this case down for the next few months."

"Right. Give me five minutes." Nick, spreadsheet in hand, was at Don's desk in two.

"Great! 2010: Families found?"

"58."

"Families interviewed?"

"Same. 58."

"Family DNA samples received and processed?"

"51."

"Hmm. We'll have to follow up on those not responding. Remains received?"

"Not that many. 7."

"Remember. They're just getting started. There was a lot of wreckage to clear before they got down to the bones. Remains identified and returned?"

"4."

"Four happy families. Something to keep us going. Where were they positioned on our schematic?"

"Right here." Nick pointed to the lower portion of the cruiser.

"Hmm. Engine area. Should have been from the bridge or upper deck... or the gun deck at the lowest judging from the way a ship usually sinks. Make a note to keep that in mind as other remains come in."

"Will do."

"So that leaves..."

"3 remains not identified/not returned."

"If we have any spare time, let's press for more family participation. And last, remains not recovered?"

"339."

"339 sailors waiting to come up for air. We'll find 'em. If we hit 50% to 60%, we'll have done well. But I'm an optimist. I always aim for 100%."

2012

Nick entered the CIL office to find Don grinning ear to ear. "You won't believe what I've found. A whole file of communications from that retired judge in Alabama who is looking for his father."

"Wasn't he the first to provide a DNA sample?"

"Yup. Twice. First, when DNA became a thing in the nineties, and then when we got this assignment and sent our first family query 'in case my first sample has been misplaced,' he wrote. Diplomatic way of telling us to get on the ball and find his daddy."

"I'd be anxious too, if I were nearing 100."

"His file contains years of cards, letters and clippings about scientific advances that might be applicable to finding/and/or identifying his father's remains. The very first one dates from 1946 when he returned from WWII. He was a Navy man too, and he was assigned to Liverpool. Remember, there had been no public announcements of our ship's loss, so he did his own investigating, traveled to Scotland, talked to folks who worked around the docks in Inverness during WWI, and came up with the 'barrage' story. 'With all due respect' he passed along his information to the War Dept. in the event he had 'discovered details they did not have.'"

"In other words, 'Don't leave my daddy behind.'"

"Exactly. And every year around the same date in September—either his father's birthday or his own, I'd guess—he'd send another communication. In the nineties, JPAC began to receive additional inquiries about sailors missing from our ship and added those to his file since he was probably behind that 'find our boys' movement. Once I assured him over the phone that we were pursuing examinations as quickly as they came to us, he sent cards instead of letters—short and to the point: 'Still here. Still interested. Still waiting.'"

Nick laughed. "After all these years, the guy still has a sense of humor."

"We could all use a dose of that. Off the top of your head, do you have a summary of our totals to date?"

"122 family DNA samples received and processed. 75 remains received. 67 identified and returned to family."

"Locations?"

"Still lower decks. 271 still missing."

"Progress. Slow progress. How do you keep all those figures in your head?"

"I've learned to be prepared."

2014

Don barged through the doors to the lab. "I've found it! I've found it! A clue to the mystery of *why* our ship went down! In the bottom of a musty box that hadn't been opened in decades. Here. Take a look. Take a look."

Nick straightened his back from bending over a microscope. "Looks like a bunch of papers to me. Old, discolored papers."

"Yes. Yes. But what papers? Look at the title. The title," Don prompted.

Nick read, " 'Wireless Transmission.' Looks like garble to me."

"Me too, at first glance. But then I got to thinking. What do we know about wireless transmissions during the 'barrage' operation?"

"None permitted during the act of mining."

"Right. Then why would this one... and only one... transcript be saved when none of the day-to-day, in port, were?"

Nick's momentary thought shifted to a gleam. "Based on its length and uniqueness, I'll stick my neck out here and guess that it was either an unauthorized or a direct-ordered transmission, possibly in a time of crisis."

"My neck is a giraffe's-length further out here than yours is. I say it is *definitely* a transmission from our ship on its fateful last voyage."

"But the garble. What good is it?"

Don slid his glasses above his bushy eyebrows. "That's not garble, my boy. That is Latin! All-words-run-together Latin. No spaces. No punctuation. Straight on letter after letter after letter. I stared at the first page until the whole thing was a blur. Went to bed. Got up and stared again. My mind must have been churning while I snored because I woke up recalling numbers in Latin and picked out those familiar words. This is how they read: sextriaduotriaduoseptem. Any enemy intercepting the transmission would think it a code, a foreign language—not English—or just a bunch of gobbledygook from someone touching the machine accidentally. But this is how those first words translate." He grabbed a pen and wrote across the palm of his hand: 632327. "How do you *read* that?"

"Six hundred thirty-two thousand three hundred twenty-seven."

"That's what I would read too. But what if we *say* it like this: six three, twenty-three, twenty-seven?" He paused and rolled his hand to urge an answer. "Come on now, six three. Six three. Think nine eleven."

"A date? June 3rd?"

"And twenty-three, twenty-seven?"

"A time? 23:27? 11:27 at night?"

"Bingo! And what do we think happened about that date and time?"

Nick's eyes enlarged with each word. "Our... ship... went... down!"

"That's right. And the *why* is in the garble between all the other twenty-threes I found at regular intervals—twenty-three twenty eight, twenty-three twenty-nine, twenty-three thirty, and so one. We have a blow-by-blow, minute-by-minute description of what happened that night."

"Wow! I can't believe our luck."

"And the genius of some radioman on the other end. Now get on that computer and see what school records you can find. There can't be that many sailors with Latin on their transcripts and radio background. I'm headed for the University to find an Ancient History professor who can translate for us. Hallelujah!"

"Done!" Don and Nick shouted simultaneously from their computers. Since their discovery three days earlier, and squeezed into downtimes in their lab responsibilities, the two men pursued separate lines of inquiry into the Latin connection. They agreed not to open the sealed manila envelope containing the translation of the wireless transmission until they determined a sender.

"You go first," Nick said.

"No. You go. Your conclusion is based on fact. Mine, on supposition. I'll be embarrassed if I'm wrong right off the bat."

Nick chuckled. "Okay. You're the boss. I was unsuccessful at finding all school records. I found those of all officers, as one would expect. Only three had taken Latin in high school. None of their grades indicated brilliance. The captain was not among them. I couldn't find all the enlisted men. I'm guessing that had to do with quitting school after eighth grade or earlier. Maybe a few orphans or runaways whose legal names and school records didn't jive, etc. I did find one who had the equivalent of four years, passed early exit exams and was accepted at a college—a Yeoman (R) for radio. That man's name is…"

"James Dickson!" they shouted in unison.

"How did you know?" Nick asked

"I checked the ship's roster. If there were no Latin whizzes among officers, there were only two enlisted candidates assigned to radio—a first class and a second. If I were a captain and did dangerous work at night, I'd want my best man's fingers on the machine then—my first class— Dickson."

"It took you three days to figure that out?"

"No. About an hour and a half this morning, but I didn't want to embarrass myself. Blushing doesn't do me any favors." He grinned while rubbing a hand over his balding head.

Nick snickered. "I should have guessed by the way you sat at your computer so silent, then all of a sudden shouted 'Done!' when I did."

"We deserve a chuckle now and again, given all the grimness we deal with every day." Don picked up the manila envelope, fanned it and gave it a sniff. "What say we tear open this baby and see what really happened?" At his partner's nod he did just that, pulled out the pages and turned to the last one.

"I think you're upside down and backwards, boss."

"Right where I want to be—the last time-reading first. Hmm. 23:41." Don glanced through the other pages. "This Latin transmission reads like a transcript of all the ship's positions and conversations on the bridge until the transmitter went dead—fourteen minutes later. Have a look."

Nick handled the priceless pages gingerly. "Rudimentary, for sure. No nautical terminology, but that's not surprising. Why would a high school class include such a thing? Basic—nouns, verbs, adjectives— common words… no punctuation, and text for lots of numbers. He uses the possessive 'mine' for the explosive, then 'go off right rear.' Then 'rad out' followed by 'lat55d33Nlong6d42W.' Position, maybe? Then 'C.' I'm guessing that's the Captain. Word for animal 'bear' then 'left' then numbers. Hmm. '23:28 mine 2 mid rear' and so on. Certainly comprehensible."

The two men spread the pages across the desk and huddled over them, pointing here and "hmming" there. A bleak scene unfolded. Strong cross currents and stormy seas made accurate navigation impossible. Atmospheric interference disabled the radio. Heavy fog and great distance prevented heading for their sister ship or communicating with her using lantern semaphore once they received 'no answer.' Mines 3 through 8 exploded within two minutes of one another, tearing multiple holes in the armored hull of the cruiser. Flooding on deck threatened to dissolve the safety pellets of mines lined up for laying. 'Winds 2xstrong.' All available hands rushed to dismantle the mines' firing mechanisms before shoving them down the track to fall overboard. Mine 9 rendered the engine room inoperative. At 23:36, the captain ordered 'all men off ship now' and mumbled, 'water 2 cold 2 last long.' More positions, until 'only mag compass works.' At 23:40, 'cross sea 2x strong move right list 45d winds 3x strong bridge move left crack break.' then 23:41 'go d….'

Nick was the first to speak. "Wow. They might have lasted a little longer with a 30 degree list, but 45? No chance under those conditions."

"Wouldn't have mattered," Don said glumly. "Any man not killed by explosion would have been gone within minutes of hitting that icy cold North Atlantic. Those old lifeboats didn't hold up well in stormy conditions, and anyone in a life jacket ended up face down in those days because of the way they were constructed. They would all succumb to hypothermia sooner rather than later."

Don rose slowly from his desk, crossed the office to the window, and gazed at the coastline. He reached in his back pocket for a handkerchief. He broke a lengthy silence with, "Looks like surf's up enough for a good afternoon riding the waves, Nick. Why don't you take the rest of the day off?"

"What about the lab work on a flight crew that just came in?"

"Not a problem. Frustration moves me along double-speed. You go out and get some fresh air. You need alone time as much as I do right now."

Without further comment, Nick left, reluctant to witness his partner's meltdown.

The shaking of his shoulders was the only indication that Don had descended to a deep, dark place just like *his* boys. For more than thirty years he had dealt with death every day. He had learned to check his emotions at the door and proceed in a clinical fashion through each case until he brought the satisfaction of closure to grieving families. That was his reward. That was what got him through. Discovering the mysteries— the secrets—the whos, hows and sometimes the whys—for loved ones left behind.

He lauded advances in DNA science that could confirm identity, in electronic ROVs with remote sensing tools that could find and retrieve an object from underwater, and in sonar that could create images from sound. And, he had to admit, in a government that supported a mission to retrieve and return remains of all missing servicemen and women.

But for *his* ship and *his* boys, this time he had invested more of himself than his psyche could handle. The discoveries were too sobering. Poorly designed life saving equipment. Explosive devices not field-tested. Faulty safety features. An operation that required largely teen-aged novices to execute precise directives in a perfect storm of adverse conditions: tempestuous atmospheric circumstances, blinding white of night, and lack of communication.

Don moved the handkerchief slowly over his face and eyes. His vision returned to the sunny seascape in front of him and all the mortals out testing their prowess against the forces of nature. He turned away. Tomorrow he would scan the wireless transmission and its translation, along with Nick's first schematic of the ship, and a new one he could whip up, depicting the result of the bridge sheared from the body of the ship and its probable sunken location. Then he would send copies by electronic mail and snail mail—just to be sure—to JPAC. For the moment, he had work to do. He headed for the lab to channel his frenzy into uniting families.

2017

Nick entered the CIL building to waves of a tirade coming from Don's office. "No! I will *not* sign off on this case yet! I don't give a hoot how anxious you are to wrap it up, and I sure don't care about DOD budget cuts. Our mission is to follow the trail to its end, and we are *not there* yet!"

He peeked through the office window to observe Don in a face-to-face videoconference with a stern uniformed officer. His boss gave the man pauses to speak but countered every argument with his own.

"We have *not* received any remains from the ship's bridge. We expect six possible, two for certain. We can identify those two positively if you'll just get down there and find them!"

Nick perked up his ears. This conversation was about the barrage ship.

"No, *we're* not holding up this case. *You* are! We *know* that the captain and the radioman were together on the bridge for the duration of its fourteen-minute sinking."

Nick inched the door open.

"What do you mean by 'how do we *know*'? We *know* our crew. We *know* the ship's position at the time of the first explosion. We *know* its last position headings at the time it went down and *when* it went down."

Nick entered quietly.

"No. We're not relying on chance or best guess. We put our trust in the ship's wireless transmission. Why do you think you've not found the bridge or any men from it yet? Because it's not where you *best guess* it is. The transcript tells you that."

Nick moved to a vantage point behind Don…

"What do you mean, 'what transcript'? From the ship's wireless! I sent it to you a couple of *years* ago! Read it, and you'll find our sailors. I *know* they are there. I *know* they stayed with their ship."

…and pulled up a stool to sit.

"Don't give me that 'lost in department reorganization crap'! *We* lived through it with all of *our* files intact. I'll resend a copy as soon as we're through here. Five minutes max. Anyone with a decent pair of glasses can read it well enough to tell that a cross current caused listing starboard and extreme wind gusts from the southeast forced the bridge to shear portside where it drifted northwest of the ship's position. Read it, and you'll find the bridge and our sailors. With all due respect I repeat, I *know* they are there. I *know* they stayed with their ship. You'll see."

Nick stifled a chuckle.

Don shook his head. "Not until I receive written authorization for an extension and *action this spring* to complete recovery. As soon as you assure us you'll follow through, we'll follow through. Then we'll have this case completed in no time."

Nick held his breath during a lengthy monologue from the other end.

"Sounds good. Appreciate your cooperation. We have families waiting."

Don turned to the younger man peering over his shoulder. "Pack a bag. Throw in printouts of the wireless transcript and *our* schematics. You can access our electronic file from there if necessary. You have one hour to get to the airfield and catch a transport. Hope you don't mind spending your days staring into the briny deep."

2018

Donald Rouse entered his office at CIL with a little more hop in his step than usual.

"You gonna wear a suit and tie to your retirement party tonight?" Nick asked.

The older man chortled. "Not on your life. I walked into this office wearing shorts and sandals, and that's how I'm walking out. If the big brass don't like it, what are they gonna do to me? Put me on deck-swabbing detail for a day?" He sat down at his for-the-first-time-in-years spotless desk. "Are you about finished with our ship's closing reports?"

Nick nodded. "All done except for a couple of questions."

"Hold on to them for a few minutes. I'd like to go over our own totals first."

"Sure. Of 383 total officers and crew listed, 231 families found. 190 DNA samples received and processed. 186 remains received. 171 remains identified and returned to family. 197 still missing. That gives us about a 45% return rate."

Don tipped his chair back and cleared his throat. "Given what we learned about how the ship went down and where the crew was probably distributed at that time, I feel an adjustment is in order. How many men do you figure were lost to the sea versus how many trapped on the ship?"

Nick shrugged. "I'd say 50-50 is reasonable."

"Sounds good to me. That leaves us about 190 to 200 possible recoveries from the ship itself. 171 identified and returned gives us... gives us...."

"An 85% to 90% return rate."

"Not bad, young man. Not bad. Validation for our process. Of course, you'll develop your own system soon, and just in time. Scuttlebutt has it that we might have a flood of remains from North Korea in the near future. You'll have to break in extra staff to take care of the load... a piece of cake for you." Don rose to pat Nick on the back. "You've been a first-rate partner, and I wish you well."

"Thank you, Don. It's been my pleasure."

The retiree reached for his handkerchief, wiped his nose and sat again with his arms on his clean desk. "Now, let's get to your questions. First?"

"Based on the transmission we discovered, who do you think decided to disobey an order and break radio silence, knowing that disobeying an order is a court martial offense?"

Don rested his chin on a fist and cleared his throat again. "Doesn't matter now. From the captain's perspective, I believe he would not openly disobey an order. Once he realized that semaphore was not an option, he'd find a way around it, maybe by a hint or suggestion that he wished he could communicate by some kind of code that did not reveal the operation or location to an enemy. Then he'd give his radioman a wink and turn his back, leaving Dickson to disobey and take the fall knowing the consequences. Or the sailor made the decision on his own in the interest of the hundreds of his shipmates rather than himself. Either way, nothing in the transcript indicates that the captain tried to prevent or stop the transmission.   To the contrary, he continued to give very detailed information to be transmitted. My bet is on the wink."

"That was my thinking too. When a young guy is staring death in the eye, he's probably not thinking about whether his decision will bring him a medal or a dishonorable discharge."

"If that's how it played out on the bridge, you do realize that Dickson disobeyed an order a second time."

Nick seemed confused. "How so?"

"The captain ordered *all* to abandon ship. Dickson did not. He continued to transmit until he went down with her. His transmission and the underwater photos confirm that. He chained his arm to his station next to the transmitter and kept on tapping until the end. Brave boy." He cleared his throat again. "Next question?"

Now Nick was uncomfortable and squirming in his seat. "I just ran a triple-check on the Dickson father and son and... either our tests are incorrect or their military records are incorrect... possibly falsified."

Don's heavy eyebrows vaulted up and his ears funneled forward. "What? Impossible! We double-checked."

"We did, and father/son *are* a match. I was putting their file in order to close it when a discrepancy caught my eye. They do not match their military records."

Beads of disbelief puddled above those eyebrows. "Explain please."

"Our DNA testing revealed that both father and son are black—father ¼ and son 1/8. But both signed their Navy registration cards, verifying that their answer 'white' was true. And neither one had the lower left corner of his card clipped. Is this one of those 'deep secrets' we've talked about?"

Stunned, Don was at a loss for words. "Is... is... the registration card the only questionable record?"

"No. Birth certificates, school registrations, a marriage certificate all record both men as white. I even checked a couple of census records. All 'white.'"

The frog in Don's throat started tap-dancing. "You might be right. Family secrets kept for generations ultimately rear their ugly heads. We're talking the Deep South at the turn of the last century. Unpleasant... and dangerous times for those of color. Many families made choices for their children in favor of opportunity. It's worth noting, as well, that many federal forms are filled out by a government employee and not the person himself. Pull out the photocopy of one of those Navy registration cards."

Nick fingered through the file, removed James Dickson's, and handed it across the desk.

"Look here. Look here. Two different handwritings. James's signature is much different from the rest of his card, so the registrar filled in all the information, much of which was based on his own personal impression. Look at some of these questions. 'Tall, medium or short?' 'Slender, medium or stout?' The registrar glances at the guy and makes his own assumptions. 'Race?' If there is no reason to doubt, he writes 'white.' If the subject has never had his race questioned before, why would he hesitate to sign? Could be this father/son pair have 'passed' since their births, and it's not our place to question how or why that happened. Was each man's a purposeful act or one of ignorance? Only they and their natal relatives know for sure."

"So you're saying we shouldn't mention this discrepancy in our reports?"

Don mulled over the issue. By rights, neither man should have had the assignment he did during his military service. Both would have been below decks in the engine room, kitchen or laundry. But both served admirably in positions for which it was assumed at that time that blacks were not capable of or suited to perform. One stood fast, carried on and sacrificed his life, along with 382 shipmates, to serve as guinea pigs in a clinical trial that may have saved countless lives over the course of a successful barrage operation and ultimately World War I.

The other, according to his military record, used creative persuasion to save countless young hot-heads from destroying their careers before they ever reached the front, and he bore witness to their lives' end when their misfortunes on the battlefield sent them his way again. From his own research of the Dickson family, Don learned that the judge focused his civilian career on juvenile justice and applying equal treatment under the law to adolescents and young men and women.

Once again, Don's emotions plopped him right into a quandary. He and Nick had labored for almost ten years to solve a mystery and in the process, they had stirred up another one. He had a soft spot for the persistent old man. For a judge, an upholder of the law, truth is paramount. Had this respected man gone to his grave not knowing, or will knowing he spent a lifetime of false representation send him to it?

Don inhaled deeply. Was he obligated to sully the reputations of two good men? He decided to follow the example of the judge's father. When in doubt, like young radioman Dickson, respond to the 'wink.' "What is our mission at CIL?" he asked Nick.

"To return the missing from America's conflicts to their families."

"How do we do that?"

"Primarily with DNA testing and any other scientific method necessary."

"In other words, we don't assume, judge or recommend. We test."

"Correct."

"Do we have scientific verification of identity and relationship?"

"99.9%."

"Is there *any* box on *any* page of the report we are required to submit that we *must* tick for 'has the soldier/sailor falsified government records?'"

"No, sir."

"Then that information is *not* within the purview of this department and therefore, *not* our responsibility to report." He locked his younger cohort in a steely gaze. "If you have a problem with that conclusion, *I'll* finish up the paperwork and sign off on it before I leave."

Nick stared back at the man he had come to respect so greatly. "No problem. I'm absolutely in agreement with your conclusion. *I'll* file the report and close this case as my first official act as head of this department."

Don could not hide a smile. "Any more questions?"

"A couple of short ones. Will you notify the retired judge of our findings?"

Don inhaled deeply again to buy time. "That is the responsibility of the Navy's Mortuary Affairs office, and they generally don't go deeply into a serviceman's file other than to notify family officially and to confirm proper burial etiquette. To be honest, I don't want to for fear that he.... I want to believe that nearly 100-year-old man is 'Still here. Still interested. Still waiting.'"

Nick chuckled at the attachment Don had formed to the judge. "Are you going to sleep in tomorrow morning?"

"I wish. My idea of the retired life is a cabana on a tropical island with seascape as far as the eye can see. But the wife has us booked for the first flight out to Pittsburgh to spend Easter with the grandkids. They're still digging out from a freak spring snowstorm that left over ten inches on the ground. And I'm supposed to hunt for colored eggs! She even made me pack a pair of long pants and boots. I'll go crazy!"

Nick reflected on how much he had learned from Don. How to surf, for sure; but more importantly, that the measure of a person is greater than his or her DNA analysis. *I'm sure going to miss that old guy,* he thought to himself as he settled down at his newly acquired spotless desk and gave a friendly wave to the man in shorts and sandals on his way out.

"Not for long, you won't," Don shouted over his shoulder as he sprinted out the office door toward retired life.

2018

I made it! Three thousand six hundred and fifty-two days from my promise to meet Charlie at the cemetery, I am mere minutes from adhering to our plan. The question is, will he? Can he? Will I find a headstone with his name on it? Or just an empty space with no note of what happened when? This is definitely my last trip here, Charlie, so please give me a sign that my journey has not been in vain.

I stare down at a cup of coffee growing colder by the minute. No matter. My stomach does not handle coffee well anymore but, still standard service at Maxine's, it arrived at our table the minute I took a seat while my children "excused themselves." I have never known a child of seven or seventy who could pass up a bathroom or a bakery on a road trip—and we have only been driving for an hour!

I guilt-shamed my kids into coming with me this trip and do not feel the least bit sorry. When they put up resistance to my coming at all and especially to bringing them with me, I threatened to hire one of those people who drive you wherever you want to go—even to Alabama. "Three days out of your lives to meet your grandmother's relatives for the first and last time is not too much to ask. You need to know where your roots lie and show gratitude for those who gave you life." Charlie told me that the first time we met, and now I am a true believer.

Funny how my kids—even though retired themselves—assume their old nuclear family roles when we three are together. My daughter struggles to get her mouth around a pecan sticky bun. I do not have the heart to tell her that the 'sticky' part will stick with her all day. My son points to a leaning tower of pancakes with ham and eggs on the side whisking past his nose. "I'll have one of those," he smiles—the first one I have seen from him since we left LA yesterday. I settle back with my acid stomach and cold cup of coffee, just thankful to be here.

The desire to show up as promised did not consume me until a few months ago. My children finally convinced me to uproot myself and move into an active-aging living community. I asked them if that meant I should actively work toward aging (I thought one aged naturally and did not have to work to hurry it along) or if I should remain active while aging (Being in a facility with so much done for me seemed counterproductive). They were not amused. They were only thinking of my safety, they said.

I relented and, in the process of downsizing, I uncovered a birthday wish come true. I thought little about the never-opened brown paper parcel I came across from time to time over the years. It was not addressed to me, so I never asked. But this time, something about the package caught my eye—no return address, only a postmark from Montgomery, Alabama, in 1943.

I opened it carefully so as not to tear the paper covering, only to find another obstacle—a second package wrapped in cellophane ready to crack and split if I did not handle it with extreme care. A mid-sized paper grocery sack nearby held more treasures. After meticulous investigation of all the contents, I determined that showing up for Charlie's 100th birthday was an imperative. I could have searched online for notice of his death, but I did not want to hear about it second- or third- or millionth-hand. I felt compelled to be there, in that place on that day, and I set out to plan such a pilgrimage. Now here I sit, children in tow, ready for that final step.

"Come on, you two," I say. "Time to move. I usually arrive between ten and ten-thirty. We won't be long, then we'll stop back here on our way out for some real homemade peach ice cream."

As soon as I glance out the window, I see that Charlie has sent me a sign. Traffic. A long procession of vehicles—some with uniformed men accompanying a hearse—fills the roadway heading in our intended direction. We exit Maxine's and stand solemnly by. My children notice my eyes fill with tears. I feel my daughter's arm find its way around my waist and my son's, across my shoulders. They are keenly aware of my sense of my own mortality, given my ninety-four years, but today my thoughts are of Charlie, a man they do not know and whose name they rarely hear.

We easily recognize the turn at the now green house by following the cloud of dust. If it were not for all the parked cars along the roadway, we might have missed the cemetery too, due to poor visibility. This graveyard is so old that it was designed long before the automobile and therefore cannot accommodate vehicles. We find a space way down the road and begin the "should we or shouldn't we" discussion.

My daughter votes for the "we should" side. "If this funeral is for your friend, and you promised to be here long ago, and you are here to fulfill that promise, then you have every right to join the other mourners."

My son begs otherwise. "If this funeral is not for your friend, and we show up with our own flowers and what all, that would be disruptive. Even asking whose funeral this is would be disrespectful, and we could hardly turn and walk away. I say we stay here until the crowd leaves."

Both children are right. I scan the area for a familiar vehicle or person. None. The crowd gathers near our gravesites, but I cannot be sure. And if we bump into anyone, I can hardly introduce myself as *"that* woman Charlie met here every ten years." I want to bear witness, to keep my promise, but I want to be discreet. For the sake of peace in the family at this very emotional time, I choose the middle ground. "We'll not enter. We'll walk back along the road as close as we can and still remain inconspicuous. When everyone leaves, we'll go in, do our decorating and express our gratitudes. If any shirttail Dickson should question us, I'll privately express my sorrow at that time."

Agreed. My daughter takes my arm to steady me on the road. My son follows with my new and improved, carryon compliant, canvas-seated walking stick that only he can maneuver. I choose a spot outside the fence where my seat and I can lean against one of those oak trees that still cannot decide which side of the fence it wants to live on.

"This is perfect, Mom," my son says. "If we were at a football game, we'd be at the fifty-yard line about 100 feet from midfield. Great view!"

Trust my son to compare just about anything to football. From his six-foot-four vantage point, he recites a play-by-play for my benefit. Seated at field level with a view of a wall of uniforms aside an open grave, I suppose, I can only imagine the flag-draped casket, color guard and seven-man firing party he describes. The three rifle volleys come as a surprise and nearly knock me off my stick. "Taps" leaves us all in tears. When the folded flag is presented to the family, I have no idea who receives it: Charlie, for his father, or Skip for his.

We watch the lingerers pay their respects and depart, but the cluster around the principals is so tight that I cannot distinguish faces enough to recognize them. At last, the mourners depart in two directions—some to their cars to leave and others to a small fenced area just beyond the north end of the grounds, new since my last visit.

My children return to our vehicle to collect the "what all," leaving me alone with my thoughts for a few minutes. I still have no clue whose burial we witnessed this morning, so I turn my attention to the surroundings. The cemetery looks fresh and new—more like a garden than a graveyard—without sacrificing its quaintness. The trees and shrubs show off a recent shampoo and trim that leave the air smelling as it does after a light spring rain. Even the live oaks fit their name, and every formerly bare patch of ground boasts new plantings of perennials that create a tapestry of rainbow colors. The rusted wrought iron fence wears a fresh coat of paint, and the graveled paths disappeared to be replaced by a pine-green-tinted concrete surface smooth enough for wheelchairs to negotiate. Whoever rests here anew is in a peaceful, welcoming place— much improved from my previous visits.

We make our way along the new pathway toward our sites, and yes, the burial we witnessed was for a Dickson, but with no stone or no name stake visible, we still do not know who rests next to my mother. I sit again and direct the children in decorating as Charlie once did for me. As I do, I intersperse tidbits about their grandmother as a younger woman than they will remember. We place a few flowers for my grandparents. "I never knew them," I say. "Never knew they existed, but I wish I had, for surely they had a tale to tell too."

I have the children arrange a nice bouquet for Lottie and tell them about her—a remarkable woman who lost a husband, her only child, and raised her grandson to become a distinguished judge, all without complaint, "or so Charlie told me." I scatter a few flowers into the new grave and place a nice bouquet where a headstone will sit soon. Decorating complete, I direct them to say their gratitudes silently, as I will, to those who gave us life.

Moments later, in the midst of our private meditations, a loud voice from behind commands, "Excuse me! May I ask what you tossed into that grave?"

I turn to watch a man stride toward us. He has the look of Charlie from the last time I saw him some twenty years ago, but my friend could not stride even then. He begins to jog and calls out, "Janie! Is that really you? Pops has had that third eye in the back of his head scanning for you all morning. I could tell he was anxious and disappointed not to find you. He even saved you a seat, but... well, here you are now and that's what matters."

Pops has... Charlie is still alive, and Jimmy rests in peace. I sigh deeply at the realization.

Skip pulls me up and into his arms for our second emotional hug, as my children stand by astounded. "You have no idea how much this means to us... to the whole family. Pops lived long enough to welcome his father home. Jimmy rests next to Lottie as *she* wished. Pops will be with our mother as *we* wished. And you helped make this possible." He sets me down gently to wipe his eyes. "I'm sorry I shouted at you. We all expected you to come alone, as usual—probably why we didn't spot you earlier."

"My son Dave and my daughter Emma don't let me wander very far on my own these days."

He chuckles. "And one of my grandsons said some strange people were messing with the grave. Glad to meet you folks. I'm Skip, Charlie's son. You're all invited to our family's birthday picnic as soon as you're finished here."

"That's very nice of you, but...."

"No buts. Don't move. I'll bring Pops right over." He trots away, taking his excited smile with him.

We do move, I to my seat and the kids, to pick up our clutter and take it to the car. They return with my precious bag in time to see Skip pushing a waving Charlie in his wheelchair as fast as his son can manage. Twenty hard years have taken their toll. He is much thinner, his cheekbones and long nose more prominent, but his blue eyes still sparkle.

"Janie! Janie! You did come!" he shouts in a raspy voice. Somehow we manage a hug despite our contraptions. "And you brought your children. Super! My celebration is complete."

Skip steps forward to make the introductions and tells us that the numerous flower arrangements piled beneath the tree that shades our plots were waiting for us to take our choice for my family, in case we showed up later… which we did. The rest will adorn Jimmy's covered grave.

I give that job to my kids while Charlie and I just sit and smile at each other, not knowing quite what to say. Dave and Emma finally decide on one with masses of blue and lilac for their grandmother and a second to place between their great grandparents' headstones. There was a time when I tried to explain to my children the importance of these visits to me. The usual reply was, "Yes, Mom. We know. Relatives. Love them or hate them, admire or disavow them, we are bound to them *by* life, so remember them kindly once in a while." But the events of the day thus far—the pomp of the ceremony for someone whom no one living has ever met, Skip's acknowledgement that I played a part in the family's expectations for this special day, and centenarian Charlie's faith that I would visit—sobered them. Finally, they are believers.

I break the awkward silence. "This place looks beautiful, Charlie. So much has changed since I was last here."

Skip gives me a sheepish look. "We followed your play book, Janie, to visit here often and with children and grandchildren. I was able to obtain approval for a memorial that has now been moved over there." He points to the party area. "Once that was in place here, we visited even more often, as you predicted, and soon brought along a few tools for our family work crew to keep the place tidy. About five years ago, Pops said, 'We're gonna do Janie one better.'" Skip blushes. "The old man figured us out."

Charlie smiles proudly. "I approached the county about setting up an 'Adopt a Cemetery' campaign. You know, like the families who adopt a mile of a highway to keep trash picked up. I reminded the board that there were several old and neglected cemeteries in the county that could use a sprucing up. They approved the idea as long as we didn't *remove* any plantings adjacent to individual gravesites. After all, how much damage could an old goat and a few of his kids do?" Charlie chuckles to himself.

"They can't do much without water," Skip chimes in.

I glance at my children who show polite interest in the strangers' dialogue.

"Pops uncovered an ancient pickup in the shed out at the farms and acquired a plastic tank for water, but after one frustrating Saturday trying to direct a bucket brigade from the outside looking in, he changed our plan," Skip says.

"I told my son that the footpaths had to come first. I had to be able to get around in my wheelchair by myself. You all figure it out!"

"That's where my sister Dee came in. She has an eye for pattern and design and came up with one that extended the main loops to and between the far corners. 'So Pops can commandeer our grandkids longer with his stories,' she said. While that was taking place, Pops searched the county records—they're all online now, you know—for ownership of that small vacant lot with the tree that used to be at the far end of the cemetery grounds."

Charlie breaks in. "Turns out, it was part of the original allocation of the ten acres for the cemetery, but when the grounds were fenced in, there was not enough material to complete the job, so the men just hooked together as much as they had and called it done. I presented the board with the evidence and offered to buy that short acre for the purpose of digging a well to supply water to the grounds proper. Our 'Adopt a Cemetery' group—the three of us Dicksons—agreed to landscape and to provide a drinking fountain and sanitary facilities if the board would approve this small plot's use as a picnic area and access to it through the existing fence by replacing one section with a gate constructed from that section."

"Many cultures do, you know," Skip reminds us, "gather with relatives at burial places on a special day to share food and memories in honor of their ancestors. We decided, why not the Dicksons too. When Pops stared at them with his decision-made eyes and told them that folks need to have a pleasant place to sit back and relax while they share memories of their loved ones and to keep trash where it belongs, well... how could they refuse?"

"The whole truth," Charlie adds, "is that with all the grandkids having kids, we needed more room to keep the young ones from running around playing hide-and-seek while we older folk took quiet time expressing our gratitudes."

"Once the water system was in, Dee went to work on a design. She has Mom's talent for gardening, and came up with what you now see, bunches of fragrant colors and textures 'that come together as a piece,' she explained. She even confiscated the wheelchair for a day to test the paths and whisk from place to place to direct the family planting crews while Pops was relegated to a lawn chair right here," Skip smiles. Charlie does not.

"Soon after the initial project was completed and on show to the public, our idea spread around the county. It started with Pops funding improvements and major upkeep of the black cemetery down the road where Maxine's family rests, including an adjacent picnic-park. Their loved ones provide tidy up crews. Our plan has grown from there to several other small, neglected graveyards in the area."

Charlie cocks his head and smiles at his most recent brainchild. "Once that took off, we started an additional project with our young ones—to research the histories of occupants here and write their stories. We hope for Historical Site designation soon under the name of Lottie Dickson with signage and maps near Jimmy's memorial in the picnic-park—a win-win-win-win all around."

My dear friend leans sideways to grasp my hand, and I meet him midway with mine, gently. His buoyant demeanor masks the frailty of bones as brittle as dry twigs, but his mind retains its sharp edge.

"I must admit, Janie, that you inspired this history project along with my curiosity about Lottie's background. Long ago you described your mother as with-dad and after-dad, but never before-dad. I wanted to be the author of Lottie's biography but soon realized that she too led three lives—with her son Jimmy, with me her grandson, and before children. I delved into records in every location I recalled her mention and could not find one identifying a Lottie Dickson anywhere. I scoured the remnants of her belongings for an old family Bible but could not find one. I even set my sharpest young ones to track her with no luck, so my line has only a recent past, not both a distant and recent one like yours. I realized that there might be others like us who seek answers to questions of their heritage, and we could help in that search—an idea that gave birth to the children's historical story project."

He gives me an encouraging smile. "Return in another five or ten years, and you may discover more clues to why your mother chose this place."

I do have clues… right beside me… but I await the perfect moment to reveal them.

Skip notices his father tiring and offers to take him back to the picnic, but Charlie objects. "No, no. You three youngers go on ahead. Janie and I need time to reacquaint. Check on us later."

My two are reluctant to leave me alone with this debilitated man, but Skip has no problem. He must have learned long ago not to disobey his father's orders.

Once they disappear into the throng of partygoers, I fix my eyes on Charlie. He does seem fatigued, so I suggest we rest quietly for a few minutes. He nods. "Just a few," he mouths. His eyelids close and he falls asleep.

I slip my arm through his and rest my head against his shoulder. How lucky I am to have found this man. *Just a few*, I promise myself, but when I feel him stir, my watch proves otherwise.

Charlie clears his throat several times before speaking. "I'm sorry you missed the ceremony. My father received a proper burial with full military honors, guns and all."

"I know. We watched from that tree over there. Very impressive."

He smiles slightly. "'Proper' means more than guns and flags. The military believes that even a couple of bones after all these years deserve a box. The opportunity to hold and caress those bodily remains of my father—simple physical contact—filled me with a deep sense of connection to the man—of belonging—even though I never laid eyes on him. I was surprised to witness a full uniform be draped over his minimal remains, but that was the man he was at the end, a U.S. Navy sailor doing his job."

"How fortunate you were provided that opportunity."

"Besides the flag draped over his coffin, I was given his medals. You'd think after all these years, there wouldn't be records to support them." He reaches into his breast pocket and retrieves a small box. "This one is father's World War I Victory Medal with a commendation star and operational clasp for mine laying sea duty. That's how he died—laying mines in the North Sea. This is a Navy Cross for extraordinary heroism— a surprise to us, for someone had to put him up for the award and it was not our family."

"What impressive keepsakes that come with a bonus—a mystery."

"Not the only mystery. We did receive an 'official report' of the circumstances of his death, but there's an 'unofficial' story too. Last spring I received a manila envelope with no return address, only a postmark from Pittsburgh. Inside was a second envelope with the instruction: 'to be opened only by James Charles Dickson, DOB 09/19/1918. If he is not living, please shred this envelope and its contents.' Inside that was a transcript of my father's last transmission from his sinking ship."

"How strange! Who sent it?"

"Someone who understood that if you don't know what happened to your loved one, you can't move on."

Charlie fingers the medals reverently, then he replaces them in their box and returns it to his left breast pocket. He presses his hand against his heart and sighs deeply. "My father is home at last. Grandmother Lottie can rest. I only wish I knew about my mother to honor her too."

This is the moment, the opportunity I am waiting for. "Your mother *is* honored. Every year. By you. I brought a gift from your grandmother to *our* mother. Now sit down—oh, you already are." Where are my wits? "You ponder what I just said while I lift this unwieldy annoyance into my lap." I open the heavy bag and unfold little bits of brown paper and cellophane to tug on just enough of a quilt to expose its corner. "Tell me what you see."

"These look like Lottie's initials." Puzzled, he investigates more closely and discovers the bumps beneath them. "What...? Where...?"

"You once told me that everyone leaves a trace: a letter, a photo, a trinket. Here are your traces. Go ahead. Open that tiny pocket."

His thumb and forefinger barely fit inside the opening but manage to remove a folded birth certificate naming his parents as James Charles Dickson and Lila Larson. "This is incredible! You mean, they were...." He points to the side-by-side graves in front of us."

I nod and squeeze his hand.

"But this certificate isn't the same as the one I've used all my life, with my mother listed as a 'Lily Lawson' I never could find." He rubs his forehead in confusion. "The Lawson one could only be Lottie's handiwork. Altering script was a specialty of hers, and she was in charge of county records at that time. But why?"

Next, the befuddled man finds a small snapshot of a young couple standing on a pier—one in a naval uniform. He notes the date on the back. Dec 18, 1917. "That's my father, and the woman is…"

"*Our* mother. Keep digging."

He does and shakes his head in frustration. "Nothing else."

"Yes, there is. The trinket!" I search, and he is right. The small pocket is empty. I search the bag. No goody there either. "Oh my gosh! What did I do with it? This mind of mine… frustrates me no end and I'd use more colorful language if we weren't in a solemn place. I swear I put it in a safe spot." I bang on my head with my fists. "Oh Charlie, it's the best ever but where is it? I can't believe…."

I clap my hands to my chest and feel a lump—a good one—a circular one with a hole in the middle. I discretely reach down the front of my blouse to pull on a chain. "I remember now. I didn't leave it in the small pocket of a sealed package in a locked carryon for fear it would attract TSA attention, so I took it out to wear like any mature woman might." I slip the delicate chain from me and place it over Charlie's head.

He carefully examines the sparkly ring hanging from it, both outside and in. "JD & LL   12-17-17." His blue eyes gradually mirror the undulating waters of the sea. "My parents' wedding ring?"

I nod and soon all of our tear ducts are gushing decades of pent-up emotion. When we finally manage to calm ourselves and inch closer, we begin to unravel the timeline and rationale for choosing this place.

"My grandfather was the first to be buried here because…?"

"The only connection I make is with others nearby from the same religious group. Then my grandmother Lottie because… she must have recognized the name and knew a little of our mother's family background. I imagine she held out the slimmest hope that Lila would one day visit the graves of her parents and identify the name of her husband on the stake she insisted that I maintain there. Remember, Lottie purchased both plots at the same time."

"My grandmother was next, and for a reason I will never understand, Mom did come for her funeral and apparently recognized Jimmy's name as Lottie planned. That solves the 'why here' question for her choice of place—the belief that someday in some way they might be reunited. Lottie and Mom both got their wishes, but if I hadn't come to bury Mom on her birthday and you hadn't been here celebrating yours at the same time, we would never have found each other. Now, how do you explain that, Judge?"

Charlie chuckles. He rests his elbows on his chair's arms and his chin on his folded hands as if in deep thought. Finally, he turns toward me. "The first time we met on my 50th birthday, I told you it was special in an unusual way, that lying at my feet was a person with whom I shared the most important event of my life. I said we had a cosmic connection, and you shivered as if you were in the company of a really bizarre fellow."

I do remember, and now I am embarrassed.

"Call it what you will, Janie—providence, the grace of God or my cosmic connection. I do believe that some power beyond our understanding brought us together all those years ago and has conspired to bring us together again for this fitting end."

Perhaps he is right. I cannot explain what force nudged me to return here again and again, allowing our memories to find commonalities.

He pats my knee. "To borrow a phrase from you, every secret that is uncovered gives birth to more. I now understand the source of Delilah's name, but I cannot comprehend why Lottie never told me that my mother was alive. Why? Is that why she asked my forgiveness at her death? I wonder what other secrets she kept from me."

I have questions too. "Why do you suppose Mom never opened this package?"

"That was during wartime. Perhaps she feared I had been killed and the package was filled with keepsakes of my young life. She couldn't face the death of her child. If she didn't know for sure, she could always believe I was alive and well somewhere."

"But that doesn't explain why she abandoned you, her newborn, in first place."

Charlie stares into me and examines my face carefully. "I have a notion you know more than you're telling me."

I try for a teasing smile. "If I told you, it wouldn't be secret anymore..." I cannot imagine that discovering one's ancestry would be anything other than reason for celebration. It certainly has been for me. But Charlie grew up at a time and in a place where the rules were different. Public knowledge of his ancestry might be problematic for any number of reasons. "... however, I do have another treasure here. *My* gift to you." I fumble in my pocket and hand him another folded paper. "My DNA profile to compare with your own. You might find some Indian blood there, but be careful who you share that information with around here. You might have secrets even you don't know."

Charlie emits a hearty laugh, remembering again our first meeting.

A quartet of our children comes to fetch us for the party. Dee's appearance—the first time I have seen her—arouses a sudden frisson of familiarity. Before I can invite her to come nearer, Charlie stops the group with an open palm and assumes his courtroom voice. Go back to the picnic. All of you! You are all cousins. Go chew on that for a while. We need more time alone. Now, go!

The four thoroughly confused adults turn and obey his command.

Charlie takes my hand and massages it between his two. "How do you feel about this revelation? About your mother being my mother too?"

This question was bound to come, so I grant myself a moment of introspection before admitting the truth. "Bittersweet," I say, and observe his expression register a disappointment he cannot fully disguise. "I can't imagine ever forgiving Mom for abandoning a child. The mother I knew would never commit such a horrendous act. But if she hadn't changed the course of her life, she never would have married my dad, and I wouldn't have had life at all, and I've lived a very blessed one. The difficult reality for me to admit is that I feel selfish... and guilty that I had her for my mom and you didn't. As traumatic as your story is, but for *you* Charlie, *I* wouldn't be here."

The instant I dissolve into tears, he pulls me as close as our contraptions will allow. His still forceful arms enfold and comfort me as he whispers in my ear. "Don't cry, little Sis. I'm at peace with the life I've led, and am now more grateful than ever for the way it will end."

Drowning in my own tears and burrowing into Charlie's life-saving hold, I understand now what he meant by simple physical contact with someone who is a part of you and yours kindling a connection... a belonging. After many minutes of visceral outpouring, we separate and attempt to right ourselves. We realize that the shade has moved but we have not, and we eat up several more minutes shifting our hardware to a more hospitable spot. We discover that blubbering and bonding transpire just as well in comfort as long as we keep handkerchiefs close by.

Charlie takes my hand to kiss. "I wish I had known her, our mother."

"You do. You've lived with or near your mother for many decades. You have Mom's bright blue eyes and her prominent cheekbones. So does Delilah, as well as Mom's wavy auburn hair among the gray, and her gentle manner. In fact, if you were to find a picture of your daughter from about thirty years ago, you'd see a mirror image of our mother."

By the look on Charlie's face, I can tell that my shocking statement demands proof. "Wait! I have one. I remember I took it out of its frame and put it in a safe place the day before we left. Where was that? Not in my suitcase because I wouldn't bring that to the cemetery. Not in this bundle that was all tied up and ready to go. Oh, where was that!"

Charlie dabs his eyes again with his handkerchief.

"Handkerchief... purse... picture! That's it!" I grovel in my purse for the photo of Mom in her bakery uniform. "See how alike they are, and how Mom shifted her left hip to the side as a mother does to rest her baby there while standing, then she tucked her arm behind it? Now watch. Dee will do the same in a minute." We focus our gazes into the party crowd. "See! I'll bet she is left-handed and has a lovely singing voice, too."

Charlie nods and points to himself with his left hand, triggering yet another handkerchief moment.

"Genes do crazy dances, and sometimes they end up in latent and unexpected pairings." I wave my hanky and burble, "Apparently... Dee inherited the Lila combo."

As expected, our snifflings turn to laughter until age and exhaustion tire us. We sigh deeply and relax. Charlie attempts to feel further inside my bag, but I stop him. "Not now."

"The truth, Janie. The *whole* truth." His vibrant blue eyes—ones that can see what is in one's mind before the thought is born—beg for, and command, the truth.

I wonder if Charlie already sees what is left in the bag, from the endearing to the monstrous. Does he envision the aged quilt that looks as fresh and new as yesterday's dawn? Can he read the card taped on top? *Your son is at war. Like his father, he may not return. You deserve to know his story for a day in your older age when you still have longings as I do.* Or the letter Mom wrote to her newborn before she walked away with her promise to love him more than anything in this world, just like she promised me every night at bedtime?

Does he watch me unfold the quilt carefully to expose its design—a Tree of Life on a background of blue with tiny yellow flowers and bordered by a two-inch wide sky blue band along each side revealing a pictograph of family heritage? Can he follow her story in the diminutive figures umbrellaed beneath lushly flowered trees with her finely embroidered stitches? Does he begin at the lower right corner's two-by-two block containing her initials and move clockwise along the lower band from a black map of Africa where boats depart to cross the seas and harbor in the lower left's corner block beneath a Confederate flag? Does his eye then follow the border upward past sugarcane fields and a blond, blue-eyed southern belle with a caramel-skinned baby in her arms, to a country store, and Jim Boy holding hands with his white girlfriend to exchange their vows of love? Does he recognize his Grandmother Lottie weeping beneath a hanging tree in her blue dress with tiny yellow flowers, her tears trailing to the roots of the quilt's central feature?

Does his sight turn right at the two-by-two block of the Alabama State flag to cross the quilt's top band displaying Lottie with baby Jimmy in front of a small cabin with a hound dog at their feet; Jimmy in uniform and a young woman with bright blue eyes joining in Holy Matrimony; and a ship resting at the bottom of the sea before it reaches the safety of the American flag in the upper right block? Is Charlie's attention drawn to his own story unfolding down the right border with Lila clutching her newborn, her tears also trailing to the roots of the quilt's central feature to mingle with Lottie's? Can he identify with the baby alone in his box, through his bike peddling years, into law school and finally the Navy just like his father, ending at Lottie's signature block with its secret pocket?

Does his mind thumb through the letters, such lengthy, loving letters between and about his parents. Does he discover that Lottie's missing letters are there too along with photographs that I had never seen before of my mother and her handsome beau at a young and happy time? What does he think of the surprise I tucked in from my own past—one I now understand?

I ponder the morality of truth-telling in circumstances when honesty will foreseeably wound the person being informed. Charlie is a man of truth, evidence and the law. Perhaps he has already scrutinized his own DNA and knows. But can he handle it, the *whole* truth? He, as well as I, wants to know the why—why our mother left him, and I do not know that truth. I zip the bag tight shut and set it on the ground at our feet. My old black baby doll, the one I treasured as a beloved symbol for my brother, bulges inside one corner.

"Let me tell you a Maxine-worthy story, Judge Dickson, about your 'truth and whole truth.'

"I once possessed another talent as well-developed as tap dancing—insatiable curiosity coupled with an ability to unwrap packages and rewrap them without leaving a tear or a trace. I usually employed this skill near special occasions. Sometimes I experienced elation—just what I wished for. Sometimes, an unexpected but welcome surprise. Sometimes, a crushing disappointment."

I pat him on the knee. "Today is a day of celebration. Your father came home. He and your mother rest together. And you lived to see that come to pass—just as you wished. Let those simple truths be enough for today."

Those eyes bore into mine still.

I take his hand. "At a time of your choosing if ever, in a place of your choosing, and with witnesses or not as you choose, *then* let your curiosity lead you to unexpected places. But understand that a full range of emotions awaits you. *This* whole truth requires a stack of handkerchiefs and is rated inappropriate for a partying crowd."

Silence. A long one, followed by "You're right. I'll...."

His intention is halted by the sound of skipping feet attached to a pony-tailed five-year-old with a backpack bobbing behind her. She halts at attention in front of Charlie. "Grandpa Lottagreats told me to tell you to come now! We're all hungry for cake and ice cream, so you better come now if you want any!"

"We'll be along in a minute, Sugar. Remember, you can't light any candles until I'm there."

"Oh. Are you the one with the birthday?"

Charlie grins and nods. "Yes, I am. I'm 100 years old today."

"Wow! That's a lotta candles." She notices me and points. "Is that lady my Grandma Lottagreats?"

Charlie chuckles. "No. She would be your... Auntie Lottagreats."

The little one claps a hand to her forehead. "Oh, no. Too many to remember!"

I join the conversation. "That's quite a load you have."

She turns around for an instant to show me. "This is my backpack, my one toy for today. We have a family rule—we can only take one toy when we travel to an outside place."

"That looks like a lotta dolls to me."

"I tied all my dolls together and put them in my backpack to make only one toy so I could obey the rule."

"What if you take one out to play with?"

"I can't! That would break the rule!"

"Why did you bring more than one, then?"

"Cuz today is real 'portant, so they all have to be here."

"Which one is your favorite?"

She shakes her head. "No favorites. One of my Greats—this one or that one back there—gives me a different kind each birthday and tells me to love them all the same, just like he does all his great grandchildren."

I sneak a peek at a blushing Charlie. "You're a very wise young girl to follow the rules and very clever to figure out how to do that."

The perky little thing smiles and says thank you. "You two better hurry up. We're all hungry for cake!" She turns and skips away, her one bulging toy bobbing behind her.

I fix my eyes on Charlie who now wears a proud, ear-to-ear smile. "What's with the Lottagreats?

He laughs. "The young kids can handle parents and grandparents pretty well, but when it comes to the greats, they don't understand how many to use. To them, there are one, two, too many to figure out. Long ago, they settled on lottagreat for anyone older than a grand. Suits all of us who qualify just fine. The older we get and the trickier the mind, we can't remember what we are either. Now, let's pack up and head for that real 'portant party." He reaches for his phone. "I'll call Skip to send a couple of the grandkids to come for us."

"Don't bother," I tell him as I put my bulging bag in his lap. "We're the Greats. Surely we can negotiate this path." I stand to stretch my back and fumble with my seat. "Here. Take this nitwit stick of mine. You may be my big brother, but you're not too big for me to push around. Now, hold on. We're going to a birthday party."

We say our final goodbyes to our loved ones. I push him slowly along the path, step by unsteady step, feasting my eyes for the last time on the colorful and restful surroundings.

Charlie twists himself in his chair, and his smirk turns into a smile. "I know how I'm going to announce today's revelation—with the truth, plain and simple. I'm going to say, 'I share the most important event in my life, the day of my birth, with my mother who was also born on this day. Her name is Lila Larson. Today my father joined our 'September 19th is Special' club when he was buried next to her, his wife and the love of his short life. I am proud to say that somehow, all of us here are related. I leave it to each of you to solve that mystery while I eat cake!"

We laugh until we cry again which seems to be our habit. Just before we cross into the picnic-park, we stop to dab our eyes. When my vision clears, I still cannot distinguish one family from another. All I see is Lottie's legacy—generations of civic-minded jubilant faces, young and old, that mirror the world's palette.

"You know, mayhem awaits when we arrive, so I'll ask you now. You granted me my one birthday wish today, but now I'm going to ask you for another."

"What could you possibly wish for beyond all this day's joyful tidings?"

"I wish for you to be my witness and my guide to unexpected places. Will you stay? For a couple of days at least? A 100th birthday deserves special consideration."

I am taken by surprise. "Stay?"

His eyes plead with me.

I pat his shoulder. "We'll see, Charlie. We'll see." I cannot imagine how to arrange it.

"Please say you'll stay with me for the setting of Jimmy's gravestone… to bring this Maxine-worthy drama to its grand finale. What can I do to convince you?"

I recall what Charlie said when we first met, that he was comforted to imagine his papa nestled between two loving mothers. Now his father is, and this newfound brother is asking for a few hours more than the bare dozen we have spent together during our lifetimes. What can I say?

I let go of the handles to hug him from behind and whisper in his ear, "Will there be peach ice cream?"

Gravity rolls him away from me, flailing his arms and shouting, "Lotta scoops, for sure!"

*

On the way to the airport a week later, my two children by my side, I reflect on my initial anxiety at accompanying my deceased mother to such an isolated, eerie place and the footsteps on the gravel path that led to a completely unfathomable relationship.

Genetic testing and analysis can determine *who* and/or *what*: John Doe, my brother, human, fox or pterodactyl. In most cases a *when* and/or *where* can be revealed: one generation removed or many; East Asian, Polynesian, Native American, European or sub-Saharan roots. Sometimes a *how*, such as a genetically linked disease, is discovered. But is there a gene for *why*? For motivation or intent?

My *why here* mystery is finally solved, only to be replaced by another. Why did my mother choose to abandon her first-born child and to carry that secret to her grave?

That enigma remains here… with Mom and a man she truly loved.

~

Note to Reader

More than a dozen crimes were committed
during the course of this whydunit.

How many did you find?

Check your answer at
www.sunwaypress.com

*

You be the Judge.

Is *Lottie's Legacy* one of

deceptions and crimes gone unpunished
or
positive values instilled

in more than four generations of one family?

AWARD WINNING AUTHOR SHERRY SCHUBERT, NAMED 2012 Writer of the Year by Idaho Writer's League and a recipient of an Editors' Choice award from Idaho Author Awards, is a graduate of the University of California at Berkeley, Class of 1967. Subsequently, she spent two years hitchhiking abroad, gathering grist for stories and a packful of dreams. "Life" called her back to her home state of Idaho where she raised a family and taught teenagers to solve quadratic equations.

Ms. Schubert's yen to write fiction during retirement is precipitated by her daughter's observation, "I have no idea who you were before you were Mom." The author specializes in fiction appealing to contemporary women, Baby Boomers and their children.

Puffin Island relates how the historical events and social issues of the Sixties shaped the author and still reverberate in her children's lives today. ***Celtic Compass, Part 1***, applies her experience in a "blended family" of the Sixties—before that term was coined—to present-day realities. ***Celtic Compass, Part II***, explores the challenge of divided loyalties faced by members of a blended family in a time of crisis. ***Celtic Circle~for Better, for Worse*** examines how antagonistic members of a blended family channel their bitterness and grief. In ***Celtic Circle~Forever***, hostile members of a blended family seek pathways to reconciliation following tragedy. ***Lottie's Legacy***, a mystery born of tragic love stories, examines the questions of ancestry, crime and intent.

In addition to her six novels, Ms. Schubert is a contributing author to the short story anthology, *Hauntings from the Snake River Plain* and to the nonfiction collection, *Family Recipes from the Snake River Plain*. All of her works are available as ebooks or paperbacks from sunwaypress.com or other online outlets.

Sherry continues to live on the family farm. For the record, she did shake the hand of President Kennedy, and she did play the guitar… badly.